Shrapnel

A Novel

JESSICA SHOOK

ISBN: 0-9980706-1-0
ISBN-13: 978-0-9980706-1-2

1

ELLE

Her husband left her. In a note.

The night before, Aaron and Elle Holloway laid in the same bed and talked about their day. She read a fashion magazine while he checked a few emails on his tablet; they kissed, said good night and fell asleep to Jimmy Fallon. The next morning, Aaron's side of the bed was cold, his sink cleaned off (that should have been her first sign), drawers and closet empty.

And an insufficient note leaving her rattled and hollow. Her whole life toppled in one note.

It was brief. That's what she hated about it most.

I can't make this work. I'll set a time to pick up the rest of my stuff.
Aaron

As if he was the only one who had tried to make it work.

With those two sentences, Elle dwindled down to a set of bones wearing designer clothes, walking around with no soul, no light, no life. She called in to work. A soulless person was useless sitting at a desk, answering phones, taking messages for her designer-suit boss. She tried calling Aaron, feeling dizzier with each ring, but predictably he ignored her. She texted him—only 20 times a day—but never one response.

Somehow she found herself on her best friend's doorstep. Sobs consumed her when she saw Marissa's familiar freckles and emerald eyes at the door. The Sheldon house always had a backing track of little girl squeals, but Elle sobbed too loudly into Marissa's thin shoulder to pause at them.

"Oh god. Oh god." Elle repeated in rapid fire. "He–left–me–" Dramatic gasps thundered through her whole body.

"Oh babe, I'm so sorry," Marissa said, brushing Elle's soft ombré hair with her fingers the way she did her children's. It didn't take much coaxing to get Elle in the house and ushered into Marissa's room while her husband, Heath, was at work. Sitting on the paisley bed-in-a-bag comforter surrounded by fringed pillows, Elle reread the note aloud to her friend. Mutual tears poured down their faces.

"Throw this out." Marissa pleaded. "Reading it over and over won't change anything. It'll just cut deeper." But as soon as she reached for it, Elle smacked her hand. No, she wouldn't let it out of her sight, desperate to read into the few words scratched down and find hope. Maybe keeping it close would remind her of the love they shared—or the anger. Either way, her freshly manicured nails couldn't touch the paper without feeling the sting of his words. But maybe she deserved them.

Heath happily took the couch that first night, then it became expected of him while Elle stayed.

Whole days passed by with Elle curled on the bed as Marissa came in and out, exchanging piles of waded tissues for fresh boxes and trying to make Elle laugh.

"I feel like Aaron and I divvied up our emotions. Like splitting property up in a divorce." Elle confessed over a bowl of vegan ice cream just after her first real conversation with Aaron post-note. "He took anger and bitterness, and left me with loneliness, anxiety and grief." She moved the bowl to the nightstand and threw her body backwards on the bed.

Marissa copied her. "Maybe it would be easier if it worked that way."

Even three months after finding the note, the thin piece of stationery carefully placed between Elle's wallet and lipstick weighed her purse down. The bag's thick strap crossed over her shoulder between her breasts, and at that moment it felt like the weight of the words it carried would collapse her chest. She reminded herself just to breathe in and breathe out.

Random anxiety attacks had become commonplace even at the

strangest, least anxiety filled moments. Here she was entering the Promenade shopping center and the thought of the envelope she'd found on her bathroom sink made her wish she'd brought her anti-anxiety medication with her. Shopping usually relaxed her, walking through the stores, handling the brand-new clothes, breathing in the therapeutic scent of the leather boots, trying on at least 10 pairs of shoes and maybe even coming home with a pair or two. This was her own personal prescription for anxiety.

In these months, the dilemma wasn't so much whether to buy anything on these curative shopping forays but instead how much to spend. It wasn't like she was shopping on Rodeo Drive. There was a fine line she had to walk—or shop as it were—until her husband returned to her. Did she want to jab at the man who had left her in a note after six years? Most of the time, yes. On the other hand, she wanted to make sure money was left when they reconciled—yes, when not if.

Walking through the Promenade to solve one part of the problem only brought another burning angst. It was December, with Christmas décor at every glance and families shopping together holding hands, beaming with holiday cheer. How had she forgotten what time of year it was?

Strolling from one store entrance to the next, none of the garb appealed to her. Another cashmere sweater wasn't going to coax him into coming home and a $180 pair of shoes wouldn't hurt his bottom line. Anything she bought would only produce another bill to come in both of their names, a reminder of her solitude.

She passed the 25-deep line of children both excited and wary of a picture with Santa. Just a few stores down was another set up for pet pictures with Santa. She rolled her eyes—at least she wasn't that pathetic.

Then it struck her. Holiday shoppers were buying gifts for loved ones. Who shopped for themselves two weeks before Christmas? Just as she turned the corner into the central open space of the Promenade, she nearly ran into a woman standing in line with a bright red garbage-bag-like sack. Elle shifted her weight and direction as she apologized to the woman at the back of the line who was giving her a terrible look.

The line was the length of two or more stores, and each pedestrian held the same type of red sack as the first woman. As Elle came closer to the front, she saw a Christmas tree with paper ornaments and finally a sign, "Tree of Hope."

With a closer glance and better understanding, Elle realized the ornaments on the tree weren't ornaments at all. They were different colored pieces of paper with names and other information on them. Elle vaguely remembered her grandmother, Norah, picking a needy child from the tree and getting them a gift when otherwise they may not get many—if any—Christmas presents. Elle had never done it herself, but in an impulsive hatred of her self-medicating shopping habits, she stopped at the table.

"Excuse me. Do you have any angels left?"

The older, plump woman behind the counter chuckled, barely looking up from the clipboard in her hand. "Plenty." She pointed to the tree and parroted with little enthusiasm, "Green is for active duty soldiers, and red is the soldiers' families."

Elle had never heard of these programs for soldiers or their families. She glanced around as if she would get caught acting out of character and plucked a red tag from the tree.

"Deadline's tomorrow." The plump woman barked, as she handed Elle her own clipboard and red sack that matched each person in line. Elle filled out her information on the forms and that of the family on the tag she held, and passed it back to the woman, who was already speaking with the next person in line.

A small pin pricked inside Elle's stomach, the feeling of pride. She was philanthropic, shopping for someone who otherwise might not have anything. Aaron would be proud. Elle found a bench far enough away from the bustle to sit and read the tag she claimed as her own Christmas miracle.

Your Tree of Hope Family: The Turner Family
Wife of Soldier (26 years old)
   Sizes: Clothing: 6-7, medium; Shoes: 7; Underwear: medium
   Needs: Flat-iron
   Wants: Digital Camera
Son of Soldier (3 ½ years old)
   Sizes: Clothing: 4T; Shoes: 8; Underwear: 4T-5T
   Needs: Puzzles, educational games
   Wants: Star Wars toys

Really? Someone needed a flat iron enough to put it on a Tree of Hope list—who on earth didn't have a flat iron? She found it disturbing that she was allowed to know the woman's underwear size but not her first name.

She could see it now, the movie playing in her mind. The beautiful woman left by her husband only to experience a Christmas miracle of helping a less-fortunate family. In her own spirit of Christmas giving, she would in turn receive the gift of love: her husband's love.

Hallmark Channel would obviously air it.

There was, however, her infamous dilemma of how much to spend. Aaron couldn't stop her from buying Christmas gifts. Isn't this what she went shopping for? Retail therapy. What's more? Retail therapy with no guilt.

Even better, she could put a little note in one of the boxes telling her Tree of Hope family how proud she was to help them through Christmas while their soldier was overseas. The gifts were supposed to be anonymous. It had said that in the paperwork. But nobody could fault her for wanting to thank this family for their brave sacrifice and share what an honor it was for her to sacrifice *her* means—they didn't need to know it was her absent husband's—for their celebration.

Elle popped off the bench with gusto, red tag in one hand and red sack in the other. Time to get shopping!

***

Near closing time at the Promenade the next day, Elle came back to the Tree of Hope feeling like a real-life Santa Claus—albeit, thin and high-heeled. She had to drag the red sack behind her, heavy and near overflowing with unwrapped gifts.

It was impossible for her to keep to herself while in line to turn in the sack. She wanted everyone around her to know just how much she had bought this family of two.

A smirk broke her lips as she noticed the woman in front of her with a sack slung over her shoulder, obviously light enough to carry and merely halfway full. Sad for the family *that* woman had picked.

The edges of the boxes in Elle's sack jutted out at every angle as she dragged it forward in line. Theatrically, Elle pulled out the red tag and a pen from her purse and began marking off each item she had purchased, mumbling to herself, but loud enough for those around her to hear.

"Flat iron, yes. Star Wars toys, check. Hmm, underwear, shoes. Check, check. Let's see. Clothes, yes. Books, of course." She paused for effect. Then louder, careful that everyone was paying enough attention, she continued, "Digital camera," dramatic pause. "Check."

She heard a small gasp from the woman behind her, and Elle was satisfied. This was way better than shopping for herself. She'd even thrown in a bit extra. The card she'd written to the Turner family slipped secretly inside the camera box, held with it a check for $50. "Perhaps to pay for your Christmas dinner or presents for your soldier husband. Whatever you see fit." A note that made her feel much better about herself and almost forget the one from Aaron sitting idly in her purse.

The note Elle penned was by far longer than Aaron's farewell sentences. In it, Elle explained her desire to get outside herself at this time of year as it was also a difficult season in her personal life. She'd included a little commentary on a few of the gifts, particularly the panties—sexy ones that Elle suggested Mrs. Turner wear when her husband came home on leave. It wasn't too long of a note—maybe it should be considered a letter. But Elle had a lot of appreciation to express for the Turner family.

Beforehand, Elle hadn't thought of the families behind the soldiers. Now she realized how amazing it was that this husband and wife could make a marriage and family work being thousands of miles apart, while her and her husband couldn't stay happy living in the same house.

The woman at the counter—same plump woman who gave her the red sack the day before—interrupted her thoughts. "Oh my." She took in the size of the overstuffed bag, barely able to pick it up to get it behind the table. "You went all out." The worker said as she looked inside the bag, not so much impressed as annoyed. "Maybe you could have spread out your generosity on more than *one* family this Christmas."

Elle's mouth fell ajar, stunned. She heard the jeers from others in line and volunteers behind the table. Everyone stared at her excessiveness. But there was no rule that said she couldn't buy every item on the list. Moments ago, she felt gratified at making this little family's Christmas wishes come true. Now all she was, was embarrassed.

Then she thought about her letter to Mrs. Turner, and pride surged.

"I see nothing wrong with wanting to make this Christmas one for the books for this family. It's not my fault or *theirs* that you are all too stingy and want more presents for yourselves instead." She huffed as she took the paperwork out of the woman's hand and signed her name. "Besides," Elle continued with another burst of inspiration, "You have no way of knowing if I already *have* done this for another family." Of course, she hadn't. The idea of taking multiple tags hadn't occurred to her, but they didn't need to know that.

Their jaws gaped as she dropped her red sack. Her smug smirk returned.

2

JOCELYN

The package sat in her bedroom next to the closet. She'd opened it and confusingly sifted through the contents. Jocelyn had no idea why she'd received this enormous box bulging with gifts. It had arrived via FedEx a week before Christmas with a note on top of the wrapped boxes, each in matching Santa Claus foil paper. The note was simple. "You and your family truly are loved. Merry Christmas from Tree of Hope."

Jocelyn hid the cardboard container in her bedroom to ensure that Ian didn't peek in and get excited as all children do at the sign of Christmas presents, just in case a mistake had been made. And she was quite sure there had been.

With the door shut, she picked into the first gift, gently pulling the tape away allowing for only small tears to which Ian's toddler eyes wouldn't pay attention if the gifts turned out to be legit.

But when she pulled out the black sheer panties with hot pink ribbons laced up both sides, Jocelyn threw them back into the box like a hot potato. This was seriously wrong! She thought of her fellow army wife and friend, Alexis. Surely she would be the only one who would have the gall to mail Jocelyn panties. But Alexis would do it with a snarky note, not through the Tree of Hope. Not to mention, Alexis was in the middle of relocating, and Jocelyn knew they didn't have the money to rain down presents on them like this.

Her long fingers rifled through all the gifts. Surely there was something, a note, a card, some sort of explanation. All the packages were wrapped, and there was nothing except the small paper from Tree of Hope. She flipped the lid to the FedEx box, and there was the return address—with her explanation in between the address lines. She shoved the presents back in the FedEx box and pushed it to her closet.

The clatter of plastic toys told her she'd have to make her call in the living room so she could keep an eye on Ian.

"What are you doing, honey?" She asked, exiting her room.

"What, Mom?"

Every time he called her *Mom* a little piece of her felt sad. *Mommy* had only lasted a few months. The first *mom* had ambushed her. Why was a three-year-old grown up enough to say *mom* instead of mommy or momma? She wasn't ready to be just *mom*. She thought she would have a few more years—at least make it to school—before she had transformed to a *mom*. But along with kids came plenty of unexpected moments.

"Just remember whatever you get out, you'll have to put back, okay?"

"Yep." He said, accentuating the *p*.

He truly was his father's son, saying the least amount needed to communicate his point. Even *mom* was a representation of that.

Jocelyn grabbed her phone, searched through her contacts, and snuck a peek in Ian's room. The sight induced a smile. Lying on his belly, little fat feet in the air, Ian had toys lined up in two rows facing each other. Dinosaur across from the army man. The robot versus a Star Wars' Stormtrooper. All prepared to fight their opponents with Ian playing puppeteer of the battle before him. "Oh Mr. Robot, Commander Rex got you. PSSHEW!" And he pushed the robot over as the imaginary missile hit him.

Even at three, Ian was an expert at sound effects. Guns, swords, cars. He could imitate them all.

"It's okay, friend, I'll help you." Army man came to the rescue. Ian never noticed his mother observing with a smile.

Building tanks, guns or any form of weapon from Legos was in his nature; the way her nature was to protect him from knowing exactly what his daddy—whom Ian of course called Dad—was doing in Afghanistan.

Walking down the hallway to the kitchen, she dialed her phone then propped it under her shoulder as she started in on the dishes from dinner.

"Hello?"

"Aunt Janie?"

"Is that you, Jocelyn?" That question was ridiculous in the days of caller-ID and cell phone contacts, but Jocelyn expected her aunt to play coy. "What has you calling this evening?"

"Why do I have a FedEx box filled with Christmas gifts in my bedroom?" Jumping straight to the point, Jocelyn's voice was filled with amusement more than ire.

"That sounds wonderful, but why would you think *I* would know about it? I'm flattered but you know I don't have that kind of money."

Her aunt's babbling confirmed Jocelyn's suspicions. "I checked the return address and you happen to live in Torrance, California. Any ideas?"

Her aunt sighed. "Why can't you just accept a nice surprise and not ask any questions?"

"You know that's not my style." Jocelyn paused for a response that didn't come. "Aunt Janie?"

"Oh fine. If you want to spoil my thoughtful gesture." That brought a small smile to her niece's lips. "I knew that Scott was still away," she whispered the last word as if it were a secret, "and wanted Ian to have an exciting Christmas. You know I couldn't make it happen alone. So," she hesitated, "I entered you in the Tree of Hope program at the shopping center."

Jocelyn gasped before she could check her reaction.

"I know it. I should have told you,"

"*Asked* me."

"But I knew you would say no."

"Aunt Janie, we aren't needy." Of which she could not seem to convince her family. They were all so worried, as if Scott didn't get paid while he was overseas or something. "Ian has plenty of gifts under the tree already. Tree of Hope is supposed to be for families who can't provide Christmas themselves. I can't believe–" She didn't finish because she didn't know what else to say.

The TV was droning on in the background of her aunt's side, probably *Wheel of Fortune*.

"But what about you, Jocelyn? How many gifts do you have under the tree? I wanted to make this Christmas special, rather than about Scott being gone."

Jocelyn wasn't mad at her aunt. She was uncomfortable with some stranger buying her and her son gifts, but she softened her response.

"They bought me panties."

"You opened them already? They were Christmas gifts!"

"Panties."

Her aunt giggled, and Jocelyn couldn't help it either. She burst out. "And you should see them, too!"

They laughed together for so long and so loud that Ian peeked out of his room. She reigned herself in long enough to explain that Mommy was on the phone with Aunt Janie. Ian shrugged and resumed his toy battle like the explanation made perfect sense.

Jocelyn sighed, feeling the stitch of soreness in the side of her stomach from laughing. "Why would a stranger buy me panties? I could never do that."

Janie explained that the paperwork asked for all sizes and she'd asked her sister Roxanne, Jocelyn's mother, for the answers. Aunt Janie had filled in her own California address to the local shopping center after explaining that Scott was stationed out of Fort Hood in Texas then personally mailed the box to the true Turner residence.

"I thought maybe I could make up for all the Christmases and showers that I've missed."

Jocelyn's heart warmed. Her mother's sister had never been close to the family until five years ago when she was battling breast cancer and needed help during her treatments. Jocelyn's entire family, who all lived in California where Jocelyn grew up, rallied around Janie and she had been trying to repay them ever since.

"You know you don't have to make up for anything." Then she added, "And you know I can't accept these gifts."

"Jocelyn Nicole," The voice that came back at her sounded freakishly like her mother. "You *must* accept them. Someone spent a lot of money on those gifts. How do you think they would feel to know that you didn't want them? Besides, you haven't anywhere to return them, and you haven't even opened them. What if there are things you need?"

"Like panties?"

They both chuckled.

"Okay, okay, I'll open all of them and keep one for each of us. But the rest of them I am giving to families who are *actually* needy."

Janie sighed. "Sometimes I think there is simply no way we are related." Another mutual chuckle. "How about two each?" She bartered.

Glancing at Ian, Jocelyn caved. "I suppose I could live with that."

***

Bath time was usually nice down time for Jocelyn, sitting next to the bathtub that kept Ian contained while he splashed around and played in the bubbles. But tonight, Jocelyn rushed through it so she could delve into the box.

"No bubbles tonight, babe." She told Ian, who put up a small fight until his bath shark distracted him.

Ian had never been a tough kid to get to sleep as long as she went through their routine. When bedtime came, Jocelyn snuggled up next to him and read the short stack of books he had selected. They said their bedtime prayers, always praying for Scott and the men in his unit.

But tonight, during Ian's prayers, he added at the end, "And let Dad be home at Christmas."

His matter-of-factness caused a rock in Jocelyn's throat. Scott had preferred to go downrange while Ian was young enough to hardly remember, but the day-to-day struggle tugged at Jocelyn's heart. She repeated how Scott would be home in March—a 13-month deployment—as seen on their homemade calendar on the refrigerator with a countdown until Scott's return.

But Ian was not yet four, and all he knew was how much he wanted his dad home.

Jocelyn stroked Ian's thick, blond hair back from his forehead.

"Can I see hims?" Ian asked, pointing at the nightlight globe on his dresser.

"Of course," Jocelyn reached over and stretched the cord of the globe over her body to the bed. She spun the sphere in her hand and stopped it with her fingertips. "Right here," she pointed just under Afghanistan so Ian could see the asymmetrical shape of the country.

Ian stared at the spot that was not much bigger than the tip of his mother's finger on this small globe. Unspeaking, he focused on it as though he could see through the plastic into the real life desert.

Staring at her boy, she wished she could leapfrog into his head and eavesdrop on his thoughts.

She had read books and blogs, even talked with other moms on how to handle deployment with a toddler. Maybe all the research eased the transitions, but in truth, nothing could make this okay for a three-year-old. "He's there protecting us and other families." They had this conversation at least once a week, but the explanation never got easier. Answering the questions of a child who's barely old enough to communicate his most basic needs, these were the things no one tells you about parenting.

"From bad guys?" Ian saw everything in terms of good guys and bad guys, so Jocelyn had learned to use his vocabulary too.

"The bad guys don't want other people to live how we do. Daddy and his friends go to help protect other people from the bad guys. Isn't he brave?"

Nod.

"We have to be brave like Daddy too while he's gone, okay?"

Ian curled his thin arms around the Daddy Doll he slept with every night while Scott was away. Seeing the doll, Jocelyn conjured the memory of the night before Scott's deployment. She wasn't surprised how intentional Scott had been about his family before leaving. Even so, when she stood in the doorway and watched him with their son, she was overcome. Scott had brought a small bag into the room with Ian and pulled out the gift for his son.

"A doll?" Ian raised his translucent eyebrows.

"It's an action figure pillow…of me." Scott handed over the foot-long pillow shaped around a fabric-printed picture of Scott in uniform standing at attention. The little pillow passed from Scott's large, masculine hands to his son's dimpled ones, and immediately Ian wrapped the pillow in a hug. "Now you can hug and kiss Daddy every night before you go to bed, even when I'm across the world." And he leaned down and kissed Ian's floppy head of hair.

That image was glued in Jocelyn's memory. The love she had in that moment for the two men in her life was what held her together during the roughest days of Scott's deployment.

Obviously, Ian would be a different child by the time Scott came home, speaking in full sentences, having lost the roundness of his baby cheeks and lingering rolls on his thighs. Scott would return looking the same, only having changed inside, taking in horrors that no one should.

This was Scott's first deployment as a father. Proud as she was of her husband, Jocelyn attempted to protect Ian from the full truth of the army and war. Scott agreed. He had known too many guys who used the army as a vehicle for their rage and anger issues. As a couple, neither wanted to introduce violence to their son too early yet Scott wanted to pass on the importance of standing up for what you believed in, to protect what you love, even if that resulted in a conflict.

With a kiss to Ian's forehead and a tug of his blanket around his shoulders, Jocelyn watched his eyelashes flicker to a close as she turned the light off.

Her protection of Ian, though, came from different reasons than Scott's. She didn't want Ian to be afraid that his daddy would get hurt—or worse—because Jocelyn knew all too well how difficult it was to deal with that kind of fear.

***

In the quiet of night—which most nights were—the fear tried to creep up her spine. Every night, Jocelyn tried not to think about what Scott might be doing. But forcing herself *not* to think of him resulted in the opposite.

Her ticking brain kept her awake, a sort of military spouse insomnia. Others she knew had it too. How could you not? Knowing your husband on the other side of the world was just waking for the day, getting all his gear on, ready to defend other families like his.

When fears tickled her mind, she had to snatch them out of her head and replace them with others: to-do lists, packages to send Scott, activities for Ian, or sometimes not thinking of anything at all, just listening to the clock tick away the dark seconds.

Middle-of-the-night waking hours spawned the craziest ideas. About a month in to deployment, staring at the blank walls of their rental, she had the grand idea to paint the master bedroom army green to show support. At the paint shop, she proudly matched a bag Scott had left behind and spent the next insomniac night painting every inch of the bedroom. As with most sleep-deprived decisions, she regretted it in the sunlight at dawn. The unfortunate hue resembled Ian's baby diapers.

Jocelyn had also developed an embarrassing addiction to midnight infomercials: cleaning supplies, work-out programs, and one unfortunate experience with a hair removal device. Their budget didn't always permit her to order, but she could watch them endlessly.

Going through the box of presents seemed like a more productive use of her insomnia. After laying Ian down on the eve of Christmas Eve, Jocelyn stared at the mass of unopened presents. They were easier to give away sight unseen, but once she opened them, they would speak to her to be kept. No doubt there would be presents she would love to see Ian open, watching his eyes light up brighter than the Christmas lights he'd helped place on the tree.

She thought about blindly selecting four presents—two for each of them—but no telling which were meant for her or the blonde-haired boy asleep in the other room. Not to mention, the mortification she would experience if she gave away panties or something. The only solution was to open them all.

Donning her flannel Wonder Woman pajamas—a care packaged birthday present from Scott—she sat cross-legged on the floor eyeing the enormous box. She tucked her hair behind her ears and began the tedious process of unwrapping the Santa paper while minimizing the rips. Rewrapping all these gifts on Christmas Eve would be torture. Her plan was to sneak a peek, write the description on a Post-It to keep track of each of them, then replace the tape.

Her heart was pounding as she opened the first present. "This is stupid," she said aloud to herself—something she did often with Scott away. "Why am I so nervous?"

As she pulled back the paper, there lay Ian's number one request: a full collection of Star Wars light sabers. Red, blue, green, purple. Her eyes watered, but she pushed the emotion back with the tape on the wrapping paper.

To clear the tears, she went back to the box with the panties. She'd rather blush than cry. Seven pairs! They kept coming out like scarves in a magic trick. Even this brought tears to her eyes, and she finally conceded to them.

Alone in her room with tears dripping down her nose and chin, Jocelyn Turner open 11 packages from a stranger, her decision becoming harder with each one.

An urge to curl up next to Scott, inhale his cologne, hear his soft reassurances overwhelmed her. He would tell her to keep the gifts, and frankly he would be as excited about them as Ian. Sometimes he was as big of a kid as their son. And he wouldn't be wrong.

The struggle heaved in her chest. She wanted to offer her son everything in the world, but she couldn't suppress the feeling that this offering wasn't hers to give. Like it was given under false pretenses.

With Scott 10 ½ hours ahead in Afghanistan, there was no way of knowing when his schedule would allow a call. She couldn't keep putting the decision off, and yet sometimes all she wanted was to not have to decide alone.

The digital camera box gawked at her. Oh the pictures she could take with it. Ian feeding ducks at the park, running through high grass, climbing the limbs of a tree. Scott and Ian the moment they saw each other again. Her visions made the decision for her, really. This would capture moments that her old camera phone would only blur. Pictures of Ian tearing the paper off these presents on Christmas Day.

If that was going to happen, she'd have to charge it overnight. As she opened the camera box, pieces of paper spilled out into her lap. A check for $50—tears swelled, her heart constricted—and a note. The latter, she hoped would explain why this stranger had lavished her family with things that others might take for granted. Jocelyn curled her hand around her knees as she read the handwritten words.

> *Dear Military wife and son, I cannot imagine what your life may be like. I can only know that the world is better because of people like you....*

If the letter was all she received, it would have been gift enough. With division over the war their soldiers faced, gratitude could be hard to come by. Even Scott heard as much disparagement as praise.

After reading the entire two pages, she wiped her eyes, folded the stationery and tucked it—appropriately—in her underwear drawer.

The missing piece was Scott by her side reading over her shoulder. But the ache for Scott was always there, the gaping ache like her ribs were being cracked open the way a coroner exposes a cadaver's heart. Sometimes the ache lasted all day; sometimes it came in an instant. The need to see the sharp edges of his face, hear the lift of his voice, feel it reverberating inside of her.

She curled up in bed and turned on the video he'd made for her. The disc was already in her DVD player from last week. She could recite his every word, but hearing his phantom voice in her head was a crumb compared to it resonating through the room.

His face filled the screen of her television, literally larger than life, and she turned off the overhead lights so that Scott illuminated the room.

"Hey Joss," her recorded husband cleared his throat and reached up to adjust the camera, making the picture vibrate momentarily. "I thought it might be a good idea to record a message for you." He'd made one for Ian, too, with silly songs and dances. "But now that I'm here, I don't know what to say exactly. Maybe I should have planned it out more like you would." He laughed to himself. "I just want to tell you how much you mean to me. You'll be with me every day. It won't be the same, but I'd like to think that we are so connected to each other that when you think of me it's because I'm already thinking of you. You'll be pulling me home. Like gravity. Or something poetic like that. I want you to–"

Jocelyn heard her own off-screen voice through the speakers, "Hey babe—oh, sorry, what–"

Not only did she remember walking in on him to put away a load of laundry, but she now had her own confused voice memorized in cadence with his. And she knew what came next.

After off-screen Jocelyn closed the door, Scott smiled at the camera, his eyes blazing like he had seen something he wanted. "God, you're beautiful." He leaned his head down and rubbed his faced with one hand, then looked squarely into the camera. "But you're even more than that. You're everything to me. You keep me standing. You keep me going. Without you, I'm nothing." He sucked in his bottom lip then delivered his last line, "You are my home."

That's where she paused: a frozen picture of Scott's face, pure love in his eyes—brown like the feathers of a wren. And she laid down looking at him, believing that as she thought of him, ached for him, he was thinking of her. His face—the picture of all her hopes and dreams and the only future she cared about—being the last image behind her eyes before sleep took hold.

3

ELLE

White twinkle lights spotted through palm trees and a slightly cooler breeze coming off the Pacific may not have seemed like December to a newcomer in area, but it was all Elle had ever known. This year she felt the season acutely.

Elle's pride was hit hard when none of her couple-friends invited her to Christmas parties or even called to wish her well. Alone with her chamomile tea and lentil soup, the apartment she used to share with Aaron had never felt as peculiarly quiet as it did on Christmas Eve.

Christmas Day was a simple meal at her apartment with her grandmother, Norah. Norah was her geographically and relationally closest family member—about 20 minutes away but rarely visited—since her own mother was barely in the picture. She was off gallivanting across the country trying to build a real estate business in an iffy economy. None of them knew who Elle's father was.

"You look like hell." Norah said when Elle opened the door.

"Thanks Norah. Merry Christmas." Always free with the compliments, her grandmother was. Elle took the mashed potatoes and rotisserie chicken from her grandmother's unsteady hands, knowing she wouldn't be able to eat them. Elle was vegan, and Norah refused to cook or eat the same way even for one meal.

"Well, you do. You're too skinny." Norah shrugged her fur coat-covered shoulders. It went along with her church-lady hat. "How's it going with Aaron?"

There was always a feeling that Norah liked Aaron more than she

18

liked her own granddaughter. She asked after him and when he gave her even a trinket, it was like he had presented her with a treasure chest. As much as she wanted to brave face it for her gran, she knew Norah would be able to see through her efforts.

Awful. "Fine." She didn't want to cry, but there was also a high chance she would at any moment.

Norah clucked her tongue. And on went their Christmas visit.

Ever since her mom took off for West Coast small towns over the East Coast metropolis when Elle was 15, Elle had been parented by her grandmother.

Although, if she was honest, it wasn't all that much different than when her mom was around, just a different house and school. Her grandmother had been at her volleyball games while her mom was working and at the school plays when her mom went out with yet another boyfriend. It was Norah who'd bought her maxi-pads for the first time, given her the sex talk, taken her to get glasses and later contacts. When her report cards needed signing, Mom would forget so Norah would sign them. When she was sent to the principal for drawing dirty pictures in her Biology textbook, Mom was called, but Norah showed up for the parent-teacher meeting. For all intents and purposes, Norah had been the mother—Elle's mother, Charlene, the surrogate.

It made no difference to Elle. She'd gotten everything she'd wished for because Norah was still a grandmother who wanted to spoil Elle with everything she couldn't give her own two children. And Charlene, well, when she did finally remember that she had a daughter, she splurged on Elle with every kind of guilt-ridden gift. Brand name clothes, the latest gadgets, gas cards directly debited from her account.

Someone had always taken care of Elle. Most recently, that had been Aaron.

See, her own money was conveniently being cashed and placed at the bottom of her tampon box (the only place she felt assured that neither Aaron nor any burglar would dare look). He'd left the apartment and moved in with his brother, but everything was on bill pay from their joint checking account.

No amount of money would matter, though, if Aaron would just come back to her. Deep down, that's all she wanted. Gah, she missed him.

A week after *the note,* she'd begged him into couple's counseling and was stunned to hear Aaron agree. Their first session was a balmy October evening. Dr. Fullerton had said they were headed straight for divorce court with the attitude they both had. Elle almost got up from that bald guy's uncomfortable chair and walk out right then. Instead she burst into tears. "But I love him so much, so, so much. I can't live without him." She'd gushed and Aaron rolled his eyes, arms crossed refusing to let anything penetrate them.

The counselor nodded, unscathed by either of their responses. "Good, good. I know you love each other or you wouldn't be here, but that is not all it takes to fix a marriage in disrepair."

Elle had tried to calm her sobbing to mild whimpering.

"If that is how you feel about your husband, and I believe it is, then you will do whatever it takes in trying to make this work."

She nodded fervently, keeping her lips sealed to not release the sobbing again.

Reluctantly and uncomfortably, Aaron had told the counselor that he felt both unheard and smothered at the same time.

Elle gasped aloud. How could that be? She had tried to talk to him every day since he'd left, and hardly got any response. How could she be smothering him when they hadn't even seen each other? She'd tried to express how much she loved him and missed him in her voice mail messages and texts.

Her only complaint was feeling invisible to her husband. He didn't express his feelings to her enough—or ever. Thus the complete blind-side of his note. If he'd ever expressed the need for her to change anything, she would have.

"I have. I tell you all the time." Aaron countered, failing to keep his voice level.

Different channels, Dr. Fullerton had said. They communicated on different channels and it was about tuning in to the same station. "Let's focus on what Elle can do first, since you left," he nodded to Aaron, "If that's okay with you both."

They both nodded, neither speaking.

Together, they agreed on three things Elle could do in the next four weeks—including the holidays—to prove to Aaron that she could change for him: 1) no more texts, 2) one call a week, and 3) if for three weeks the first two worked out, they could meet in person. Week four, the two would reconvene in the counselor's office and discuss their progress.

When they were walking out, the counselor held Elle back for a moment, which irritatingly kept her from walking Aaron to his car. Maybe it was by design. Dr. Fullerton cautioned her, "I know you are hoping for an easy solution to all of this, Elle, but I want you to know that it is going to take time. This first month is about opening Aaron back up to the idea of you two being together. You are going to need patience." He said with a nod that Elle copied.

Although difficult, Elle knew it was the perfect opportunity for Aaron to realize how much he missed her throughout each day, how sweeter his life was with her in it. She was confident that one month from that day in December, Aaron would be ready to get back together.

***

"What the hell do you think you are doing?" Aaron's volatile inflection pierced Elle's ear through the phone.

"Happy holidays to you too, husband. How was *your* single Christmas?" She responded, dripping with sarcasm.

"Don't act like you don't know why I'm calling."

"I have no idea what you mean?" She really didn't.

"I got the credit card bill."

Her smile dropped. Not exactly what she was hoping for from his first phone call—one that went against the counselor's rule, by the way, but she wasn't going to say anything.

"You have to pay for this, and you have to pay it with all the money that you aren't depositing into our bank account."

Elle shifted the phone to her shoulder so the manicurist could file her fingernails. "How do I know that you didn't spend a bunch of money on yourself and are nabbing me with the bill?"

"At Victoria Secret's?"

Elle gasped in mock horror. "How dare you use our money on your mistress."

"This isn't funny, Elle. You spent $700 in one day."

"I miss you."

"Yeah, I can tell by your shopping habits."

"Aaron," Her voice just above a whisper, she pulled her hands free from their treatments to cradle the phone. "I *do* miss you. I can't do this anymore. I want to be with you more than anything in this world."

His voice dropped all venom. "Just as always, Elle, it's all about you." Deep breath. "Now pay the bill."

The line went dead, but Elle said it anyway, "I love you."

She looked around the nail salon, desolate the day after Christmas. All the technician's eyes were on her. Their heads bobbed back to their busy work.

"My husband," she justified to "Maggie," the American name for the young Vietnamese woman filing diligently at her nails. "Are you married, Maggie?"

Maggie shook her head, apprehensive.

"Probably better for you." This was the most Elle had spoken to anyone in the salon about personal matters. Usually she only had complaints for them—nails were too short, wrong color, or needed a redo. Nail technicians could be like hair stylists or bartenders, right?

"People always say marriage is hard, and they aren't kidding."

Maggie's head stayed down, but Elle continued talking to the crown of Maggie's mop-thick black hair. "Everything started perfect. The wedding was beautiful. I mean, the department store pasted a wretched mask of makeup on the bridesmaids, but thank God that was fixable."

She paused when the salon phone began to ring.

"Of course my styles have changed. I would never have silver and blue now. Plum and ivory would be perfect."

The ringing of the phone became piercing.

"Do you need to get that?"

One of the women rushed to the front and answered in broken English. No one met Elle's eyes.

"He acts like I'm the problem, but I really don't even know what I did." She paused, "He never said he was unhappy."

And she barely took a break ranting until her manicure was done. When she didn't feel like she'd verbally purged enough, she asked for a pedicure.

***

Too heartbroken to be seen at a party, Elle's year ended skimming a marriage book with Ryan Seacrest muted on TV and a glass of Champagne—which she didn't like—in her hand.

Her new year began with a headache and puffy eyes.

Around 11 in the morning, her phone chimed with a "Happy New Year" text from Marissa to which Elle did not respond. Mid-afternoon Elle finished the bottle of Champagne and fell asleep until her phone buzzed and woke her. This time it was Aaron. A text. From Aaron. In an instant, she was awake and sober—mostly. It was simple and to the point. "Happy New Year, Elle." This was the first unsolicited communication from him. And it wasn't a mass text. It was personalized. That was something.

She remembered how the counselor cautioned at their first appointment not to expect Aaron to come around right away. And yet within three weeks, Aaron was making a step forward.

All evening she obsessed about her husband and was certain he couldn't stop thinking about her. By midnight with more Champagne, she was texting Marissa. "Aaron can't go a week without sex, nevertheless three. You think he misses me?"

"Of course he does."

By two o'clock in the morning, she was using the spare key over the door to slip into her brother-in-law's apartment—Aaron's new residence. She snuck into the spare room and took the time to stare at the man before her. The stubble of the new goatee he was growing—she'd tried to tell him that wasn't in style anymore, but oh well. The parenthesis of his eyebrows over his closed eyes. Just for a moment, she wanted to touch him, insert herself into his dreams, then maybe she would lay down to sleep next to him. Maybe when he woke next to her warm body, he would want her again.

Elle lowered herself onto the empty side of the bed. As his chest lifted in sleep, she gently touched it, to feel his changing heart beating. One touch, one second.

"WHAT THE—Elle, what are you doing?" Aaron jumped out of bed faster than Elle even realized he was awake.

She smiled. "I thought you might miss me. In bed. With you."

"Get out."

Pause, not entirely believing his request.

"Elle, get out NOW!"

Now she heard the demand it was. Humiliated, ashamed, disgusted, she stood, snatched her purse from the floor and took one last glance before heading for the door.

"OUT." As though he was sending a dog outside to poop in the yard.

Elle's ears hurt, her heart hurt, her pride hurt. When the apartment door slammed behind her leaving her husband on the other side, she wanted to hide. She felt a spotlight on her, as if all the neighbors saw her vulnerability displayed on the front porch. Could she hide from herself, from her own stupidity? Anything to mute the thoughts screaming at her in Aaron's enraged voice. But she'd been drunk plenty, smoked pot once, and none of that would drown this. She'd still wake up sober knowing she practically signed her name to divorce papers unless she mended this junk yard she'd dumped herself in.

***

The morning was a blur of headaches and bright lights, but she managed to dress in matching clothes for work and glance through the piled-up mail. Junk. Bills. Aaron's name all over the stupid envelopes, making her hangover throb as bad as her humiliation last night.

Tucked in between two bills was a green, handwritten envelope. From Texas. She didn't know anyone in Texas. Probably a marketing ploy with a handwritten font. She opened it anyway, curiosity reigning.

The envelope held a simple white card embossed with a pink flower and "thank you." Even more intrigued, Elle opened it and looked at the signature before she read the body of the note. "Jocelyn Turner." Her mind registered the last name, and her eyes popped to the beginning.

> Ms. Holloway,
> There are no words to express how appreciated your Christmas gifts have been. This Christmas was going to be difficult, but your selflessness changed everything for us. Capturing a picture of the surprise on my son's face when he opened the light sabers was a gift in itself. So my thanks to you. I hope that your holidays were as special as you made ours. God bless,
> Jocelyn Turner

There was an actual tear spilling over Elle's eye by the last line, but she wasn't crying for the Turner family. She was crying because she wanted to feel as valuable to someone as the gifts were to this woman. Where was karma? Or "give and it shall be given to you"? When would she get her return on that damn investment?

***

Dr. Fullerton made it clear Elle had to respect Aaron's boundaries for things to work between them, but those boundaries screamed at her from their invisible line asking her to push them in whatever way possible.

A boundary laid in front of her, a battle she didn't know if she could win. When he wouldn't listen to reason, Elle had always been able to soften (or harden as it were) him by dressing in lingerie or kissing him in just the right spot.

Admittedly she had messed up Dr. Fullerton's mandate to not meet in person, but he also encouraged some healthy contact in mending their relationship.

So sending a text in hopes that he was missing her would only be right. Healthy even.

Hey it's me, how was your day?

She pressed send and waited with her stomach fluttering to the point of nausea. Minutes ticked by while she stared at her phone. Then it buzzed with a response.

Fine. Yours?

Maybe she read too much into the waiting time and the condensed response, but she had a feeling he had mulled over whether to respond at all, and then what perfect words to use to convey his interest and disinterest all at the same time. In turn, she needed to pick her words just as carefully while making it clear that she wanted him, needed him.

Couldn't get my mind off of you. Made it hard to get anything done.

The second response time seemed even longer. She was taking a risk, but she knew it would either bring them one step closer or it would crash like a jet without an engine. She held her breath until her phone vibrated a response.

What are you doing now?

That was it. That was her opening. She knew Aaron enough to know what he was asking. He was missing her, thinking about her, wanting her. She took advantage of this thin crack in his shield and wrenched the opening even larger, reminding him of their best connections.

She jumped to her feet, found the best lighting she could in her apartment, angled her phone above her head where her whole body was in full view of the forward-facing camera, and clicked the perfect picture of herself…naked. Then before she lost her nerve, because even someone as brazen as Elle had brief moments when they questioned their methods, typed:

This…

Attached the picture and clicked send.

Her stomach spun in a U-turn but knew there was no way to get it all back from the cyber world now, so she rolled with it. Scanning back over their brief text conversation and the thought of him picking his phone up, seeing her picture and groaning the way she knew he did, made her heart thump out of her chest. He loved her body. Let's be real, *she* loved her body. She worked hard for it and he appreciated it, in more ways than one. And there was no doubt that he had been missing this part of her, even if he could do without other areas.

Okay, so climbing in bed with him at his apartment had been romantic but he had seen it as a little intrusive. She got it. But this was visual. Men—Aaron in particular—were visual. There was no doubt she would catch not only his attention but his desire as well.

Her phone buzzed but not with a text, this time with a call. She giggled, did a little victory dance then holding the phone close to her chest, took a deep breath before answering in her sexiest tone, "Hey,"

"What. The. Hell. This has got to stop, Elle." He whisper-yelled, in that restrained way that told Elle he was avoiding being overheard.

"I thought," she stumbled over her words a bit. It was disorienting flying high then drowning in the depths of the ocean in a split second. "I thought you missed me too."

"For Chrissake, Elle. I'm in a meeting."

Elle's breath glitched.

"Couldn't you tell by my texts that I was busy?" There was a roughness in his voice and a fair amount of noise in the background. "I'm at dinner with colleagues and a potential client."

Elle wanted to cry. "I thought because you were responding–" Her voice sounded like a child. She wished she could be one of those strong women who knew she didn't need a man. Why couldn't she be one of those women? "This was always what we were good at. We could always connect like this. And I've tried every other way. I thought you would miss this." *Miss me* was what she really meant. The tears were coming now, and she couldn't hold them back from her voice either.

Through the speaker, she heard him scratch his chin, a nervous habit of his that she'd always found sexy. But this time picturing his fresh goatee wounded her in a place she couldn't name.

"I wish you could understand, Elle, it takes more than sex to keep a marriage." He sighed, and his breath came out ragged. "There's things I've been missing that are deeper than that."

"Just tell me what. Please."

A man's voice boomed in the background. Aaron muffled his response by covering the mouthpiece to talk. Then he was back with her. "I have to go, Elle."

She wasn't ready for the end. Not yet. "Please tell me. I want to know. Really, I do." She grasped for a rope to bring him back to her. She was capable of change if she only knew what change he wanted to see in her. "You could come over after your meeting."

"I can't. I should get back to dinner. We'll talk," He paused then said, "I can't."

The line went quiet.

She curled up on her bed, still holding the phone against her ear. If she held it there long enough, would he call back? Could she will him to say what she needed him to say? With no blanket over her, letting her body be as physically vulnerable as she felt inside, she lay all alone on the bed she had hoped to share with him again.

4

JOCELYN

There was a time when Jocelyn's dates were like anyone else's: dinner, movie, holding hands, feeling the electric warmth of her date's body next to hers. And over the years she'd been on quite a few of those with Scott, but these days her dates took on a different tone.

For one, her date was shorter, pudgier, with sticky hands and crumbs stuck on his chin. He preferred pb&j at a park to filet mignon in a sit-down restaurant. And she was no longer the one with a curfew; her date had a bedtime.

Once a week, Jocelyn spent two hours with her phone tucked away in her mommy-purse—practically a diaper bag minus the diapers—and focused all her attention on her son, who was nearing four and becoming more and more entertaining.

"Mom, swing me!" Ian shrilled as they raced from the playground to the swing set.

On their first date of the new year, Jocelyn and Ian picnicked at a nearby pond, tossing out stale bread to the ducks, learning to count how many times the turtles snuck their heads above water. Even in Texas an outdoor date this early in the year was a rare opportunity. They took full advantage of the sun as it danced in Ian's blonde hair.

Sleep deprivation had tempted her to reschedule with her son, but their future held a day not too far away when Ian would rather spend his time with friends. When that day came, Jocelyn would wish for the age when he still needed her help putting on his shoes or swinging on a playground.

She hadn't heard from Scott since before Christmas. Now in the new year, her stomach lurched at the thought of him, but she knew there was nothing her worrying could do. As soon as they were home from the park, she couldn't reach for her phone fast enough. A deep relief saturated her as she saw an email from him and read,

> *Hey babe,*
>
> *I'm sorry I missed our Christmas Skype. You would think after missing so many holidays with you both that it would get easier. But instead it seems like each one is harder and harder to miss. They had us out on a mission after a terp was kidnapped. It lasted longer than any of us expected. I didn't even realize it was Christmas Day when we were out. One of the houses I patrolled near had a small Christmas tree up and I could see the lights through their window. It reminded me of home. The guys had saved some Christmas dinner for us. It was nice, but it wasn't like being with you and Ian. I miss you both so much. I received your care package and one from Mom and Dad and your parents as well. Please tell them thank you for me. I'll have some down time now, so let's Skype tonight, your time.*
>
> *With all my thoughts and love,*
> *Scott*

At his invitation, her stomach squirmed. Those few words revived the part of her that was a woman first and not only a mother or house keeper or home manager.

By bedtime, Jocelyn had taught two tutoring sessions (for extra income), drowned in household chores, mowed their small lawn, plus date night. She could have fallen asleep standing up. She tucked Ian under his Star Wars blankets with his Daddy Doll of Scott wrapped in his arms. He'd fallen asleep before the last page of *Goodnight iPad*. A bit of her still felt the new-mom impulse to check on him as he slept, to make sure he wasn't close to falling off the bed, that he was warm enough with his bare feet tucked under his blankets. But she'd learned to enjoy these rare, quiet moments when the pressures to keep him safe were lying low.

Hot cocoa in her hands and a blanket over her sore feet, she sat on the couch ready for the remainder of her date night. Skype opportunities with Scott were rare, and the call wouldn't last long. But any chance to see her husband's face would keep her awake into the wee hours.

The empty side of the bed where Scott would have been still had a rut in the mattress. She thought of how she would press her foot up against the bottom of his like pressing down on a gas pedal, just to get a reprieve from his snoring, even if only for a few minutes. Even that, she missed.

She sipped her hot cocoa, letting the steam rise to her face, feeling her pores welcome the warmth. Without knowing if Scott was yet awake at dawn in Afghanistan, Jocelyn wondered if she should pick up the book on her nightstand; its worn pages having been pored over again and again for years. Just as she was about to pull the blanket back and flip through the book's pages, a trill rang through the speakers next to her. The screen showed Scott's Skype number.

With nerves in her belly even after all these years, she fluffed her hair and checked her light makeup in her reflection at the bottom of the screen, showing what Scott would see thousands of miles away. As she clicked the green "Answer Call" button on the screen, Jocelyn exhaled, relishing the gnaw in her stomach.

There was Scott's face filling the screen before her—his beautiful, beautiful face. Even military short, his light brown hair was matted down—from being under a hat or in bed, she couldn't tell—but she wanted to run her fingers through it, to ruffle it while she kissed him hard on those full lips.

"Hey gorgeous," His voice made her body tingle and her throat thick.

A bottle of his cologne sat on the side table next to her, and making sure she did so off camera, she pumped a squirt into the air. A week after Scott deployed, Jocelyn had received a package in the mail, her name and address handwritten by her husband. In it: a t-shirt he'd worn to sleep in, a bottle of his favorite cologne and a pressed daisy. Ever since, she sprayed that cologne when they Skyped. To others it may have been silly, but to Jocelyn it brought her closer to this man.

"Was tonight date night with Ian too?" His connection was clearer than usual.

"It was." Jocelyn pulled out their new digital camera, and pointed the viewing screen at the webcam. "Can you see it?"

"Gosh, he's getting big." Scott said, squinting at the screen.

"I know. You want me to wake him up?"

"Next time. Tonight's for us."

Warmth flushed through Jocelyn's body. "Only a couple months and it'll be in person!"

"Counting down the days, are you?" Scott grinned.

"Always," Joss said. Her strength wavered when she glanced back at her husband. She wanted to push her hands through the screen and touch his rough chin, stroke his full eyebrows with her thumbs and line her fingers down his square jaw. The memory of the last time she had touched him seemed so real she could feel her fingertips pulse.

Instead she continued talking, taking advantage of every second she had with him however they came. "We made a new calendar for this year, and Ian put stickers on different days so he could keep track of when you'll be home." Scott's tour of duty ended in March, and Jocelyn's chest wrenched when she thought about it too long. She hated wishing the days away with an ever-changing little boy, but looking at her husband, she yearned for spring.

She filled him in on all things Ian. "Most recently," Jocelyn said, "we had an interesting conversation after dinner tonight. Randomly, Ian told me that his 'boy parts,'" she made air quotations, "were getting too long and big, and he didn't want them to get bigger."

"Oh no," Scott said with a chuckle.

"I tried to tell him that he would want them big when he got older, but he didn't believe me."

Together they laughed, and it felt good to co-parent, even for just a moment.

Scott turned the conversation to his wife. "What about you? What have you been up to?"

Jocelyn laughed lightly, "Um, gosh, let me think. I've just been to so many parties I don't know if I can remember them all." She tried out her best nasally Kim Kardashian impression. Then rolled her eyes. "Not much more than being a mom."

"Well, you're a great one." Her husband said.

She smiled her thanks, then added, "But wait, there was something. A FedEx man came to my door a couple days after New Year's and delivered a package of bubble bath."

"Really?" Scott asked with mock surprise. "Sounds like you have a secret admirer."

His wife pretended to consider the possibility. "You think?"

"You know what you should do?"

"What's that?" Jocelyn raised her eyebrow, knowing the answer would be amusing.

"You should take a picture," Scott paused for dramatic effect.

"Uh-huh." Joss said.

"Of yourself in the bathtub with bubbles and email it to–" He cleared his throat, "your secret admirer, so he knows you're getting use out of the gift."

Jocelyn mockingly dropped her jaw. "You wouldn't mind?"

Exaggeratedly, Scott shook his head.

"You know, I have something better in mind."

Scott's eyebrows went up. "You do?"

"Yep." Jocelyn moved the laptop facing away from the bed and switched on a cued up track of music. With the first thump, she was grateful Ian was a deep sleeper. Although she couldn't see Scott's face, she heard his "No way" and a giddy chuckle. Her cheeks blushed, but she was committed now.

She stood in front of the webcam holding the blanket around her waist, swaying her hips to the beat. Scott had taken her dancing before, sure, but she had never done anything like this. After six years of marriage and some stranger buying her panties like the ones she wore under the blanket, what better time to get over her inhibitions and match the seduction of his long-distance gifts.

Her hands rubbed against her abdomen and pulled at the bottom of her black camisole as the music moved through her body. Then she dropped the blanket.

"Oh," Scott groaned when it revealed the black and pink panties—like nothing she'd ever worn before.

Turning three quarters so he could see the laced-up back, she bit her lip watching his reaction.

"Jocelyn," he laughed as he put his hands like blinders on the sides of the monitor screen and looked over his shoulder, then whipped his eyes back to the screen.

"Better than a bubble bath picture?" She asked as she swiveled her abdomen and hips in his direction.

"Yeah, way better."

Jocelyn giggled. She could see the curves of her body in the small box at the bottom of the screen and felt pride in her fitness regimen even while Scott was away. The knowledge that in a few months he would be home to lavishly touch all over her body kept her going.

His wide, brown eyes fixed on the screen. Scott looked as though he could laugh, cry and explode simultaneously.

Nothing actually came off her body, because she was a little concerned that other eyes might see. But Scott knew what was under the black camisole and his smile said he was remembering in detail.

As the song concluded, she brought her lips to the webcam and kissed it. Scott moaned a mixture of frustration and ecstasy. "Get. Me. Home. To. That." He pulled at his short hair.

"When you come home, you'll get way more than that." She said, biting her lip in a smile.

Scott rubbed the tips of his fingers against the morning scruff of beard on his face. "Yes," he growled.

Jocelyn let her smile drop a little. "I love you, Scott Turner."

"And I love you." Then he laughed, "I don't want to turn it off."

Jocelyn winked. "Just think about me all day."

"Will do." Scott said unable to remove the toothy grin from his adorable face. Even more reluctant than usual, they both clicked on the red "End Call" button.

Her heart racing from the dance but mostly from the hungry look in those caramel brown eyes, Jocelyn fell back on the couch. Then aloud she said, "Thank you, Miss California." And giggled to herself, smiling bigger than ever after ending a call with Scott.

5

ELLE

Whoever created the Mary Poppins type purse that fits your entire arm in and still barely touches the bottom, Elle cursed them. Who needs a purse so large anyway? She had one—Louis Vuitton—and she hated it. Okay, most of the time she loved it, but at this instant, she hated it. More than a purse, it had become the natural place to put anything and everything—makeup, hairspray, combs, toothbrush and paste, spare shirts, gum wrappers—come on, all she wanted was a receipt and she must have had fifteen pieces of paper in there.

Marissa had come along as moral support. Not only did Elle need the extra cash, she thought if Aaron saw the effort she was making in returning what he had called "frivolous garbage," then he would see how much she wanted him back and that she could change.

Although, for the record, the Chanel blouse she was returning was in no way frivolous garbage.

The counter in front of her was covered in random items she'd pulled out of her bag searching for the receipt. She did feel like Mary Poppins minus the cheery disposition and propensity for quaint situational songs. The woman behind the counter glared at her.

"Aha, here it is." Elle pulled the slippery paper out in triumph and handed it to the woman, whose glare had not subsided in the least.

The woman picked up an envelope that had fallen from the countertop. "Is this yours?"

Elle snatched it from the woman.

"Oh perfect," Elle said to Marissa as she scanned the forgotten letter. "Listen to this, 'This Christmas was going to be difficult, but your selflessness changed everything for us.' Seriously? Welcome to the club. Apparently Christmas sucks. And so does selflessness."

Marissa took the note from Elle and read it for herself. "Elle, this is amazing."

Elle scoffed. "I know. I wish it wasn't. I should be able to blame them. If I could return all of those gifts, I wouldn't have to return this beautiful blouse." She grabbed the sleeve and cradled it gently between her fingers. "I'm happy just touching it. Imagine how it would feel to wear every day."

"You know this shirt costs as much as two weeks of my grocery budget." Marissa pulled the sleeve out of her friend's hand.

Elle scowled.

Waving the letter in the air, Marissa added, "You gave this little boy a Christmas he won't ever forget. That's priceless."

Elle seized the letter and shoved it back in the abyss of her purse. "This is where it all started. If I hadn't bought all this, Aaron wouldn't be so pissed. I mean, what needy family asks for a digital camera. Or Victoria Secrets' panties." Elle's volume rose and people were starting to stare, but Marissa had grown accustomed to Elle's dramatics.

The saleswoman plunked the pen and paper down for Elle to sign the credit back to her card.

"You know you didn't have to buy everything on the list. You could have just stuck to the inexpensive things."

Elle swiped the receipt off the counter and threw her hands in the air. "Then how selfless would I have been?"

Years of practice with Elle's emotional—and irrational—rants taught Marissa how to see through her friend. "You're just upset with Aaron, and maybe yourself. You don't need to take it out on strangers. If you let it, this whole situation could give you a new perspective."

Elle's cell phone buzzed, muffled in her purse. She'd seen it multiple times when she'd been digging with the gusto of an archeologist excavating a site to find an ancient treasure. Again, she began pulling things out and setting them on the counter even though the next customer was already being helped. Her hand groped for it as it buzzed the last time.

Seeing the missed call, Elle said, "Oh thank god it was only Norah." She returned the items haphazardly to the oversized handbag, all to be lost once again.

Marissa tried to help but only got in the way. "How is your Gran? I miss her."

"She's fine." Elle shrugged. They walked toward the exit.

"Have you talked to her about Aaron?"

"Not since Christmas."

The phone buzzed again. This time it was on top of the mound in her purse. "Hello Norah," Elle answered.

"H-h-h-p-p meee."

Elle stopped walking, cut short by what she thought she'd heard. "Norah, you're breaking up. Do you need help?"

When she heard a thud on Norah's end of the call, Elle grabbed Marissa's hand and pulled her along toward the exit. Marissa got the idea. Elle heard commotion on the line, voices, then someone grabbed the phone.

"Hello?" a voice said, an edge of panic behind the word.

"Is my grandmother okay?" Elle asked, following Marissa's search for the car in the parking garage.

"She slipped and fell in the grocery store. I think she hit her head on one of the shelves." The woman's voice was soft, making every effort to stay calm. "I've already called an ambulance. What's her name?"

"Norah Webster," Elle responded, now seated in the passenger seat of Marissa's minivan, pushing her free hand against the dashboard as though that would help the van move along faster.

"It's okay, Norah," she heard the woman repeat on the line. "We're going to get you to a doctor. Shhh. Don't try to talk right now. I'm talking with your granddaughter."

Listening to the woman, a flash of a memory flooded Elle's mind. Norah lying over a crying young Elle, brushing her hair back from her face after her mother had left for a week of traveling. "Shhh, it'll be okay." Norah had said in the same way.

More muffled talking on Norah's end, then the woman was back. "The ambulance is on their way. They are going to take her to Torrance Community Hospital."

Elle confirmed she'd be there but wanted to stay on the line until the

EMT's arrived on scene. Tears prickled her eyes as Elle glanced at Marissa watching the road soundlessly. She inhaled deeply the smells that seemed sharpened by the moment, Marissa's pine tree air freshener left over from Christmas and a hint of hairspray. She knew this was a moment she would be haunted by forever.

***

The hospital was quiet when Marissa dropped Elle off, the hallways empty and few people working to tell her where to go. She didn't make a point to visit hospitals—they had funny smells and not enough signs— but she always pictured them like they were on TV shows: bustling nurse's stations, overstuffed waiting rooms, multitudes of people whispering.

But here she walked the halls alone. Like a horror movie. She followed the signs and arrows to find the room number she'd been given, passing a nurse's station where no one asked her if she needed help.

Elle opened the door where Norah was in the back bed behind the drawn curtain. The television was on, a game show if she heard right. But still Elle tiptoed, feeling the need to keep the volume of the hospital room low. When she pulled the curtain back slightly her grandmother's face looked up at her, as though she was the one sneaking in on Elle.

The image of her grandmother sitting in a hospital gown, fragile and small in the bed, made her feel as though decades had flown by in an instant. Her throat constricted. The last time Elle had walked into the hospital with Norah, Charlene had still lived in the area and Elle thought she was going to lose her only grandmother.

"Oh Norah," Elle said, not knowing if it was relief in her voice that her grandmother was awake or sadness that they found themselves in this room at all.

"Moooommmma." The word came out slow and labored. There was a square bandage taped to Norah's forehead which concerned Elle. Had Norah lost her memory?

"No, it's Elle. I'm here now."

Norah wobbled her head. She used the hand that was not wrapped up past the wrist to adjust the blanket over her legs. "Ccc-aaa–"

Elle's phone buzzed, which earned her a frustrated glare from the nurse, and when she pulled it out of her purse the screen read: Aaron. She popped out of her seat and said, "I'll be right back" without even looking up.

"Aaron?" She answered.

"Hey Elle." He sounded casual. Like calling out of the blue wasn't completely abnormal. Like it didn't make her heart jump out of her throat to hear his voice. Like they were husband and wife talking on any average day.

"Listen, I need to talk to you. It's important." Of course. It couldn't just be to call and say, "I'm sorry. This was all a mistake. I want you back."

"What is it? I'm sort of in the middle of something." No, being at the hospital for her grandmother was not more important than talking to her husband, but she sure wanted him to think it was.

"Oh. Sorry. Is it a bad time?"

Bad time? Every minute of the day is a bad time until you come home and take me back. That's what she wanted to say. But instead she said, "I'm at the hospital with Norah."

His voice changed, "Is everything okay?"

Sometimes the feeling between Aaron and Norah was mutual. Sometimes it seemed Aaron liked Norah more than his own wife. Well, right now he probably did.

For a few minutes while she gave him an overview, she was able to pretend that he was her husband who lived in her home and loved all her pieces.

"Keep me updated. Maybe I can stop in and see her."

"You could come see both of us." She didn't expect him to agree, but she had to throw it out there.

There was silence in the air. Then she heard him sigh. "The reason I'm calling is," he paused. "I need the apartment."

"Like for a meeting?"

"Mike's wedding is this month. I have to be out by the time they get back from their honeymoon."

Elle had forgotten about her brother-in-law's wedding. Of all times for Aaron's little brother to be getting married. "I guess I'm uninvited then, right?"

"Not that I know of."

"Do you already have a different plus one?" She might have meant it as an angry jab, but it came out more charged than she wanted.

"Elle, stop." He sounded angry. The way she had wanted to sound.

"I think it's a fair question."

"No."

"No, it's not or no, you don't have a plus one?" Elle asked.

His voice escalated. "No plus one. And no, it's not a fair question if you know me at all."

"It is when you consider that you haven't even told me why you left. Obviously, I don't know you like I thought."

"You had to know this was coming. I've told you over and over. It's you who's not listening." His words rushed together, "That's not why I called. I need to stay at the apartment. I've been moved out for months, and I think that after the wedding it's fair for us to trade and you move out."

"What? You want me to move out? Where am I supposed to go?" Her words boomed through the car and echoed in her ears.

"I found my own place, so yours isn't really for me to figure out." His voice was on edge. "You haven't paid for a single bill in the last month. I'm sure you have some money saved up by now."

Elle was never speechless. Until now.

He tried to soften. "Look, I wouldn't be doing this if Mike wasn't getting married. But it's not unreasonable, Elle."

Even if she went through with it, she would never say it was okay.

"There's more." Aaron said.

Dread seeped out of Elle's pours.

"I cancelled our appointment with Dr. Fullerton. And before you whine about it, Elle, just think about it. You know why."

Elle knew how crazy she had been. It had been more than just sneaking in to Aaron's apartment or sending him naked pictures. After recovering from that, she had taken off work early to get to Aaron's office while he was out and had waltzed to his desk to replace the screen saver with a risqué photo of them together from…before she had lost him. In bed, hair tousled, love-drunk faces, sheets strategically placed on her but enough showing to make him look. And linger.

"Stop saying that about everything! If I knew why, then I wouldn't be asking. This was an important appointment." She was flustered and the pitch of her voice was all too revealing. Week four, Dr. Fullerton had said, would be the week they discussed how she and Aaron were to proceed from here. They were finally supposed to be able to meet in person.

In contrast, his voice was steady. "I cancelled *all* of the appointments because you haven't succeeded at one step that man gave. From day one, you bucked every rule, looking for loopholes instead of answers, and I'm done paying for it."

The hurt cut so deep that Elle's eyes started to fill. "Are we not a good enough investment?"

It took him so long to respond that Elle thought the line had cut off. Finally, "I want you to think back over our life and tell me what was missing? And I don't mean your perfect job. I mean with us."

"Right now?" But inside she answered, *I didn't think anything was missing.*

"That's what I wanted you to be doing over the last few weeks."

"What could I learn from you being gone that I couldn't have gotten from a really good conversation with you?"

"Are you still not listening? I kept a second job just to pay for this counseling. If I don't quit paying your way, you won't ever learn or change. I'm not your sugar daddy. That's not what I signed on for."

Infuriated, Elle bit back. "Oh no. You signed on for 'sickness and health, better or worse,' but clearly you didn't mean it."

Aaron's voice was tired when he was responded. "I thought I did. But that's for partnership not parenting."

At that, Elle hung up.

***

When she re-entered Norah's room, the television was blaring and the nurse was taking Norah's vital signs.

"Would you like some another ice pack on your ankle, Ms. Webster? We've got to keep the swelling down if you want to get back in the dancing scene." The Smurf-wearing nurse looked straight out of nursing school—not to mention why would anyone older than 12 want to be seen in public with Smurf's all over their body?

Norah laughed as much as she could in her state.

When Smurfett finished taking Norah's pulse through her wrist, she continued to hold her hand. "The doctor will come in shortly to go over your CT scan and MRI. He might decide to do an EKG because of your history."

Elle knew the nurse was referring to the stroke Norah had a few years back. It had put her out for months and scared Norah into daily walks and eating healthier—if you considered microwave Lean Cuisine meals healthy.

The nurse turned to Elle and said, "Your grandmother took quite the fall." She patted the back of Norah's hand, "I'll be back to check on you a bit later, Ms. Webster. Get some rest."

Golden curls drooped on either side of Norah's face in true Ethel Mertz style. Elle wasn't sure what to do. She fidgeted then asked, "Since I'm here, is there anything you'd like me to do?" Too late she recalled the communication barrier.

Norah's thin lips twitched, like she was fighting the words from coming out. "Cllll-ooo–" She took a break and started again. "Ccccll-ooo-ssss–"

Leaning forward without even realizing it, Elle tried to decipher. "Clothes?" Slowly Norah nodded and Elle smiled. "You want me to get your clothes? Sure." If there was anything Elle was good at, it was clothes.

***

Weeks had passed since Elle had stepped through her grandmother's front door. Maybe more like months. Could she have been so preoccupied in her plight with Aaron that she'd forgotten to stop by and help Norah get caught up with her laundry or clean the hard to reach corners of the apartment that had become Elle's job since Norah's back had given out one too many times? Months, and yet Elle hadn't noticed.

A dusty wreath hung crookedly over the peephole when she approached the front door. It was the same floral wreath Elle helped Norah hang in high school.

The key ring in her hand held entrance to this house, but the spare key, Elle knew without looking, was stowed away under fake grass in the potted plant to the right of the door. She could hear Norah's words of caution, "That fake plant cost me $50, so only use that key if it's an emergency."

This had been Norah's home for as long as Elle could remember. So when the nurse at the hospital had pulled Elle aside to hand her a brochure for a nearby assisted living facility, Elle had handed it right back. Year after year, Norah made herself clear to Aaron and Elle when they visited, "Don't you ever even think of putting me in one of those *homes*." She'd said it like a dirty word. "I'm a grown woman, and I want my own space."

Norah would never leave this place. It was more than a house, at this point. This long-standing, well-maintained home was a symbol of Norah herself.

Barb, the neighbor, passed along the sidewalk to the joint mailbox sifting out her mail, stirring Elle to the present. Ladies on this street were quite nosy, and Barb's inundating questions could send Elle running into traffic. She plunged the key into the lock and opened the door.

There was a particular smell that Elle had become accustomed to in Norah's home. A mixture of antique furniture and citrus cleaning products. But that was not the smell that welcomed her. Quite the opposite. A sour, pungent odor burned her nostrils. She nearly vomited right there in the white-tiled entry way. Proceeding into the home she was so familiar with, not one knickknack was out of place. Yet it wasn't the home she'd known.

The glisten of the sun pointed out a thin layer of dust covering the furniture. The garbage can which was usually emptied at the end of every day sat filled to the brim, and the source of the horrible smell was a litter box by the back door that hadn't been changed in who knows how long.

The cat! Momma, the black and white cat Elle had never bonded with, must have resorted to spraying the old green chair in the corner, because it reeked. That's what Norah was trying to say at the hospital. This cat meant more to Norah than any other possession. Elle hadn't even realized that this little woman spent her time sitting alone with only Momma to keep her company—a cat who was as feeble and elderly as her owner.

This home had always been perfect. Always. Not only was her house kept, but Norah presented herself immaculate in every way. Her car was spotless. Her closet was color and season coordinated, with jewelry to match and shoes that she had dyed the exact color of each outfit, kept pristine in their shoe boxes.

Looking around, there was a lot more to do than pick up some clothes to take to the hospital. She didn't know why Norah hadn't kept up her home as of late, but what she did know was that before Norah could return, the home had to be brought back to its original state.

Wrinkling her nose at the bleach smell of the latex gloves, she pulled them on over her gel-manicured hands to start at the litter box. Flashes came to her of growing up watching Norah with yellow rubber gloves just like these, scrubbing something, anything and everything. There was nothing unscrubbed in Norah's home.

But it was too much for Elle. The gloves came off; she pulled out her phone, sifted through her contacts and dialed her cleaning service. "I need an entire house deep cleaned, everything, today. I don't care how much it costs."

***

While the cleaning lady worked, Elle took a walk around the familiar house. As she entered the living room, memories cascaded over her. Every turn could have brought her to tears. Instead she took the moment to remember simpler times when everyone was healthy and she hadn't screwed up a marriage, when she and Norah could dance around the room singing "New York, New York" and laughing at each other.

It hit her then, and she couldn't believe she hadn't thought of it until that moment. She found the cleaning lady hunched in the shower and because Elle trusted the woman with her own home, left her to finish the job alone and returned to the hospital.

Her hands felt dry and in dire need of lotion as she gripped the steering wheel, but even that didn't take her mind off of her new plan. It was so obvious. How could she not have thought of it immediately?

She couldn't get to Norah's side fast enough. And all the way, she planned what she would say. When she stepped around the curtain in Norah's room, her grandmother was sleeping peacefully. And while that should have been a relief, being that the doctor had explained how much rest Norah's body needed, instead Elle rolled her eyes. She pulled the seat up closer to Norah's bed, not making any effort to be quiet, and sat on the edge of the seat, drumming her polished fingernails on her knee. How long had Norah already been sleeping? Wouldn't she fall back asleep in no time if Elle woke her up now?

Elle looked at the door, saw no nurses nearby, and casually dropped her keys on the tile floor, clanging them to the ground. But Norah didn't stir. She scooted the chair up a bit more, the legs grinding against the tile in that awful way. But nothing.

She grabbed the TV remote from the bed and turned on reruns of Norah's favorite game show, *Deal or No Deal*. For good measure, Elle turned the volume up a little too loud.

As though the contestant's terrible decision to not make a deal had reached into her subconscious, Norah awoke with a snore.

"I haven't been here long," Elle answered as if Norah had asked the question. She held the water and bendy straw up to Norah's lips. Norah's swallowing abilities had returned, much to the doctor's delight. "Has the doctor been in to talk with you?"

Norah shook her head with a groggy *no*. Elle didn't know whether it was a good sign that Norah was responding or a bad one that the doctors had no idea when Norah would be able to get out of here.

"I've been thinking," Elle began, hoping to see a sign of understanding and agreement, "you know, Dr. Forsythe said that when you get out of here, it'll be hard for you to get around by yourself. He even recommended putting you in a home."

Fear showed itself in Norah's pleated face.

"I know! I told him he doesn't know my gran." Elle played to her audience. "So what if I was to be your roommate and help take care of you?"

There was a pause, and Elle decided to seal the deal by adding, "It's the least I could do after all the years you cared for me."

She grabbed Norah's knobby hand with both of hers and smiled.

6

JOCELYN

"Turn it up. Dis is Dad's favorite song!" Ian hollered from the back seat.

Jocelyn smiled as she turned the dial on the car radio up. She wished Ian knew Scott's love of music by being around his father, but instead it came from her saying those words over and over to keep Scott's favorite things close. The blogs and books said that was a healthy way to keep a military child connected to their parents and ease the transition to the military parent returning home.

So they played all his favorite styles of music, watched Sunday night football even though it bored Jocelyn, and made Friday night spaghetti night. To keep Scott close.

They had just visited a nearby shelter, donating some of Ian's toys now that he had a whole new set taking up his toy bins. The night after Christmas, she asked him to sift through his toys for ones he no longer played with to give to kids who didn't have as many. It was important for her to teach Ian to give back, that not only soldiers or doctors or someone with an influential job could make a difference. Everyone could make a difference in some way.

He gave little resistance. In fact, just the opposite. He came out with even more toys than expected. Hugging one, he had told her, "I love dis one. I hope somebody else loves it too."

Then they had loaded up the boxed toys with a hand drawn card to the Helping Hands shelter which housed homeless families. Jocelyn was taken aback by how many children were there, keeping warm by the fire while the outside weather changed without notice.

The shelter's director, a woman who had enough gray hair to tell her own painful story, talked with Jocelyn for a while so that Ian could play with his new friends. He could make a friend anywhere and everywhere much like his dad. When she asked if they had other needs, the director answered, "Anything, really." Without knowing Jocelyn's husband was serving in Afghanistan, the director explained how many veterans came through their doors and the heartbreak—this time of year especially—to see them without homes.

This shelter spoke to why Joss struggled to take gifts under the guise of needing something, when families like these all over the country were in true need. She thought about what it would take for a man—like Scott—to lose himself after retiring from the military, unable to hold a job, unable to care for his family, rendered homeless. A mother sat on the couch with a ball cap over her bleached hair, watching her children play paper, rock, scissors with Ian. The sight tugged at Jocelyn's heart. In the woman's eyes, Jocelyn saw a possible future for herself. One that she would do everything in her power to prevent.

* * *

From the shelter, Jocelyn and Ian began their trek through the day's chores. Next stop was the Commissary for groceries. Even though they lived off the army post, the Commissary was close and the prices were much nicer on her budget. She went straight to the produce section where everything was bought local and stocked fresh.

Over the mound of bananas, she caught a glimpse of Elizabeth Cryer whom she knew as the wife of Captain Stewart Cryer—the Commanding Officer of Scott's unit. Mrs. Cryer led the unit's Family Readiness Group where Scott and Jocelyn had attended events with the unit and their families. However, Elizabeth and Jocelyn did not have the same interests. To put it nicely. While Scott looked to Captain Cryer like a second father, Jocelyn saw Mrs. Cryer as a mouth, the one with news on the latest army divorce, which happened all too often, or gossip on who made the biggest faux paux at some societal party.

Seeing Elizabeth's neatly cropped auburn hair triggered Jocelyn's unnatural crouch behind the bananas in hopes that she was as invisible as she felt at most army social events.

She made it through the produce without a run-in but saw Leanne Hargrove with her daughter waving in Jocelyn's direction.

"Hey there, Grace," Jocelyn wheeled her cart carrying Ian over to them. She babysat Grace last year during Leanne's deployment while her ex-husband worked. "How's kindergarten going?"

Grace shrugged. "Pretty good. For school."

The two mothers chatted a bit while the kids made faces at each other before rolling down different isles.

Headed to check-out, Jocelyn said a brief hello to Becky Lake with her three-month-old in a sling around her midsection. Her husband was training in Fort Lewis, Washington. She saw the purple crescents under Becky's eyes and remembered what it was like to have an infant while her husband was away.

An army post was like a small town. If you lived there or spent much time around the facilities, then you ran in to someone wherever you went and a lot of the time they knew your business. A lot of names to know, but none she called friends. Not since Alexis moved. Without Alexis or Scott, she was on her own. And she wasn't sure yet if that was a good or bad thing.

Living off post kept her off everyone's gossip train. Plus, using their housing allowance money to rent a duplex that was less expensive than their allotment saved them a little extra every month.

Jocelyn didn't recognize the cashier, a man with short gray hair who couldn't have been older than 50. She started to introduce herself when she overheard the familiar tone of Elizabeth Cryer's voice one register over. The tone said Elizabeth had news and wanted you to know she knew. Elizabeth had cornered another army wife in line, Nina whom Jocelyn had met at the last FRG playdate, and although Jocelyn couldn't see Nina's face, she knew the curious expression it held.

Captain Cryer's wife had lured Jocelyn before with that same tone of voice, but Jocelyn was never one to take the bait. She didn't care what juicy piece of gossip Elizabeth was frothing with. Although, today, her ears perked up when she heard the words "commo black out." Those words sent a chill through her. It meant that there had been an injury or casualty and communications from all units had been blocked until the families were notified. Being the head of the FRG, Elizabeth was tasked with keeping tabs on the soldiers and communication with their wives. If there was news, Elizabeth would know.

"Of course, this is all hush, hush." Elizabeth said to Nina, and Jocelyn rolled her eyes so hard it hurt. If the Captain knew the gossip his wife spread, Jocelyn wondered if he would trust her with any information at all. And if this was the "hush, hush" information she told people, what didn't she tell?

Then Elizabeth's voice turned to a faux whisper that Jocelyn could still hear. "There are rumors that the commo black out originated near our unit, so I haven't slept since I heard the news." *Our* unit was Captain Cryer, Scott and Nina's husband's.

The genuine worry—albeit coming from a worry monger—resonated in Jocelyn's ears as she left the Commissary and drove home.

Her fingers drummed on the steering wheel, her brain whirling with possibilities. She knew better than this, she told herself. She knew where this treacherous thinking could lead.

Early in Scott's first deployment, before they were married, she had glued herself to every news report on anything in the Middle East, and she had worried over every crash or injury or death that was reported. Every single one. She fell asleep imagining his whereabouts: Teaching himself to become accustomed to the sound of midnight explosions the same way she had learned the creaks in her apartment all alone. All new sounds to learn to sleep by. Except his were the splatters of machine guns and hers were the barking of the neighbor dogs. Young Jocelyn had worried herself into not eating, hardly sleeping and losing a good 15 pounds before Scott returned. This time she had to shake the obsession before it started.

Pulling in to her duplex driveway, piles of leaves mounded in her yard showing the grass beneath that had turned brown since she'd last seen it. Yard work was one of the many things she allowed herself to forget about while Scott was away—not that she had ever made it a priority.

Her duplex neighbor stood in the front lawn, bulky gloves covering his hands leaning on a rake standing tall next to him. She had always thought his hair was too dark to be natural but now he'd grown a matching mustache. He waved as she turned the car off and made his way toward her. Scott did not like this guy and that alone gave her a sinking feeling every time he tried to talk to her.

"Hey there, Jocelyn," Kirk said, a single leaf attached like a leech to the hem of his jacket.

"Hi Kirk," she said as she unbuckled Ian from his car seat. *Freaking Jody.* She could hear Scott's voice in her head. Scott always grumbled about Kirk—never calling him Kirk though. Jody was what soldiers called the man back home who was trying to sleep with their wives. (The term, Jocelyn had learned, dated back to World War II. These were the things Alexis had always filled her in on. The military was a world with a language of its own.) Not that Kirk had ever made any advances.

Kirk gestured toward the piles of leaves without taking his eyes off Jocelyn but not in a creepy way. Too friendly maybe but never creepy. "I was raking up my leaves, so I thought I'd work on yours too if that's okay."

The yard disagreed; he hadn't waited for her approval. "Yeah, it's fine." She moved to the back of the car and opened the trunk.

"Here, let me help you with those," Kirk said of the grocery bags. When she looked up to say, "That's okay," he had already wedged the rake against a tree and was pocketing his gloves. She smiled a thank you, not knowing what else to say.

In her head, she held a full conversation with Scott.

I bet he'd like to rake your leaves. Scott would have said.

Even at the thought Jocelyn rolled her eyes. *What does that even mean?* Her mind asked, familiar with Scott's if-you-know-what-I-mean euphemisms.

I'd like to rake his face. Scott's voice was clear inside her head. She laughed to herself. Her imaginary conversations kept him close, and maybe made her crazy. But she had known him for so long, she knew exactly what he would say. After all, she had loved him since seventh grade.

Putting the grocery bags just inside the door, she turned to Kirk behind her and grabbed the ones he carried. "Thank you for your help." She said, blocking the doorway. She had never and would never let Kirk inside. Even though she didn't suspect his motives the way Scott did, she wouldn't leave an ounce of opportunity for Scott's impressions to be correct.

"Yeah," Kirk said, grabbing his gloves from his pocket and patting them in his palm. "I'll just get back to the leaves."

Jocelyn nodded and closed the door with a gentle shove.

Ian was already trying to lift the bags from the ground. "I got dis one."

"Look how strong you are." She said, following behind him.

On she went about her routine as though everything everywhere was normal, as if she didn't repeat the words *commo black out* to herself every few minutes. That was the job of a mother—military or civilian. To set the world at peace for her little one, even when she was sick, when she was crushed, when she was exhausted. She was the only view Ian had.

Ian propped his little feet up on the cabinet door and pushed upward to climb to the counter and set his grocery bag on top.

"Be careful," was a common phrase that came from her lips having a fearless little boy. Sometimes his antics made her heart leap in her throat, but better him be fearless than never explore what he could accomplish.

"Be careful." She whispered under her breath as she thought of Scott. Wherever he was, whatever he was doing, being a soldier always came first. As much as her job as a mom was to not show alarm, his job as a soldier was to not allow the alarm to get in the way. His unit—men who had become brothers, a second family—and his job to serve the country came before his own wellbeing.

One of the reasons she'd fallen in love with him was his ability to make everyone around him feel safe. Not only because of his height or strength, but because he was willing to step up in the middle of a situation for a cause. In high school, it made him a champion tight end football player and a swoon-worthy boyfriend. It was the reason that when he confessed his plan to enlist she knew it was the right path for him. For them.

They were seniors in high school, at the time, and had been dating for a little over a year. She'd been sitting in the bleachers doing her AP Anatomy and Physiology homework, watching him finish up his football practice in the dry heat of September. It was the anniversary of the 9/11 terrorist attack and the video coverage of the airplanes hitting the Twin Towers was on every television. "We Will Never Forget" pictures were all over social media. She had driven up to school that morning to see the 9th graders lower the school flags to half-staff.

Scott climbed the bleachers, still in his football pads, his typically spiked hair matted and sweat-soaked against his forehead. He landed a sloppy kiss on her cheek and nuzzled his nose in her neck. "You smell good."

"Of course I do. You've been tackling sweaty teenage boys for two hours." She only looked up from her notebook for a second, but she couldn't help a smile.

"I gotta shower, but I want to talk to you." He had grabbed her notebook from her—the one she had doodled I-HEART-SCOTT all over—and closed it. That's how she knew it was important. She tucked her purple pen behind her ear.

The look in his eyes was a mixture of excitement and nervousness, but he was keeping his composure for her sake. "This is crazy, but it isn't a rash decision. I've been thinking about it for a long time. I think I've always known, but I haven't ever talked with you about it."

While that didn't surprise Jocelyn because Scott wasn't the most talkative type, it peaked her curiosity.

"I'm enlisting in the army."

Jocelyn started to say something, but she didn't even know what, so her mouth sat open for a few too many seconds. She closed it to swallow. His expression exposed the serious thought he'd put into this decision. Somehow she felt it wasn't her place to argue.

"When?" was her simple request for explanation.

His graduation was in December, so his answer didn't surprise her. "January."

There was nothing left to add. He needed her support. Even at 17, that's what love was all about.

"Has my stench incapacitated you?" He smelled his gray undershirt and pretended to gag. He could always turn a tense moment into a joke. "I should shower before it renders you unconscious."

Jocelyn smiled with weak cheeks. She felt struck with a sudden case of the flu.

"Wait for me," Scott said with a wink.

That statement held more weight than either of them wanted to admit. And their future flashed before her eyes: Scott in his army uniform, his notoriously spiked hair buzzed close to his scalp.

Wait for him. She could wait for him forever if that's what it took. She felt like she already had. She'd loved him since she was a gawky seventh grader with glasses that were so big they touched her eyebrows and cheeks simultaneously. She'd waited for him since before he outweighed her.

If it were a movie, the girl would've answered the boy with something like "Today, and always." Jocelyn knew that because that's what she was thinking. *I will wait for you today. I will wait for you every day of my life.* But the catch in her throat told her that she would never be able to get the words from the hopeless romantic lobe of her brain to her mouth. So she nodded. Because that's what girl's do in real life. They think the cheesy lines, but they never say them. There was always something left unsaid.

***

Ian splashed around in the bathtub that evening, and in between his squeals and overspray, Jocelyn found herself sitting phone-in-hand on the closed toilet seat. She scrolled the screen with her finger through every news report she could find on Afghanistan. Searching for any piece of information, any link to Scott's unit in Jalalabad. But she came up with nothing. Waiting for Scott was one thing. Waiting for him to come home to her. But waiting for others to tell her whether he was alive and safe was a different story.

Frustration culminated as she slammed her phone down on the sink. Ian looked up from his sloshing bubbles. Turning her attention back to her son, she helped him shampoo his hair and the business of bathing. When Ian was done and swaddled up in a towel with only his wet head and wrinkly feet sticking out, the electricity of the phone drew her back. She'd created a habit during Scott's deployment to never have her phone away from her so she never missed a call from him. Without it, she felt naked, vulnerable. With the commo black out still present in her mind, the phone had been far away for too long already.

Ian's bedtime couldn't come soon enough. As soon as she closed his door, her fingers brushed the edge of her phone. She needed to talk to Scott. And she couldn't. So she did the next best thing.

Oh babe, you always say not to worry. I've been doing this too long to let triviality get me going, but I overheard Elizabeth Cryer gabbing about a commo black out today and it has me hypersensitive. I'm helpless here not knowing anything, but I believe in my heart you are okay. You have to be, you know, because Kirk asked to rake the leaves and who knows what else, and I need you home to show off your muscles to him. Anyway, all this makes the gap between us seem even bigger. But we are doing alright. You would be proud of your son.

He was so happy to give his old toys to the homeless shelter today. He has such a beautiful example set by his father of selflessness, it shouldn't have surprised me. I love you and can't wait to feel your arms around me.
    Jocelyn

Sent. It was out there now, commo black out or not. If Scott— correction—When Scott read it, he would get back to her when he could. She had to believe that.

With her emails already opened, she scrolled to the folder that held every single email Scott had sent her during his two deployments. Some of them were airy while others were upsetting. She scrolled passed one subject line that read, "Really Bad Day." Those could have been the hardest to read but sometimes in them she felt closest to her husband, reading his emotions put delicately into words, almost being able to see what he saw, to feel a little of what he felt. Those were the worst and the best somehow.

She opened an email from about three months in to his first tour in Afghanistan, when they were both learning what this life would be like, before each of them knew how strong the other really was.

I've got about an hour before we are rolling out and I wanted to send you a message first. I think about you every day. I promised you before I left that I would tell you everything I could, that I wouldn't hold things back from you, but babe, it's hard. One day on patrols we'll be greeted by locals, kids asking for candy, then a few days later the village will be empty. We always expect an ambush. Some days it comes. Some days it doesn't. Those kids that were coming up and hugging us a few days before are now trying to kill us. I can't tell you any more than this. I don't wish these feelings on anyone. I think of you and see your face every night before I go to sleep. I hope to dream of you and our future, instead of our present. I love you.

That was the first email 20-year-old Scott let down his protective humor-in-everything style. Everything else was about the DFAC—dining facilities—and chow hall, the FOB facilities being better than expected, the contraband alcohol they found during a patrol but was prohibited on base and conveniently never made it to the FOB. She scrolled to the next email.

Hey beautiful,

Today I encountered my first sandstorm. Women back home pay big money for the kind of skin exfoliation I got today. A big brown wall of sand came right at us. The horizon rose to welcome us to Afghanistan. Once it hit, visibility was zero. We had to hide out in the tankers. I can still feel it burning my eyes. But my skin feels like a baby's butt. Maybe I'll jar it up and bring it home to you. You can have a spa day, compliments of the 'Stan. I'll send more pictures soon. I love you.

Now though, she could distinguish the tone of his emails. The soft ones didn't mean he was safe or unafraid—fear was an everyday experience in war—but he could make light of it for her sake, for his own sake, to keep them both sane. The lighthearted ones scared her when he hid his feelings behind the guise of sand storms and video games. When he could put his emotions into words and be vulnerable, he was less concerned with shielding her.

More than anything, she felt fortunate his position in the army allowed him to email her frequently and with candor. Some milspouses knew nothing about their husband's assignments. That would have driven her to drink.

One by one, she read email after email until her eyes closed themselves. She slept, clutching her phone as though it were the only connection to her husband.

Ding.

The sound and the vibration in her hand woke her with a gasp. Her eyes fell to the army green painted wall in front of her, trying to find her bearings as to what time or day it was.

Her phone had buzzed, she realized, and it was an email from Scott. Her heart stuttered. Any communication from Scott was good news, right?

Seeing Scott's name in bold as the Sender put a groggy smile on her lips. She held the phone with both hands. Her eyes stung as she read.

Love from the 'Stan. I'm as happy to be emailing you as you are to be reading it, I'm sure. I'm sorry you were worried about me. It was a different unit involved. There were two casualties on our side, though I didn't know them. I wish I could have emailed you. The commo black out was lifted this morning. It is all quiet here—which means we haven't left the base. For now, we are busying ourselves with the plethora of video games the guys got over Christmas. Some guys never grow up. I've been watching out for the new guy, Xavier. He reminds me of myself back in the day. Green but fiery and ready to go. He's getting bagged on pretty bad. I've got to show him the ropes and make it seem like we do more around here than play Halo.

Let me know what's going on at home. Tell me everything. Every detail the way you would if I was sitting with you on the couch.

And tell Kirk to kiss my ass. I'll bet he wants to rake your leaves. Stay away from that one.

I miss you and Ian more than I could say. Don't hole yourself up in the house. Get a babysitter and go see a movie. Take care of yourself. You need your strength for when I get back. Ha!

You are my gravity pulling me home. Love, Scott

P.S. I'll keep my head low to the ground...just in case.

7

ELLE

Evenings out on the beach weren't the same without Aaron. Redondo Beach had always been Aaron's favorite, so taking in the orange flames of the sunset with co-workers only made Elle sad. What Jenny from human resources and Neil from accounting thought were vibrant, beautiful clouds, Elle saw in monotone. The crashing waves became white noise. The food at the restaurant on the pier tasted bland.

They used to come here with Marissa and Heath. They used to walk the pier with fishermen lined up on one side and street vendors on the other. They'd had their caricatures drawn once.

Those images wouldn't leave her alone as she pretended to listen to office gossip. When her friends were ready to move on to the next location, Elle declined. "I'm just going to go home."

Jenny, her blonde dreadlocked hair falling midway down her back, looked at Elle sympathetically—or pathetically, Elle couldn't tell which. "No, come on," her friend begged.

Elle still declined. She needed to be alone.

Even at home, she couldn't shake the feeling that her life was changing against her will at an accelerated pace. Spinning her wedding ring around her finger in that way Aaron hated, she heard his words. *Tell me what was missing.* Still there was nothing. All she missed was him.

Her vision swam, but that didn't stop her from filling up her wineglass. She grabbed her phone and tablet while she curled her legs up under her on her chaise lounge.

Her fingers tapped out a brief text to Marissa in case she was awake. After fifteen minutes of the text remaining unreturned, she knew her friend was sleeping, gearing up for another day of taking care of her little humans. As much as she loved Marissa, they had little in common any more. Elle couldn't imagine how Marissa could survive a day taking care of two daughters, how her eardrums were still intact considering how loud those children were every time Elle called. Marissa was either the most patient person in the world or desensitized to reality.

On these lonely nights, she wished for a mother to call and cry to. But her mother wasn't like that.

From the outside, Elle looked like she had so many friends, but now she realized none of that was real. They were girls to get mani/pedi's with or hang at the bar or beach. They were drinking friends and shopping buddies, but not deep secret, kindred spirits. None of them knew her beyond the pretty façade of lush hair, mascara and bronzer.

Her marriage counselor had said writing letters or journaling helped take inventory of her feelings. She opened a blank page on her tablet. The white screen resurrected her anxiety. Millions of texts had made her quick with a touch screen keyboard, but her fingers were paralyzed. Where to start. Closing her eyes, clearing away the fog of wine, she tried to put herself in Dr. Fullerton's office. Why hadn't she taken more notes? "Write your feelings," she heard him say. "Use feeling words."

I feel alone.

I feel like life has played one big joke on me and this is the punch line.

I feel like I am a living lie. Maybe Aaron's right and I am the most selfish person there is. I've let everyone down.

I feel like no one understands me. Even Marissa. Her life is different from mine. I can't measure up to her. Sometimes I don't even know who she is anymore. Or why we're still friends.

I feel like I'm the only screw up. No, I guess everyone has lies they're living too. Marissa resents Heath and the kids for keeping her from her doctorate. Rachel cheated on her husband the first year they were married. Liz had an abortion to get that big promotion. Lena's filing for her third divorce. And Jenny hides money from her boyfriend in case

they ever split. Maybe that's what I should have done, but I never
thought this would happen.

The truth is we're all messed up. I'm getting a divorce. There it is. I
said it. My husband left me because I'm a selfish, spoiled brat. I wake
up every day wondering if today will be the day I get the papers. Because
he's right. I'm so selfish I bought gifts for a needy family I didn't even
know to punish my soon-to-be-ex-husband. I considered asking for
those gifts back when Aaron told me to pay the bill. What kind of
disturbed person does that? Me.

No wonder Aaron doesn't want to be with me.

There it was. The ugly truth. It flowed out of her in one big rambling
of consciousness, and she didn't feel any better. Just sad. Damn shrink.
Didn't know what he was talking about. She turned off her tablet and laid
it on the bed next to her. She downed the rest of her glass of wine, turned
the TV on to drown out the thoughts chewing in her mind, and wished
for sleep.

***

Saturday she invited herself to Marissa's for lunch. Everyone was home,
but Elle didn't mind. The kids were holed up in their rooms. The seven-
year-old, Hailey, had gotten an American Girl doll for Christmas, and
there was no separating them. She was changing the doll's clothes and
braiding its hair when Elle arrived. Heidi was napping. Elle thought at
four, Heidi was a little old to nap, but she wasn't a mom. Heath was
working in the garage fixing something greasy on the undercarriage of
the car.

Elle set her purse down on the counter where Marissa was preparing
lunch and helped get plates out. Every one of them was cracked.

"I brought you coffee." Elle handed over the large paper cup and
noticed how much older Marissa looked this morning with her hair
pulled up in a harsh ponytail and no makeup to cover all those freckles.
Elle could see the darkness under her eyes and knew the exact concealer
she would recommend if the opportunity arose.

Marissa downed the coffee like it wasn't scalding hot. "I should buy
stock in coffee. This is my fifth cup." She slathered the peanut butter and

jelly on half a loaf of bread. Heath had been working extra hours all week on a big project, so she'd been doing double duty at home. Elle didn't know exactly what that entailed, but there were small pieces of paper and swabs of glue on the counter, so she gathered it involved some craft project.

Marissa ate her pb&j with some carrots sticks while the kids had a side of potato chips instead. She'd learned long ago not to make her friend food since Elle was a vegan and only ate organic.

"Have you talked to Aaron?" Marissa tended to jump to the point, no small talk, no fluff pieces.

"No," Elle spit the word out of her mouth.

"Do you think he'll change his mind?" It wasn't an accusatory tone. It was an honest question.

Elle considered it. Nothing had given her any concrete evidence to think that he would, but she hoped nevertheless. "I'm moving in with Norah, but I'm not giving up."

Her friend patted her hand then squeezed it. "You haven't failed. I know that's what you're thinking, but it takes two to make a marriage work."

"It only really takes one for it to fall apart." Elle added.

"He moved out with no warning. He quit counseling. He isn't innocent here."

Elle looked down at their hands, her friend's skin shades lighter than her own.

"I wish it was different. I have tried everything I can think of."

Marissa laughed her agreement. "You have been brazen in your efforts, that's for sure!"

The laughter was contagious, and before Elle could stop herself, she was giggling along with her dear friend, reliving every stunt she'd pulled, imagining Aaron's face reacting to each one. The giggling turned to raucous laughter which turned to belly-hurting hysterics until tears were pouring from both of their eyes.

Elle shook her head. "I don't know what I was thinking."

Marissa giggled like one of her daughter's friends. "I'd like to have seen Aaron's face when he showed up at work with your picture on his screen saver."

Elle shook her head. "I heard his voice. I can imagine his face."

"You know before he got mad, he was–" Marissa looked over her shoulders as she spoke to make sure the children were out of earshot, "turned on."

"Not from my text during a business meeting."

"He probably blew it up and put it in his bathroom."

Elle gasped and laughed. "Stop!"

"Moooooooom!" Hailey hollered to Marissa from the other room. "Heidi got into Aunt Elle's purse."

Elle's eyes grew saucer-wide. Her dear friend blushed as she jumped up to assess the situation, but that didn't make Elle feel any better.

"Oh my." Mar said, picking Heidi up who screeched at being caught red-handed, literally. Red lipstick covered her hands and mouth in Joker fashion, as well as covering Elle's iPhone being squeezed in Heidi's surprisingly strong grasp.

"That lipstick was MAC!" Elle shrieked, pulling the phone and demolished lipstick tube from the toddler's hands.

"I'll pay for it. I'll buy you a new one. I'm so sorry. I thought she was still asleep. Sometimes she is so sneaky." Marissa was flustered in a way Elle hadn't seen.

Elle's shoulders slouched in a sigh. "It was last season anyway. Aaron never thought it was my color. It probably looks better on her." She studied the mushed paste. "Why don't you keep it?"

Heidi's eyes brightened up at the exact moment Marissa's eyes panicked. "Oh no, she doesn't need to–"

"It's fine, Mar," Elle said, thrusting the stick back into Heidi's waiting hands. "Every girl needs a good red!" Elle demonstrated a proper pucker and helped smear more red on Heidi's tiny lips.

Marissa was not one to suppress her candor, but it was different with her children. "She's four, Elle, she doesn't need red lips yet."

But Elle didn't hear her—or at least didn't acknowledge her. "Look how beautiful you are! The right makeup makes the girl! Go look in the mirror!" Elle said, thinking perhaps she should give Mar's tired eyes a makeover too.

Only a couple seconds passed before Hailey came running, "Moooom, that's not fair. She's four and *she* gets play makeup. I want some!"

Marissa shook her head emphatically. "You know the rules."

"But she's four!" Hailey shrieked.

"Oh Heidi," Elle put a gentle hand on the girl's shoulder.

"I'm Hailey." The seven-year-old said flatly.

"Hailey," Elle corrected herself, eyeing Marissa. "You're only a couple of years away from wearing a full face of makeup. It'll come soon enough."

Hailey slouched her shoulders but relented, stalking off.

"A couple of years?" Marissa gave the all-too-familiar look that Elle was wrong.

"Sure. She's seven. I see girls who are wearing makeup before they wear training bras. You really should get her some makeup to play with so she can learn how to use it properly. It makes a huge difference."

Her friend ignored her and finished wiping the lipstick off of her iPhone with a wipey. "I'm not sure if I should tell you to be around more or to steer clear of them. But you do need to learn their names."

Elle rolled her eyes and grabbed the phone out of Mar's hands. "Well that's your fault. Hailey and Heidi? And Heath? How do you expect anyone to keep them straight?"

Even Marissa had mixed them up in the heat of a holler.

Scrolling through her phone, Elle sighed. "Some of my apps are deleted."

"Yeah, she likes to do that." Mar nodded, head tilted. "Consider it pay back for giving her red lipstick that I'm likely to find covering my walls and carpet. You should probably check your texts too. She likes to play with the typing."

***

After a few errands, Elle stopped by the hospital to check on Norah. If she was going to move in with her grandmother, she had to start making more of an effort.

The Smurfette nurse was leaving Norah's room and as they passed, the nurse gently asked her to put her phone on silent since Norah was resting. A streak of rebellion to say *I'll do as I please, thank you very much* surged within her, but she complied. Although her grandmother was quite awake when she entered. She was dressed in white starched pants and teal blouse with pumps to match. The teal ensemble was complete with earrings and watch—a wardrobe which she had detailed on hospital letterhead for Elle to bring her seeing as Elle's choices apparently weren't wearable. Only Norah would be this dressed up as a hospital patient.

Norah fiddled with the sheet next to her and patted her hair as the nurse walked out. Then she looked up at Elle, "That's Dawn. Isn't she a doll? She's worked here for three years, and she has the best bedside manner of any nurse I've ever had. I think if I was to come back to the hospital, I would want to come during her shift." Well, her speech was back in full force.

"How are you feeling today?" Elle practically tiptoed in, not knowing if it was because Norah was supposed to be resting or if she had become accustomed to walking on eggshells.

"I wish somebody would shoot me in the head." Norah said, throwing down the TV remote.

Mouth dropping open, Elle didn't know if she should scold or laugh. "Well it can't be that bad."

"If one more person comes in here to poke me with something, I'll make a scene. You get this age, you take a little fall and they think you're dying and put you in a hospital. I just want to be home. I don't need all of this fuss."

Elle almost laughed. She pulled up a chair next to the bed and changed the subject. "Well before you leave, make sure to ask as many questions about the tests as you can." They still didn't have a clear answer on whether the fall was a caused by a mini-stroke or not. Norah's speech patterns had created quite the concern.

Norah shook her head, "Everything's fine. They're just keeping me for observation. Barb's husband—you remember Barb that lives next door–"

"Yes, I used to live at the house too."

"Her husband broke his hip a couple years back; oh, I want to say in 2012. They gave him a prescription or two and told him to relax until it healed."

"Well everyone's case is different–" Elle said.

"You don't think I know that?"

"Never mind." Elle grumbled. Her grandmother could be so difficult. This was why they didn't see each other often. "I interrupted my day to check on you, so–"

"Well, I didn't ask you to do that."

"I know." Elle took a deep, calming, yoga breath—even though it had been weeks since she'd been to a class.

The door opened and the doctor popped in to express his hope that Norah would be released the next day. One last test had been done, and the results were taking longer than expected.

Elle looked pointedly at Norah. *Observation only, huh?* Glancing at her watch she jumped out of the chair. "Well, I've got to get going and pack for the move, you know, but I'll pick you up tomorrow when you're released."

Norah's voice split through the room, right past the doctor. "Elle Holloway, it is the weekend; you have no children; you are separated from your husband. Whatever are you running off to that is more important than your hospitalized grandmother?"

Even the doctor's eyebrow arched before he escaped the room. Manipulation hung in the air and vacuumed every excuse out of Elle's head. "I'm only a phone call away, Norah."

As if Elle hadn't said a thing, Norah swatted at the air. "The nurse brought in the newspaper this morning and these overhead lights are terrible on my eyes. Read it to me, will you?" She grabbed the folded paper from the nightstand and held it out in her knobby hand to Elle.

There was no arguing. She snatched the paper, stalked back to the chair, threw her purse on the floor and began to read page one while Norah held her head high in victory.

By the time Elle finished the local and nationwide news sections including the obits, the sun was low in the sky out the second floor window. Norah's eyes were drooping in combination with fatigue and medication, only after stubbornly staying awake for hours in Elle's company.

She kissed her gran on the forehead, as she had done when she was a teenager, then promised to come back the next day. Manipulation or not, Elle was glad she'd stayed.

With Norah's door closed behind her, she pulled her phone out, turned the ringer on and while bee-lining for the elevator notice she had five voicemails. Weird for a Saturday.

She pressed on her voice mailbox only to hear shrieking. "Who in the hell do you think you are, Elle? Why would you do that to me? I don't even know what to say right now. I thought we were friends. Is this some kind of horrible revenge? You better have a stellar excuse or we are done. DONE!"

The shock on Elle's face reflected in the elevator door as it closed. She couldn't identify the voice from all of the shrieking, like the high pitch anger had distorted the nature of the sounds. Before she could dissect it, the next one started.

"Hi Elle, um, it's Rachel," Aaron's sister? They hadn't talked since, well, you know. "We obviously have, um, a few things to talk about. So I guess, give me a call? Um. Okay. Bye."

A few things to talk about? Had Aaron done something? What was happening?

The next voicemail came on and she immediately recognized the voice that was sobbing throughout the message. "Elle, it's Jenny. I don't know—I just don't know what to say. You were the only person on the earth I told about the money," her voice went to a whisper, "Henry got your email first then broke it off with me. He said if I couldn't trust him, he couldn't trust me. I don't understand why you did this. Call me, please."

Email? What email?

Then a jolt of lightning hit her right in the chest. Rachel. Jenny. Liz must have been the one shrieking. She knew it was her journaling. But she couldn't piece together how an email was sent. *Think. Just think.* She told herself, trying to remember any way that she would have sent it out drunk or by accident.

Lena. Crap. Why had she written about her boss? She opened her emails. There were so many unread. She scanned the first one:

Well, it was sound wisdom to not spill any of my gossip to you. Although we all know who to get the scoop from at the water cooler on Monday.

Then the next one:

I hope I'm not on your list for the next email outing.

Wow, Elle. Just. Wow.

Embarrassment blew her over like a tsunami and threatened to knock the wind out of her. How had this happened?

The subject line drifted before her eyes.

Kkjihlmbimmjasdfh

Her stomach plunged to the ground floor. Heidi. Marissa's four-year-old. Red lipstick on her hands and on Elle's phone.

Elle had written the rogue journal entry on her tablet at home, but it synced with her phone so that everything was accessible on both devices. With fumbling fingers, she opened the email sent folder. There it was. The last email.

Subject: Kkjihlmbimmjasdfh
Time: 12:42 pm
To: All Contacts

Right in the middle of the hospital elevator, her knees almost buckled. She might have let out an audible groan when she read the *Sent To* line.

So many calming breaths. Once the fog in her brain cleared, she logged in to Lena's office email to which Elle had administrative rights. Her fingers moved across the touch screen of her phone out of instinct. The indicting email sat in the inbox, in bold, unread. She deleted it and emptied any history or trash where it could possibly be stored.

She followed suit with all of Aaron's email accounts. Thankfully he hadn't changed any passwords yet. He could *not* see how out of control she had become. He couldn't read those defaming words.

Next, Marissa. There had been no call, no email from her friend. Elle hoped that in the business of being mommy, she hadn't seen it yet. But there was no avoiding her reading it eventually. What she had written about Marissa wasn't as life altering or blackmail-ish as the other girls. But it would be friendship altering. The others were fair-weather friends anyway. Work associates. Old college buddies. People that would pass through life one month to the next.

Not Marissa. Marissa was her constant. The one who not only held her up when her legs or heart failed her but was willing to call her out in love and honesty. Elle needed Marissa for survival. Maybe she hadn't realized it until the possibility of losing her or hurting her detrimentally was so present.

As she found herself on the ground floor of the hospital, stepping out of the elevator, Elle took a deep, courage-building breath and dialed Marissa's number.

The ringing lasted forever, grating on Elle's impatience. There was a click when the line picked up followed by fumbling, and for a second, Elle thought her dearest, longest friend had answered and hung up on her. Her heart sunk past the basement floor.

"Mooooooom," There was a rustling of feet. It had to be Hailey. "Moooooom, it's Aunt Elle."

The sound of a door opened. A sigh. "Hey. They don't even let me go to the bathroom in peace." Marissa said. "Sorry. I don't know why she didn't just answer and tell you I was *going to the bathroom*." Elle could imagine the mom-look on her friend's face. The words she wrote about Marissa came to her. *Marissa resents Heath and the kids...*

"So," Elle didn't know where to begin.

"You figured out the email." A statement not a question, made in a flat voice, a tone Elle couldn't gage. It wasn't Marissa angry voice. So what was it?

There was no other way to approach it. "I am so, so sorry." Elle meant it. "I never should have even written it. It was some technique the counselor mentioned. I thought it would help." She almost laughed at the absurdity of that statement, then continued in a whisper, "It obviously didn't."

"Oh Elle," Marissa jumped in. "*I'm* sorry."

"What? Whatever do you have to be sorry for?"

"I thought you would be furious with Heidi." Marissa continued without a breath between words. "When I saw the subject line, I immediately knew. I feel horrible. I know she was a mess today and ruined our lunch. I already disciplined her. I know how you don't like kids, so–"

"Wait! I don't like kids? Since when?" Elle barked.

There was a pause before Marissa spoke, almost laughing. "You've never liked kids, Elle. It's pretty obvious."

"How is that obvious? I work for a baby décor company. I'm surrounded by kid and baby stuff all day long."

"And you complain about it every day."

It annoyed Elle the way Marissa never candy-coated things. Ever.

"At first I thought it was just my kids, but no, I'm pretty sure you dislike all children."

"I have come to every function of your children's I possibly could. I have bought them the best toys and clothes–"

"But you don't *talk* to them." Marissa interjected, with no hint of bitterness. "You don't hold them. If they are even a little dirty, you draw back when they get anywhere near you."

Elle scoffed. "I sound like a monster."

"That's not what I'm saying, Elle."

They both paused. Elle didn't have anything in retort. So Marissa was the next to speak. "And for the record, I do not resent my husband or my children. I loved the idea of a career and a doctorate, but I love my family more. And I'm okay with it. I'd rather be home for them every time they need me. No resentment."

"I never should have written it. I'm sorry."

"I'm kind of glad you did so I could clear that up. Next time, though, just talk to me. I love you, Elle. *That's* why we're still friends, and this email isn't going to change that." The way only Marissa could, she spun the mushy moment around. "Although, if I had been one of those other girls you wrote about, I'd have driven right over to your house and bitch-slapped you."

Elle laughed, even though she felt like she might cry.

***

Legs crossed under her and tablet in her lap, Elle wrote yet another email. She'd called Rachel, Liz and Jenny to apologize profusely. They were three of the most difficult calls she'd ever made. Rachel and Jenny were gracious. Liz, on the other hand, was irate and nothing Elle said or did would change that. Now she decided to follow up with an email to all recipients.

With as little thought as she had put into the original email, she tapped out an apology to be sent to the same group. Her first draft read:

Hello all of you who read my unfortunate, wine-induced accidental email. It was the product of one too many glasses of wine and a depressing evening. Better than an illegitimate child though, right? Ha ha. I know it was humiliating for those of you mentioned in the email.

It was for me too. Obviously it was never meant to be sent, but sometimes kids playing with your phone don't care about that. I'm sure my reputation has taken a hit. I hope you all know I am sorry.

Even she knew it sounded flippant and disingenuous. More than anything, she wanted it all to go away. She wanted to lay down after another night of too much wine, sleep hard and wake up to realize this was all one big nightmare, worse than any Halloween movie.

Rubbing her eyes, pulling her hair, biting her nails, she tweaked the apology until it resembled sincerity.

All of these people, some she knew and frankly some she didn't, had all seen her at her worst. Her most judgmental and critical. Inner thoughts that she wouldn't dare share. Like she had opened her shower curtain to an amphitheater of people from her life. All their eyes on her, naked—and not good naked, but pruny with old lady boobs. None of them could ever unsee what they had seen. It would never go away. Years from now, when people from college would think of her, they wouldn't remember that time she'd worn the elegant dress she'd designed herself. Nope, they would remember Elle Holloway, the girl who sent that drunken email.

Oh god, if she ever finally made it as a famous designer, this is what would be her skeleton in the closet. She could see it printed in the magazines. All of her beautiful designs reduced to this one moment in time.

What else could possibly go wrong?

Shaking her head like it was an etch-a-sketch, she cleared away the thought. She didn't want to jinx herself.

With another sip of wine—oh who was she kidding, it was a chug—she examined draft four or five of the apology. Who *was* she kidding? What else was there to lose? Her husband? Her reputation? Even though she had successfully deleted the email from Aaron's account, Rachel was his sister. They were practically conjoined; she told him *everything*. This was bound to come up in conversation. If Aaron read this sad excuse of an apology, he would know that nothing about her had changed. And she would like to think that *something* in her was different. Could she at least fake it?

Blank page open. What would she say if she knew Aaron was going to read it?

Dear Cyber world of friends and acquaintances,

No doubt you have all read and maybe even reread my last email. So have I. I'd like to blame the wine I drank that night or stress. Unfortunately, I can't. Because I wrote it. And let's face it, I believe every word. I know that's shocking for me to admit being that I named other people and their problems not just mine. But I figure at this stage why not add a dash more honesty. Isn't that what an apology should be anyway?

I'm a mess. So what. My life is in complete disarray. As is my closet. How is that different from any of you? Oh right, I wrote it out and sent it to my entire contact list...or at least an unnamed four-year-old did. Maybe I will die friendless. Or maybe I will find a single person in the world who doesn't know about this indiscretion and befriend them. Or maybe the one friendship that matters most will survive only slightly scathed.

Here's hoping for good things...and that this never happens to any of you.

Elle

Before she knew it, Elle was no longer faking.

***

The weekend was fleeting. Monday came before Elle was ready. As much as she wanted to cover her head with blankets for one more day, the sun peeked out over the mountains in the distance and beckoned her back to life.

Although her apology had lightened her step, returning to the office was going to be challenging. While she brushed her teeth, she heard Gossip Train No. 1 gearing up.

Out of all the "victims," Jenny saw her every day, but Jenny acted normal. Not a hint of hostility in her greeting. In fact, not one person made mention to Elle. Could it have blown over?

Okay, maybe not. Her inbox was full. FULL. Responses across the board. "So proud of your honesty. We need more of that in this world." "Who do you think you are to compare your humiliation with the people you exposed?" Interestingly—yet not surprising—she hadn't received any response from her mother.

One email was notable, though, because she didn't have a glimmer of recognition at the name. She opened it with caution, but within the first couple of lines, her shoulders relaxed.

Ms. Holloway,

You should know I never do this. Email a complete stranger. Never. But after reading your latest email, I felt impressed upon to respond and share that I admire your courage.

I admit that your first email appalled me. But how was my reaction to you any different than your honesty about the women in your email. For that, I am sorry. You wrote the way we all think about others and ourselves. Women judge each other far too harshly, but we are our own worst judge and jury. Don't give yourself life in prison. Be lenient. In life, few are. Give yourself that gift, as you gave to my family.

Sincerely, Jocelyn Turner

Elle blinked back surprise. Jocelyn Turner—the woman from the Tree of Hope. She clicked back to her original, accidental email. She knew it was there and her heart thundered when her eyes rolled over the words, *I'm so selfish I bought gifts for a needy family I didn't even know to punish my soon-to-be-ex-husband. Then thought about asking for those gifts back when Aaron told me to pay the bill.*

She let out an audible groan. Never once had she considered Jocelyn Turner as one of the victims in this horrible situation. She didn't even remember until now entering Jocelyn Turner's information into her contacts after receiving her thank you note.

Couldn't she cop out? Text Marissa and say, "Heeeellllppp!!" and do whatever Marissa said to do. But she had gotten herself into this situation, so she was going to have to deal with it herself.

Dear Ms. Jocelyn Turner,

How gracious of you, even after what I wrote. You, who I have never met, handled this more graciously than people I've known for more than a decade. I appreciate it, even though I'm terribly embarrassed.

I will work on leniency. Obviously I'm not good at that. Currently giving myself life in prison…better than the death penalty. Maybe I'll get off on parole. Ha!

I hope you and your son are still enjoying your gifts. Per your thank you note, my Christmas was indeed memorable.

Elle Holloway

To avoid losing her nerve, she hit send before rereading it. Of course, that was a terrible mistake. She raked her fingernails over her cheeks as she read what she sent. *It's* whom *not* who. *I have* got *to stop sending emails!!*

Once again this stranger had plucked a string in her heart, and she couldn't get the woman out of her head.

On her break, Elle was scouring social media for Jocelyn Turner. Social media stalking was the way of the world these days. She found a Jocelyn Turner in Texas whose profile was private, but there was a picture. Elle enlarged it on her screen. The woman before her, posing outdoors with her young son, was a natural beauty. Her thin layer of makeup accented her gray eyes, blonde hair pulled into an easy ponytail, with a smile that complimented the graciousness of her words.

Elle had never felt so drawn to someone without having met them. For a moment, she pretended they could become friends. This woman had everything together, a smile that made everyone around her at ease, a perfect toe-headed son, and a heroic husband. If only Elle's life could be as perfect as Jocelyn Turner's, then things would work for her. Her friends wouldn't hate her. Aaron would love her again. If only.

8

JOCELYN

Jocelyn pushed a stray piece of her hair back into its messy bun and the greasiness that she felt on her fingertips curled her stomach. She hadn't gotten out of her pajamas until afternoon to take Ian in his stroller on their daily jog around the block, and was shamelessly contemplating putting them back on even though it wasn't quite dinner time. Some days Jocelyn felt like she spent every spare moment in front of a screen. This was that kind of a day. The world around her kept moving on its axis, but she was in one seat paying bills, working on last year's taxes, putting out a new advertisement on Craigslist for her tutoring services since one of her clients had outgrown their need for her, and now she was working on their budget.

This was the hour of day Ian was not pulling on her, as though sitting in front of the computer put a neon sign over her that said, "Interrupt me! Cling to me!" He'd sat in her lap while she did taxes, trying to click the buttons on the computer and moving the cursor all over the screen. More than once he had thrown a tantrum about wanting to go swing even though winter weather had rolled in. Jocelyn wanted to pull her greasy hair out all day. Finally, Ian was sitting next to her, coloring Darth Vader solid black in a coloring book and mumbling things to himself about fighting the dark side.

Her home smelled of the tortilla soup that was cooking on the stove as she sat at the kitchen table with the budget spreadsheet opened on her laptop. Her eyes were starting to cross looking at the same numbers over and over, trying to find extra money where there was little to none.

If Scott were home, he would pull Jocelyn out of her seat, singing loudly off key and force his wife to dance with him. He had this way of moving his hips with hers that made her laugh and blush at the same time.

They had gone dancing on their first date in 10th grade. It was her first date ever. She had been nervous, hardly able to believe that the boy she had crushed on for three years had finally noticed her and asked her out. They'd eaten Italian cuisine at a restaurant where you could draw on the table cloth and had written lines from songs back and forth all night. Before dessert, he had taken her to the corner of the room where the dance floor was empty and swayed with her to the music. She had known then that she wanted to dance with him for the rest of her life.

But tonight Scott wasn't home to dance with. She would have to take a cue from his memory and give herself a moment's break from all the numbers. She stood, stretched her arms over her head and behind her back, then checked on the simmering soup, took a slurp and determined it wasn't done yet.

"I want a bite." The only valid distraction from Ian's intent coloring was food.

"It's not quite ready yet," she said. Before Ian could whine at her about being hungry, she added, "How about dessert first?"

His eyes widened, then he stuck his tongue out like a lapping dog.

Jocelyn laughed. "Okay, down boy." She pulled out the vanilla ice cream stuffed in the back of the freezer. Usually she only offered up dessert as a bribe for finishing dinner, but she wasn't worried about the growing boy finishing his favorite soup. She scooped out a rounded bowl for each of them and sprinkled some sliced strawberries on top of hers and chocolate sprinkles for Ian.

Once Ian dug in, he didn't say a word. She watched with a smile as he took small bites so as not to freeze his mouth then licked the spoon clean between every bite. While checking her emails on her phone, she took her own bite.

The first email in her inbox was unexpectedly from Elle Holloway. Jocelyn hesitated to open it, remembering the emails she had already received. After the gifts, Jocelyn had imagined the kind of woman who would spend so much on a family she'd never met, and although she expected her imaginary Elle Holloway was inaccurate, the real one had proven to be a bigger disappointment.

But the second email Jocelyn received from Elle was different. Honest. Refreshing. Jocelyn wished she had the bravery to be so real.

And Jocelyn had responded in a weird, email-induced afterglow. Now it seemed they were exchanging emails. Her curiosity about Elle Holloway was higher than ever.

With another bite of ice cream and a glance at Ian, who was starting to make a dent in his chocolate sprinkles, Jocelyn got on her social media accounts and searched the name Elle Holloway just to see a picture. Only a woman would do such a thing. Scott would never look up a stranger, except for the time he googled his own name and checked out all the other Scott Turners.

She scrolled through a couple Elle Holloway profiles until she found one in California. The woman's profile picture was no surprise after the emails she had received. Her picture was a selfie in the driver's seat of her car, but her face could have been in a makeup ad. The woman was all lips, eyelashes, cheekbones. And cleavage. Perfect, perky, round, never-had-a-baby cleavage.

Dipping in for another bite of ice cream and turning the spoon upside down in her mouth, Jocelyn looked down at her own boobs, hidden under a threadbare workout shirt and sports bra. Only plastic surgery would ever give her cleavage like that again.

What kind of a man leaves a wife that looks like that?

She caught her reflection in the corner of the screen. Yesterday's mascara crusted on her eyelashes and smudged under her eyes. Early fine lines creaking their way across her face. Maybe there were days she should be thankful Scott wasn't home to see her. She tossed her phone on the counter in disgust, then took another big bite of ice cream.

There was a knock on the door. Ian looked up from his bowl and ran to the front. They rarely had visitors so he was as bad as a yappy dog when anyone came to the door. Jocelyn's tongue was frozen from the ice cream that lingered in her mouth. She tried to chew up the strawberries but they were cold against her teeth.

The door to their rental didn't have a peep hole or windows so Jocelyn pulled it open, expecting FedEx or something.

But it wasn't. The first face she saw was Elizabeth Cryer. The first thought she had was of her own unkempt appearance opposite this immaculate woman.

The second face was a man she had met several times at the unit's get togethers, recently a potluck Christmas party. Lieutenant John Wilkins was Scott's unit Rear Detachment Commander. She knew what it meant that an officer from Casualty Affairs and their FRG leader were at her door step.

"Good evening, Jocelyn," he said with a sharp nod.

She didn't respond. She couldn't. The muscles in her face fell slack as she looked back at Elizabeth Cryer. Elizabeth's eyes were glossy, but her smooth red lips remained motionless.

The chill of winter wind blew toward them. Jocelyn's senses were suddenly heightened. She could hear the beating of her heart so clear she was sure her visitors could as well. There was a strawberry seed stuck between her molars. A moment she would remember forever and yet a fog descended over her head and rested on her shoulders ensuring that just as many of these memories would also be lost.

Certain impressions would be engraved on her mind, though. The thin line of Lt. Wilkins' lips. His asymmetrical beret gripped under his arm as she let him inside her home. Wanting to scream for her husband as the Lieutenant spoke, "I'm sorry to interrupt your evening."

There was no doubt this moment was about to change her life. No matter what else they said, she knew there was a short list of reasons they were at her door, and none of them were good.

Ian pulled on her leg as the two visitors passed through the entryway to the living room. She offered them a seat on the couch while her mind ticked away how she could distract Ian from their conversation. There was no way she could let him hear what they said. Whatever it was.

Forcing words from her mouth took Herculean effort. "Why don't you go finish your ice cream before it melts."

She was grateful that he did as she said. Her eyes turned back to her unexpected guests, begging them to spare Ian the pain they had to bring. She perched herself on the edge of the reclining chair—Scott's chair—pressing her palms together between her knees for support. She was going to need it.

Lt. Wilkins began, "I'm sure you are guessing all the reasons we could be here, so I'll get right to it. Scott's company was ambushed on a patrol, and Scott was wounded."

Jocelyn seemed to know it before the words were even spoken. She met eyes with Elizabeth Cryer and in their meeting, Elizabeth's face melted with pity.

Her breath sped up in her chest with a shot of adrenaline. Should she feel relief that he was alive or should she be crying? But her instincts were right; her life would never be the same.

She couldn't sound frightened, couldn't panic or Ian would feel it, and she needed more information before she could tell him anything. She stole a glance behind her to make sure Ian remained in the kitchen. She had to hold it together for her little boy. Even though she wanted to collapse on the ground and let the tears escape, she couldn't give in.

"Is he okay?" The question seemed illogical. Of course he wasn't okay. He was wounded. But she couldn't think of any other words to string together. The strawberry seed irritated her gums but also grounded her in the moment.

Wilkins answered with a brief nod. "Sgt. Turner's vehicle was hit with an RPG. He was outside the vehicle but was caught in the explosion."

Jocelyn breathed through her mouth, slowly, pushing the breath out because otherwise she may not breath.

"They stabilized him, and he is en route to Germany for further evaluation."

Her chin quivered imagining Scott unconscious, helpless—a term she never would have applied to her husband before—at the field hospital in the middle of the desert thousands of miles away, but she pushed the images away and held strong. If she spoke now, her voice wouldn't hold. Her eyes bounced between the visitors.

Elizabeth's pale face had softened. She reached out and grabbed Jocelyn's forearm. "We don't know a lot of details right now. As soon as he's able, I'm sure he'll contact you."

Jocelyn pursed her lips to trap the sobs rising. A shadow moved in her periphery. She turned and saw Ian peeking around the corner, with his empty ice cream bowl in his hands. His face was her booster shot of strength.

"All done?" She asked him, grateful to focus on something…else.

"Is Dad okay?" Ian asked, the bowl tilting toward the ground in his dimpled hands.

Jocelyn was out of her seat before the last syllable was out of Ian's mouth. "Oh honey," she said as she set the bowl on the tile floor and wrapped her arms around her boy's slender body. "Daddy's okay." She didn't believe it was a lie. He was alive. That should be enough.

"Is he coming home?" Ian asked against her shoulder.

After all the times Ian had asked that, this time the answer had changed.

As elated as she should feel with him returning sooner than planned, there was no joy or relief. Her mind jumped from news reports to soldier's she had known who returned missing limbs or with bodies burned or mangled.

Her thoughts steadied on the boy in her arms awaiting his dad's return. "Soon," she said, "he'll be home soon."

Ian pulled back and whispered to her. "Are they staying for dinner?"

She jumped up, remembering dinner on the stove, but when she stirred the soup, a thick crusted layer had burned to the bottom of the pan, ruined. Tears sprang to her eyes. They never came when they were supposed to. She bit her bottom lip, willing the tears to evaporate before anyone saw.

Footsteps tapped on the tile entering the kitchen. She felt a presence behind her, a gentle hand on her back. "Why don't I order pizza for you both?" Elizabeth said.

Jocelyn could only nod.

Minutes ago Elizabeth Cryer was the last person she wanted to share this moment with, the last person she wanted to depend on, and yet here she was.

Turning, Jocelyn asked, "Would you like to join us?"

Elizabeth bobbed her gaze from Ian's expectant face back to Jocelyn. "Oh, I haven't had pizza in years. That would be a great treat."

Together they returned to the living room where Lt. Wilkins remained seated.

"Would you like to stay for pizza, John?" Jocelyn asked him.

He jolted out of his seat. "I appreciate the offer, but no ma'am. I have some other things to attend to this evening. You all enjoy."

Jocelyn found it amusing when her elders called her "ma'am" but she couldn't find the strength to smile at him. Suddenly, she felt tired.

Wilkins stopped at the door before leaving and turned back to her. "I am so sorry, Jocelyn." He held his beret in his broad hand, fingering the edge of it as he spoke. "If there is anything Sandra or I could do for you, personally, please let us know."

She thanked him as she closed the door behind him, then returned to Elizabeth and Ian in the kitchen.

"That was my first time to order pizza through an app on my phone." Elizabeth announced, then nodded toward Ian who was turning on cartoons for himself in the living room. "This one requested cheese, and I got veggie for us." She placed her smart phone back in her purse— custom army camouflage, with her husband's rank "Captain" embroidered in gold on the side.

Jocelyn collapsed into a chair at the kitchen table. Elizabeth busied herself putting the small amount of salvageable soup in a Tupperware container then washing out the pan. Jocelyn didn't speak. Her thoughts were too muddled. Finally, Elizabeth sat down, not seeming to expect conversation but just there. Jocelyn had never witnessed this woman quiet for so long. She and Scott had nicknamed Elizabeth "The Mouth" after meeting her, when every other statement was a piece of gossip. That reminder sent a streak of panic through Jocelyn's core.

"Please don't tell anyone." The words spilled out of Jocelyn's mouth, and then she realized how ridiculous they were. Of course everyone would learn what happened to Scott. But Jocelyn wasn't sure if that was the part she wanted Elizabeth to keep quiet. Was it the burned soup, Jocelyn's tattered appearance, or her inept reaction to all of this? Or all of the above.

Elizabeth patted her arm. "Of course."

That reassurance was not entirely convincing, but the panic ceased.

The woman left her hand on Jocelyn's. "You are only as alone as you allow yourself to be. There are times when it's okay to ask for help." They met eyes. "This is one of those times."

The image of pity-filled glances directed toward her and Ian brought the panic back. Help was difficult for her. Even when Lt. Wilkins' offered moments before, she thanked him for his kindness but had no intention of collecting. A thought popped in Jocelyn's mind, and she blurted it out. "Lt. Wilkins had somewhere else to be. Scott wasn't the only one, was he?"

The FRG leader's eyes dropped. "No, there was one young man killed in the ambush."

***

Bedtime distracted Jocelyn as she laid down next to Ian, swallowing her emotions. The sound of dishes clanked down the hallway. Elizabeth offered to clean up the kitchen while Jocelyn put Ian to bed. One step toward accepting help.

The longer Scott had been deployed, the longer Ian's nightly routine had become and she had given in to "just one more book" so many times they now read four every night. She picked up the first one, *Good Night, Moon* and then *Good Night, iPad* which was Scott's favorite, but she had a hard time getting through it with Scott's Daddy Doll face staring at her from under Ian's arm. Would his face be the same when she next saw him? They hadn't commented on his injuries, and it haunted her. She wanted details, concrete information, things that she had long ago learned not to expect from the army, but now it was different.

"Dis one, mom." Ian reached for Scott's recorded book.

"It's late, honey. Mommy's tired. Why don't we skip Daddy's tonight? Tomorrow we can listen to it twice."

"I want Dad to read to me too." Ian would not give up. They had listened to it *every single night*, and on some nights, twice.

"Okay," she pulled the book off the nightstand. Its weight was an anchor dragging her to an ocean of hurt. She opened the first page and braced herself as Ian pushed the play button.

The sound she ached to hear bellowed from the nickel size speaker at the bottom of the book. His familiar timbre induced goosebumps on her skin.

With voices for every character, his delivery was akin to a Disney film. She attempted to control her breathing, to control her tears. Control was her thing. She was good at control. But somehow tonight she couldn't do it. Tears raced down her face with a mind of their own, down her temple, wetting her hair and Ian's pillow beneath it.

On page three, Ian's favorite voice was introduced. It was the same goofy voice Scott used for his childhood dog, a frumpy golden retriever. She didn't know if it was worse to close her eyes and see his face glowing behind her eyelids or to have his eyes glaring into her from the doll.

A hand caressed her hair away from her face and wiped the line of her tears. What she thought was her imagination, she found when she opened her eyes was actually her son. Ian had closed the book. "It's okay, Mom." He said. "It's okay to be sad." His big brown eyes stared at her from beneath the fringe of his eyelashes—Scott's eyes staring back from this little face. "I get sad sometimes when I hear his voice too. He be home soon."

Her not-so-little boy parroted what she had said to him on nights when he woke up crying out for his dad. "You can sleep with him if you want to." His small hands, once dimpled and chubby, held out for her his Daddy Doll with Scott's picture standing at attention.

When she opened her mouth to answer, a sob threatened, but she had an ounce of control left to restrain it. "You keep it tonight, babe. But thank you."

She held him in silence for a while, his head nuzzled against her shoulder, his hand rubbing up and down on her bare arm. Jocelyn reveled in the warmth and comfort of a warm body next to her, as Ian played with the monogrammed necklace she wore, the one Scott had given her for their fourth wedding anniversary. She was acutely aware of him everywhere she looked.

When she thought Ian had passed into sleep, she swung her legs out of the bed and adjusted her weight to lift herself up. Ian's voice called out into the darkness, "Will Dad be home for my birthday?"

It was a question that he had asked no less than once a week, and the answer had always been no. But now, their lives were pooled with uncertainty. She didn't know what kind of hope to give.

"Maybe he will be." It was truthful. And she and Scott had always vowed to be truthful with Ian. She couldn't promise more than that.

His mouth moved into a half smile. She kissed him at his thick hairline wanting to cheer, "Daddy's coming home," but what version of Scott would be returning?

***

Her phone cradled in her hand. She wished it could dial on its own since her fingers were paralyzed by dread. Their families needed to know, but she couldn't move from her hunched posture.

Elizabeth produced two cups of hot tea and set Jocelyn's on the table.

"I'm sure you could wait until tomorrow–"

Jocelyn cut her off with a sharp shake of her head. She needed to rip off the proverbial Band-Aid. But first, a question. "Who was he?" She didn't take her eyes off her phone, as though Scott would feel her and know to call. "Who was the man who died?"

Ribbons of steam rose from the teacup on the table. In Jocelyn's periphery, she saw Elizabeth take a stalling sip anyway. "His name was Xavier Martinez." The teacup clanked as she replaced it in its saucer. "This was his first tour. He was 19."

An exhale leaked slowly from Jocelyn's tight lips. She would call Scott's parents and her own. Even through the sobs emerging from his mother and the silence from his dad, she would tell them how lucky they all were, because Scott was coming home. Nothing else could matter. Because there was a mother in a different state getting a different call. A mother hearing that she had hugged her son for the last time, that she would never look into his eyes, wild and alive, again.

She thought of Ian, and how Xavier was once that young and innocent. That his mother once laid him down for bed, maybe read to him, maybe kissed the crown of his head, smelling his shampooed hair. And now, she would lay that grown son to rest, knowing he was no longer in the cold body that she pressed her lips to one last time. Jocelyn's tears dripped in harmony with her image of Mrs. Martinez standing over her son's coffin.

They were lucky. Their soldier was returning while Mrs. Martinez would mourn hers.

9

ELLE

Shadows cast three years of memories along the walls of her living room as Elle was packing. She planned on only taking clothing items and a few personal belongings to Norah's, because she intended on returning soon. But no matter the amount, it still felt like she was leaving behind her life, and Aaron with it.

On more than one occasion she had been told the apartment looked like a magazine. No rugs, limited furniture, signature pieces, everything white. That was Elle's style. What Aaron called antiseptic, Elle called minimalist. The modern staggered wall shelves with few decorations and even fewer books on them. The floor length ornate-framed mirror that was too large and heavy to hang so it leaned against the wall instead, which she liked even more.

Streaks of light shown through the white wooden blinds and reflected against the opposite wall. She wondered what this place would look like without her presence to keep the counters clear of clutter and clothing confined to the bedrooms.

Elle had dreamed of moving up the hill above Rolling Hills toward Palos Verdes. Since she had been a little girl, she had imagined a white house with a Spanish tile roof overlooking the water with a peek at Catalina Island.

Three years ago, Aaron had surprised her with a lease on this apartment instead of renewing their one bedroom. It wasn't at the *top* of the hill, but she was much closer.

When they had walked through, Aaron showed the second bedroom and painted a word picture for her, "We'll get that sewing desk you've been looking at and put it right here by the window. And the manager said we could add shelves, so it can be organized the way you like it." He was as excited as she'd ever seen him. And she'd jumped into his arms and kissed him open mouth, right in front of the guy giving the tour.

She'd made three new pieces within a week of taking occupancy. A local boutique bought the pieces but never confirmed a second order. She'd set up an online store through a national website and was thrilled with the quick responses. But the orders petered off. Before long, she stopped spending as much time in her studio and would sit by Aaron on the couch, watch TV, doodling a few designs here and there.

Now, a year had passed since she used her sewing machine, and the dust along the binding of her sketchbooks showed she hadn't drawn in them for months. The room turned into storage for rolls of fabrics that sat piled under winter coats she'd never worn on trips they'd never taken.

Though she couldn't pinpoint when, she'd lost the joy in wearing her own designs, and instead spent more money than she made in a day on pieces she wished she'd designed.

Until now, she hadn't thought anything could hurt worse than Aaron leaving, but packing up her closets came close. Each piece carried a memory in the folds of its fabric. The cut-out dress she wore when Aaron took her to the art gallery opening. The plunging jumpsuit that revealed enough cleavage to get Aaron's attention during his award ceremony, yet not inappropriate for a work event.

A tear dripped down her cheek. Not for the clothes. Not for the apartment she was packing up. The tear was for the life she'd imagined when they moved in, the life she saw slipping through her fingers one piece at a time. First Aaron, now the place they had tried to make their home.

Surely there was a trigger that last night before the note, the last night they'd spent together. Some fight they had, some foreboding sense she overlooked. But there was nothing. Just the morning after. The empty bed. Her empty heart. The aching loss.

The freshness of an unworn garment in her hands couldn't extinguish the feeling that she was a damaged, hole-ridden item thrown to the back of a closet to be forgotten.

There was one picture frame on the bookshelf of them together, happy and smiling, that she wanted to take, but propped against it, there was an envelope with her name scrawled across the middle.

Aware of déjà vu, she opened it with care like it could rip her skin if mishandled and leave a gaping wound. And she supposed it could.

I know you are going through a lot right now. So consider me the dick who couldn't find a way to tell you this in person. I'm getting rid of the apartment. The lease is up at the end of the month and they are upping the rent. Honestly, we don't have the money to keep it. We are going to have to let it go. I'm sorry.
Aaron

We are going to have to let it go. Letting go was so easy for him, while she was white-knuckling her entire life.

She couldn't find the energy to be mad. Instead, she took one last look at her unboxed home, like at any moment it could go up in flames and these memories would be lost forever. Her lungs felt heavy like she was breathing through terrycloth. He had given her no choice. This door had to close.

This time she threw the note away. The pain of holding on wasn't worth it. She left the picture frame in its place, leaving the couple in it to stare Aaron down while he packed up his own memories. Let them whisper to him of happier times.

*****

The last day of their lease landed on a bleary weekday. Elle waited until that last day to move her boxes out of the apartment ever hopeful for Aaron to change his mind. She came home from a long day of setting appointments, changing appointments, proofing and ordering seasonal catalogs, approving website changes, and the list went on. Her neck hurt, her head hurt, her eyes hurt. But the busyness had kept the dread at bay.

Marissa's husband, Heath, pulled the rented moving truck in front of the apartment at 6 pm, and Elle unlocked the door with a forlorn twist. The shock of a bare room made it all real. Dividing up property: their first step toward finalizing a divorce she never wanted. Her boxes were stacked against a bare wall. He'd moved his boxes out early and taken the furniture. Even the curtains were pulled down leaving empty brackets for curtain rods. A shell of a home matching her shell of a life.

She didn't cry for Heath's sake. The poor man was already swimming in estrogen at home; the least she could give him was the decency of a tranquil evening. Together they began the tedious process of hauling box after box down the sidewalk into the truck bed like a funeral procession.

Heath only paused to wiped his sweating bald head with a rag. Until the last box sat alone against the entry wall. She couldn't touch it. It would electrify her fingertips. Every muscle was tight with apprehension as Heath walked up behind her, his steps quiet with the experience of tiptoeing near a sleeping baby.

He placed his hand on her shoulder, a gesture that could have been awkward but wasn't. No words nor any movement. Just the hand on her shoulder. Even though she never had a brother, that one touch was what she imagined it would be like.

After enough time passed, Heath spoke but didn't move his hand, "You want me to get it?"

Everything in her screamed *YES! PLEASE!* It was just a stupid box, but it was so much more. It was her marriage taped up, closed and ready to be put on a shelf. But she wasn't ready.

"It's okay." She sighed. "I'll get it."

Still she stared, feeling her most potent memories whooshing around her like ghosts.

"I'll be in the car," Heath said, running his hand over his prematurely bald head that was shaved to the scalp. Thankfully he had the features for it. "Take as long as you need."

After the sound of his footsteps drifted, there was no way of knowing how long she stood there. The sky had grown dark and only the light of the porch shone through the windows. Even once she forced herself to grasp the box between her arms and heft it to her chest, surprised that there was no sting involved, she still couldn't bring herself to hear the horrible, final clunk of the door closing behind her.

A neighbor came down the staircase across from her. "Oh here," he said seeing her arms full, "let me get that for you." And he pulled the door closed before she could respond. The dreaded clunk resounded in her ears, and the neighbor asked if she needed help with the box.

"No," she cleared her throat, "It's okay."

As they moved in different directions, she called over her shoulder, "Thank you." It was the last day they would be neighbors and she didn't even know his name.

***

Elle tucked the box on her lap in the passenger seat, not wanting to let it go now that she finally had the courage to pick it up. On the way to Norah's—her new home—they pulled into a gas station and she handed Heath her credit card.

He returned wearing a grim expression. "The card was declined."

She blinked back shock and passed him another card. It was declined as well. Panic seized her. She handed Heath her wallet. "Try them all."

Heath shook his head, glancing toward the man at the neighboring pump, then pulled out his own wallet.

"No, Heath, it's the least I can do to pay." Elle said, clamoring out of the truck. But he insisted despite her rampant apologies.

They drove in a different kind of silence than before, and when they turned the corner arriving on Norah's street, Elle's heart sputtered. Aaron's car stood alone under the lamplight. Heath recognized it too; Elle knew from the grunt as Heath cleared his throat.

When they pulled in the driveway, all he said was, "I'll bring the boxes in. You can go check on Norah." Elle caught the implication and was grateful for it.

Her shoes stomped a little too hard on the walkway leading to the door, and maybe she burst in the house like she was going to catch them breaking the law.

"Oh. Aaron." She said. "Why are you here?" Maybe her tone was too accusing, but she couldn't restrain herself. It was all too much.

Norah interjected before Aaron could speak, her abrasiveness evaporated in Aaron's presence as it always had. "He brought me dinner knowing I was home alone after a hospital stay." Guilt oozed from her words. "And flowers." Norah's raisin fingertips brushed the edges of the white roses.

Aaron avoided his wife's gaze. "Trying to make up for missing you in the hospital." He said to Norah.

She waved away his comment, "Oh you wouldn't have wanted to see that."

During the small exchange, Heath came in with his first load of boxes and whispered to Elle for directions. She gestured up the stairs then turned back to Aaron, "Can I talk to you privately?" Her eyes wide with implication.

Norah's guilt rang louder, "You are *not* going to let that man move all of your boxes himself, are you? That is certainly not how I raised you."

Elle wanted to ignore her but knew it wouldn't work. "You can help him if you'd like." Feeling every bit of the 15-year-old who moved in with Norah over a decade ago.

"Elle," Aaron reprimanded under his breath.

Nostrils flaring, Elle turned back to her grandmother who was cozy on the couch with a throw blanket and remaining bites of cherry pie. "I'll be right back to help him." Then she dragged Aaron to the garage—the only place they could have any privacy in this house. In years past, she had stolen away to this garage with boys—even Aaron during college— for make-out sessions. Now her teen years were mocking her.

The garage air smelled of wet leaves and laundry detergent. Even this room was immaculate, with its shelves housing labeled containers. As the door shut, Elle turned on Aaron. "My credit cards were declined today. Every. Single. One. Do you know anything about that?"

"I've told you to stop spending so much, and you haven't. So I cancelled them."

Her chest burned at his nonchalance. "My debit card didn't work either."

He nodded calmly. "I moved my money."

"*Your* money?"

"Yes, mine." He cut her off. "You haven't made a deposit since September, so I took it all out. I can't close it with your name on it, but it's empty."

Anger was overrun by agony. "How could you do this to me? First my apartment, then my accounts." Her voice nearly a whisper, "Why do you hate me?"

But Aaron remained unchanged. "This isn't about hating you. This is about self-preservation." He plunged his balled hands into his pockets.

Months ago, she could have found the childish gesture adorable. Now it was infuriating. "I'm out of money."

Her throat went dry.

"Norah and Charlene, they let you act like money reproduces itself." He exhaled a puff of absurdity. "I've told you a hundred times we'd run out with the way you spend it. A dozen times I've cut up your credit cards, but you sign up for new ones. You go on a shopping spree for *retail therapy*, but you put us both in a deeper whole."

Elle rolled her eyes. It always came back to this. "That Christmas shopping wasn't for me!"

His frustration bubbled to the surface. "WE DON'T HAVE ANY MONEY!"

His IT job made him six figures and with her promotions, her pay wasn't bad either. "Why would we have no money?"

"You don't get it!" His hands flew into the air. "I took side jobs just to pay for your Louis and Chanel, but it didn't help." He kneaded his eye sockets. "I refuse to pay your way through every boutique in Southern California. That's not what a husband is for. I'm not Norah."

"That's not fair." She didn't need a sugar daddy. She had her own ladder that she was climbing at Lena Designs—although her money hadn't been deposited recently. If it would change Aaron's mind, she would raid her tampon box and give him all her rolled up cash.

"Really?" He struggled to keep command of himself. "You know what's not fair. I put all my plans on hold for you and *your* dream. I got a grown-up job to pay for the bills so that you could work your way up in the fashion industry. You promised me over and over that you just needed the right job to get enough experience. So I put *my* stuff on hold for you.

"But every day you come home and all I hear about is how unhappy you are and how much you hate your job. There are two of us in this, Elle. I don't love my job either but it's paid your way until you hit it big. Now you aren't even trying."

His voice boomed around the garage, rattling her.

"I am trying. I try every day. Why do you think I drive an hour to get to work and sit behind a desk answering phones for people who are doing exactly what I want to be doing?"

"I have no idea. Why do you?" He shifted his weight, leaning against a shelf of laundry supplies as though his strength to fight was gone. "You have a talent, Elle. A gift, really. You have notebooks full of sketches of clothes that you used to be excited about designing."

She dropped her eyes.

Aaron took a step toward her, switching to husband mode. "They would have rivaled anything sold in the stores. Instead you stowed all that talent away like the supplies you bought. Waiting for what?"

Quick to answer, she straightened, "I am waiting for the right opportunity."

"You really think you're going to get an opportunity when you haven't been designing? You have to work to get where you want to be."

Elle's arms flailed with exasperation. "And do what exactly? Make a design a week, sew a few things together and sell a couple a month online? I tried. I can't make it big that way."

There was a knock on the door of the garage, then it opened revealing Heath's round face. "Sorry to interrupt. Do you want all of the boxes in the guest room against the wall? None of them are really marked."

Elle stole a glance at Aaron, paradoxically embarrassed that he was watching her relocate, even though he was the reason she had to do so. "That's fine."

Heath started to close the door, then poked his head back in, "I put the suitcases in the closet."

She nodded at him, and he returned with a wink, then left the couple back to themselves. Elle rivaled between relief and awkwardness. Her feet caught her attention so she didn't have to look at her husband.

Without hesitation, he jumped right back to where they were. "I didn't care about you making it big. I cared about you. And your dream. And our life together. I thought that was important to you, too."

"That's how I was going to make our life together. My whole life I've wanted to be a designer, Aaron."

"Do you even remember what I wanted? What we talked about while we were dating and engaged and first married?"

"Aaron."

"Damn it, Elle, I wanted a family. I wanted a daughter who looks like you and runs around in the backyard wearing your gorgeous handmade dresses. I wanted a house that had a studio so that you could work whenever you had inspiration. I wanted crappy vacations together and memories and photo albums. I've worked my ass off trying to get us there because you're still looking for the *right* opportunity."

His hazel eyes revealed the pain of a broken man.

"We've only been married for *six* years. We have plenty of time for a family." Then she recognized her missed opportunity to echo his desires. The moment passed her by.

"You haven't talked about it in five years."

The care in his voice and her missed opportunities should have softened her, but instead it infuriated her. "Well, I'm sorry that I didn't find the perfect job as quickly as I'd hoped. Believe me, I'm sorry. It hasn't been easy going for me either. I wanted to design gowns and dresses and things that make women feel glamorous. And instead I work for baby bedding designer. I'm surrounded with hideous pastels and have to listen to everyone *oo* and *goo* over the baby models whose slobber I have to clean up. And I don't even like babies."

Silence. A hideous, bulbous silence.

"That would have been good to know six years ago." The emerging deadness in Aaron's face constricted Elle's throat.

"You know what I mean."

"Yeah, I think I do. Finish unloading your boxes, Elle."

Elle was stricken by his words, his implication, but Aaron didn't stick around to notice. He was out of the garage and out of the house before Elle could pull herself together.

They'd had fights before. She'd thrown a coffee mug at him once, he'd slammed doors and punched walls. But she had never walked away feeling like it was so final, so over. Her body sagged against Norah's Cadillac, hidden away in a quiet garage with the glow of one lone light bulb overhead. The idea of being seen, having to face Norah or Heath, each knowing or at least sensing what had gone down, it was too much for her.

She wanted to hide forever, never face her new future colliding with her past, moving in with the woman who raised her, hiding away in the same garage she had found comfort in as a teenager. She'd drawn the "back to start" card. Do not pass go. Do not collect $200. And she could really use that $200.

By the time she donned the courage to go inside, Heath was gone and Norah was sitting alone watching a news show. Elle flashed to being 15, dropped off on Norah's doorstep like a delivery package as her mom kissed her on the cheek and waltzed out to catch her next real estate opportunity. The 15-year-old Elle hadn't taken the time to unpack the few possessions she'd brought, but curled up next to her gran on the couch, for once knowing who would be there when she woke.

"I gave Heath $100 out of your wallet before he left." Norah said, then moved her quilt, opening a free seat next to her, as though the same moment 11 years before snuck through her memory too.

A hint of a smile swept over Elle's lips. She sat, legs curled up under her and breathed in the familiar scent of gardenia air freshener. As she laid her tired head on Norah's boney shoulder, she found a place where she belonged.

***

Temporary. She told herself when the digital clock sitting on the white nightstand screamed 1:30. Sleep evaded her as she curled under the stark white comforter on her first night sleeping in the room that had started as her mother's bedroom decades ago. Passed down like a family heirloom. The walls like the rest of the house were painted an offensive shade of peach, impossible to find in a paint store without color match. Still the color wasn't as terrifying as the closet door's floor length mirrors opposite the bed. The thought of what those mirrors had seen, particularly featuring her mother, caused an involuntary shudder.

This had to be temporary. Aaron would take her back; they would find a new rental—even if she had to move lower on the hill. The dream of living at the top of the hill where everyone had an ocean view, where even your address spoke of your importance, would have to wait. She could only work on one dream at a time.

A tree clawed at her window, the wind creaking against the old home. Something else creaked too. Without peeking out the door, Elle recognized the sound of old floorboards from too many teenage nights sneaking out. A light flipped on that shone under Elle's door, and she suspected the morning would find her gran asleep on the office couch.

Temporary. She reminded herself. It had to be.

Pulling the cloud-like comforter over her, she grabbed her phone to dull her mind enough to force sleep. Her social media newsfeeds sifted through a life separate from hers. Single friends dancing with strangers, drinking into wee hours of the morning. Families on Disney vacations. Then a picture posted by her sister-in-law Rachel of her six-year-old daughter riding Uncle Aaron's shoulders at a park. He was smiling wide with the beginning of crow's feet reaching under his eyes. He looked happier than she had seen him in…she wasn't even sure how long.

That smile haunted her even after she closed her phone. She wanted to see that smile shine toward her, to feel it warming her like the sun over Redondo Beach.

Thoughts of Aaron would consume her if she didn't replace them, before she found herself on his doorstep or in his bed again.

She typed the first name that came to mind in the search bar: Jocelyn Turner. The woman's name came to her at random times, and the desire to befriend her grew stronger in sleep deprivation. On impulse, Elle messaged her.

Hi Jocelyn,
Delete. That sounded too friendly.
Hi Mrs. Turner,
Delete. She wasn't Elle's teacher for heaven's sake.

Hi Jocelyn,
You don't have to respond to this. I hope you don't think I'm creeping on you. Well I guess I was, but not in a stalker way. I'm just up in the middle of the night and don't know how to keep my mind out of places it shouldn't go. I know our husbands are absent from our beds for very, very different reasons, but I thought you may have suggestions for keeping the worries at bay.

If I'm completely out of bounds here, let me know. You owe me nothing. I'm just low on friends these days.
Elle Holloway

10

JOCELYN

The television screen beamed a cleaning product infomercial while Jocelyn sat on her laundry-covered bed. She had dozed off and awoken a couple hours later as though she'd had a cat nap. Thus began the insomniac hours where loneliness crept its way through the house like a low, billowing smoke, extinguishing every bit of light and happiness around her if she let it.

Her phone buzzed with a text from Alexis, her friend reading her mind from a different time zone—Colorado to Texas. Both of them suffered from military spouse insomnia even though Alexis' husband was retired from the army. If Jocelyn had learned anything from her friend going through the process of re-civilization, it was that army habits didn't die overnight.

"You wanna run to the corner and grab a Panini? I've been craving one like no other." Alexis texted.

Their communication carried on as if they still lived blocks away, giving in to a fantasy world. In the military, one needed to be good at making friends quickly, though rarely did the friendship last through the moves and miles. But the talent for making friends had skipped Jocelyn. She had no other real friends since Alexis and Paul moved. She wasn't the making new friends type. She was the stay-at-home and survive the day with her little boy type. Alexis had been the Texas-style thunderstorm that forced friendship upon Jocelyn, seeing the gaping hole of missing comradery inside her and filling it whether Joss liked it or not.

"Oh god, yes. Maybe we can get our nails done too." Sometimes the fantasy overtook Jocelyn. She could almost remember what it was like to indulge in a mani/pedi.

"I don't even want to think about what your toenails look like."

Glancing at her misshapen nails and chipped red polish, she texted back, "No you don't, and I haven't shaved my legs in months."

She could imagine Alexis lying in bed while Paul snored next to her, the dim glow of her phone lighting up her caramel face. Jocelyn wished for sleep, but even more she wished for the warmth of her own husband lying next to her.

Her phone buzzed with Alexis response. "Even for the webcam show you gave Scott?"

Jocelyn blushed. "I didn't get that close to the camera."

Thoughts she attempted to avoid sprinted across her mind. The webcam was the last time she had seen Scott. Post-injury, she had to hold her imagination in check. If she let herself, she could concoct answers that the army wouldn't give. Was Scott's mangled body covered in bandages, or his skin burned beyond recognition? Would his face be the face that longed for her through the webcam?

"Have you heard from him?"

"Not yet."

Alexis had been her last call the evening she found out. Saying the words the third time wasn't any easier than the first.

"Have you talked to Ian?"

The texted words lingered in front of Jocelyn's eyes without response. The courage to tell Ian eluded her. She'd said the words enough over the phone for a lifetime, and every time they stalled in her throat. The effort would be worse looking at Scott's eyes duplicated in his son's.

"I can't." She typed. "Not without more information."

"You know the army. Don't expect that anytime soon."

Waiting was the juggernaut. If she knew what had happened to her husband, what to expect when she saw him, then she could see a mosaic of what was to come for her family. But the plethora of calls she made resulted in dead ends. No one who knew anything would talk with her.

"I wish I could be there with you." Alexis said. "I'm so sorry."

There wasn't anything else to say. They both knew Paul and Alexis didn't have the money to visit, and their new jobs were too fragile for vacation time.

An email notification broke through, and she was grateful for it. It was an email from Elle Holloway asking for tips to deal with insomnia. One sentence from the email struck her, "I know our husbands are absent from our beds for very, *very* different reasons..." Jocelyn closed her eyes and in that second saw a white hospital room with rows of beds, rows of men just like Scott with families just like her, waiting to see their soldier; Scott one among many.

Half-folded laundry spread across her bed. If anyone knew about insomnia, about keeping your mind out of the trenches, it was Jocelyn. Filling the void with anything was better than leaving it empty. The response was easy.

> *You caught me having the exact same kind of night. Here are some things I do: (Disclaimer: I don't exactly recommend them all.)*
> - *Laundry and cleaning. It keeps the hands and mind busy.*
> - *Move furniture. I've rearranged my house no less than 20 times.*
> - *Develop an embarrassing addiction to infomercials.*
>
> *For normal insomniac suggestions, I recommend reading, relaxation techniques or...infomercials!*
>
> *Hope they help. And honestly, this is what I think social media is for, connecting with people you would otherwise not be able to. But if you show up at my doorstep, I will consider you a creepy stalker! Sleep well.*
>
> *Jocelyn*

Pressing send, she swallowed the hurt she shared with this woman, unwilling to reveal that some nights none of those things helped.

***

A shrill sound woke Jocelyn to piles of Ian's pajamas and underwear on the bed not yet folded. Her phone rang, trumpeting through the quiet house. She fumbled to answer before it woke Ian.

On the screen, Scott's name and phone number glared at her. Her finger couldn't hit the Answer button fast enough. "Hello?" Her voice sounded childlike, unsteady, hopeful.

"Joss?" It was Scott's voice, quieter than normal, but still Scott's.

All her tension released. "Oh god, Scott." Her free hand pressed into her eyes, like she could push the tears back from where they came. She tried to emulate the strong wife she usually portrayed with him, but her strength had seeped out of her like helium from a pinhole. "I thought–I don't know–I didn't–"

"I know, babe, I'm sorry." His voice was as raspy as a first morning sentence. The line was clearer than his previous calls but that could have been her ears attuned to his voice after being devoid of it for too long. "I'm okay."

Jocelyn took a deep breath. She tried to hold on to the *I'm okay* part, but it wasn't enough. A tear ripped past her cheek and down her neck in record time. She wiped her face and focused on her husband's voice. There was no need for her traditional cologne spray. His voice triggered all her senses to conjure Scott's scent, his taste, his warmth against her skin.

He took a labored breath. "They come and talk to you?" The words slurred.

"Yes, Elizabeth Cryer and John Wilkins came. But that was days ago."

"I would have called earlier, babe, but I've been in and out." Scott's slurred speech continued. His meds were undoubtedly strong. "I'm foggy on the details, but they did surgery. A couple, I think, but I don't remember. The last thing I remember is suiting up."

It was Scott, but not Scott. His voice was flat, and as much as she could blame it on medication, she theorized it was more.

"They have me scheduled on a flight outta here in a couple days." Pause. She could hear him swallow. "I'm coming home, babe."

There was a smile in his voice, a smile that was burned into her mind forever. She exhaled relief, knowing he could hear it across the ocean in Germany.

"You remember when we were in school," Scott said, his words slowing down, dragging him into sleep, "and we would stay up all night on the phone talking until we fell asleep."

Her affirmation was quiet, remembering the clear case phone she had by her bed, the one that showed all the wires and bells inside, that fit easily between her ear and her pillow. She laid down, positioning this smaller phone the same way. Her words would be muffled, but that didn't matter now.

"And we would ask 'would you love me if' questions until we couldn't think of any more." Scott sniffed into the phone. Could he be crying like she was? It had been so long since she'd heard him cry.

"I remember."

Would you love me if I gained 300 pounds? They would ask each other. *Would you love me if I had no eyebrows or eyelashes? Would you love me if I lost my arms and couldn't hug you anymore?*

They had been kids, asking morbid, preposterous questions at ridiculous hours of the night—although Scott's were always light and funny. *Would you love me if my lips never stopped growing?* But now, some of the other scenarios seemed too close to home.

"I love you no matter what, Scott Turner." She said. A tear dripped over the bridge of her nose and pooled in the other eye. Scott didn't respond, his breathing thick and steady. He was asleep. Jocelyn laid with the phone against her ear, listening to him breath. In. Out. In. Out. And that breath was the best sound she had heard in her life. With closed eyes, she could imagine it was Scott's chest her head laid on, wrapped up in him, listening to his breath. In. Out. In. Out.

***

The airport pickup area was sparse, although a parking space had been hard to come by. Jocelyn's hands fidgeted with her keys while she waited for her mother to walk through the rotating doors. She had delayed her mother's visit long enough. The delay wasn't because she didn't want her mom coming in from California. In fact, when her unannounced email came through with flight details Jocelyn felt lighter. Her hesitancy came from the inevitable talk with Ian. She still hadn't told him about Scott's…incident, but her mother's visit would bring questions.

Ian stood at the windows next to the rotating door, squirming to catch a glimpse of his Grandma Roxanne. "Can I go around just one time?" He asked, pointing to the glass doors as they twirled in front of him, teasing him like an amusement park ride.

"No, babe, we aren't supposed to go in. They are only for people coming out." She smiled at him as he resumed his post. "Don't put your mouth on the glass, Ian."

Checking her phone for a message from her mother, Jocelyn jumped when Ian started chanting. "I see her. I see her."

"Okay, good. Not so loud." Jocelyn glanced at the surrounding business people with their button-down shirts and briefcases contrasting her yoga pants and ponytail.

Moments later, her mother came walking through the doors, searching the faces for Jocelyn but Ian finding her first. He ran to her wrapping her legs in a hug. "Were the doors fun?"

Roxanne's round eyes looked at Jocelyn from under her thick bangs in confusion. Jocelyn laughed, tiredly. Thank goodness for this little boy. He kept the spark of joy in her life.

Simply seeing her mother allowed her to breathe easier and filled her with a sense of home. Ian attempted to roll his grandmother's bag to the car. Driving away the women made small talk to avoid the topic looming over them all, while Ian made a game out of spotting airplanes that dotted the sky.

"Mom?"

"Yes."

"When I get big and strong like Dad, I want to drive airplanes in the army."

Small talk came to a halt, and Roxanne looked at Jocelyn with glossy eyes that showed worry, fear that Ian would end up like Scott. However that was.

Jocelyn moved her eyes to the road and squeezed the steering wheel with both hands the way some squeeze a stress ball. "That would be cool, Ian."

What Jocelyn didn't want from her mother was another voice of worry. Her own cargo hull was maxing out her strength. Scott's parents were on the brink of falling apart and she was baring their daily calls on shoulders that were weighed down even before Scott's injury. And her shoulders weren't all that broad. She couldn't add her mother to the mix.

"I wish I had an extra room for you to stay." Jocelyn told Roxanne when they arrived home.

Her mother surveyed the duplex. Heat reached Jocelyn's cheeks when her mother answered, "It sure is cozy, isn't it?" knowing it was meant in the nicest way.

"I don't mind the couch." Roxanne said with sincerity. "When Scott gets home, I'll get a hotel so you can have family time." She was careful with her words. Careful with his name. As though his name could perforate her daughter's heart.

"That could be a while. I have no idea how long he might be at the hospital." She whispered too, to keep Ian from hearing.

"It's good I'm retired then." Roxanne had been retired from teaching for two years. After a beat, she added. "Your dad wanted to come."

Jocelyn bounced her head up and down. She wanted to avoid this topic. "It's okay, mom."

Her dad was not supportive of Scott's army career—not because of Scott but because of his politics against the war. Jocelyn stayed out of politics, siding with Scott that war was rarely all right or all wrong. While her dad had a lot of respect for his son-in-law, there were many dinner table dissertations that Scott sat through with clenched jaw but only one he ever excused himself from. Not usually one to confront a situation, Jocelyn had turned to her father and reminded him, "Your son-in-law is a soldier for the United States Army. When you disrespect the army, you are disrespecting him. And me." She'd left it at that and finished her meal.

That was the last time they had seen her dad before Scott's deployment.

"I wasn't mad at him. I was just tired of hearing it all the time." Jocelyn answered the question dangling in her mother's face.

"Is that why you didn't come to Christmas?"

"Not at all. We didn't have the money, and I knew you didn't either." Roxanne opened her mouth to speak, but Jocelyn cut her off. "I was not going to ask Brad for it." Her younger brother found success owning his own pool company in Las Vegas—although that didn't mean that he was loose with his money. On top of Brad's high earnings, he had a notion that his older sister was in the lurch. But the pity that looked at her through Brad's eyes made her sick.

Jocelyn changed the subject to give her mother a tour of the modest house. Modest didn't mean plain. When Alexis still lived on post, she had taught Jocelyn how to make the small space her own. Together they had painted every wall—"Life's too short for vanilla" was Alexis' motto—and watched a slew of YouTube videos on refinishing furniture. Jocelyn's home was full of mismatched pieces found in trash piles or at garage sales that the two friends had spent hours sanding, painting, refinishing and distressing. Roxanne noticed each piece that she'd been sent pictures of over the years.

But their tour was interrupted by Ian grabbing his grandmother's hand. "Come. See my room."

As they entered, Ian presented to her every toy bin. Each one labeled with words he wouldn't be able to read for at least another year but knew by heart. He showed off his Darth Vader bedspread, his Star Wars rug and lastly Scott's Daddy Doll.

"I love it." Was all Roxanne could manage before she had to step out of the room for a breath. Jocelyn felt the same way every time she saw the small face of Scott staring up at her.

"The women in the FRG, the Family Readiness Group I told you about, they have offered to help with anything we need. Meals, house cleaning, watching Ian."

They were in the kitchen now, opening the chalkboard painted door of the pantry to hide away from Ian's ears. Roxanne whispered, "Have you told him yet?"

Jocelyn shook her head. "I will. Tomorrow." She knew her mother's next question would be if she wanted her there, but this one she needed to share with Ian alone. "I don't want to scare him." Tears threatened, so she stopped there.

Roxanne turned to look at the stacks of labeled storage bins holding all her pantry needs. "Hm," she let her eyes scan the shelves. "I think you need to come organize my pantry."

A smile lifted Jocelyn's lips and spirit. "The label maker was my best investment." Of course, she bought it from an infomercial.

***

There were only 48 hours ticking away before Jocelyn would see Scott's face. His arrival information came through email; the black words glared against their white backdrop. He would be leaving Landstuhl, Germany where he was being treated at the American military hospital and arriving at Andrews Air Force Base. From there he would be transported to Fort Hood. Home. A knot twisted her stomach every time she thought of it. First from excitement, like awaiting a first kiss. But that quickly soured into jittery nerves.

After a rare breakfast out—Roxanne's treat—the three of them hopped over to the FRG playdate. Dread settled heavy in Jocelyn's stomach atop the harvest pancakes she'd eaten. The moms at the playdate were women she'd brought soups to in Tupperware containers when they had the flu, watched their children grow inches, and met with once a month for a playdate like this one. They were the closest friends she had in this home away from home. Which didn't say a lot. Shame bloomed on her cheeks knowing that she hadn't called a single one of them to meet for coffee outside of this setting, to talk about their husbands, to make any true connection, even for support after Scott's... She interrupted her own thoughts. Her shoulders had grown the size of boulders carrying this herself, and yet these army wives with husbands in Scott's unit no doubt knew of Scott's situation. Her situation. Their eyes would greet her in pity, seeing their own nightmare in her sagging smile.

If it wasn't for Ian's excitement about seeing his friends and her previous commitment to bring a food item, then she would have backed out in a passive text. Instead, she toted her mom and Ian along with the promised fruit salad.

Jocelyn hadn't stepped out of the parking lot by the time Ian was pummeling toward his friends, lightsaber in hand, her motherly call to *Be Careful* trailing after him. A little girl cartwheeled by and the sidewalk was covered in neon chalk drawings.

Her fitbit would certainly collect a million steps from the parking lot to the pavilion where the other mom's clustered. That's how far it felt. One by one they noticed Jocelyn with a prism of reactions.

A squatty redhead, newer to the group than Jocelyn, herded her two little ones to a table toward the back of the pavilion. *It's not contagious.* Jocelyn wanted to snap at the woman. *Your kids won't catch a curse by playing with my son.* But stoically, Jocelyn proceeded past the woman. Angie Byrne waved above the crowd, a hopeful wiggle of her thin hand. She stood next to the food table, where children and flies alike were gathered. Angie took the fruit salad from Roxanne and tossed a grin Jocelyn's way. "This looks wonderful." Angie said, and Jocelyn was grateful it wasn't *I'm so sorry.*

She tried, really she did. She tried to be a part of their flowery conversations, but she tired of them as quick as cheap bubble gum loses its flavor. The glaring typos in the last FRG newsletter—which Jocelyn rarely read; inconvenient location of the next fundraiser—which Jocelyn never attended; the child who was struggling to potty train; the construction on post causing traffic issues.

Their banter pinballed around Jocelyn. When someone looked her way, she nodded with a plastered smile. Then she noticed Elizabeth Cryer alone for once on a bench by the splash pad. She excused herself, with a gentle pat on Roxanne's hand. If she was bored, how terrible a time must her mother be having. Roxanne headed toward the playground to find Ian.

In all the months of FRG meetings and events, Jocelyn had never approached Elizabeth. Now she was stealing away to sit in the sun with this woman. Elizabeth was crisp with a button-down white blouse and khaki mid-length pants—at a park! Her hair was pinned in a chignon just above her neck, making her look older somehow.

As Jocelyn sat next to her, Elizabeth sounded as surprised as Jocelyn was. "Is everything okay?"

A shrug lifted Jocelyn's shoulder then dropped. "Fine. You?"

"Yeah, fine." Elizabeth's unusual low-energy matched her own.

Could the same situation be weighing heavy on Mrs. Cryer? "How is the Martinez family?"

Elizabeth's board-straight back straightened at the question if that was possible. "As expected, I suppose." Perhaps the first time Elizabeth Cryer did not share every piece of gossip she knew. In contrast, her stare focused on the fountains of the splash pad standing at attention, awaiting the summer months to splash on children and elicit squeals of delight.

It struck Jocelyn how paradoxical this woman's situation was. To be the head of the FRG, to plan and attend mother's events and play dates with no child of her own. To support the families who lost their own child, when she has never had the fortune of raising one. The total of a woman was never what she appeared to be on the exterior. Even Elizabeth Cryer.

A gaggle of laughter rose from women huddled around the table of food. Jocelyn scanned the park for Ian and saw him on the swings with Roxanne pushing him and smiling. Her chest throbbed at seeing so many women carelessly happy while she could hardly focus on sitting up straight. Jocelyn straightened her back in protest. Maybe she and Elizabeth had more in common than she'd ever thought.

"Have you heard from Scott?" Elizabeth asked.

"Just arrival details from his CO." His CO, Elizabeth's husband. Jocelyn couldn't postpone the question that had nudged her toward this bench. "Do you have any new information?" She regretted the question as soon as she'd asked it. She sounded weak, incapable of handling her own circumstances. "I just—I can't get any answers. I don't know what to expect."

"I don't. I'm sorry."

Jocelyn cringed at those last words.

"I know there will be a lot of medications, a lot of hospital visits, but he's strong enough to get through this. Whatever it is." Then Elizabeth's well-manicured hands were holding her own. "And so are you, Jocelyn."

***

Five white 4x4 trucks drove down the Texas highway around her as she made her way to the army post as though she was being escorted by the Star Wars Stormtroopers that Ian played with daily. Texas wasn't all cowboy hats and ranches like she'd imagined when she learned Scott had been stationed at Fort Hood, but the roads certainly were crawling with trucks regardless of gas prices.

Yes, she was using the act of counting trucks on the road as a distraction from her destination. She was en route to meet Scott at the on-post hospital. Despite her plans to meet him on the tarmac as he arrived from Andrews Air Force Base, she received a call from Lt. Wilkins early this morning *after* Scott had been processed and admitted to the hospital. Pushing back the betrayal she felt for the army not giving her more information along the way, Jocelyn thanked Wilkins and canceled every plan she had for the day.

Her eyes flickered to the digital clock on her dashboard, ticking away the approximate thirteen minutes it would take from her location to get through the security check point at the gate entrance and wind around to the hospital. She had only ever been to the maternity ward to visit new moms, and for those visits her palms had never sweat.

The morning had been hard, leaving Ian with her mother. He wasn't away from Jocelyn often, maybe Sunday school when Jocelyn made it to church, but otherwise they were practically attached. Together every day, all day.

Maybe that bond was the reason he had swallowed the news about Scott easier than she expected. She'd sat next to him on his bed and explained, "Daddy was hurt doing his job, so he is going to the hospital where doctors are helping him get better." The explanation was simple, but it was all Jocelyn could handle while looking into Ian's round brown eyes.

"Do I get to see him?" Ian asked. Hopeful.

"Not yet." It wasn't all a lie. She couldn't take Ian yet. She wanted to do a better job preparing her son than the army had prepared her.

Much of the morning was spent on FaceTime with Alexis, begging for wardrobe guidance. Her nerves ricocheted across her closet. Today would be the first time Scott had seen her in months.

"He wants to see his wife. I don't think he'll care what you wear." Alexis said, biting into her breakfast toast. They hadn't FaceTimed in weeks; everything seemed different. Alexis' natural curls were straightened and flowed like black oil past her shoulders. Her mocha skin needed no makeup, but her lips were a perfect shade of red.

"He may be hurt," Jocelyn told Alexis, "but I'm pretty sure his eyes still work fine. It's the first time I've seen him in person. I wanna look *nice*."

"You're headed to a hospital, Joss. You can't wear a cocktail dress with garters."

Jocelyn had rolled her eyes. She'd never worn garters in her life.

"Girl, he would be happy to see you even if you showed up in flannel pjs and your robe."

In the end, she had selected skinny jeans, boots and cinched chambray button-down. For the first time in weeks, she wore a full face of makeup. When she came out of her room with her purse on her shoulder, Ian sidled up alongside her.

"We go see Dad." He said.

Her stomach dropped, but Ian was smiling, excited for the day he had been waiting for.

"No, honey, I'm sorry. I'm going to the hospital by myself. He still needs help from the doctors before he can play with you. Grandma's going to play with you today."

"But I wanna see him." Ian whined. Tears pooled in his eyes. "I wanna go." He raced to the door and reached on his tip-toes to unlock the deadbolt.

"Ian, you have to stay here today." Jocelyn tried to be firm, but her heart was fracturing like glass with every word, every wail.

Even she was guarded in seeing Scott for the first time, uncertain of all his injuries. She couldn't do that to Ian. Squatting down to the level of his square face, she noticed the pudginess of babyhood had almost evaporated. "I know you want to see him, honey, just not today."

Ian screamed at her, flailing one arm around and swatted her on the shoulder. Before she could react, he hit her again, his arms spinning like helicopter blades. "I wanna see Dad. I go see Dad."

"Ian Scott Turner, you do *not* hit your mother." Roxanne jumped in. Jocelyn was too stunned to move when Roxanne picked Ian up and took him toward his room. She glanced over her shoulder at her daughter with such strong emotion in her eyes and nodded.

Swallowing the hurt with understanding, Jocelyn grappled out the door and to the car. In her seat, she allowed herself a rare moment of quiet. An inhaled breath stuttered in her throat. She leaned back on the headrest. Her family was changing, already on day one. Everything was changing. She would *not* allow herself tears, though. She had worked too hard on her mascara to ruin it. She was going to see her husband today. She should be celebrating. He was alive, returning to her when others had returned to their families in flag-covered coffins.

That's why she counted the trucks on the highway. To distract herself.

At the security check point entrance at Fort Hood, she rolled her window down and held out her Department Defense-issued ID to be scanned. She'd done this hundreds of times, for shopping, for FRG play dates, for meetings. But this time it felt more official somehow. Like she was now a part of a weird club, one that lived the dark side of military life.

Her car seemed to park itself in front of Darnall Army Medical Center. She took a breath before getting out and walking into her new reality. Reminding her body to inhale and exhale slowly, keeping her shoulders back and tension out of her neck, she stepped down the white-tiled hallway toward Scott's room.

She could see the door. A couple of steps and she would be within reach of her husband. Each step was deliberate, to keep herself from running, to keep her stomach from doing back flips. Those same feelings stopped her a few feet away from the door. She smoothed out her shirt, pulling on its hem. A burning panic surged in her stomach as the door glared at her. Scott was inside, lying on a hospital bed. Closing her eyes, the image of his face on the Skype screen projected behind her eyelids. The last time she'd seen his face. What would she see when she opened the door?

"Mrs. Turner?" a voice said from her right. She turned and noticed the nurses station. A woman in a white medical coat reached out a slender hand in Jocelyn's direction. "I'm Captain Lyle, Sgt. Turner's doctor." When the doctor smiled, her skin stretched wide showing all of her teeth. "He's been talking about you."

Jocelyn turned back toward the door, but the doctor reached out and touched Jocelyn's forearm with a gentle touch. "First, I'd like to brief you on his injuries, if that would be okay." Finally, someone wanted to brief her.

With a flip of her stomach, Jocelyn nodded. She didn't trust her voice to speak yet.

Dr. Lyle didn't have to look at Scott's chart to begin. She explained how Scott's right leg had taken the brunt of the blast. Field doctors had set the bones in his leg and done preliminary surgeries to remove some of the shrapnel throughout his body. "Shrapnel is just a fancy word for metal fragments, glass or any kind of debris that would have dispersed from the blast." The doctor's voice droned on. Jocelyn had waited, even begged for this information, but now a magnetic pull was drawing her toward the man behind the door. Just like the words Scott ended his emails with: *You are my gravity, pull me home.*

Now Dr. Lyle flipped through a chart for a missing piece of information. ". . . left some of the pieces of shrapnel imbedded deep in his thigh muscles in hopes that they would begin to move further toward the surface on their own. Surgery that deep into his muscle would have caused more damaged than leaving the pieces in place."

Jocelyn felt her stomach roll at the thought. These were the risks; she had known of them before she had said "I do." But this couldn't be real. She looked around the room to stay grounded, but she was floating out of her body toward him.

The long fingers of Dr. Lyle reached up to her own ear as she explained the damage to Scott's right ear, parts of his face and all the way down the right side of his body. "...seem to be healing nicely–"

"Can I please just see him?" Jocelyn interrupted. The doctor's words had turned into mumbles in her ears. "I've waited so long."

The doctor tilted her head with sympathetic eyes. "Certainly," she said.

Jocelyn unlatched the door and walked into the room expecting a curtain up to ease her into the scene, but there was no longer any barrier between her and her husband. He was just ahead of her, angled in his bed like a protractor, his left profile all she could see. And he looked just like her Scott. A hospital uniform instead of the ACUs she'd seen him in last.

Her eyes panned to his lower body. Jutting out of his thigh and shin were small metal bars shaped like chopsticks propping up two larger foot-long metal braces that formed an X above Scott's bandaged leg.

Maybe he heard her heart thundering as she took in the scene or maybe he perceived her in the room. He turned his head slowly in her direction. She took a deep breath. *He is still your Scott.*

"Hey," she said, wanting to be the first one to speak to show she could handle this. She walked closer, taking in more of his injuries with each step. His lips were grotesquely swollen and split; a chunk of his bottom lip was missing, sewn together with black x's. They were not those soft lips that she had waited so long to kiss.

His nose must have been broken and reset—not the first time—leaving an indigo trail under his right eye and around the curve of his cheek. That's where the bandages started, tucked around his ear and all the way down his neck, disappearing beneath the white gown. The only part of his face that seemed untainted by the blast was his chin, scruffier than the army allowed. Its blunt edge beckoning her to touch it, kiss it, but she was suddenly unsure. Would her touch hurt him?

"Hey," he said back. A blood vessel in his eye was broken, blood swimming around the brown iris like an ink spot.

"Your hair looks good." Jocelyn said with a small smile, jumping to their light, sarcastic banter.

He laughed—or at least tried, letting out a huff of air from his mouth like a laugh—but then winced. "Yeah."

She spotted a chair in the corner of the room and drug it next to him, the legs scuffing against the tile. Before this awkward uncertainty, she would have sat right on the bed with him, maybe laid with him, but now the moment held the ambiguity of a blind date.

"Let me guess, I should see the other guy." Jocelyn repeated the line he'd used so many times when coming back with scrapes and bruises, even a broken nose, from training. Too late she realized she'd chosen the wrong quip.

Scott turned his head, and it felt like he was turning the heat of the sun away from her. "Not this time." His words were quiet. And they shut her up.

Her eyes scanned over him, taking in everything she could. Stitches up his neck into the brown of his hairline. His arm was wrapped in gauze and tape, twice the size of his other arm. The hospital gown covered so much.

For reasons she couldn't pinpoint, she had to remember what it was like to be a wife. His wife. Was it the shock of his injuries? The length of time they'd been apart?

What do I do? She asked herself. *What would I have done before?* Words came easier to her; she'd been having conversations in her head with Scott since he deployed. Their banter had kept her loneliness at bay. But touching him? She hadn't done that for an entire year.

Her eyes fell to his hands. It was like being on their first date again, wanting to feel his palm against her own skin, wanting to intertwine their fingers and never let go, but unsure how to make the first move.

This would be their first touch all over again. It seemed momentous, even though she couldn't recall their first touch after his last deployment. Certainly it had been a hug, a kiss, like normal couples. But this moment was anything but normal.

"How's Ian? Did you tell him about me?" His voice had the roughness of morning's first words.

She nodded, the place where Ian had slapped her arm flared with heat at the thought. "He wanted to come today, but I didn't think it was a good idea."

Scott shook his head. "I don't want him to see me looking like Two-Face." He licked his lip, but it didn't help the dryness.

"I have some chapstick." She went to digging in her purse, giving her hands something to do, and stood as she found the tube. Stepping to his bedside, she realized she didn't want their first touch to be lathering chapstick on lips that she should have been kissing. Without another thought, she reached out for his hand, feeling the callouses of his fingers against her soft skin.

Sitting down on the edge of his bed, she tried not to put her full weight on it and brought his nearest hand to her lips. Touching her lips against each of his scratched knuckles. With that one touch, she couldn't understand how she'd forgotten. Touching him felt right. And she never wanted to let go.

He breathed deep, contented.

Another jagged gash just under his collarbone peeked out from the top of his hospital gown. It was crisscrossed with stitches. How many stitches had it taken to put this man back together? To bring him home to her?

"I'm glad you're home." She said, meeting his eyes. Looking at the startling red stain in the one eye made her cringe, but it couldn't hurt her a fraction of how it hurt him.

"I got here as soon as I could." He answered with a lift in his cracking lips.

11

ELLE

The pergola above Elle shaded her grandmother's patio from the California springtime sun. The wooden slats were painted gray to matched the home's siding complementing the splashes of pink and purple blooms. Ivy climbed the beams and clung to the retaining wall along the yard's perimeter; thick oak trees like sentinels blocked the world beyond this third-of-an-acre lot. Strawberry plants hung from the edge of the pergola, swinging with the breeze.

There was a magical feel to it, this secret garden of Norah's. Pictures of decades past showed Elle putting her nose up to the yellow roses that grew along the pebbled pathway as she learned to avoid the thorns. She'd spent hours watching her gran pluck and prune, dig and sweep in this lush yard, but Norah's green thumb gene had skipped a couple generations.

Moving from her knees to her backside, Elle took a break from weed pulling. Norah's bulky gardening gloves may have kept Elle's manicured hands intact, but they made it difficult to wipe the droplets of sweat threatening her eyes. "I've never understood why you don't hire someone to do all of this."

Acting strictly as supervisor from her wicker lawn chair per doctor's orders, Norah took a substantial sip of guava juice through her bendy straw. "Why have a garden unless you're willing to put the work in to enjoy it?"

Momma, the wild cat, scuttled across the stone retaining wall. Elle shrugged, "You can enjoy this without having to break your back over it. They have landscaping companies for that."

Norah shook her head with a light laugh, "Why do you kids always skimp on the work and expect the same results? You get cliff notes instead of reading books; you pay people to do the work that you deem too hard. How will you ever learn the lessons you need to make it to a ripe old age like me?" She waved her hands over her body. "Wisdom comes through work."

"Ah, you think you're wise?" Amusement implicit in Elle's voice.

"Wiser than you'll ever be if you keep paying everyone to think for you."

Ugly weeds needed to be pulled and a bag of plant food ready to be spread, but as long as Norah was talking instead of cracking the whip, Elle relished the intermission.

"In my day, you worked hard or you didn't eat."

Elle heard little of Norah's depression-era upbringing other than these little quips. But these, she'd heard all her life.

With a grunt, Norah continued, "In my day, you stuck things out even when they got hard: jobs, marriages, everything."

Letting the verbal slap skim past her, Elle bent her head back. A lone ray of sun peeked through the leafy ceiling and soaked her face. For days Norah hadn't mentioned Elle's marriage. She should have known it was coming. She was surprised her gran hadn't erupted like an advice-giving volcano.

"You didn't see the divorce rate at 50% when people were willing to get married and stay married and take it serious."

The teenager in her wanted to throw the gardening gloves down in a tantrum and run through the sliding glass door into the house stomping her feet. But the adult in her spoke up, "I'm not going to do this right now."

"When, then? Marriage is work and no one wants to put the work in any more. You can't run away when it's not making you happy."

"I'm not running away from anything."

"Well you didn't move in with me to help me. I knew in the hospital when you brought it up that you were only asking to help yourself."

The pain in her gran's eyes at that simple admission took Elle's breath right out of her. "Norah,"

Norah waved both hands in the air, waving away the conversation. "Get showered. I want to go to dinner." She got out of her chair with much effort but was unwilling to accept Elle's hand for help. Norah never had been willing to accept much from anyone.

After taking off her dirty shoes and gloves, Elle followed through the sliding door into the living room. The same framed pictures Elle had seen for decades occupied the walls. Black and white photos of Norah, her husband Larry who had died when Elle was a toddler, and their two children, Charlene and Bruce. One of Uncle Bruce and his family who lived across the country. One frame held a picture of Elle and Charlene; the only one on the wall that didn't have a man in it. A wedding photo of Aaron and Elle's sat on the side table under a brass lamp.

This house was a time warp that Elle had hastily escaped as a teen. The only updates were the flat screen televisions and computer upstairs, oddities in a home that stood like a museum from childhood. The same navy couches covered in a preserving plastic, a chocolate brown quilt folded over the back cushion for chillier nights.

Near the entry sat the same out-of-tune piano Elle had clanked on as a child and wished to play as a teen. Its keys were yellowed like Norah's unpainted finger nails. A painting of a lake with a girl seated in a small boat hung on the wall above the piano. Only the back of the girl's auburn hair and cornflower blue dress were visible in the picture. Elle always envisioned her own face on the girl, although her grandfather had purchased the painting before Elle was born.

There was a sudden sense of urgency in Elle's chest, like her ribs were shrinking. Her life was revolving backwards, returning her to the dependence of childhood. All sense of control and freedom was being repossessed. Deep breaths.

Dinner out of the house would be good.

Although they didn't make it far. Norah refused to crawl into Elle's compact hybrid car, and Elle refused to sit in the passenger seat with Norah's jerky driving. Compromise made, Norah passed the Cadillac keys over to Elle, inevitably telling her granddaughter how to operate a car and where to turn. Every comment became an opportunity for an argument, but the reminder of Norah's frailty prevented Elle from seizing them.

"There," Norah pointed at a restaurant around the corner. Good thing, because Elle couldn't keep her lips sealed much longer.

They pulled into the shopping center that housed the Brine Buffet. She hadn't been there in years, although Norah was a regular. Elle remembered being too short to see over the counter of the buffet line and Norah held tightly around her waist to boost her up so she could scoop endless amounts of tapioca pudding and steak onto her own plate. Steak on a buffet was questionable to Elle now, and come to think of it, could have been the origin of her veganism.

The manager greeted Norah by name, who asked to be seated in Chris' section. There was a chance that Norah alone kept this establishment running.

"You remember my granddaughter?" Norah asked Chris as he brought her usual black coffee and a glass of ice water.

"Yes, it's been a while." The portly server responded with a warm smile. He was in his late 40's, mostly bald, and procured an enormous amount of pity from Elle without even knowing it.

She smiled at him, pretending to remember. Inside she hoped she wasn't in a dead-end job at 40.

Being vegan left little for Elle to eat here, although California these days was so full of dieters and vegetarians and vegans and every type of allergy that it wasn't hard to find a restaurant that catered to specialized orders. Just not Brine Buffet. Elle poked at the salad bar, cringing at the browning lettuce edges. "I'll have water and eat at home."

"No, you will not." Norah demanded and pointed at the buffet, "Why don't you have the steak? It's your favorite."

"I don't eat meat or animal products and haven't since I was 20." Elle said.

"I was hoping that was a phase. That's why you're too skinny." Norah poked a hardened fingernail into Elle's ribs. "I can see your bones."

And I can see your varicose veins. Elle imagined herself saying, knowing it was a terrible comeback.

The two women sat in what should have been silence but wasn't as Norah chewed the well done wad of steak. It wasn't Norah's fault; it was the steak's. Reiterating why Elle's veganism was *not* a phase.

"Why didn't you ever get remarried?" Elle blurted. It was a loaded question, but she couldn't listen to the gnawing of teeth and saliva any longer.

The fork clanked on the plate and Norah wiped the edges of her mouth with the black linen napkin. "I didn't choose for the marriage to end and couldn't imagine being married to someone else."

If Elle bit down any harder on her tongue at the obvious jab, it would have bled.

After chomping on salad with clumpy blue cheese dressing, Norah spoke again. "I read a quote by some lady author that said it is some satisfaction to be able to have as much water and mud in the house as a person likes. I figure that's probably true. After you get used to being alone, it gets to be more convenient that way."

A smirk pulled at Elle's mouth. "I've never known you to let much water and mud in the house anyway. And I can't imagine a husband would track it in any more than a teenage girl did."

Norah met Elle's eyes, taking the challenge. "I liked having you around. I knew you'd keep me young." The lie came easily to her grandmother. And it *was* a lie, Elle knew, just like she had known when Norah was lying to her at 15.

They'd sat together on the kitchen barstools, leaning against the white counter top the first morning after Elle's mom had dropped her off with a kiss on the forehead and a suitcase of clothes. Norah had poured them each a cup of black coffee.

"Mom doesn't let me drink coffee." Elle's 15-year-old self had said.

Norah had nodded. "When she picks you up, she can decide." It was a typical grandmother move: giving her things her mother didn't allow, not terrible things but coffee along with chocolate covered cherries and sugary cereal and processed chicken nuggets.

When they had drained the coffee pot and only the grounds were left for cleaning up, 15-year-old Elle had mustered the nerve to ask, "She's not picking me up this time, though, is she?"

The lie came from Norah then too, "Until she does, you're welcome to drink as much coffee with me as you like. I'm right here every morning."

"It's a date." Elle had said, liking the company more than the coffee.

Those coffee talks hadn't lasted once Elle moved out. By 18, she had packed up and moved on the same way her mother had.

***

Sleep descended on this quiet neighborhood with the sunset, it seemed. Even Momma the cat curled up on the patio mat sleeping.

It was laughable how different this was from the life Elle left behind—or was forcibly removed from. Dance clubs pulsing with music. Boutique grand openings. Art exhibits. And Elle Holloway sat on a couch, eating her baked sweet potato sprinkled with cinnamon in utter silence.

The wind blew outside the paned window, and the chill of it passed through her skin, a ghost reaching her heart. Another reminder that she had no one to call. No husband to turn to. She'd hurt everyone who meant anything to her.

She would never have pictured herself living back in this house, and now it was the morning fog clouding her way.

A photo album under the corner table caught her eye. The album itself was a memory calling to her. She caped the blanket around her shoulders and pulled the album on to her lap.

Her hand hovered over the maroon album cover. She wanted to look inside but an invisible hand stopped her. The first picture was embossed on her memory the same way the gold leaf embossed the album's edge: Norah standing with her arm wrapped around Elle's mother's waist, resting just under her ribs. Elle could feel that hug. It was unique to Norah, back when she was strong enough to do so.

When Elle was younger she would squirm around, "Gran, that hurts."

But Norah would squeeze and say, "When a hug is this big, you feel it for days."

Cradling the cover, Elle opened the photo album. Three faces smiled up at her, but instead of filling her with warmth, her insides ached. Norah, Charlene, and in the middle, sitting in Charlene's lap was little four-year-old Elle. Back when the three of them could be in the same space and still smile. It had been so long. Where was her mother now? Gallivanting around the country, looking for new real estate to flip, having her dinners paid for by any man who would offer. *What is wrong with me that my own mother doesn't want me?* With one glance at the 4x4 picture, those childhood feelings rushed back. How could one person be so selfish?

The words flew back at her. Hadn't Aaron said exactly that to her? Had she become another version of her mother?

They were cut from the same fabric roll. Charlene had never kept a man, didn't even know who the father of her only daughter was. If anyone could understand Elle's loneliness, it was Charlene. They finally shared a commonality.

She pulled at her purse and her phone toppled out.

It rang twice. Then picked up to clinking dishes and murmuring of a restaurant. "This is Charlene."

"Mom? It's Elle." She rolled her eyes. Only child. She was the only person on earth that could call Charlene *mom*. But speaking to her mother again was like being tongue-tied talking to a first crush.

"Oh Elle, hi honey," As though she talked to Elle every day, yet it had been months without an email, text, anything.

"I was calling to tell you that Norah, um, Gran isn't doing too well."

There was a loud clatter on the other end. "What, honey? Sorry, I'm in a restaurant."

"Oh, it's okay. It sounds loud there. Do you need to call me back?"

"No, no, what's up?" Always so casual.

"Norah had a fall. She was released from the hospital earlier this week."

"Oh no." There was fumbling on the line and a muffled "Excuse me for a moment." Then a few seconds later the restaurant clatter was gone. "How serious is it?"

Does it matter? Instead Elle answered, "Well she's 84, and she was in the hospital for days. So there's that."

"Elle, stop being childish. You know what I'm asking."

She reverted to a child, wounded by Charlene all over again. "She hurt her leg and wrist pretty bad. I'm staying with her." There was a moment before her mother responded when Elle wanted to confess, to burst the bubble of hurt expanding in her chest and have her mother glue her back together.

But the moment passed, and Charlene responded, "Good. I'm glad you're there with her so I don't have to–"

To what? To take care of your mother. To help your daughter. To be responsible for someone other than yourself.

"–stop what I'm doing right away." The low hum of restaurant chatter resumed in the background.

What could be so important? Work? Vacation? She knew so little about Charlene; couldn't remember if she had received a Christmas card from her own mother or noticed the return address.

Maybe selfishness was in their blood. Only it skipped Norah's generation.

"Okay. Just wanted you to know."

"Thanks, honey. Keep me updated." Charlene's tone was all business now, like she was asking for a spreadsheet report.

"Yes ma'am." Elle couldn't resist, but her sarcasm didn't land. Charlene had ended the call.

The brief conversation had siphoned her energy. Treading softly back to the living room to turn the light off and replace the photo album, her eyes could scarcely stay open. She would rather crash on the couch as Norah often did than trudge to her empty bed. How she longed for somebody to lie next to again, the closeness of someone who cared for her. It had been so long.

With creaking floorboards underfoot, Elle tiptoed to Norah's bedside then slipped beneath the peach sheets next to her grandmother and pulled them up to her chin. Each of her muscles relaxed, absorbed in Norah's peach cocoon, a safety she hadn't felt in months.

12

JOCELYN

Scott's square fingers intertwined with his wife's as Jocelyn sat on the edge of the hospital bed next to him. Their bodies rested closer than they had in over a year, and the two held hands in silence. The nurse just left the room, verifying that she could remove Scott's bandages and some stitches in front of Jocelyn. It stung when he wrestled with the idea.

His uninjured hand squeezed around hers, preparing her, keeping her close, begging her to love him still. Her words alone hadn't convinced him that nothing had changed, but her presence *should* mean more than trillions of words.

Jocelyn moved her thumb over the white crescent moon of his square fingernails. Some moments it felt like they were the only part of him untouched by this war.

When the nurse returned—Jocelyn couldn't remember her name; this was only her second time to see her—with a metal rolling cart holding her supplies on top, she smiled at them, clear braces encasing her teeth. No doubt she was qualified to be here—she had to be, right?—but Jocelyn fought the urge to educate the young nurse as to why Scott's care was most important. These wounds wore the proof of the man he was, the reasons she loved him so.

The nurse's thin fingers gently pulled the adhesive from the bandages on Scott's mummified leg. Scott focused his gaze at the ceiling.

He believed her thoughts were written in the curves of her face. She could say the same for the way she read his eyes. Maybe it came with the years of familiarity. But motherhood had changed her. With a preschooler came mastery of the poker face she had never before perfected: Masked seriousness when Ian was found hiding behind the couch smeared with chocolate from creased neck to earlobes. An inward smile when he cried "Owie, owie, owie," in his sad little voice. She'd developed a pretty good poker face.

"Are you ready to see your new husband?" The way his voice bounced against the ceiling tiles back to Jocelyn's ears sent a chill through her.

"You will always be the man I married." She said.

His profile revealed a stunted confidence in her words. It crushed her. She had waited for him, made a life with him, knowing what the consequences could be. Would the weeks and months of recovery prescribed to heal his body also heal his opinion of her?

"I talked to Dad today." Scott said while the nurse was careful to sift the bandage under the metal bars raised inches above his leg.

"He wants to see you." Jocelyn spent hours reassuring her in-laws about things that she was unsure of herself. They'd called almost every day since the news of Scott's injury.

"What would he do? Take off work, spend tons of money on a plane ticket to sit here for a couple hours."

"They want to know you're okay."

"I'm okay. I told him I'm okay."

Scott squared his shoulders—almost a wince—when the nurse lifted his leg to unwrap the last layer of bandage from under his calf. His eyes fixed on one place above his bed. His reaction made her wonder if he had seen his own body, the way it was now. So when the nurse pulled the gauze away, Jocelyn was steel.

Two holes where the metal bars burrowed into his legs were now exposed. Rising like a scaffolding concreted by Scott's bones. Jocelyn swallowed back the rising bile. It looked barbaric, like bloodletting with leeches or boring holes in the skull. This, however, was keeping Scott whole. She kept her eyes moving.

The surface of his skin beneath his knee was uneven with red meteoric chasms, sections where portions of damaged skin, muscle and possibly even bone were removed. Bright red lines snaked their way up his leg, showing where her husband's body had been split open.

Even with the bruising and light swelling of his misshapen leg, Jocelyn could see entry points freckled across the surface where shrapnel lurked. The thought of pieces of scrap metal, maybe someone else's bones and whatever else making a home under Scott's skin, deep in his muscles and tissues, made her stomach roll. But she worked to keep her breath even. Scott reacted when the nurse touched what would obviously end up a lifelong scar to clean the wound. Jocelyn watched the nurse's every movement, wiping gently across the bulging stitches—too many to count—cleaning, sanitizing, warding off infection and bacteria.

She wished it were so easy to ward off the infection plaguing Scott's thoughts, memories, worries. His confidence in her and their marriage waned like an immune system subdued by a virus.

"I know Mom and Dad want to see me, but I don't want to see anybody except you." He said.

Peeling her eyes away from Scott's leg, she saw that he was no longer looking at the ceiling but at her. Poker face. Their eyes met. She could get lost in those cavernous eyes, and she would have let herself for a moment had they not born the swirling red sign of injury.

"You look beautiful." He said simply. "Have I told you that?"

Jocelyn raised an eyebrow. In the days she had been coming up to the hospital, she had prepped less and less. Her hair was back in its typical messy bun, with yoga pants and flowy t-shirt. She felt a mess until he looked at her like that. He looked at her like she was more than she had ever thought of herself.

Jocelyn kissed the palm of his hand. This was her Scott.

The nurse sighed, her eyebrows pulling together like she was watching a romance movie. Jocelyn blushed and looked down at her feet, suddenly uncomfortable.

Drawing attention away from his wife as though he'd read her mind, he wiggled the fingers of his injured arm. He had yet to close them in a fist. "Would you still love me if I got the tattoo sleeve I've always wanted?" He said, lifting his arm up a little. "I'll get your name right here." He let go of her hand to point at his bicep.

She made herself laugh and joke to cover up her notice of how much muscle mass he had lost in his arm. Not because it was important to her, but because it was important to Scott.

With a little examination of the nicely healing marks on Scott's forearm, the nurse moved on to removing the sutures on Scott's neck and jawline.

When the phone in Jocelyn's pocket buzzed, she jumped, moving the bed and jerking Scott slightly as the nurse pulled the first suture from his neck.

"Sorry," Jocelyn said sheepishly and grabbed her phone.

"It's Mom." She said, keeping her voice even-keeled. "I'll take this outside and make sure everything's okay with Ian." With care, she eased off Scott's bed and steadied her pace to the door. She inhaled deep, gulping fresh air, once she was around the corner. Her pride soared for holding her composure with Scott, but it was sweet relief to be out of the room that burned her nose with chemicals.

She answered her phone.

There were squeals in the background. Good ones. "Hey honey, how are things there?"

"Fine." Jocelyn recognized that her voice was too high pitched but couldn't get it down an octave.

Roxanne didn't seem to notice. "Leanne just dropped off dinner with her little girl. Grace is so sweet, and she brought her little doctoring toys over. Doc McStuffins. I don't know who he is, but Grace and Ian played so well together."

"It's a she."

"I know Grace is a she. That's what I said."

"No. Doc McStuffins is a she."

"Oh. Well, anyway. I told Leanne to let Grace stay and play with Ian so she could have some alone time, and that little girl has Ian following her everywhere. It reminds me of you and Brad, the way you used to boss him around and he'd just nod his head and do what you said." Roxanne chuckled.

It didn't surprise Jocelyn that her mom had invited Grace to stay. Children loved Roxanne, and 24 years of teaching elementary school had taught her how to stay in control while being as sweet as cherry pie.

When the call ended, Jocelyn took another fresh air breath before turning on her casual exterior and reentering the room. By then the nurse had moved up to Scott's ear.

"Everything okay?" He said, meeting her eyes, testing her again. The ameba-shaped blood splotch swam in his eye.

"Yeah," Jocelyn shrugged. "Mom added a kid for a playdate." He nodded as if he didn't hear the words and only saw her face working to be casual. It felt like high school drama class, having to stay in character.

"Hey. About Ian." She started, breaching a subject he had put yellow crime scene tape over.

He sighed. She ignored it.

"I know you don't want him to see you like this," as the words came out, the nurse pulled the bandage off of his ear, exposing the stitches where his missing earlobe ended. The line was jagged, like someone had bitten it off. A matching row of black stitches lined his jaw where the shrapnel ripped through him. Seeing it, Jocelyn was surprised his jaw hadn't been effected more than a little popping when he opened his mouth or chewed.

"But Ian needs to come. It's been almost a week, and every day when I leave to come see you, he–" *screams, shrieks, throws a tantrum.* She searched for the right word. "cries for you. He wants his dad more than anything."

Her effort to lessen the blow didn't seem to help. Scott's head hung over his chest. She wanted him to look at her so she could decipher what he was thinking, but he wouldn't.

After adding adhesive tape where the stitches had been to keep the skin healing, the nurse threw the bandages and suture pieces from the tray into the bio-hazard lidded trash bin. "Just a couple more days for the sutures on your torso." She said to the couple, ignoring their conversation. She pumped two squirts of the hand sanitizer pump attached to the wall into her hands and rubbed it in thoroughly. "And remember today is your first physical therapy appointment for your hand."

They nodded and she took her leave.

Scott clenched his stitched-up jaw, and nodded ever so slightly. "Okay," his voice low, cautious. "Bring Ian tomorrow."

With his agreement, Jocelyn felt relief. And dread. Probably the same as Scott.

***

"I go see Dad! I go see Dad!" Ian chanted while running through the house, pumping his arms in the air. He wore his footie pajamas and

Jocelyn kicked herself for telling him right before bedtime. She and Roxanne giggled watching him cheer louder than they had ever seen him. She could have calmed him down for bed, but he deserved this celebration.

Ian's bedtime routine took quite the delay with a growing reading list that Roxanne had become accustomed to, and even after both women had kissed him on the forehead and said his prayers with him—"Thank you, God, for bringing Dad home, and thank you I go see hims."—they could still hear him through the closed door jabbering on. Jocelyn wondered if Scott would even recognize this boy of theirs; he had grown and changed so much.

Her mother crashed on the couch by 9:30, but Jocelyn was awake in her room for hours planning how she could prepare Ian for what he would see. Maybe she should have told him from the beginning and kept him fully aware of how Scott was healing, but it hadn't seemed as crucial until now. Images plagued her, ones of Ian not recognizing Scott or hiding from his dad behind her legs. Staring up at the ceiling the same way Scott had to avoid looking at his bare leg, Jocelyn grabbed her phone and opened her messages.

Elle Holloway had started a pretty long thread of insomniac messages with Jocelyn. Joss felt like she was in a platonic, modern day *You've Got Mail* scene. The night before she'd left off telling Elle about growing up in California and that until Scott joined the army, she had never been out of the state—Elle replied that neither had she. Elle asked about Texas, the weather, the number of cows roaming, the usual ideas of the state.

Talking about herself always felt uninteresting. Everything about Jocelyn had been ordinary. A Norman Rockwall painting of mom, dad, one boy, one girl. Scott was her wild storm, her great American novel, her epic story. He was the greatness in her life. Every extraordinary moment she experienced was because of him.

Jocelyn's most recent message was about the year before when a winter storm hit and she and Scott took Ian out sledding for the first time on the cul-de-sac at the end of their street. Ian squealed that day, with his nose Rudolph red and his teeth chattering between "Again" cheers.

Opening the messenger, Jocelyn found a new reply.

"Such a lovely family. How did you two meet? Was he already in the military?"

As Jocelyn sent her answer, Elle's account switched to *active*. This wasn't the first time they'd been online simultaneously.

Elle's response was immediate. "It must be nice to be so sure of each other. I wish I had been. I married Aaron at 23 (too early) but I don't think we ever lived up to each other's expectations."

It must be nice to be so sure of each other. The words slapped Jocelyn in the face. They *had* always been so sure of each other, of their life together. She missed the feeling of solid rock beneath her feet.

The screen showed that Elle was typing. "I know your life isn't easy with a husband in the army, but sometimes I envy the happiness you have. I envy you guys knowing what you wanted in life, going after it and getting it. Grass is always greener, right?"

After these long recent days, she felt furious at this woman, furious at her perception. "I don't know what my life *in pictures* looks like to you, but it is nowhere near enviable. The happy faces posted on social media are out there so my family doesn't worry, so they don't pity me. And sometimes because of it, I struggle all alone. Don't make that mistake."

Oh the relief found in admitting that. *I struggle all alone.* Jocelyn had buried those words, those thoughts in the dark when she had no one to turn to. Scott was a son, brother, friend, son-in-law. They leaned on her. Even though she was limping. She could only hold about as much weight as Scott's metal-barring leg without losing it.

Elle's response, "I'm sorry you struggle alone. I guess from this angle you seem like Superwoman. Why can't we be honest with the people around us about hard things? I guess I'd have to be honest with myself first."

"I have to be Superwoman." Jocelyn typed. "My son depends on me. And my husband. I want to prove to him that I can match his strength. But it's not always true. None of its true. That's the downfall of our social media generation. We want people to think the best of us, so it's what we put out there. When behind the scenes, we're falling apart."

"Is that true for you? I feel like I'm the only one."

Jocelyn didn't hesitate before typing, "Hell yes."

The doorknob to the bedroom twisted and creaked. Jocelyn threw her phone on the nightstand. The clomping of Ian's footsteps padded across the bedroom. He didn't make a sound but pulled on her sheets with all of his upper body strength until he lifted himself onto the bed. Jocelyn rolled toward him and watched his eyelashes flutter back to sleep, safe in her shadow.

Ever so lightly, she put her hand over his heart. The day he was born, she remembered her nurse telling her to put Ian skin to skin against her chest so he could share her warmth, hear her heartbeat and feel secure. All these years later, she curled up against him, letting their heartbeats mingle. She felt his heart beating against her palm and matched her breath to his. In moments like this when they were all each other had, he was the one who gave *her* security.

***

By the time breakfast was served, Ian had dressed himself—the buttons of his shirt were off and his shoes were on the wrong feet—and climbed on to the sink to "do his hair" by wetting it down and slicking it to the side. A part of Jocelyn wanted to leave everything exactly this way for Scott. Instead, she took a picture.

Ian carried a toy bag stuffed with things he wanted to show Scott. With pride he presented his mother a "Welcome Home" sign in bubble letters that he and Grandma Roxanne had colored.

Roxanne helped Ian in the car, buckling him in his seatbelt and giving his forehead a kiss. "What you do when I gone?" Ian asked his grandma.

"Gosh, I don't know. Maybe read a book."

Ian nodded in approval, "You can read mine."

Driving toward the hospital, Jocelyn glanced at him from the rearview mirror to see him staring out the window. His feet bounced at the edge of his car seat.

"When we get to the hospital," Jocelyn began the preparation conversation that kept her up half the night, "Daddy will be in a bed because he can't walk on his own yet."

Ian met her eyes in the mirror, and he looked so much like Scott she wondered if there was any of her in him at all.

"You can give him a hug, but be careful because some of his body still hurts." She thought of the marks on Scott's face, the blood in his eye, the metal rods jutting from his legs. How do you prepare a child for that? "Parts of him may look a little different right now, but he's getting better every day."

Ian nodded his head.

He kept a tight grip on her hand from the car all the way inside, his other hand holding his bag. He didn't say a word about pushing the buttons as they went into the elevator, didn't jump like he normally would when it started moving to feel the leap in his stomach. When Jocelyn pointed out Scott's room from down the hall, his grip on her hand tightened. She smiled for him when he looked up at her. With hesitant steps, they entered the room.

Scott was seated on the edge of his bed with his back to the door, one foot flat on the white tile floor.

A member of the medical team, whom Jocelyn had never met, was squatted down in front of Scott. He watched the mother and son walk into the room. "You must be Ian." The man said with a robust smile that illuminated his teeth against his chocolatey skin. Then he took a few steps back, retreating from this important moment.

Scott twisted to see Ian, but the pain of the motion looked like a stab to his side. His uninjured hand jerked to hold his ribs, another broken part of him.

In a glance Ian didn't look scared even though his feet were bolted to the ground. His eyes scanned the scene in front of him, checking things out, as though he was waiting to see if this was really his dad or just one big hoax.

"Hey buddy," Scott said, ignoring his own pain. He couldn't rotate his head to look over his shoulder because of the adhesive tape on his neck and chest, so his voice bounced off of the back wall of the room. "Come on over and sit by me." Scott patted the bed next to him. Ian brightened at the voice that read his bedtime story every night. With short, slow steps, Ian came up alongside Scott.

In the quiet of the room, Jocelyn heard her husband's intake of air when he saw their son's face. From the door, she could only see a portion of this face—the side that had been protected from the blast—but she saw the muscles in his jaw working to compose himself.

Ian's eyes moved all around, looking at every part of his dad.

"Look how tall you are," Scott said, helping Ian up on the bed with his working arm. "Pretty soon you'll be as tall as me."

On the bed Ian positioned his legs exactly like Scott's, hanging off the side except his feet didn't touch the ground. He placed his bag next to him.

Watching the scene from the doorway, Jocelyn held a hand to her lips. She'd waited so long for this moment between them. Scott, the broadness of his back and shoulders unable to be hidden by the white paper gown, and Ian, so small next to his father. Her world, sitting right in front of her.

Ian craned his neck to look all the way up at Scott, then glanced back at his mom like he was making sure this was all okay. Then he barreled his body at his dad and swung his short arms as far around Scott's waist as they could reach. Scott wrapped a hand around Ian and picked him up with his one arm, ignoring the wince that came. He lifted Ian into a full bear hug, Ian's little face pressed against his dad's shoulder. Then Scott kissed Ian's soft hair. "I've missed you so much."

Ian's response was muffled against Scott's body.

The medical staff member made his way over to Jocelyn. "He's been talking about this all morning." He said in a low voice so as not to disrupt the reunion. "I'm George Holt, the physical therapist."

Jocelyn shook his extended hand.

"We finished up some therapy today, working on the grip of his right hand and strength in his right leg." He bobbed his head while he spoke, a subliminal message of positivism. "We want to get him out of here and home to you both as soon as possible."

"We'd appreciate it." Jocelyn said with a weary smile. This only reminded her of the long road of healing they had ahead of them.

The low murmurs of her boys talking a few feet in front of her captured her attention again. The moment between them felt so intimate, so organic that she didn't dare intrude. At Scott's gesture, Holt helped him move his legs back on to the bed as Ian crawled to sit next to him. The boy dug through the bag he'd brought and showed his dad the Welcome Home sign he'd colored. Then dug some more. When he finally pulled it out, she couldn't see what it was from this distance as he held it in his hand.

"Mom say you gots hurted. Was there blood?"

Scott nodded.

"Mom say I can only have a Band-Aid when there's blood." He opened his small hand and in his palm held a Doc McStuffins Band-Aid. "Do you need a Band-Aid?"

With soft eyes, Scott nodded again.

Ian moved to get on his knees and with pre-school dexterity worked to open the packaging. Twice he glanced at the bars sticking out of Scott's legs—there were no longer bandages or stitches over the healing wounds—then his eyes moved over his dad's body. He seemed to know exactly where to put the purple and blue Band-Aid featuring Doc McStuffins smiling face. As he leaned over Scott's body, Jocelyn knew it pained him but Scott didn't so much as flinch. He intently watched Ian's face. Then once it was in place just below Scott's cheekbone over a deep crimson line, Ian kissed the Band-Aid the way Jocelyn always kissed his.

The two adults met eyes across the room. In Scott's expression was the same adoration that Jocelyn witnessed in his eyes the first time Scott held his son.

Ian's innocent voice rang through the room. "Is you's leg gonna be a robot leg like Darth Vader?"

Scott took an amused moment to evaluate the comment. Jocelyn held back a laugh when he looked at her. "Probably not." Scott said.

"Mmph." Ian mumbled in disappointment.

***

It was a long day with Scott before Ian and Jocelyn returned home. Roxanne was seated on the couch with the television on when they walked through the door around dinner time.

"Are you two hungry?" Roxanne asked, getting up to help Ian take his jacket off. "I made chicken enchiladas."

"No!" Ian said. "Tonight is spaghetti night."

"Oh honey, I think we're out of spaghetti, so I made what we had." Roxanne said. Jocelyn followed them in to the kitchen, too tired to step into the scene. Until Ian screamed at his grandmother.

"No! We eat spaghetti!"

Jocelyn stepped between them. "Ian, no screaming." But that didn't stop him. He repeated himself until full-size tears fell down his cheeks. She looked back at her mother, but their expressions held the same question. Jocelyn should have known what was wrong. She was with him every day. She knew him better than anyone. But her body felt too heavy and sluggish to translate this outburst.

She pointed her finger at him—never having wanted to be the finger-pointing type, yet here she was. "There is no screaming in this house. If you want to talk to me, you need to calm down." Ian couldn't even hear her over his wailing. Giant tears dripped out of his tightly closed eyes, and his round tomato face looked like it could burst.

Thinking of nothing else to do, she grabbed him and hugged him. Maybe she needed it more than he did. Ian didn't move to hug her or to push her away; he just kept crying, rubbing his tears and probably some snot on her shoulder. She let him cry, rubbing his back until the sobs turned to snivels. "Will you tell me what's wrong?"

Snivel. "Spaghetti night is Dad's favorite. Dat's what you always say." Ian pulled back from his mother's comforting shoulder and rubbed his nose with the back of his dimpled hand. Roxanne leaned down and handed him a napkin as he continued. "If we have no spaghetti night, maybe Dad won't come home."

Jocelyn skipped a few breaths. Tears pinged the back of her eyes wondering how long he'd held this reasoning in his little mind. Had she planted the seed with her need for routine and watered it with her own worries? "No, baby. Dad's coming home. He just has to get a little bit better." Ian's worried eyes looked at her, wanting to trust her. "Let's have spaghetti tomorrow, okay?"

His little head bobbed a nod, and Jocelyn pulled him back to herself. How confusing it must be for him. She didn't know what was right any more, what would make things easier. Nothing about this was easy.

Even on her worst days, there was no room for giving up. Because giving up would abandon the little one standing next to her. Motherhood teetered on the line of giving up and growing stronger. Every day held the question, which side will we choose?

Roxanne made a plate for Ian and sat him at the table while Jocelyn put her shoes away. If they could break the routine of spaghetti night, maybe she could bend another rule to induce a smile.

She donned stealth mode, searching the toy basket until she found what she was looking for. She hid around the corner taking a breath, then popped into the kitchen with a loaded Nerf gun. A Styrofoam bullet shot out at her unsuspecting son and the orange tip landed right in his enchilada sauce. His surprised face looked up at her, his mouth opening in shock.

"Run for your life, it's a nerf war!" She laugh-shouted, picking him up from his seat football style, putting the gun in his hand, tossing him on the couch then taking shelter behind it with her own Nerf gun. Roxanne hid in the kitchen squawking in laughter. Jocelyn heard Ian's giggle as he tiptoed to find her hiding spot. Dinner could wait.

13

ELLE

The date had not escaped her. How could it? Flowers had been delivered to nearly every woman in her office, and being the executive assistant to a female boss, she'd signed for several deliveries for Lena alone: flowers, edible arrangements, chocolates from clients and associates as well as the newest Mr. Lena. Elle had piled them high on her bosses' desk, overflowing to the credenza. With each new delivery, Lena's eyes betrayed the pity that grew towards Elle.

On previous Valentines, Elle had been the one dropping heart-shaped vegan chocolates on every desk and shaking her head disapprovingly to the bitter members of the office who wore black and held depressing single woman events to snub their noses at the Hallmark holiday. But this agonizing year she understood them.

For once she found herself looking forward to a quiet night at home with Norah's equal lack of suitors.

The word *home* brought with it the comfort of a deep breath. As soon as she hit the door, before Norah could even greet her, Elle's jewelry was off and high-heels scattered. Sweat pants and a braless tank welcomed her like a blanket. The plan was to watch as many *I Love Lucy* episodes from Norah's collection as she could.

Until the doorbell rang. Not a common sound around this house.

A look passed between the two women, simultaneous confusion mixed with excitement. Norah took too long to walk to the door, so in

Elle's impatience, she bolted ahead without checking the peephole before swinging the door open. When she saw Aaron looking *almost* sheepishly across the threshold, her heart leapt so high in her throat she couldn't utter a single word.

Norah had shuffled her way to the door and pulled Aaron inside. "Am I happy to see you? I thought I was going to spend the evening with this gal crying over Lucy and Ricky."

Her grandmother's attempt to ease the hanging tension felt like a stab of betrayal. She wasn't that bad off.

As she closed the door, their voices trailed into the kitchen.

"Just dropping these off for you both," he said as Elle rounded the corner into the kitchen, his back facing her with two bouquets of flowers in hand, unaware of the amused smile creeping across her face. The scene was so reminiscent of the first time she brought Aaron here that she almost checked the year.

Norah silenced him with her signature hospitality move of fresh shrimp cocktail. Then she swooped the bouquets of white and pink roses away to place in one of her many Depression glass vases.

Only then with a shrimp between his teeth and a drip of cocktail sauce on his chin did Aaron catch eyes with Elle. Her smile wavered, but there was a hint of lift at the corners of his mouth in return. Norah chattered about how few visitors she had these days, how Elle never had houseguests. If Elle didn't know better, she would have thought her self-assured grandmother was nervous. Or maybe she was nervous *for* Elle.

Norah opened the fridge, unhappy with the mere offering of shrimp cocktail, muttering about Elle's crazy veganism not rubbing off on either of them. Her shaky hands collected cheese cubes and packages of crackers, strawberries, blueberries and yogurt dip. She directed Elle to retrieve the china serving platters and bowls. Norah's hands worked expertly, arranging things as if there was a party in the next room. She poured Aaron sparkling water without needing to ask.

Elle grabbed a strawberry, only to notice the infestation of mold on the whole batch. Her face twisted in objection at Norah's offering when Aaron caught her eye.

Don't. His eyes demanded with a shake of his head.

Yes. This is disgusting.

Please don't. Aaron's eyes pleaded. He glanced at Norah with a bit of sadness.

"Is this all okay? Do we need more?" Norah said with a light touch to each plate. Her eyesight was too poor to notice the blatant rot of the strawberries. Elle wondered what else in the fridge had gone bad under Norah's unwell eyes.

"No," Elle spoke regardless of Aaron's dispute. He sighed deeply. "These strawberries are all moldy. How long have they been in there?"

"Oh," Norah said. Her shoulders slumped as she whisked the package away from the counter and into the sink. Elle and Aaron exchanged more nods and shakes and eye gestures. Then Norah not only washed the berries down the garbage disposal but all of the fruit, shaking her head and muttering to herself.

With the disposal's loud grinding sound, Aaron pulled Elle by the arm into the next room. "Why did you have to say anything?" Aaron whispered.

Elle found the answer obvious but said it anyway. "Because they *were* rotten. Did you want to eat them?"

His hand still gripped her forearm. "No. I would have thrown them out myself without having to embarrass her."

"You are so passive."

"And it spares her humiliation. Then again you don't care about sparing anyone." His whispered words bit at her with teeth sharper than a piranha.

The disposal turned off, and only the sounds of Norah shuffling dishes remained.

"Why'd you even come?" Elle didn't bother to whisper.

"It didn't seem right to ignore my wife on Valentine's Day."

"But every other day it's okay?"

Aaron deflated, the way heart-shaped balloons delivered across the country would in a few days.

I'm sorry. She thought as she bit the inside of her lip in penance. But the words stuck in her throat. Why didn't the mean words get stuck instead?

"I should have had the flowers delivered. My mistake." With that Aaron returned to the kitchen, gave Norah a light kiss on the cheek. A few mumbled words to her and then he was gone. The door clicked behind him while Elle stood fastened in the place where he'd left her. Again.

Norah sighed as she returned the untouched food to the refrigerator. "I don't know why you can't give him a break."

"Why is everything always *my* fault?" Elle said, but instead of bounding up the stairs to her room, she rushed out the front door after her husband.

"Wait," she called to him, even though his door was closed. But he saw her. She stood by the door until he reluctantly opened it and got out. Only then did she continue, "I've thought about what you said. What I was missing." Elle was cautious with her answer. She didn't want to make him mad, but she had to be honest. "I've given it a lot of thought, but I wasn't missing anything."

Aaron scraped the sole of his shoe against the concrete driveway. "That's my answer then, isn't it? We want different things. Because I am missing something. A lot, really."

The wind blew through her hair, but she didn't bother correcting the wild strands. "Why didn't you talk to me?"

"I told you in a hundred different ways."

"Maybe I'm just hardheaded." At her own statement, Elle laughed. "Ok, we all know I'm hardheaded. Maybe I needed you to say it more directly."

"Was me leaving not direct enough?"

That cut so deep she felt a hole oozing in the wake of his words.

He shrugged, unapologetic. "You weren't listening any other way."

Maybe he was right. She had been caught in her own atmosphere.

Standing on the driveway as her husband drove away was more than she could take. She should have gone with the Anti-Valentine's singles and drank herself into oblivion wearing the black of mourning. Even that would have been better than this.

***

The end of the week came slinking along with its host of opportunities for Elle to pine after Aaron. She yearned for a night of dancing past midnight and drinks on the beach, but she refused to go alone. So when some of the girls at work invited her out, she almost squealed her response.

She'd been out every night, shopping or working late, and come home to Norah asleep on the couch with a TV tray of empty dishes and the television blaring at what Norah thought was a normal volume. So it could've been guilt bringing Elle home that Friday night before joining her co-workers. Elle's own loneliness made her wonder about Norah's.

The house was quiet—which wasn't abnormal—when Elle tossed her keys on the plantstand by the garage door. But it was the familiar moaning floor boards above her head that set Elle on edge, the creaking of Norah's deliberate steps on the second floor.

She hurried up the steps, tempted to take them two at a time. The movement made her sure that Norah was okay, but the doctor hadn't cleared her to take a flight of stairs solo. Her strength hadn't returned enough to make that trip alone. Only two days before, Norah had slipped in the shower. It had been twenty minutes before Elle found her, water pelting her from the shower head and Norah flush with embarrassment at her feeble, naked body.

The incident had spurred Elle's suggestion for one of those Life Alert necklaces with the emergency button, but Norah scoffed at the commercials. "I will never be one of those old women who says they've fallen and can't get up." With a laugh and nod, Elle had let it go.

The thought of Norah trying to make it up the stairs alone but falling, breaking a hip or worse made Elle ill.

"Norah?" She held her voice in check, dodging panic by only a syllable.

A warbled voice returned from the master bedroom, "In the closet."

Elle rounded the corners from the hall to the bedroom; the closet was at the far end with its mirrored sliding doors that made the master bedroom feel twice the size. There was Norah fully clothed, bent over, backside in the air, fishing coral pumps out of a shoe box.

"What you doing up here?" Elle realized her accusing tone too late.

"I'm in *my* bedroom. What business is it of yours?" Norah didn't turn around as she responded, next digging through a drawer for pantyhose, a requirement for every Norah ensemble.

Elle endeavored to calm down—or at least appear to—by lounging on the bed. Although doing so was difficult as Elle was sucked into the puffy white cloud of the bedspread. "I was concerned about you making it up the stairs by yourself."

"Oh," Norah shook her head, but Elle couldn't decipher if it was purposeful or the common shake of old age. "No need to fuss. Brandon helped me."

Elle's forehead wrinkled. "Who's Brandon?"

"He's the sweet boy that comes every week to help me get around." Norah clucked her tongue at Elle's confusion. "Ever since that episode," (Elle assumed she meant the stroke the year before) "my doctor requires him to check on me once a week and take my blood and such. I thought it would be a woman, but I am perfectly okay with it being Brandon." She said suggestively.

Gross.

Sounding chipper, Norah continued, "I'm going out tonight."

If Elle had been drinking something, it would have spurted out her nose—then Norah would have told her how unladylike that was.

"That's right. I'm going to the Clubhouse." Never missing a step, Norah continued getting ready. Her starched white slacks held a crisp crease down the front. Her selected pumps identically matched her coral knit sweater, gold and coral watch, and she rummaged through her four-foot-tall jewelry box to find the matching bangle and beaded necklace. The colors changed with each ensemble, but the style remained the same. Every day. She had this exact outfit in every color that complimented her skin tone. Norah was even known to buy white pumps and have them dyed to match a new sweater.

Trying to sound detached, Elle asked what the Clubhouse was.

"A group of us get together there to play gin rummy," was Norah's casual response.

Parental instinct that Elle had never known exploded with questions inside of her. *How often? Who is in this group? You are not gambling.* The words stayed trapped behind her closed mouth. She was not the parent here or even a guardian.

Instead, she offered—more like demanded—to drive so Norah wouldn't put the entire city in danger. She only needed to change her clothes.

In contrast to Norah's, her own closet was unorganized and overflowing, not to mention two cases full of shoes on the floor and all the special occasion stuff in the garage.

Hanging the pinstriped slacks and ivory blouse on the hanger in exchange for distressed jeans and white v-neck blouse, she was interrupted by a light knock. One leg was already clothed in the skin-tight jeans, and there would be hopping and possibly falling involved in order to get to the door. She called her grandmother in and continued to dress herself.

Norah cracked the door and poked her face into the opening. "I need some help," she admitted as she held up her pomegranate colored lipstick.

"Just a sec," she said, relishing Norah's appreciation of her makeup skills. In hopes of updating her gran's thinning hair from the roller curls that lined Norah's creased face, she brought some hair products along with a makeup bag to the master bathroom.

"My hands are too unsteady for this today." The first bit of weakness Norah had spoken of in days.

A glance at the bathroom countertops showed the same powder puff Elle had dabbed against her porcelain face as a young girl and next to it the hand mirror passed down to Norah from her own grandmother. Elle knew without looking that the mirror had a hairline crack in it from when young Elle dropped it after being caught with said powder puff. Every turn of this house held a lifetime of ghosts.

The staple Estée Lauder lipstick worn by Norah daily needed an accompanying lip liner to avoid Norah's telltale ex-smoker's lines around her thin lips.

"Can I try something?" Elle's voice and gaze softened toward her grandmother who rarely allowed herself to be this vulnerable.

Norah nodded.

In quick response, Elle sifted through several options in her lipstick bag. She smoothed Norah's lipstick on the back of her hand then drew parallel lines with each shade of lipliner until she found the best match. Holding her fingertips to Norah's chin to steady them both, Elle looked at her grandmother's worn face. She could not remember a time since childhood that she had been this intimately close to her grandmother, feeling warm breath on her face. Asking Norah to part her lips, Elle outlined them then added Norah's shade. She turned toward the mirror, and Norah followed suit.

"I haven't been able to do that because of my hands." Norah held them up and showed how they lightly trembled. Then pointed to her eyes where years ago she had her eyebrows and eyeliner tattooed. "This too."

Looking at the elderly woman reflected in the mirror, Elle smiled.

"You look nice."

Under the uneasiness of a compliment, Norah stood abruptly and dabbed perfume on her neck. "You were always able to do makeup."

That was the closest she was going to get in the way of a thank-you or compliment, so she took it.

"Clothes too. I saw that closet of yours."

"I learned from the best." Elle said. It was true. *Never leave the house without mascara and lipstick,* Norah had drilled into her.

A small sigh escaped the freshly lined lips, one that Elle could have sworn sounded sad. "Maybe I should have taught you differently."

"Don't be silly." Elle reassured her as she closed the lipstick and put her supplies away in the bag. "You helped me discover how much I loved fashion. Wearing it *and* creating it."

Her hands moved from the makeup bag to her grandmother's hair, fluffing up the curls a bit. "Would you let me do your hair the way I used to play when I was a kid but for real?"

Every weekend Elle stayed with Norah, they would curl up on the bed, turn on *I Love Lucy* and Elle would sit behind Norah playing hairstylist. She used her fingers as pretend scissors against Norah's hair, making the cutting noise with her mouth, then put sponge curlers in, and finally she would use the antique mirror to proudly show her grandmother the finished product.

It had been over a decade since their last "appointment."

With her fingers, she combed through her grandmother's hair like the old days.

"No." Her grandmother said sharply, swatting Elle's hands and nostalgia away. In an instant, she was grabbing her coral clutch and ever so slowly making her way to the door. Not a battle she wanted to argue, Elle simply followed.

* * *

Acting as Norah's driver was like living through the terror of learning to drive all over again. *Stop Elle,* she'd yelled as the light turned yellow. *Turn here* a mile away from the actual turn followed by a *Put your blinker on.* Norah infiltrated Elle's eye line with her claw-like pointer finger, leaning all the way across the console when the turn was approaching. And to top it off, Norah held the door's crash bar like she was driving through a war zone gasping and groaning with every acceleration.

By the time they had reached the retirement home's clubhouse, Elle was ready to run far, far away or strangle her grandmother.

As calmly as Elle was hysterical, Norah got out of the car and headed toward the clubhouse entrance, hollering over her shoulder, "You can pick me up in three hours. That's usually what time we're through."

Mouth gaping, Elle realized that her grandmother had used her as a taxi. So that's what it felt like.

"Excuse me," Elle said, throwing the car into park and hopping out of the car after Norah. "The least you could do is let me walk you in and introduce me to your friends."

Norah turned and hollered back, "And let you embarrass me? Absolutely not."

The familiar tone of voice and words gave Elle a chuckle. She had said those words verbatim to Norah a hundred times. Elle stared over the roof of her car watching her grandmother shuffle away. She inspected the building in front of her. It horse-shoed around the parking lot, a soft salmon color of stucco with a Spanish tile roof, reminding her of a hotel. The sweetness of roses and fresh cut grass lifted to her nose, and she pictured herself visiting Norah here.

Another car drove up and a couple in their seventies emerged, walking to the entrance. The woman had a fur coat over slacks with contrasting bright red pumps, and she laughed freely as the doors opened letting the couple inside. Strands of Big Band music twirled through the open doors and cut off as they closed. It was like an old-timer's nightclub, and for gin rummy no less. Everything about the place seemed perfect for Norah.

After a quick shopping foray and tofu Asian salad for dinner, Elle returned earlier than Norah had requested. She checked her teeth in the car's rearview mirror for the third time and breathed deeply. She bolted out of the car toward the Clubhouse front door. As it opened, the scene surprised her. Her imagination had wandered when she'd dropped Norah off and she expected to open the door to a blue's nightclub with cigar smoke in the air and a piano player in the corner. But this was a regular recreation center. Linoleum floors, white walls and fluorescent lights. There was a folding table against the wall covered with a plastic table cloth and refreshments. Music played from speakers in the corner and a handful of couples shuffled their feet in time, holding each other close as if remembering years gone by.

A round table sat in the opposite corner with its folding chairs all occupied. She recognized the back of Norah's coral sweater and light hair, the gestures of her hands as she spoke, the backward tilt of her head as she laughed.

Elle stood at the entrance, unaware how people were watching her. She was more occupied watching her grandmother, alive like she hadn't seen her in years. A man seated next to Norah wore a smile as big as his plaid bow tie. He watched Norah's every move and laughed with her every word. His white wingtip shoes coordinated with his few wisps of white hair.

When the game concluded, the man was out of his seat and helping Norah out of hers with a gentle touch. Norah swatted her hand at him the way she did anyone who attempted to help her, but he scooted her chair back and held her hand as she stood nonetheless.

Elle liked him immediately.

Norah's eyes caught Elle's as soon as she turned from the table, and they squinted with disapproval. She moved toward her granddaughter faster than Elle thought she was capable. The wingtip man followed.

"Hello," he said. His voice sounded younger than Elle expected; over the phone, she may have imagined him an entire generation younger. "Is this your granddaughter?" He asked of Norah, but not in the condescending way that people ask of a young granddaughter. His was genuine.

"Yes, hel–" Elle began but Norah cut her off, grabbed her outstretched hand ready to introduce herself and pulled Elle out the door.

"What are you doing?" Elle asked while being dragged to the car. It was almost impossible for her to hold back a fit of giggles. Norah was acting like a teenager, and Elle knew exactly why.

When they were secured behind closed car doors and windows, Elle asked, "Who is that man?"

Norah ignored the question as she put on her seatbelt.

"Why were you hiding him from me?"

The question was met with silence.

Elle put the car back in park and crossed her arms. "I'm not driving home until you answer." Norah focused straight ahead but as Elle looked passed her gran's staunch profile, the wingtip man stood by the entrance door casually watching their car with his hands in the pockets of his pleated pants.

"Maybe I was hiding *you* from *him*." Norah said and leaned over the console to shove the car back in gear.

Elle bit back a smile at the response and at the longing in Norah's simple glance out the window toward the wingtip-wearing man.

It appeared Norah had a beau. What Elle wouldn't do to have those fluttery feelings back.

***

Her first sunrise yoga session since the split with Aaron nearly brought her to tears. She'd missed the crisp air at sunrise with the breeze coming up from the ocean that couldn't keep the sweat away. And she'd missed Jenny's soothing voice barely audible above the ocean's tide. Jenny had a decade of yoga experience, plus the taut muscles and unwavering balance to prove it. Pulling in to the office parking lot, Elle felt muscles in her back and legs that she'd forgotten could be so soft and strong at the same time. The calm that resided in her was only matched by the still water of the morning ocean.

That calm was disturbed when a woman jumped in front of her at the entrance to her building.

"Elle Holloway?"

"Yeah, what?" Elle replied, fresh yoga feeling gone and instant annoyance at this BlueTooth wearing, makeup abusing, blonde's approach.

"You've been served." The blonde shoved a stack of binder-clipped papers at her.

"Seriously?"

The woman's glossy mouth pursed as if Elle was a bother. "Yes."

"No," Elle glanced at the cover letter from a law-firm she had never heard of, then tried to give the package back. "I don't accept."

When the woman turned her back on a desperate Elle, there was no other option. Elle tossed it at her like a game of hot potato. "Take out the BlueTooth and maybe you'd hear me. I don't accept."

The blonde turned, looked at the papers on the ground but left them in place. "It doesn't work that way." And she walked away.

Elle's heart felt like her yoga legs, stretched and broken in ways she didn't know existed.

Her head knew what the papers were, but if she didn't pick them up they couldn't be hers. If she didn't look, then it wasn't really happening.

"Ma'am," a man who worked on her same floor stood beside her. She wasn't aware how long she'd been standing there unresponsive. "Did you drop this?" He was holding the vile papers in front of her.

But she didn't want to acknowledge it, touch it, possess it. "I guess I did." She said, without extending her hand.

"Do you need help?" His concern was quite genuine.

"Yes," But she quickly replaced the answer with, "No." And though it took every piece of her will, she reached out and took the envelope. "Thank you." The words tasted like poison as they passed over her tongue. Like thanking a police officer who just issued you a ticket.

"Hey, aren't you the receptionist–" He was talking, but it didn't register in her brain, as it took all her concentration to move her stiff body safely to her desk on the third floor.

With every call she answered, appointment made, message delivered, she attempted to push the thought of opening the seal of the envelope further away.

At times she thought the sun was standing still, but the clock finally ticked to lunchtime. She locked herself in the bathroom, phone in her hand.

"He filed." It was all she could get out when she heard Marissa answer. Her voice crumbled with the verbalization of her worst fear.

"Oh Elle, I'm so sorry."

"Some bimbo blonde served me the papers." They sat next to her on the white tile floor of the bathroom, taunting her.

"Have you opened them?"

"No," squeaked out.

"Stay on the phone with me while you do. Even if you don't want to talk. I just want to know you're okay."

Even with all the things in their lives that were polarizing, Marissa was Elle's one person.

Her hand hovered over the mounding papers, her fingers close enough to touch his name listed just above hers. She remembered what it was like to touch him the night she'd snuck into his brother's apartment.

"Why would he do this?" She asked. The fury in his eyes that night lit her memory, the way his words gouged a whole from her ears to her heart.

Marissa was quiet for a bit, but when she did speak, her voice echoed in the otherwise quiet background. "Things can change. I still believe that. You know, California has a six month cooling off period after the papers are filed, so maybe in that time it will change."

"I thought I was doing what he wanted."

There was no response.

"You don't think I tried either, do you?"

"I think you went about it the wrong way." Marissa's tone was careful. "If you could actually *talk* to him, none of the sneaking around or fighting or winning him back. Just try to be understanding."

Elle shoved the stack of papers across the tile. "Sure, it's easy coming from the perfect Marissa Sheldon home where there is no fighting and nothing ever goes wrong."

She could hear her friend's heavy sigh. "You know that's not true."

"Yeah. I know. You have big problems figuring out how to get stains out of the carpet and how many coupons you need to lower your grocery budget. Forgive me if I think being asked for a divorce is a bigger deal."

"I can't believe you just said that." Marissa could have sounded exasperated, but she didn't. Hurt, but patient. "All I was trying to do was help."

"That's okay. Go back to your children, Marissa." Elle hung up, throwing her phone on top of the dreaded stack of papers. Even as the words echoed off the bathroom walls, she wished them unsaid.

She was a shotgun. Her hurt splayed in every direction. People should stay far, far away.

If she could only tell Norah. Grandmothers could be bulletproof.

"Hello," Norah grumbled into the phone.

"Norah," Elle held her voice steady.

"Oh Elle," Norah said. "Is this important? The Pearl Show is on."

Elle laughed through the thickness in her throat. "No, it's okay. I'll see you after work."

She made her way back to her desk and tapped out a message to the one person her shotgun couldn't reach. Jocelyn.

I was served papers today. Apparently, I'm getting a divorce. Gah, I never thought this would happen...

But she knew that was a lie. She'd imagined this moment over and over. It had kept her up at night gripping her heart with fear tipped claws. She'd sensed it was coming. She'd thought she was powerless to stop it, but that was a lie too. The power had been hers all along, and she'd failed once again.

14

JOCELYN

Echoes of Scott roamed through the house, like a ghost strolling down the hallway, even though he wasn't to be discharged until the next day. His presence followed her home every time she left that antiseptic hospital room, and even though he smiled and kissed her before she walked out, she felt his soundless request for her to stay.

But Ian was always waiting.

She swiveled her head around to look at the clock, checked her phone but her insomnia buddy wasn't online. Elle had messaged her such awful news, and though she didn't say so in her response, it gave Jocelyn a renewed gratitude. Scott was being discharged the next day now that the scaffolding-like bars had been removed from his leg and replaced with a two-piece cast, leaving his marred knee exposed, groping for mobility. George Holt's therapy was his newest nemesis even though it had strengthened his grip so he could finally maneuver himself on crutches.

The last day Scott was in this house pre-deployment, he stood—without any cast or crutch—in front of their bathroom mirror as he shaved until his face was almost as soft as Ian's. He'd had earbuds in his ears, his unclothed shoulders broad and a towel covered hips swaying to a song. Jocelyn wished now she knew what song it was. Ian, who had been old enough to walk at the time but not talk in full sentences, had waddled up next to his dad. In both of his strong arms, Scott had picked Ian up effortlessly and sat the little boy on the sink with him as he shaved, putting one earbud in Ian's ear. Together they had bounced their bodies to the music.

She had imagined Scott returning home, dancing around the house, stepping to the beat while she was trying to sweep crumbs off the floor or singing off key against the nape of her neck while she put on the little bit of makeup she wore. But that was all different now. A bit of the light in his eyes was missing.

Maybe a shred of light was missing from hers too. And Ian's.

Now that Roxanne had returned to California, offering to take Ian with her for a couple of weeks which Jocelyn denied needing, strangers spent the days with her son. Not complete strangers, of course. Women of the FRG. They had set up a schedule to help with Ian, and Scott's hospital walls were covered with pictures Ian had drawn, proving he was adjusting to not being with her. But every day she was missing some new piece of her son. Yesterday he'd learned to draw Darth Vader. He needed her less and less. Wanted her less.

When she told him that his dad was moving back home, he had said nothing in return then screamed at her when it was time to lay down. It could have been his age, not wanting to go to sleep. But there was a change in him. He ran from her when she reached out to him, woke up asking for Scott instead of her. He had cried himself to sleep the night Grandma Roxanne had flown back to California, inconsolable.

The changes, the emotions were cracking Jocelyn's strong surface. They kept her awake at night. Which was kinda okay, because she was back to moving furniture at midnight. Less insomniac and more about making the house accessible for Scott's crutches. She moved everything away from the doorways and got rid of all rugs. She did not want to think about what would happen if Scott somehow slipped on them. It was like baby proofing the house all over again.

That's when she sat up in bed. Scott would hate the paint on these walls. That one irrational, insomniac decision to paint their bedroom walls army green that she always regretted. But she'd never painted it back. Now there was only one night left. She tiptoed through the house to the shelf in the garage where the old paint cans sat. She grabbed the Sand Castle paint and supplies, then tiptoed back to her bedroom. The painting would make for a long night—she knew because she had done it once before—but it would keep her mind focused.

One coat on all four walls, and Jocelyn was barely able to keep her eyes open. She washed the paint speckles off her hands and the couple on her cheeks, then laid down grateful she'd paid extra for the non-toxic paint. She had barely dozed when the alarm went off.

Her first thought: Today Scott would come home. The next time she laid down in this bed, he would be next to her.

***

"Well, Sergeant, looks like you are heading home today." A male nurse came in with a wheelchair to confirm Scott's discharge. "Late Valentine's present?" He looked from Scott to Jocelyn with a smile.

"Dammit," Scott said, ignoring the wheelchair and looking at Jocelyn. "You didn't get a Valentine."

Jocelyn smiled. "I think you had a good excuse."

When she and Ian had arrived, Scott was already changed into a Metallica t-shirt. She swore it used to be fitted against Scott's arms. She couldn't decide if it was her memory playing tricks after not seeing him in civilian clothes for so long or if the shirt actually hung loose along his chest and shoulders showing the muscle mass he had lost in a month. He wore athletic shorts that fit easily over his leg cast. She wondered who helped him change, who had seen him practically naked before she had.

"I already sent your Valentine's care package before–" She didn't quite know how to finish the sentence, so she didn't.

"No naked pictures, I hope."

The male nurse chuckled, and Jocelyn obliged her husband with a smile and shake of the head, but even the voice behind Scott's humor wasn't the same.

The nurse brought the wheelchair next to the bed and put a hand out to help Scott, but he was already lifting himself. When he was seated, his above-the-knee cast awkwardly extended past the footrest.

Ian perked up. "Can I sit in you's lap?"

The nurse didn't wait for Scott to answer. "Sorry little man," he laid the crutches over Scott's lap, then looked back at Ian. "You want to help me push?"

Ian glanced at Jocelyn as though he expected her to tell him no, then nodded his answer. He moved behind his dad, the top of Ian's head barely seen over the handles of the wheelchair, but he reached up and held on to the gray grip next to the nurse's hand.

The muscles of Scott's jaw went to work in disapproval of the wheelchair. Jocelyn beat him down to the ground floor and pulled the car around front for him, and the nurse wheeled him to the passenger side door while Jocelyn put the crutches in the trunk along with Scott's taupe duffel bag of remaining items he'd had at the hospital.

Scott grumbled when his wife sidled up next to him, seated in the wheelchair with a sour expression. "I'm a soldier. If I'm going home, I should be able to walk to the damn car on my own. Not sit in a wheelchair for every gossip on post to see."

Jocelyn bit back a smirk. Scott hadn't seen a problem with the hospital's policy of wheeling all patients to their car when Jocelyn birthed Ian.

The drive home was anything but quiet. Ian had made a playlist, with Jocelyn's help, of all Scott's favorite songs. Ian mouthed the lyrics as they drove, but Scott didn't seem to notice. He didn't hum or pad his thumb against his thigh to the beat. All he said was "Yes sir," when Ian asked if he liked the songs as they arrived home.

It was like an awkward first dance, the way Jocelyn helped Scott maneuver the cast out the door, then his body weight up out of his seat, and tried to grab him under his arm to help him stand while she handed him the crutches. "You got it?"

"Yeah," he said, not meeting her eyes, focusing on the grip of the metal crutches.

Every move felt awkward. Scott couldn't get a rhythm to walk, to move the crutches, to lift the cast on his leg, but he grunted "I got it" when Jocelyn tried to help. He was only a couple of steps from the door and Jocelyn's head was buried in the trunk digging out Scott's bags when she heard a familiar voice.

"Hiya, Scott. Good to see you home." It was Kirk, the neighbor.

Freaking Jody, she could hear Scott's thoughts.

Jocelyn wanted to curl up in the trunk and hide. Kirk's timing was never good, but this, well this was near suicidal.

She heard her husband's voice, flat but heated. "Kirk."

The crunching of shoes on the gravel came toward her. "Joss, here, let me grab that for you." And before she could answer, Kirk had grabbed

Scott's bag out of her hand. He was behind Scott with the bag before Scott could make it two more steps on the crutches.

Breaking into a quickstep, she met up with Kirk. "I'll take them. You can go on home."

The neighbor didn't take the hint—he *never* took the hint—and opened his mouth in retort.

Scott released one hand's grip and turned toward Kirk. The crutch Scott had let go of clattered up against the doorframe as Scott ripped the bag out of the man's hold. Then a growl seeped from his lips, "Go."

"Whoa," Kirk's hands went up in surrender. "Just trying to help."

"*We* don't need your help." Scott wrapped the bag's strap over his shoulder and reached out for the crutch. Jocelyn wanted to help him, but he would hate how that would look. She heard him mutter, "I'm perfectly capable."

Kirk opened his mouth but she met it with a sharp shake of her head, then she followed Scott into the house and closed the door on Kirk.

"I guess the leaves got raked." Scott said after the door was shut, passing by the "Welcome Home" sign she and Ian had made with little more than a glance.

Jocelyn didn't respond.

***

Through the grapevine, she heard there was an FRG meeting being held this week. Not that Jocelyn had to attend now that Scott was home. Meetings were only once every three months, and she always preferred the virtual FRG website instead. But this time, in her absence her name would be whispered through the rows of army spouses. Milspouses all over Texas seemed to know Jocelyn was living out their nightmare. Well, one version of it.

A yellow ribbon appeared around one of their tree trunks in the front yard, and several bouquets of flowers had been delivered over the past few weeks signed by the FRG. Not to mention the freezer full of dinners delivered through Elizabeth Cryer from the group.

"You should be grateful," Alexis told her when she complained over FaceTime. "I could tell you plenty of stories about the FRG's I've been a part of that would make you hug every woman in that group. During

Paul's first deployment, I didn't even know there was an FRG until the month before he came home. Nobody ever contacted me."

They'd had this conversation several times. Before Paul retired, Jocelyn tried to convince Alexis to volunteer for her FRG and set things straight. Alexis would've ironed those women out but in the meantime run them all off.

"They're nice enough," Jocelyn admitted, "but I don't want a bunch of women that I only sort of know in my house. I want people I know and love in my home. I want people I trust."

Alexis clucked her tongue. "I wish I could be there Joss, but you've got to let people in when they're trying to help you. That's what the FRG was created for. They're trying to be there for you. Let them."

Now she wished she'd accepted their offers, with Scott home and little to no conversation between them. At least a woman would talk with her.

Scott had retreated to the bedroom. Everything sapped his strength and created more than enough frustration. So there he was until Ian came in wearing pajamas.

"Dad, watch," Ian laid on the floor next to Scott's pullup/pushup bar by the bed. Ian wrapped his hands around the curved handles and did ten push-ups, his hips and legs grazing the floor while he moved his upper body up and down. It wasn't the best form, but Jocelyn never corrected him. When he was done, groaning, Ian stood up and flexed his mini biceps. "Feel my muscles." Pronouncing it *mus-culs*.

Scott high fived him.

"I want you to lay me down." Ian said.

"It'll take me a minute to get in there. You go ahead and get in bed." Then he looked at Jocelyn, almost hanging his head. "When I left I could do one armed pushups, and now that I need that skill, I can't–"

The ache in his voice tore at Jocelyn. She tried to respond positively, but it took longer than she wanted to find the right words. "At least you have a little workout partner now." He nodded, smiled at her with appreciation, and then as soon as she saw it, the look was gone. He pulled himself up on his crutches, struggling but not looking to her for help, and went to Ian's bedroom.

Jocelyn followed him but hid around the corner listening to Ian inform his dad of their long routine. When Scott cut the bedtime reading to only one book, Ian didn't complain.

When they were done, he moved out of Ian's room, knocking the crutches against the wall and the door jams.

"He's still sleeping with that doll even though I'm right here." Scott whispered too loud when he saw Jocelyn in the hallway.

She wanted to explain how difficult it had been for Ian, how hard it would be to change his routine now that it was in place. She imagined Ian would sleep with that Scott-shaped pillow for months to come. But she stayed quiet.

A wave of butterflies pulsated through her body when she realized what came next. They would go into the bedroom together, husband and wife. They would get ready for bed, lay next to each other, listen to each other's breathing.

She went to the drawer for her pajamas but changed into them behind the closed bathroom door. In the mirror, she caught her reflection and held her own gaze. Not all that long ago she was brave enough to do a strip tease for this man over Skype. Why did she suddenly feel so shy about lying next to him in bed wearing simple pajamas? She took a deep breath, drawing on the bravery that the Christmas panties had given her.

When she opened the door, Scott was propped against the bed with his back to her, using his left arm to unsuccessfully tug his t-shirt up over his head. Her mouth twitched.

She moved nearer to him, his seated stature making her breasts eyelevel. "Here, let me help you," She tugged the hem of his t-shirt gently. Too late she realized she was sweating profusely. Her palms and armpits were slick.

Her stomach lurched when her eyes moved over his bare stomach and chest while the t-shirt lifted to his neck. She had always known her husband to be muscular, chiseled even. He had been in football since she'd known him and the word *obsessed* could have described his workout regime even before the army. Underneath the multicolored bruises and lines of scars crisscrossing his skin, his muscles were different now. He was thinner, leaner.

She helped him lift his arm, her fingers brushing against the skin over his ribs then the inside of his bicep. The shirt tugged at his jaw but got stuck caddy corner on his face, over one ear but pulling on the other. When his mouth revealed under the neck of the shirt, he was making a face. A giggle spilled out of Jocelyn, then he helped pull the shirt over his ear.

Still smiling they paused, looking at each other until Scott cleared his throat. "I know there have been expectations for my coming home. But," his eyes drifted down to the carpet.

"I'm just helping you get ready for bed." She interrupted, not sure she was ready for more yet either. The heat once between them was unusually lukewarm. Baby steps.

Athletic shorts were next, and she reached for the elastic waist, her fingers feeling cold and hot against his skin simultaneously. She wasn't giggling any more, but her armpits were sweaty as ever. The fabric was slick under her touch. Her cheeks went red. Her heart pulsed in her fingertips. She had seen this man naked many, many times before. If she closed her eyes, she could see all of him right then. But this was different.

A breath stuttered out of her lips as she separated his shorts from his boxer briefs with her fingertips and pulled only shorts down his legs, over the cast and around his covered foot. When she looked up at him, he was watching her.

"This isn't how I pictured my first night back." He said. "Not how I pictured us undressing. I'm sorry."

An eyebrow raised. If only he knew the show she had thought of giving him. The relief she felt scared her. She held his arm and reached around his waist avoiding his cracked ribs, wanting to help him sit, but he tensed. "I've got it." He said with severity that nipped at her.

She stepped back and went to her bedside, crawling under the blankets.

Their mattress had lost its firmness over the years, so maneuvering his body took more upper body strength than even the crutches. But he deflected her attention by sniffing the air. "It smells like paint. Did you just paint?"

His nose had always been like a basset hound. "You would've hated the color, so I painted it back."

"And you moved the furniture?"

A year had gone by, and he still noticed. "Yes, but that happens every few months."

With five pillows stacked around his back and neck, Jocelyn felt the awkwardness return. What to say. Where to put her hands. She felt like a 10th grader again at the Italian restaurant.

He patted the inches of sheets between them. "Why are you all the way over there?" He grabbed at her arm, pretending to pull her closer. "I've waited a long time to lay in my own bed next to you."

She gave a guarded smiled. "I don't want to hurt you."

"I'd rather hurt all over than not have you next to me."

Scooting closer to him, she curled her body up next to his, feeling the hair of his legs tickle her smooth skin. Her head fit against his chest like the crevice under his shoulder had been made for her and her alone. Her nerves dissolved with each *thud, thud, thud* of his heartbeat. Underneath this damaged skin of his, the same heart she married was beating strong.

Her hand went to his cheek, the lines of his jaw and ear covering the scars on his skin. With a hunger in her belly that she held off, she kissed him gently on his broken, split lips. But they felt the same way they always had. Soft, full. He kissed her back. Then pulled back. "See, this is torture." He kissed her hair on the top of her head. "But I like it."

They laid together until his breathing was that of deep sleep. She thought having him home and safe would spur sweet, easy sleep. But no, new worries filled her mind. How long would it take them to find their new flow?

Jocelyn rolled on her side and watched as Scott's eyes fluttered in his sleep. She wondered. Still no one had given her answers about what happened—least of all Scott. He remembered so little. She had spent years convincing herself he would tell her all she needed to know. But now, now she had a deafening desire to know every single detail. To know his dreams, his nightmares. To know who he was now. To know him better than…before.

15

ELLE

A sharp rapping on the front door interrupted Elle's new Thursday night ritual of watching game show reruns with Norah. Elle barely had the door open before her mother was bursting through the entry like a steam engine. Charlene invaded the living room with her big, swarming presence—especially for such a small woman—before the front door was closed behind her.

"Game shows," Charlene said peeking at the TV before greeting her mother or her daughter, "Things around here never change." She added in a sing-song voice that tried but failed to make the words sound less critical. Coming from a woman who was changing her hair and home every year or so, the condemnation didn't land.

"Hello dear," Norah said at the same time Elle asked, "What are you doing here?"

If Charlene noticed the tone in her daughter's voice, she chose to ignore it. She looked at Elle and said, "After your disturbing call, I knew I had to change my schedule around to come see my two favorite ladies."

"How sweet." Elle said, unimpressed with the delayed gestured. Norah's eyes narrowed at her, though, conveying that her sarcasm was not welcomed this time.

"I'll make you something. Have you eaten?" Norah went into full hospitality mode.

"Mom, don't make me anything. I don't need your shrimp cocktail. I ate on the airplane."

"You flew here?" Elle joined in.

"Well you didn't think I would drive all the way from Oklahoma, did you?"

It was preposterous to even begin to picture her glamorous mother in Oklahoma. "You live in Oklahoma?"

"Oh goodness, no!"

Her response was met with two blank stares.

With a flip of her hand, she laughed. "I just finished brokering the purchase of an apartment complex there. It's my first commercial property, and the deal was quite extensive which is why I couldn't come until now."

Her almond shaped acrylic nails scratched Elle's back, a sign she did in fact remember being a mother to the girl standing next to her. The girl who still didn't know where her own mother actually lived.

"How admirable that Elle could come stay," Charlene's smile complimented her condescension. "But I'm here now. You can go home to your husband and show him a little appreciation." Her eyes widened and her shoulders shook suggestively.

The following silence spoke the truth.

"Uh-oh," Her sing-song voice returned.

Shame kept Elle's eyes from meeting her mother's, but only long enough to remember how unsuccessful her mother's own love life had gone.

"We're finding a new apartment, so Norah let me stay here…until then." None of it was a lie.

Realtor Charlene Webster appeared, and Elle knew what was coming. "You should buy a place. I've been telling you that for years. I can help you find a good investment property and you can fix it up the way I do."

Elle shut it down with a *not now* hoping that would hold until Charlene fluttered off to her next endeavor.

It was like a well-dressed health inspector had entered their home the way Charlene surveyed the kitchen, her floral cardigan flowing behind her like a cloud. Elle noticed how her grandmother left the couch to tidy up the living room which was already in pristine condition. Folding the throw and replacing it on the back of the sofa, straightening the magazines on the coffee table, wiping an imaginary layer of dust from the television. Long ago Elle remembered her mother scurrying the same way to clean every inch when Norah would visit.

A sense of protectiveness fell over Elle. The Great Wall of Elle standing between the elderly mother and her daughter, both of whom had taken their turns raising and protecting her too. Because now, Norah and Elle shared this new thread: they had both been abandoned by this woman, forgotten.

A gentle touch on Norah's shoulder reminded her grandmother to relax and return to her show. In Elle's eyes, she conveyed her best *I'll take care of it* look. Then with a deep, collecting breath, she breached the kitchen entrance.

"What are you doing here?" Elle asked Charlene, her words low and guarded.

"I told you. I'm here to take care of Mom."

"Where are you living now?"

An airy, uncomfortable laugh. "Is this an interrogation?"

"I'm entitled to know where my mother lives." Elle said.

"I'm in North Carolina, right off the coast. I just finished rebuilding the back porch and I can see the water from it. It's like living in a Nicholas Sparks' movie." Charlene said, followed by a trill of laughter.

"How long have you been there?" She hated it, but she heard how much her voice resembled an abandoned little girl hiding away.

"About a year. I sent you a postcard." Charlene said.

A postcard. From her mother. In the age of texting and emails and social media. A postcard was for vacations and breathtaking pictures, not intermittent mother/daughter communication. But there was no point addressing it. Charlene always justified; she was always vindicated; she always won. It's what made her a successful realtor. But a crappy mother.

"Unless you'd like to, I'm going to help Norah get upstairs and to bed." Elle said.

"Already?" Charlene said the way a child might. "I just got here."

Elle lowered her voice, not so much for secrecy as to draw her emotions back, "Norah is still recovering."

Charlene's volume matched her daughters. "You said it wasn't serious. Did you lie to me?"

"No. But she's 84." Elle said defensively. "And I have work in the morning."

"Oh come on. Call Aaron and let's all go out for drinks after Mom's in bed. It'll be fun." Charlene swiveled her hips and filled Elle with dread.

Fun. Ha! Her estranged mother, her estranged husband and her all together in a bar. Sounded like the beginning of a horror movie. She agreed to go but talked Charlene out of inviting Aaron along. It was the lesser of two evils.

***

The night air was crisp with the smell of salt water as the breeze rushed up the beach from the ocean. She had to hand it to her mother; Charlene knew how to elicit perfect service from a bartender without showing any cleavage. Fruity cocktails in hand and shards of shells poking Elle's sandaled toes. Taking off her shoes would give Charlene the impression that she was enjoying herself.

Low-slung chairs lined the beach, while lights hung on invisible wires twinkling like stars above their heads. The rushing sound of the ocean waves were louder in Elle's ears than the music or chatter of the bar's patrons. This. This is what she loved about living on the California coast. She could spend every night like this.

The ocean was a stunning paradox of waves crashing violently on the shore and serenely sweeping back to where they began. Ebb and flow. It was a paradox Elle knew well. Her life violently colliding with martial tragedy and sending her back to the home that gave her a start. Now seated next to the woman who launched it all.

She was satisfied with a wordless evening, but her mother, as usual, had other plans.

"Tell me about Aaron." Charlene broke the silence with a sledge hammer.

Elle took a substantial sip.

"His work is going well. Some businesses have asked him to do side jobs so he might start his own IT business if it keeps up like this."

"No," Charlene said sharply. "Tell me about you and Aaron."

As if Charlene could be gone for over a year, move to a new state without contacting her daughter, but rebound into Elle's life over a cocktail.

"There's nothing to know." A stammer betrayed her.

"None of us Webster women have been good with men." Charlene said matter-of-factly, staring into the black of the distant ocean.

But it wasn't true. Norah and Grandpa Larry were married for decades before he died when Elle was too little to remember. Maybe Elle romanticized it, but Norah had been faithful to him even after death. It was a fairytale kind of love that shown in Norah's eyes whenever she talked about him.

Fairytales always had tragedy, didn't they? Cinderella's prince could have mistakenly chosen any woman in the kingdom whose foot fit the shoe. Ariel's Prince Eric almost married the sea witch disguised as a lovely singer. Even in the perfect fairytales, there was loss, and still they ended in happily ever after.

In Disney princess world, she and Aaron still had a chance. Didn't they?

"It's not the same." Elle boldly retorted. "You and Norah chose life without men. I didn't."

"So he's left you."

Elle's silence was admittance enough. She didn't feel the need to hash it out with the woman who welcomed free dinners and drinks from a different man every weekend.

"As I say, we don't need them." Charlene said with a lifted chin.

As much as Elle wished she could subscribe to a comradery with her mother, to feel security in singularity, Elle was Aaron-deficient. He was her vitamin. He made her better, her brain healthier. And she didn't want to give him up.

***

Morning shone bright through the white-lined curtains on the window over Elle's bed. It was a terrible design, in her current opinion, but that opinion could be tainted by the hangover. She didn't plan to drink so much, but her mother kept the glasses full and talk of Aaron kept Elle draining them.

Her phone alarm was beeping a deafening tone. Breaking the phone to shut it up seemed logical, right?

Stumbling through her morning dress routine, she dangerously balanced on her Prada heels down the stairs to the kitchen, pushed the brew button on the coffee pot and dug out the Tylenol. In the cabinet sat the miniature Dixie cup of Norah's daily vitamins and prescription meds. She filled up an amber glass with ice water and a bendy stray, setting the Dixie cup next to it so Norah wouldn't forget.

Driving through the outskirts of LA traffic with a hangover was bad enough, but Elle arrived to preparations for an early meeting with the folks from Baby-On-Board chain store. *A beer is the best cure for a hangover*, Aaron's voice echoed as she pulled an aspirin out of the first aid kit in the office kitchen then followed it with a swig of lukewarm coffee. It'd have to get her through the meeting until she could run down to the bottom floor café for a soda (which was Marissa's hangover solution).

God. She sounded like a sorority girl listing off this many remedies to a hangover.

Right as her headache seemed to subside, the clock flashed to closing time. The day had absorbed itself.

But nothing could absorb the sound of her mother and Norah yelling—not even the front door.

Welcome back, headache.

"….gin rummy…don't care…"

"…you came…the hell…"

Enough listening at the door. She'd better go in before they started throwing valuables.

Charlene saw her first. "Oh thank God, Elle, talk some sense into her."

That probably wasn't going to happen.

"It's Friday night, and she won't let me take her out to dinner." Charlene said.

"It's gin rummy night, and I am not going to miss it." Norah said.

Elle couldn't place which direction Norah's voice was coming from.

Charlene didn't turn but yelled into space. "You can go to gin rummy any time. Your daughter is only here for one weekend and you can do me the courtesy of coming to dinner."

Then a man appeared from around the kitchen corner, his legs so long it only took him three steps to pass through the living room to the entry. Elle almost screamed until she saw his name badge clipped to the pocket of his scrubs. His expression was amusement as he wheeled a case behind him.

"You must be Elle," he said.

"And you," she stuttered trying to remember his name, "must be–"

He smiled at her effort. "Brandon."

Charlene grumbled again about Norah.

Elle widened her eyes at their guest. "I am so sorry." Not hiding the apology from Charlene.

"Believe it or not, I've seen worse." Brandon shook his head, hair dark with streaks of gray. He was clean shaven, and his eyes bespoke an adventurous spirit.

Warning alarms went off when Elle saw her mother turn at Brandon's voice and take in his lean build.

Just as Charlene opened her mouth to charm him, Norah appeared at the top of the stairs, with her gnarled knuckles gripping the banister. A fresh Band-Aid creased at the bend in her arm. Elle supposed it came from Brandon's visit. There was a determination of strength in Norah's face; the same look she gave when she refused to live in a nursing home. Elle knew what Charlene didn't: Norah hadn't walked down these stairs by herself since the fall.

Unsure of what to do, Elle looked to Brandon. He was grinning wide toward Norah.

The set of Norah's chin spoke as if through telepathy. *Do not help me,* it said.

Each step of her turquoise pumps, the ones dyed to match her blouse and jewelry, moving deliberately from one stair to another was a clear victory to Norah. One that Elle inwardly shared. Charlene on the other hand bounded up the stairs like a bratty teenager. "Oh good lord, Mother, would you hurry up." She grabbed Norah's arm without noticing Norah's free hand pushing her away, the turquoise bangles protesting against her gold watch.

Of course, they didn't move any faster together than Norah would have alone, but Charlene's impatient outburst did its job in robbing Norah of her independence. By the time Norah's feet arrived at bottom of the staircase, her shoulders slumped and her head hung as if she had aged a decade in those few steps. It could have been the strain, but Elle recognized it as defeat. Because she knew the feeling.

With a squeeze of Norah's hand, Brandon took his leave. His easy smile was gone.

In Charlene's way, she badgered Norah toward the garage. "Fine. I'll take Elle out for dinner. We'll drop you at your silly game on the way." There was no question in her voice.

Elle never made it out of the entry before heading out again, still donning her pinstriped pencil skirt and button-down shirt smelling of the baby powder from the office.

The complaints began within minutes of backing out of the driveway in Norah's Cadillac. "I don't know how you can drive this thing. It's like navigating a ship." Charlene said.

"Not everyone wants to drive a toy car." Norah muttered. But when the last word came out, Norah recognized the direction they were headed. "This isn't the way to the Clubhouse."

"Oh you can miss one night to spend with your girls. I'm buying." Charlene said.

A mixture of anger and panic swam in Norah's beady eyes, as if Charlene had locked her in a car taking on water.

"Mother!" was all Elle could say. Even in this small action Charlene's repeated betrayal was there, rearing its head.

Norah stayed quiet. There was nothing to say.

"Mom, your hair!" Charlene commented at a red light as the low sun illuminated the thinness of Norah's hair. "I can see your scalp!"

Norah fingered through her hair, trying to do the impossible and conceal what had been exposed. "I just–"

"You should have worn a hat." Charlene spoke over her mother. Then her eyes donned an idea. "How about I take you to the beauty shop tomorrow? My treat."

It was never *Can I?* or *Do you want to?* With Charlene it was always a statement, a demand.

The Cadillac weaved between lanes as Charlene took the turns of the Rolling Hills at the speed of her sports car, all while chattering about every detail of her home renovations. Either oblivious or unconcerned with the silence around her.

When they pulled past the harbor and up to the restaurant, the sun had already set on the charming view of the port. If you timed it just right, you could dine outside by the dock and watch the boats under the setting sun.

Their reservation awaited them—a table for three, Charlene's plan all along. Norah only spoke long enough to ask for her favorite waiter and introduce him to her dinner companions.

"Today while you were at work," Charlene said to Elle after her last bite of salad that she scrutinized the waiter over. "I got to thinking that the house is a bit too much for Mom now. She can't make it up and down the stairs even to get to her own bed."

Elle wondered why Charlene wanted Norah at dinner at all if she was going to talk like they weren't seated next to each other.

"So I did some research and there's a retirement condo only two miles away that has two vacancies. I think we could *update*"—her eyes widened emphasizing that Norah's home was stuck in decades past—"the house and sell it. My prediction is that it'd sell within 60 days and then we could move Mom over to a smaller, more conducive condo."

Elle's eyes bounced from her mother's to her grandmother's and back again like she was stuck in a sing-a-long. Panic veiled Norah's eyes. *Say something.* Elle thought. But Norah was hunkered down in the corner of the booth, wearing the pained eyes of lost puppy unable to voice any fears.

Charlene only stopped to sip her Moscato then carried on, "With my apartment deal done, I really don't have to be home. I could video conference the contractors working on my kitchen next week, and that would free me up to work here. We could have all of the painting done and furniture moved in a week and a half, two weeks tops."

"You can't do that." The words exploded out of Elle.

Her mother's mouth gaped open, hand frozen mid-gesture.

If Elle railed on her mother the way she wanted to, it would make a scene. They may even be asked to leave the restaurant. Instead she put her napkin to her mouth taking a moment to wipe invisible crumbs and to collect herself.

Then looking directly into Charlene's eyes and no place else, Elle began, "This is the one place Norah has lived for, well, as long as I can remember, and she's been clear that she never wants to live in a home-"

Charlene moved her finger to interject, but Elle left no room.

"Or a retirement community. She is perfectly happy where she is." An awkwardness followed as Elle took a substantial gulp of her own wine. She needed the warmth that coated her core.

"That's ridiculous." Charlene said once she had regained her senses. "Who cares how long she has been there if the house is impractical. And frankly on her fixed income, she *should* sell and downsize."

"She doesn't have a fixed income anymore. I'm living there, and I'm pitching in." The lie popped out at her mother before she thought it through. There were those groceries she brought home, but hell, Elle was practically on a fixed income herself.

Before she could take her statement back the way she returned Chanel earrings, her eyes caught a glimpse of Norah, sitting up straighter than she had all night, with a smirk on her orange-lined lips. You might even say that her grandmother looked proud.

"Does Aaron know this?" Charlene called her bluff.

Considering he separated his money from mine, I don't think he'd care.

"Has my money or my marriage ever been your business?" Elle's chest heaved at her audacity, but she couldn't let Charlene notice. She sat upright, her shoulders pinned back like she was having a floor-length dress altered.

Charlene tossed her napkin on top of her plate and stood, scuffing the chair legs across the floor, muttering about a ruined evening. But Elle's regret of the night was not strolling along the docks with Norah as the water lapped at the pier. Elle leaned in to Norah, "Why didn't you say anything?" Elle glanced toward Charlene who was tapping the toe of her high heels at the waiter printing off the check.

"You did a fine job." Norah said deadpan.

"No thanks to you. It's your house, you know."

Norah tilted her head a little. "And yours too, it seems."

***

The car ride home matched the quiet weekend. When Charlene graced the house instead of her Palos Verdes hotel, she sequestered herself in the office with the door closed, periodically shouting about the hand-scraped wood floors costing more than quoted. For once Elle wished she would change her ticket and fly home early.

Her mother's judgment seeped like a vapor from around the closed door. The clothes Elle wore didn't seem designer enough. Elle lost count of how many times she changed before dinner every night. And when they did finally eat together, she saw Charlene's eyes tsking her for how much oil and vinegar dressing Elle put on her salad.

When Departure-Monday arrived, Elle couldn't contain how pleased she was that her mother was back on a plane with her suitcases of criticism heading to the opposite coast. The lightness in her shoulders and the lift of her face caught the notice of some coworkers after the weekly staff meeting.

"So how are things with Aaron?" Jenny asked, a new mermaid tattoo gracing her shoulder.

Elle shrugged. "The same, I guess." It embarrassed her that everyone knew. She would have talked to Jenny about it anyway, but that wretched email still made her blush.

"Oh," Jenny said, seeming disappointed. Her bleached dreadlocks brushed the middle of her back as she tilted her head. "You seem happier today, and I was hoping you two made up."

Elle could only wish. Explaining her mother's visit seemed exaggerated coming from her mouth, but it wasn't. "Mom and Norah, me and Mom, at the same time as me and Aaron; it can all be a tangled mess."

Jenny's expression changed to sympathy. "Mother/daughter relationships can be touchy. At least your grandmother is such a gem."

Elle simply nodded.

The afternoon proceeded as Elle flew through her task list for the day and started in on tomorrow's. Boutiques were called, new orders confirmed, online store edits sent, appointments set, Lena's dry cleaning picked up. Before Elle knew it, her coworkers were clocking out and the doors were clicking shut around her.

No amount of Los Angeles traffic could damper her mood. She felt so productive, so light and airy, almost carefree, that she rolled her windows down on the drive home and sang off-key to Pink's latest song blaring from her speakers. Elle pulled up in the driveway, finally empty of her mother's rented sports car, and waited for the last note of the song before rolling up her windows and turning the engine off. The birds chirping a greeting to her as she stepped onto the front porch, key in hand. Then the door opened and a woman—*her mother*—bounded down the front steps at her.

"You're here. What took you so long?" Charlene grabbed Elle by the arm and dragged her inside, the heels of Elle's Chanel shoes scraping on the pavement in protest.

Surely it was a dream. Surely she had fallen asleep at the wheel in rush hour traffic, maybe died in a tragic accident and this was her hell. Yes, that was it.

"We have news to celebrate." Charlene said, pulling her daughter into the dining room where Norah sat in one of the dining chairs diagonal to the table.

"Where is your car?" So many questions and this was the first to pop out of Elle's mouth.

"In the garage." Charlene answered, as if it were obvious.

"But there is no room. Norah's car is in there."

"Oh dear, you are spoiling the surprise." Charlene shook her head and laughed. "We sold the car!" She shouted, arms up in the air, like she was shouting "Surprise!" for a party.

Elle looked to Norah. "What?"

As usual when Charlene was in the room, she assumed everything was directed at her. "I listed it on Craigslist this weekend and I've been emailing a couple of buyers. Then today one of them came, test drove it, loved it, and paid cash!"

Norah didn't meet Elle's gaze. She stared at the hem of Charlene's bohemian-print dress.

"But why?"

Charlene dropped herself onto the couch next to her mother as though the telling of a magnificent story was too much for her feet. "With mom being on a fixed income like we discussed and *you* not being willing to sell the house, I brainstormed a few ways to make her some extra money. Mind you, the Cadillac was an older model but being in pristine condition we easily got Kelly Blue Book value." She threw out *we* as though they had been in on the whole ordeal together.

"Besides," Charlene continued, waving off Norah like she was an infant who couldn't understand, "she can't drive the car with her eyesight anyway. The only reason she still has a license is because it hasn't been up for renewal. She'll lose that in a few months too."

"I can't believe you did this without consulting us." Elle was indignant.

Charlene made a face. "I talked to Mom about it on Friday. She was on board 100%."

A thick sludge squirmed in Elle's stomach. There was no way Norah agreed to another chunk of her independence being taken away. This Elle knew. What she didn't know was why her grandmother hadn't fought. If the idea had been Elle's, Norah would have bared her pearly whites.

"But there's more! I changed my flight to stay for at least a week more!" *Oh god,* it was the never ending Charlene show. "With the sale of the car, we figured even though we aren't selling the house, we can still update it. Get rid of this god-awful peach. I'm thinking new paint, new couches and maybe a couple other things. We can list some of this stuff online since it worked so well for the Cadi."

Charlene's voice droned on, but Elle's lens was focused on the deep wrinkles of sadness, of loss on Norah's face. Her eyes glistened enough to make Elle question if it was tears or her medicated eye drops. She saw a flash of Norah's future in a home that no longer looked like her own, that might as well be the nursing home she protested for years.

Not that Elle hadn't had all of these same thoughts. It was a god-awful peach, and Elle hoped that she never laid eyes on this color anywhere else in the world. It was the color of her nightmares. And a couple of weeks ago, Elle might have made the same suggestions if she'd thought of them. But now, seeing the brokenness reflected from Norah's eyes, Elle had to stop her mother. This woman knew how to ruin everything. She'd already ruined a family, abandoned a daughter, lost her daughter's father. Elle couldn't let Charlene break her own mother.

She interrupted whatever was being said, "Can I talk to you upstairs?" Any other place in the house and Norah was sure to eavesdrop.

Confused but unsuspicious, Charlene agreed.

"Tonight's not a good night," Elle said after she closed her bedroom door behind them, tucked away in the room they once shared as mother and daughter. "*Dancing with the Stars* is on, which means its meatloaf night, and those two combined pretty much makes it Norah's favorite night of the week."

Still confusion reigned on Charlene's face.

"You got rid of her car and most of her independence, isn't that enough change for one day? Can't you let her have her dancing show/meatloaf night and put the rest off until later?"

With a reluctant shrug, Charlene conceded. But before returning downstairs, she looked back at Elle and asked, "Do you make the meatloaf?"

"God, no." Elle moaned. "She gets the microwave stuff. I can't even look at it."

They both cringed a little. At least they shared that. The rest Elle would have to figure out tomorrow.

***

The next day when Elle came home, Charlene had shopped at Elle's favorite organic market and made mouth-watering vegan brownies that even Norah ate.

But the next day, when Elle opened the door she panicked. Her painting. The only item in the entire house that made her feel like she belonged here. The painting of the brunette girl looking out over the water. It was gone.

She rushed to the kitchen where Charlene sat on a barstool laughing into her phone. Elle clunked her Louis Vutton bag on the formica counter top, hoping the sound would jostle her mother's attention, to no avail. She waited, nails drumming, foot taping, every cliché tactic she could think of.

"Welcome home, dear." Charlene said when she ended her call, taking no notice of Elle's behavior. "That was a church down the street who has been kind enough to take this piano as a donation. They are going to give Mom a tax-deductible receipt."

The painting, the piano, this sent Elle over the edge. Getting rid of the peach was one thing. Elle protested that on Norah's behalf. But these were the only things in the entire house that held sentiment for her. Charlene was stepping on the toes of Elle's memories now.

"That's enough." The simple words inflated and pushed Charlene back a step. "You have to stop. In a couple of days, you'll be gone and I'll be left here to taxi her around because she has no car and to watch her wither away because you took all sentimentality out of her home. These are our memories. If you convert everything to 'Charlene-style' then you might as well put her in a home. How selfish are you?"

The outburst was met in silence. Charlene's expression revealed nothing. She turned and ascended the creaky stairs leaving Elle to her vindication. And guilt. The momentary victory didn't feel like anything. It didn't purge the anger or the abandonment. They were still there, pulsing like individual organs in her body.

Her thin fingers graced the edge of the piano. She didn't know a single person in her family who played. Rumor was Grandpa Larry had, but Elle had no memories to prove that, not even a picture. The piano, yellowed like stale, unused ivory, sat as the cornerstone of the formal living room. Every seat angled toward it, awaiting any potential performance.

Aaron had sat down on his first visit to meet Norah—he didn't meet Charlene until they were already engaged—and tinkled out *Fur Elise*. His fingers had brushed the keys the way a hummingbird touches a delicate flower, smooth and sophisticated. Even then the piano sounded like a warped record. When she marveled at him, he said he'd played for a few years in high school but stowed away a couple pieces in his finger's muscle memory. He'd never played it again.

If the piano only sat as an ornament to the past, was it fair to keep it? So much had been lost. Another constant she would have to say goodbye to. Neither of them could take losing any more of their past to the future.

When she felt the heat of eyes on her, she found herself on the piano seat without realizing she'd ever sat down. Over the slope of the piano lid she saw Norah watching her from the bottom of the stairs. The silence resonated between them. There was so much Elle wanted to say, to yell. *Why do you let her do that to you? Why does she control you?* Yet under Norah's scrutinizing eyes, Elle felt as though she had been wrong, somehow. Norah shook her head for a moment, so slight that Elle thought she imagined it, then turned to make her precarious journey up the stairs, leaving Elle alone. She tapped Middle C, and like her, it was still out of tune.

***

The days of Charlene's visit slipped away, but not quick enough for Elle. They only passed each other in the halls, slinking away like a high school ex-boyfriend without a word. A peace came in returning to the ignorance of her mother's life. Charlene's final visit was on Saturday before her flight took off that afternoon, and there was an unspoken obligation that Elle see her off.

When the knock at the door came early Saturday morning at the end of Elle's yoga practice amongst the backyard blooms, the relaxation she had sweat for faded. The tension between her shoulder blades and the knot that bothered her squawked its disapproval. Elle straightened her posture and swung the door open with a calming breath.

Charlene moved into the house without pause, holding in her hand an accordion folder and last season's Betsy Johnson purse that Elle eyed with amusement. So flashy with its bright, quilted hearts and leather bows, it screamed Charlene.

"I put this together for you." If Charlene felt Elle's tension toward her—after the silent week they'd had, it was impossible not to—then she didn't let it show. "There are copies of the documents for the Cadillac in case anything comes up."

She shoved the folder into Elle's arms and turned toward the kitchen. It was as though Charlene had all of her conversations in the kitchen. Elle trailed like an obedient puppy, even though she wanted to tuck tail and hide. Maybe the same feeling paralyzed Norah in Charlene's presence.

"I realize I was hasty in getting rid of the car. And I don't want your young life to be chained to her for the rest of hers. So I got her an electric motorized chair." Charlene opened the folder and pulled out a neat stack of papers clipped together. A picture of the black and grey glorified wheelchair centered the page, complete with joystick instruction and charging details.

"Fifteen hundred dollars? Doesn't that use up a huge chunk of what you got for the car?" Elle asked. The knot in her back flared. For once she was concerned about the price of something.

Charlene tapped on the paper with her pointed fingernail. "List price five thousand dollars, so this was cheap."

Ever the deal maker, Elle thought.

"That doesn't matter anyway because I got it through her Medi-cal."

Elle looked up from the paperwork. "Norah has Medi-cal?"

"Oh good lord, Elle, of course she does. You didn't think she paid for hospital stays and Brandon's visits and medication in cash, did you?" Charlene all but laughed.

"I just—I didn't know." Elle stammered.

"Her prescriptions from that stroke alone are hundreds of dollars." Charlene pulled out a barstool at the counter and sat, anyone else would have stumbled in her size heels but Charlene moved with the grace of a dancer. "Five days in the hospital with all of those tests…" Her sentence trailed off.

"How?"

"I've been Mom's power of attorney for years. Did you not know that?" Charlene asked.

Elle couldn't find a response as her mother explained the authority she'd been given to act as Norah's voice in financial and medical actions if necessary.

Although, Charlene must have recognized the shock on her face and capitalized on it. "I live across the country, and I talk to her regularly, follow up with her doctors, and stay on top of her bills. I work with her social security, Medi-cal, her retirement funds. Who do you think checks in with Brandon every week?"

Elle's mind rattled. She couldn't put the pieces together fast enough. "Norah said–"

"'Norah said,' huh? She's protecting you. She always has. And look how well it's served you." Charlene laughed at her daughter in disgust. "I've taken her to two doctor's appointments on this trip alone. Did you even know she had appointments? You lived less than an hour away and what have you done?"

Elle tried to think of some reply. Any reply.

Charlene beat her to it. "Who's the selfish one now?"

She dismounted the swivel barstool and propped her bag on her shoulder. "I'll drive myself to the airport. Bye, Mom." Charlene kissed Norah's cheek and said goodbye.

Elle hadn't heard Norah shuffle into the room and didn't turn to look. How foolish she was to not know Norah had doctor appointments, or any of those things. Suddenly she felt like Norah had done her a disservice in protecting her, or whatever she was trying to do. They shared a house, and yet all Elle had paid attention to was Norah's awful snoring and unhealthy eating patterns.

A stinging, profound shame hung over her. Elle felt its presence stronger than her own. It swallowed her. The truth in Charlene's words, in Elle's own selfishness. What had been so wrong with Elle that Charlene was willing to care for her mother over the long distance but couldn't extend her daughter the gracious information of her own whereabouts. She was a small child all over again, her chin tucked against her chest and hair fell in her face. Norah's younger face formed in Elle's mind, her less gnarled finger tipping Elle's childhood chin up and looking into her big eyes. The woman who had always been willing to care for her. And

Charlene, the woman who had always been willing to leave.

"What is so wrong with me that makes it so easy for her to leave me?" Elle had asked Norah once. And Norah's response, "Nothing is wrong with you, dear. She is trying to make a better life for you both."

She's protecting you. She always has.

Until that one time Norah had said, "It's not you she is leaving." The statement left Elle spinning with more questions, round and round, until she was dizzy trying to focus on an answer.

So much Elle didn't know. And she never asked.

But there was a night junior year when Elle couldn't sleep. Those words spun in her head. *It's not you she is leaving.*

With only the moonlight coming through the blinds above her head, it came to her. The answer. It was so obvious, so crazy she hadn't realized it before. Charlene was running from Elle's father. Or the memory of him.

Elle tiptoed over the creaky floorboards to the office next to her room. She sifted through the filing cabinets to find her birth certificate. Under the Father heading, it read: Unknown.

Canvassing the neighbors and old friends of her mother's, none of them had any information to give, hadn't even heard from Charlene but were happy to see Elle so grown up and looking so much like her mother at 17. Norah had never stopped her but never offered anything either. After one too many pairs of eyes stared back at her with pity as they said the words *I'm sorry* in one variation or another, Elle gave up.

Now watching her mother again turn her back and leave, she knew. Elle was a demagnetizer. Those who should love her, couldn't. Not even long enough to kiss her goodbye. All the years of not knowing who her father was but knowing too well who her mother really was. And neither of them wanted Elle at all.

Did anyone really?

She texted Marissa, "Wow, just got reamed by my mother. And the worst part is I think she's right. Once again I'm terrible and I can't take it back."

Elle's phone buzzed with a call. "Hey," she found it impossible to hide the defeat from her voice.

"Is this about your mom or Norah?"

"Both." Elle relayed the conversation, huddled in a corner of the garage for privacy and maybe a little penance. The garage felt vast without the Cadillac housed in it.

"I've been stressing over my own problems, but I should have thought of what Norah has gone through too." She ran her hands through her thick hair. "I don't know which is worse, that Mom thinks I've been entirely inactive or the truth that none of this with Norah even occurred to me."

A hush suspended between the phone lines.

"It's bad, isn't it?"

Marissa was careful with her words, which made Elle feel worse. "It's not bad. It's just that you've never gone through anything like this. You've never been sick or had to have someone be caretaker for you, so you don't know how to handle it."

"I should have been taking her to doctor's appointments and helping with medications though, right? I should be doing more than heating up her microwave dinners and watering her bushes."

Marissa whispered to her children who were actually quiet in the background, then returned seamlessly to Elle's conversation. "You can't change yesterday. You can only move forward and be more aware from here."

Without warning, a tear slipped out, and in the solitude of the garage Elle let it fall. The brimming shelves and the washing machine had always been good secret keepers. "I'm all the things they've said about me. I am selfish. I am an embarrassment."

"Well you know me. I'm not going to tell you that you're a selfless saint."

Elle spat out a laugh.

"Sure, you've done a lot of selfish things. You've made some silly mistakes. But I mean, who hasn't! You know who what you want to be. You just got lost in the mix of life. *Show them* that you aren't what they say about you."

Silent tears rippled over her cheekbones. More followed, down her neck, pooling in the hollow between her collar bones.

"You are not what your mom says about you. Don't listen to it. Don't let your mother put her failures on you. I know you hear me. It's going to be okay."

Elle made her cheeks big with air then exhaled slowly, blowing the hair that had fallen in her face. "I think it's going to take a while to make up for this."

***

Her brain was a fog; her eyesight wasn't much better, forced to adjust to daylight after leaving the garage. A clatter in the kitchen sink cleared the fog for just a moment. She walked in to find Norah with her dirty breakfast dishes. Elle joined her at the sink. "Let me do that for you."

"I can do it." Norah responded, grasping with white knuckles for her independence.

"I know you can. Just let me help." With a gentle touch, Elle took the dishes and scrub brush from her grandmother's gloved hands.

The white porcelain was slippery in her hands. She scolded herself for choosing this moment to act chivalrous. She hated dirty dishes and held the devout belief that if the caked-on food didn't come off, the dishwasher wasn't good enough. She wanted to wash dishes the way they did in the Cascade commercials.

Her finger grazed the remnants of Norah's runny eggs and bile might have jumped up her throat. But she closed her eyes, replaying Marissa's pep talk. She scrubbed them clean—which made putting them in the dishwasher pointless but this was supposed to be about Norah. She felt her grandmother's eyes watching her every move, and what would normally make her feel micromanaged instead emboldened her to prove she'd been paying attention all these years.

After her hands were dry, Elle traced the edge of the sink and faucet with the hand towel, drying off every droplet of water, then folded the towel into a square with the embroidered "N" on top. Placing the towel next to the faucet, she felt certain that Norah was scrutinizing her, but when she glanced at Norah, the tilt of her lips formed the smallest smile.

"Thank you," Norah said.

It may have seemed small to anyone else, but Elle could do the herky cheerleading jump that she'd never gotten right in high school.

Because this, this was a victory.

16

JOCELYN

She had never broken a bone, never so much as had a cavity, so she was clueless what to expect the day Scott's leg cast was being removed. The easing of jitters was excuse enough for making Scott's favorite breakfast. His crutches tapped an odd rhythm against the floor as he entered the kitchen.

"Smells good," he said, leaning against her at the stove. He could have been talking about the bacon sizzling, but his nose was in her hair.

His touch beckoned her, but the Turner men hated overcooked eggs. She scooped up yellow mounds flecked with pepper on to plates adding bacon and biscuits alongside them while he brought the forks over. Working together again felt right.

"I'll do it." He said. His hands grazed her thumbs as he grabbed the plates from her. Then he nodded in reassurance.

"Okay."

En route to collect Ian for breakfast, the kitchen erupted with clattering and crashing behind her. "Scott! You okay?" She hollered his name, panicked, running back to the kitchen. Scott stood motionless over shards of ceramic plates and unappetizing piles of scrambled eggs. He stared at them like he could move them with his mind.

Her instincts had told her he wasn't steady enough to balance the plates and maneuver his crutches at the same time, and she chided herself for discarding them. "Watch out, you're bare foot." She said as she touched his forearm to help him move away from the broken pieces.

A shirtless Ian checked on the commotion.

"Stand back, babe. Let me clean it up." Jocelyn said.

With the arm she was holding to steady Scott, he reached up and pushed her shoulder back into the cabinet with the force of a man who had started working out his upper body again. Jocelyn stumbled backward and her backside bumped into the refrigerator.

"Scott!" She hollered, shocked by his reaction.

The sound of her voice brought him back to himself. He lifted his eyes for the first time since she had returned to the room. He exhaled releasing whatever paralyzing toxicity he'd experienced through his breath. "Sorry," he said, "I didn't want you to step in the pieces."

They both knew that wasn't what happened. But neither of them voiced the truth of it. Jocelyn reached for the broom and began sweeping with Scott in her peripheral. This shimmer of anger unnerved her, even though a vein had been running under his clean-cut surface since he had come home.

Using his crutches, he hobbled out of the kitchen, leaving the spilled breakfast on the floor and his barefoot wife cleaning up the pieces of his mess. He passed Ian standing in the doorway, wide-eyed, holding his Scott-shaped pillow under his arm without a word.

***

Before they loaded up in the car, she had a missed call from Alexis. Jocelyn couldn't remember the last time she had missed a call. While Scott was gone, the phone was plastered to her hand. She listened to the voicemail.

"Joss?" Alexis' voice wavered in the recording. "Something's happened to Paul. Call me."

Jocelyn's heart skipped. She grabbed Scott's arm, leaning on him a bit too much. He steadied them both. "It's Paul," she breathed the words while tapping Alexis' number into her phone.

On the second ring, Alexis picked up. "Joss?"

"What happened? Is Paul okay?"

"He is now. We're at the hospital."

"What happened?" Jocelyn repeated, pushing her hair back from her face, feeling the worried creases in her forehead against her fingertips.

Scott tapped his watch and mouthed, "We've got to leave. Talk on the way."

Jocelyn nodded but listened to her friend intently.

"I came home from work and he had swallowed every pill he could find in the house. He had stolen some prescriptions from his parent's house and taken those too."

"Oh Alexis," Tears spring to Jocelyn's eyes.

"When I got home last night, he was on the bathroom floor with vomit all over his face, like his body was on my side fighting to keep him alive. They pumped his stomach at the hospital, and he's already doing better."

Why didn't you call me last night? Jocelyn wanted to ask, but she knew their closeness, not only geographically, had waned in the last year since Paul's retirement and their move from Fort Hood.

She didn't know if it was insensitive to ask her why Paul would do such a thing. What do you say to a friend when her husband attempts suicide? She listened instead.

"He's on suicide watch at the hospital because there was a note and everything."

"What did it say?" Jocelyn said, getting in the car and starting it, hoping Alexis didn't notice the background noise.

"That he knows he hasn't been the same since leaving the army. That he was unhappy and I was unhappy and that I deserved better. He'd already bought a plot to be buried in because he didn't think he deserved a place in a National Cemetery." Her friend's voice cracked. Jocelyn had never heard Alexis cry before. "He had his SGLI paperwork lying under the note. He said he wanted me taken care of financially but not to be dragged down by him."

Jocelyn knew about the army life insurance Alexis was talking about. It could secure up to $400k since Paul had still been paying into it. Alexis had told her that Paul was having a hard time adjusting to civilian life even after taking his SFL—Soldier For Life, which were basically recivilization classes before his enlistment was up. Alexis had never felt at home as an army wife, and didn't appreciate the way the army treated her or Paul. Jocelyn didn't know the details because Paul had put a stop to Alexis' bad mouthing.

"He's okay now though." Alexis said. Jocelyn wondered if Alexis was telling her or convincing herself. "He'll be okay."

"I'm coming." Her eyes were on Scott's reaction. But his only reaction was to nod his agreement.

"No. You have a lot going on."

"Alexis, let me come help you."

"No." The word was clipped, fierce. Then she lightened. "But you can make me a new budget." Alexis snorted through the pain in her voice. "I'm the big breadwinner now. Me and my bartending job at 35."

Pulling the car up to the check-in gates at Fort Hood, Alexis heard the familiar interaction from the station guards.

"I'll let you go. I wanted you and Scott to know."

Jocelyn protested again, but her friend insisted.

"Tell Scott hello. I hope he's feeling better."

"I love you, Alexis. Call me anytime." She said, feeling desperate to persuade her friend. "You know, I'm always up at midnight. I will come out there if you need me. You know I will."

There was silence on the other end, but Jocelyn knew her friend was still there. "I thought getting out would fix all of this, but it doesn't."

Jocelyn glanced at her husband, with his damaged leg and body that would never be the same, and for only a moment she wondered if it was all worth it. But Scott's resolve straightened her back. He believed it was worth it. He knew the risk, and he blazed on. So would she.

***

Their day was painfully silent. Alexis' call had stalled them. Other than with doctors and therapists, Scott seemed like he'd rather ignore that there was a situation.

She tiptoed around her husband, as though the pathway to him was covered by shards of ceramic plates. If she stepped wrong, she'd get pushed away. He still spoke in her head, that sarcastic flavor that made her smile. While he holed away in his room, she'd considered putting on the video he'd made, just to have a piece of him home.

Ian did the same thing by carrying around his Daddy Doll. He took it with him to Leanne and Grace's again while his parents went to have Scott's cast removed. If Jocelyn had a hard time asking for help before, now she was relying on it for survival. Like a death in the family, even the FRG mothers moved on. Only three of them were offering help anymore, and for the first time in her motherhood, she was considering a Mother's Day Out program. Their budget spreadsheet showed more red than black, and she wasn't sure how they were going to make it to the end of the month without the added expense of MDO. Not to mention her revamped dry erase calendar screamed at her with its physical therapy appointments three times a week and her taxi-ing Scott to and from work starting next week.

In the exam room among the nurses and assistants, Scott was uncharacteristically demure. Exposing his leg was more intimate to Jocelyn in this moment than being naked together. She remembered exploring his eyes when she was in labor with Ian, in her most vulnerable, most pain-filled moment, and seeing his love in the tears in his eyes. That was the closest she could come to imagining what he could be feeling.

The nurse put the surgical mask over her mouth and safety goggles over her eyes—was this an episode of HGTV home makeover show? It was as though they weren't even in the room when she turned on the saw. The grinding was louder than Jocelyn had expected in the small exam room, and she understood why the nurse had eye gear on when the plaster dust covered everything in its vicinity.

Her hand squeezed Scott's to reassure him, but he didn't move, his eyes fixed on the wall ahead. The nurse made several cuts along either side of the cast with a round saw that reminded Jocelyn of an episode of *Criminal Minds* then pried apart the plaster. Scott squared his shoulders when the nurse lifted his leg to remove pieces from under his calf.

"Sorry," the nurse said, acknowledging Scott's flinching. Jocelyn breathed through her mouth, so she didn't inhale the plaster dust. And to concentrate on what was in her control.

The white skin of his leg appeared, pale next to his desert tanned body. When the doctors had removed the bars from the bone and placed the cast, they'd screwed the bones in place and fused a metal bar along his femur. "Very Wolverine," she'd said to him. But he wasn't in the mood for joking. With therapy, he would get most mobility back in his leg. Most.

"Looks like its healing well." Jocelyn said.

Agreeing, the nurse smiled. "It is. It looks great."

"Pfft," Scott blew through his lips.

The nurse's eyebrows pulled together. "I know it isn't the same as before. The muscles are tight and have some weakness from nonuse, which is normal. All of that will change with PT. Soon. We'll keep you on crutches for a bit longer until you strengthen up those muscles."

Scott grabbed his crutches and was out of the room before Jocelyn could thank the nurse as she wiped up the plaster dust from the surfaces. Like he was racing to his physical therapy appointment, forgetting all patience or gratitude in the wake of discomfort. A lot packed in one day, just the way Scott liked it.

Together—and yet separate still—they headed to meet George Holt in the therapy clinic. A few steps into the journey, Scott's strength waned, as did his speed. Jocelyn wanted to drive around or get a wheelchair, but he refused. His jaw worked as hard as his healthy left leg. She could see his triceps as they contracted gripping the crutches with each step. A sweat spot had bloomed down his back by the time they breached the doors of the clinic.

"Hey Hooch. Welcome back." Holt said with a sly smile. Hooch was the army nickname Scott had earned; he told her it was a play off the Tom Hanks movie *Turner and Hooch,* but she had a feeling there was more to it. George turned to her, "Jocelyn."

"Take care of him today." She said with a wink at the therapist. She had yet to be in their sessions. Scott had told her he didn't want her there, not wanting her to see him that way. *That's crazy. You've seen me on my back pushing out your baby.* He rebutted that Ian needed her more. *I'm more than just a mother. I can offer so much more to you.* Nothing she said had convinced him.

"The leg looks good."

"Shut up." Scott said, flicking the towel from around Holt's neck. It seemed like Scott's rapport with Holt came easier than with her.

Kissing her husband, the kind of kiss she would give him before a high school football game, tasting sweat on her lips after they parted, Jocelyn left the room. She walked the halls and called Alexis. There weren't many people she could trust with the question she was about to ask.

When her friend answered, happy to hear from her, she apologized for calling so early. "I never remember what the time difference is."

"No big deal. I'm on my drive to work."

"How's Paul?"

Alexis tsked. "Acting like nothing ever happened. What's up?"

"Can I ask you something? I don't want you to read into it."

"Anything."

"Should I be worried that Scott doesn't talk to me about being hurt? Or let me help him? Or touch him?" Jocelyn spilled the words out faster than she could even keep up. She'd been holding them on her tongue for days.

"Oh hun," Alexis smacked her lips. Lips that Jocelyn knew were always painted bright red against her mocha skin. "I wish I could answer that one. Our men are all different. Paul still hasn't opened up to me about anything over there, but some men have to talk it all out. Maybe he's waiting on you to ask, to know that you're ready to hear it."

"He doesn't think I *can* handle it. It's like he's testing me over everything."

"Just give it time. It's a hard transition coming home from all of that. It's a new world. I don't nag Paul. Can you imagine how much worse he would be if I had? He's seeing a counselor now. All I can do is hope that if he ever needs to talk to me, he will."

Was that right? She didn't want to be a nag, but she didn't want to wait and see either. A weight in her chest pulled at her. "Do you ever suspect Paul could have PTSD? I mean, do you think Scott could?" She hated the stigma of all soldiers having post-traumatic stress disorder. She hated that she was buying into it, but she couldn't help from wondering.

"Hun, I don't know how someone could survive a war and not be traumatized."

Jocelyn should have known that's what Alexis would say. It was one of the reasons Alexis had pushed Paul to retire from the army at the end of his enlistment.

"But somehow, they can compartmentalize it. Has he started his reintegration classes?"

"Sure. He's done everything they tell him to. Sometimes I think he goes to all this stuff just to get out of the house. I'm more of an über driver than wife or mother right now." Jocelyn glanced at the clock on the wall.

"Well, are they helping? They're supposed to help identify PTSD in those classes."

"I don't know. I just don't know anything anymore."

The conversation turned to lighter topics until Alexis arrived at work and had to end the call. "Let's do this again soon. I've missed our little talks."

Jocelyn agreed. They hung up, and Jocelyn waited on a bench in the hallway outside of Scott's PT room. She thought she could hear his grunts, but that could have been her imagination. All she knew was that when Scott did finally open the door leaning on his crutches, his ecru t-shirt was streaked with sweat on his back and chest, his face so red with excursion it was almost purple.

"I hate this man." Scott grumbled as Holt, smiling with pride like it was a compliment, walked him out to the hallway.

"Do you need to towel off or anything?" Jocelyn asked him.

"I already did."

"I'm having flashbacks to the car rides after high school football practice." Jocelyn teased.

Scott raised his eyebrows. "What does that mean for me?"

Jocelyn weaved her arm around his crutches and encircled his waist, regardless of the sweat or stink like she used to in those same high school years. Then she leaned up and kissed his lips, abused as they looked.

"Get a room," one of the other PT patients walking through the hallway quipped.

"You got one close by?" Scott hollered back.

Jocelyn laughed and all, but she knew they hadn't made love since his return.

*　*　*

Ian's birthday snuck up on her with Scott home. The plan had been to celebrate it after Scott returned from deployment, but now that he was home, Jocelyn was feeling a major mom fail. Until, that is, Elizabeth Cryer offered to throw him a party. She had gotten close to Ian watching him nearly every week. Being that she and John had never had children of their own—Jocelyn hadn't the nerve to ask why—she told Jocelyn that she'd never had the chance to use all the child birthday party ideas she'd pinned on Pinterest. The thought of Elizabeth Cryer on Pinterest threw Jocelyn, and she hated to lean on Elizabeth yet again but the stress was mounding so she couldn't say no.

On the party's eve, the house was anything but quiet with Ian helping make the party favors for his friends. Elizabeth relinquished this one piece of the work at Jocelyn's insistence. Although Scott headed straight for the bedroom after a quick turn in the kitchen to grab a beer. Every drink tugged at her stomach reminding her how much medication he was on, but he insisted it was fine.

"What are you doing?" Jocelyn asked, when she saw the bedroom transformed into a range of mountains formed by Scott's clothes.

He hunkered over his drawers pulling more out, throwing them over his shoulder adding to the pile. "I'm getting rid of all this."

Her eyes bounced around the room deciphering the meaning between his words and actions. There was a pile of shorts, and the pieces began to fit themselves together in her brain. "Why are you throwing out all of your shorts?"

"If you don't want me to throw them out, you can give them to one of your shelters."

"That's not what I'm asking."

"Well, I'm not going to be the guy everybody says skipped leg day at the gym because I've got chicken legs."

"Scott,"

He interrupted, for the first time looking up from the drawers. "I've got no need for shorts anymore. That's it."

Jocelyn wanted to tell him to stop throwing fits, to stop acting like Ian. Her shoulders dropped in defeat. She had too many things going on right now to deal with his crisis of shorts. A little boy in the other room was counting on her for his birthday, for his routine schedule, for everything. As much as she wanted to be able to help her husband too through this whole thing, he wouldn't give her much more than a grunt when she asked him to talked to her. Scott was a big boy. If he wouldn't open up to her and let her in, then she was going to go back to putting her energy into the little boy who did.

***

Elizabeth Cryer's house had been transformed into a Star Wars dream and therefore was perfect for Ian. There was a photo booth with the black sky of space and stars and spaceships as a backdrop. Jocelyn and Ian took a picture wearing Princess Leia buns and Yoda ears respectively. Ian even pulled Scott in for a picture with lightsabers. The cake was covered with black fondant and little white fondant stars, with a little Luke Skywalker and Darth Vader (whom Ian called Dark Vader) fighting with lightsabers as a cake topper. Plus, there were cake balls of each character's face.

If Jocelyn was in awe, then Ian was in Star Wars heaven. There were paper crafted lightsabers for a battle in Elizabeth's backyard, and she catered to the young age children better than Jocelyn could have anticipated.

The other parents in attendance *oo*ed and *aah*ed too, but Jocelyn had trouble reading if they were sincerely there for her son or if this was a pity appearance. For Ian's sake, she didn't care, but for her own and Scott's it mattered. A couple of the women tried to talk to Scott, whose bruises had faded to a hint of yellow above his cheekbone and the blood in his eye was only a crescent hanging from his iris. She couldn't read his eyes but his jaw clenched and released every couple seconds. If she had to guess why, it was because he felt—and maybe they felt—he'd left their husbands downrange.

Not long after passing out the paper lightsabers to each of the kids who were all want-to-be Jedi's now, a knock came from the back door.

"Well who could that be?" Elizabeth said, feigning surprise.

When she opened the door, a full size, real life Darth Vader stepped out, iconic inhale-exhale combo and all. The kids were cheering, jumping, shouting. Ian charged at him with his little paper lightsaber, but Vader was ready. After a jab and block, a clash and hit right in Vader's arm, the towering villain turned to Ian and said, "You have done well. There is still good in me after all." Then he turned. But before leaving, he stopped next to Scott on the back porch and in a resonating declaration said, "Scott, I am your father."

Scott laughed a little, shaking his head.

Then Darth Vader disappeared into the house.

The "Before Scott" would have been in the backyard jumping around, swinging a lightsaber himself fighting with Ian and all the other kids. He would have made some snarky comment at the photo booth about Jocelyn needing Princess Leia's gold bikini. He would have been the one dressed up as Darth Vader or led the resistance against him. But now,

Scott was seated in a rocking chair on the back porch drinking a beer, watching his son's 4th birthday party instead of partaking in it.

Farther from him than ever, Jocelyn moved in Scott's direction to make her own gold bikini insinuation. But the back door opened in front of her, and it was Mike, Scott's father, in the doorway. And Jocelyn realized, the same time Scott did, that Darth Vader was in fact Scott's father. Scott hung his head for a moment, hiding his emotions, then pulled up on his crutch to stand and give his dad a bear hug.

The presence of the woman who made it all happen crept up next to Jocelyn and spoke low enough for only the two of them to hear. "He called one day while I was at the house watching Ian, and Ian let it slip about the party. I didn't encourage Mike to come because I wasn't sure how Scott felt about it." She paused. "But I didn't discourage him either."

Jocelyn winked at Elizabeth. "Thank you." But those two words could never express the fullness of her heart or the gratitude it held. "Can I hire you for every birthday party forevermore?" The two women laughed.

The party breezed by while Jocelyn busied herself with taking pictures as an escape from talking to any adults. Including her father-in-law. He was there for Scott and Ian, and as much as she loved him, they needed to be together. Oh, that Ian would remember this birthday forever.

When everyone had cleared out, Mike and Scott were still in the rocking chairs on the back porch, and knowing those two, less talking and a whole lot of rocking.

"It's really great that your dad came." Jocelyn said. Mike was coming back to the house for dinner but was staying at a hotel. Jocelyn was grateful for that too.

"Yeah," Scott said. A hint of sincerity was missing.

A red light blinked inside Jocelyn. The piece of her that could read Scott was malfunctioning. The car was still parked in the Cryer driveway while Ian was driving home in Mike's car. If she was going to ask him, now was the time. Jocelyn inhaled courage. "What's going on? You acted like you didn't want to be at your own son's birthday party."

There was a pause. A long one. Scott looked straight ahead at nothing in particular.

"I shouldn't be here. I'm supposed to be there." Scott said.

"You make it sound like you don't *want* to be here."

"I don't. Not like this."

She saw his body shift when he realized what his words sounded like to her, but he didn't take them back. She inhaled, swallowing her wounds, waiting for him, prodding him with her eyes to continue. Begging him to let her in.

"Some of those kids in there, I watched them grow up in pictures just like Ian. The wives looked at me like I could give them something. Like I could tell them about their husbands. But I can't. I left my men over there. Doing the job that I should be doing. But I'm here at my kid's birthday party, while they are still sitting in their CHU watching some ripped movie missing their wife and kids. It's not right."

She almost understood. If she had been one of those wives, maybe she would feel that way. But she wasn't. Her husband was home, alive, and shouldn't she be relieved? Shouldn't he be home with his family sans guilt? He was hurt. He lived. He was home. Was she wrong to revel in his return?

"Let's go home." Scott said.

They would return to the house, eat BBQ with Mike, act like everything was fine. Act like they weren't being ripped apart, like the RPG hadn't shattered more than Scott's leg.

***

Out of exhaustion and avoidance, she laid down next to Ian's tiny body. His chest rose and fell as he slept. Her emotions were doing the same thing.

How many nights had she laid waiting for Scott to fill her bed again? Now he was, and she hid away in her son's twin size bed. The man in the other room was as stubborn and handsome and irrational as he was before, times ten. Before, they laughed things off together. Before, she would have walked in on him throwing his shorts in a pile, and his response would have been to throw a pair at her starting a shorts-throwing fight until he tossed her body on to the bed laughing. Before, he would have been up all night helping her decorate a birthday cake for Ian like a picture she'd seen online with no clue how to make, and at midnight he would have figured out the solution. With her.

With only the moonlight peeking through the blinds, Ian's skin was smooth as velvet. A freckle relaxed in the hollow of his collarbone that she swore hadn't been there before. When had the pinprick dot appeared and discolored her son's smooth, fresh skin? She brushed her finger over it. Anything could change in the most ordinary of moments.

In ninja fashion, she slid her legs off Ian's bed. The stalking quiet of the house was her only midnight companion. Laundry took a back seat to their new schedule, and it was piled high on top of the dryer in their tiny utility closet. Folding towels and sorting socks felt familiar, her thoughts drowning in the fresh citrus scent. Scott's army duffle bag, which was as big as Ian, had returned home with him and was shoved in the corner of the utility closet. She hadn't had the wherewithal, or frankly the time, to unzip it until now. His desert tan army boots laid on top, a light dusting of Afghanistan sand brushed off as she held them up. The last time he'd worn these he'd taken a hit, the day that changed their lives. She didn't even clean the boots off, just set them on the shelf above the washing machine. His ACUs and other clothes were folded in perfect squares on top of each other. They were already clean but a light musty odor clung to them from being zipped up next to the boots. Someone packed the bag with care.

Hidden between his folded clothes lay Scott's laptop. Adrenaline pulsed through her body at the sight of it. This could hold everything she wanted. The secrets to Scott. A pang stung her chest. Should she open a doorway to Scott's thoughts without his permission? If only to understand him better? Her hands hovered over the black case, conflicted like a parent holding a teenager's unlocked diary. With a glance toward the hallway thinking of Scott sleeping, dreaming of experiences he wouldn't share with her, she shrugged off the guilt and worked at getting the laptop open and plugged-in. When the word processor booted up, there were all his journal entries, filed and saved by date, waiting for her. Only one click away. There was no way to unlearn what she might read in these pages.

All of Scott's questions of her rewound. Was she ready to see her husband like this? Could she live with what he had been through? But the notion would never fade until she read every word. She opened entry number one.

17

ELLE

The time had come. Elle was desperate enough now to work out her money situation. With her credit cards cancelled, bank account withdrawn and cash stuffed in her tampon box, she was done. Early Saturday morning with black coffee being the stiffest drink in the house, she snuck into Norah's office with a Trader Joe's brown paper bag in hand. The starched brown bag folded at the top hid her stash of unopened credit card bills. And there were a lot of them.

She sat at the desk. A fairly new computer sat atop it, along with a desk calendar covered in Norah's scratchy handwriting. The space was more organized than Elle's workspace, but that was no surprise. Next to the desk was a small table where Norah's typewriter sat. It was amusing to see this new technology alongside its vintage counterpart. Alongside the opposite wall was a couch and television. More old photographs framed the wall.

The computer booted up; cursor expectantly blinking for a password which shouldn't have surprised her. In a commendable decision Elle's mother had pushed Norah to buy a computer and take classes at the local community college a few years back.

The crackle of the floor boards alerted her to Norah's approach. Elle hollered out to the hallway and asked for the password.

"It's written on the label at the bottom of the screen so I don't forget it."

Again the paradox. As Elle typed in the letter/number combination, Norah joined her, lowering herself on to the leather couch.

"Why do you still have this old thing?" Elle touched her fingers to the corner of the avocado-colored typewriter. "You could probably make some money if you wanted to sell it."

"Oh dear, no." Norah shook her head. "Your grandfather gave me that. Some things are more valuable than the money they represent."

Christian Loubuton shoes made Elle feel the same way.

"I still use it." Norah said absently. "My hands aren't all that steady, so I type out birthday cards and such with it; make out my checks with it, that is, the ones I don't pay online."

An eyebrow rose at the 84-year-old who paid bills online.

"Yes, Elle, I know how to use the Internet. Quite well actually. I took a class. I may have an old typewriter and an old body, but I believe you *can* teach an old dog new tricks."

Laughing, Elle shook her head.

"It's true. I make a newsletter twice a year for those of us still around who graduated college together. There aren't a lot of us left, but we like to stay in touch. All but one of us still lives in Southern California."

The insinuation that so many of Norah's peers had passed on made Elle uncomfortable and unsure of what to say.

With effort Norah climbed off of the couch and opened the black metal filing cabinet next to the desk. "I have some of the past issues in here. I try to include pictures of some of us throughout the year." Her unsteady hand passed a four-page newsletter to Elle. Clipart borders, word art and fancy fonts filled the page. A black and white photo of a dozen seniors centered the page with fine inkjet lines pulsing through it.

Clicking the filing cabinet drawer back in place, Norah gazed over Elle's shoulders lost in nostalgia. "I know it isn't like print work you put out at your office, but it's just a little something."

Elle wanted to cut her off, wanted to take away any insecurity her grandmother felt. "It's great." She said with true pride. "Do you do this with anyone from your high school class?"

A neighbor honked a horn outside but it didn't deter Norah's response. "No, no. I would never do such a thing." She started for the door in her shuffle walk.

The response was definitive and typically Elle wouldn't pry. But she was searching today. "Why do you do that?" Her voice soft and not at all accusatory. "When you know everything there is to know about my life but I hardly know anything about yours."

Without turning Norah answered, "I'm not like you. I'm from a time where we talked little about ourselves."

That was not good enough for Elle. "Well I'm not. Now, you can tell me why you have such deep negativity toward your high school classmates or I can pester you every day about it. You will give in eventually."

Norah laughed a sweet sound that Elle had missed. "Well then." She shuffled back to the couch.

"My family was poor when I was growing up. We worked on a farm in Arkansas."

"I can't picture you anywhere but California."

Her gran smiled. "Got here as fast as I could. The girls at my high school were snobs. My parents worked for their parents. Hell, after school hours *I* worked for their parents, and they knew it. I was feeding pigs while they were taking car rides with boys. Every day they dressed to the nines, all the latest fashions—for Arkansas anyway—and I only had a few changes of clothes."

Norah painted a picture clear as Waterford crystal of the girl she once was, graduating high school and heading off to university taking classes on bookkeeping. "I might have still worked for those girl's parents for a time, but at least I'd do it as far away from pig slop as I could get."

Her twenty-something self had worked her way to independence and enough money to buy whatever clothes she wanted, then followed a job she heard about from the countryside of Arkansas to the Oceanfront of California where the fresh air smelled of salt and sand. Worked her way through finishing college classes.

"Even then," with a distant look in her eyes, Norah said, "I could never have gone to my reunion with those girls."

"But why?" Elle shook her head. "You moved to California, the land of Hollywood and celebrities. Every picture I've ever seen you were as fashionable as a movie star. You would have shown those girls up."

The distance in Norah's eyes stretched over the years, "I never wanted to look in their faces again." Maybe she was afraid she would have seen that poor farm girl again. Maybe everyone was running away, or maybe it just ran deep in Elle's bloodline.

As if shaking off a trance, Norah moved her attention back to Elle. It seemed to make them both more comfortable. "I'm interrupting what you were working on. What did you need with my computer?"

Embarrassment flooded Elle, and lie after lie sprang to her mind. But the room was still fragrant with vulnerability. As knifelike as the words were coming out of her mouth, she pressed on saying them aloud for the first time. "Apparently I am out of money."

That was the simplest way to put it and any more would have been stabbing a gaping wound.

She unrolled the top of the brown paper bag and dumped the contents out on the floor. The pile mounded higher than her ankles. She expected a gasp, a disapproving shake of the head.

Instead, Norah said in her way, "Well at least you aren't feeding the pigs yet" and handed over her silver envelope opener.

***

Elle woke, startled and disoriented after dreaming the houses at the top of the hill came alive and were avalanching the houses below. She was buried alive under the rubble of one-of-a-kind paintings and decor that filled the walls of the homes she had wished to live in.

Even her unconscious self was killing her off in a tomb of things she coveted but couldn't afford.

Her eyes opened to the darkness, a hint of moonlight reflecting off of the horrific full length mirrors on the opposite side of the room. Many nights growing up, Elle had awoken from nightmares to those mirrors. And many nights they had kept her awake in horror of what lurked in their reflections. But now the only reflection she was afraid of was the one looking back at her, the lonely, lost girl with so much to prove and so much to learn.

Her tongue was grimy against her fuzzy feeling teeth. She needed a drink of water, maybe a gallon of water in her face to shake the sensation of high end rubble pressing down on her chest.

In her silk shorts, she navigated the creaky stairs like a teenager sneaking out. Even as the ice cold water poured down her throat, she knew it wouldn't help. Nightmares and dry mouth were only symptoms of what ailed her. Night hours were the hardest, the ones when her situations screamed at her, her loneliest bit, the hours when she was stuck in this house of peach-hued ghosts and not Aaron.

When she made her way back up the stairs, she knew there was no way she'd be going back to sleep soon.

Messaging Jocelyn with a simple, "How'd Ian's birthday go? How are you?" Elle found herself smiling at the an unexpected comrade in this woman who shared her insomnia. As much as Elle wanted to show up at her house and force a friendship on her—she could see Jocelyn, Marissa and herself hanging out at the beach drinking green tea and laughing over how awkward their first meeting was—but no, Elle wasn't that crazy. She *did* have boundaries.

This time, though, she heard nothing back from Jocelyn.

***

Driving in Los Angele traffic—even in the suburbs—made it easy to get caught up in the cut offs, road rage and brake lights instead of noticing the beautiful mountains in the distance or the palm tree that speckled the edges around the highway. Elle skipped stopping for a cup of organic espresso or a quick browse through a favorite store and picked Norah up for an opportunity out of the house. Since Charlene's visit, Norah hadn't been out at all.

Together they decided on heading to the market. Elle wanted to make them dinner. "None of that tofu crap," had been Norah's only response.

Everything took longer with Norah. Even driving, somehow. Alone, Elle could have been to the market and back, chopping up the jicama, almonds, arugula and strawberries that she planned on tossing together in a salad. She took a deep, patience-reviving breath, then noticed Norah swatting at chunks of her hair trying to move it back and forth, trying to cover up spots in her hair so thin and light that her scalp shown through. Her gold bangles clanged together with each tussle of her fingers in the near-sheer strands of her hair.

An invitation had arrived for Norah to attend a roof-top party at the Clubhouse in a couple weeks. Already prepping her possible wardrobe options, "I'll wear my new pearl necklace" Norah had said. But Norah's consciousness of her hair's inadequacy had come from Charlene.

"How hungry are you?" Elle asked on a whim.

Norah shrugged her shoulders. "How hungry do I have to be to eat one of your special salads?"

Elle smirked. She was immune to Norah's responses.

"Let's make a quick stop first."

"And put off eating a plateful of grass? By all means."

Elle jerked her car into a parking lot, and Norah's face crinkled in response.

"It's on me." They were at a hair salon, but Elle had other ideas. They entered to the typical store chime and salon chemical smell that burned Elle's nose.

The two women, with a generation between them, passed the reception desk, the sales ladies and walked to the section covered by shelves full of decapitated heads of beauty with lush locks of shiny hair. Elle stood to the side of the shelves with an uncontainable smile and turned to Norah, whose eyes were wide taking in the unexpected expanse.

Elle floated to one of the shelves in full Vanna White mode. "Look. They have your color." She said presenting the row of champagne colored wigs in a wide variety of styles, long flowing curls, a pixie cut, chin-length bob, shag cut ala '90s Meg Ryan.

"Or we could be adventurous and try a new color." Elle giggled pointing at a high shelf with the "vivid colors" of blues, purples and pinks. There were shelves of chocolate brown, strawberry blonde. It was like an ice cream parlor for hair.

Norah said nothing. So Elle took the initiative to grab an employee and ask if they were supposed to manhandle the wigs themselves or if there was a different protocol.

The employee stepped over and introduced herself as Sandy. "Is there one that you want to try on?"

Norah stood transfixed.

Elle jumped in, unable to hold back her excitement. "What about this one?" Pointing to the short champagne-colored bob.

Norah bore no expression. The reaction made Sandy uncomfortable enough to let the ladies know to call her over whenever they were ready. But Elle didn't give in that easy. "I think you might have fun with a bit of a change. What about the strawberry blonde? It compliments your skin tone."

The more Elle talked, the more distance Norah put between them. Finally, "I think we should get our dinner." She said and turned to leave.

Baffled, Elle thanked Sandy and told her they'd be back soon. Hopefully. By the time Elle exited the store, Norah was already buckled in her seat. Elle got in the car speechless and drove to the market. Every attempt to converse with Norah failed. So Elle matched her on the drive home, trying to pinpoint what could have hit Norah so negatively. Then, Elle saw it. "I was being like mom, wasn't I?"

Norah didn't look Elle's way but her age spotted hand was suddenly on top of Elle's smooth one, and with a light squeeze Norah spoke without a single word.

**

Sunrise yoga on the beach bathed Elle in serenity, but by the end of the work day, Elle was exhausted. She planned on curling up with a cup of chamomile tea and watching whatever Norah watched on a Wednesday night until she fell asleep.

Except that when Elle opened the door home, Norah jumped up as quickly as an 84-year-old could, purse in hand, dressed to go out. "I talked to Brandon about it today, and I want to go back to the salon."

"It's okay, Norah. You don't have to."

"Well, I'm going. If you don't want to go, hand me your keys." Norah put her palm out but not quite flat due to the arthritic curve she never admitted to.

Elle breathed out through puffed cheeks. "Fine." Then as they made their way to the car followed up with, "What made you change your mind?"

"Oh I haven't been able to get mine to do anything," Norah huffed. She subconsciously twirled the bit of hair by her ear as she gazed out the window. The car wove around the hills. Elle had ever seen Norah twirl her hair like a lovesick girl, but she knew better than to mention it. "I think it might make a nice accessory next to my new pearl necklace at the rooftop party." Norah said.

Elle managed to keep her smile a subtle curve.

"You're back!" Sandy was up from her stool the moment she saw the two women enter and accompanied them to the wall of wigs. "Have you come back for one in particular?"

Elle angled her body toward Sandy and asked, "Do you happen to have one in a peach color?"

The question hung in the air, Sandy not knowing who to look at or how serious the question was.

A smile breached Norah's lips when she caught Elle's eyes. Then Norah was bellowing in laughter. Elle joined in. It was the first time she had made her gran laugh since moving back, and it was a beautiful laugh. A full-bodied laugh.

Sandy still seemed a bit unsure what to do, so she repeated her mantra from their last visit to let her know if they needed anything.

They could hardly hear her over their giggling. Other customers were looking at them, but neither woman cared.

With laughing tears in her eyes, Norah grabbed a wig off of its disembodied mannequin complete with full face of makeup. It was the pixie cut, and she stared at it in the mirror sitting atop her own head. "Well it doesn't look as good on me as it does on her." She nodded her head toward its bodyless home.

Elle wiped her own eyes. "You have to put it on right." She adjusted it over Norah's delicate hair, tucking the last few belligerent strands under the mesh lining.

"There you go."

"Not much better." Norah said, deadpan. "Remember when you came home with that haircut in junior high."

Elle murmured her undoubtable acknowledgement.

"You took one look in the mirror and said you looked like a boy."

"And you said that was impossible." Elle added before Norah had the last word out.

"This time it is." Norah pulled it off with gusto and threw it at Elle, who put the wig back and brought the short bob down. But Norah didn't like this one either.

"I could try the dark brown." She met Elle's skeptical look with, "It's your natural color, isn't it?"

"Who even knows anymore." Elle said.

In the end, the shag was left. As much as Elle didn't want to like it, it fit Norah perfectly as soon as it was in place. The silky strands that could have easily been seen on the red carpet fell perfectly across Norah's forehead and by her ears.

"Jackpot." Elle said with a proud smile matching Norah's.

"You're still paying though, right?"

With the swipe of her new credit card—the one she opened in her name only, the idea struck her to text Aaron and let him know that this purchase was not for herself. But it was too late for that. And too little. If she had considered it when they were co-cardholders, when he loved her, when it was *their* money she was spending, if she had thought of it then, she may not be here spending money on a wig, or even living with Norah. She may never have remembered the grandmother she had been missing. If only she had seen both roads when it had mattered. If she had thought at all of Aaron instead of centering on the feel of cashmere against her skin or the weight of Louis Vuitton leather.

Aaron would never know this change she had even seen in herself, because he would never see the bill with the line of payment to Beauty-full Salon. But the moment was bigger than Elle and Aaron with their money problems.

Sandy placed the wig for Norah and handed her the black ribboned box with instructions for care. Everything about Norah transformed, the way a princess might on coronation day as the crown is placed atop her royal head. Her back straightened like a girl's in etiquette class, her shoulders as graceful as a dancer's. This was no returnable cashmere sweater.

***

The evening of the rooftop party, Norah called across the stairs to Elle. "Help me with this, will you?"

Standing in the doorway of her bathroom fully dressed, Norah held out her new hair piece. Sitting misshapen in Norah's grip, it looked like a shiny clump of roadkill, but it had already gotten plenty of use. She'd worn it every day, to the grocery store, the pharmacy, dinner out or at home, and church on Sunday morning.

But Elle was chagrined to walk in from work the first few times to see the beautiful wig exposing the mesh lining on Norah's forehead peeking out from under her new bangs. After reading instructions and watching YouTube tutorials with Elle, Norah had gotten okay at it, but like cooking or driving, she always relinquished the job to her granddaughter whose fingers were nimbler and whose eyes could differentiate better between skin and the tan colored lining.

Norah handed Elle the new pearl necklace after her hair was in place. The cultured pearls in their natural freeform shape were variations of subtle pinks, purples and copper.

"I think this is my favorite of all the pearl necklaces you have." Elle said as she clipped it around Norah's neck. The string of gems landed just below Norah's collarbone.

"It should be. It cost enough."

Elle's eyebrows wrinkled. "I thought you were on a fixed income?"

Norah shrugged as she sat in her vanity chair. "Your mother doesn't have to know everything." She held out her lipstick and liner, and Elle knew what was expected.

"Why do you let her control so much?" Elle asked, breaching a tender subject when her grandmother couldn't escape.

The woman waited to respond until Elle had lined her thin lips with a springy red. "She's not controlling. Not really. She just has a lot of ideas."

Elle tilted her head down at Norah as she donned her best *you've-got-to-be-kidding* look. "When she was here she controlled your every move and every decision."

Norah didn't disagree or shake her head, she just replied, "She's done a lot for me over the years. I know you don't believe that," she continued before Elle could argue, "But it's true."

Elle chewed her cheek, deciding how far she could go before Norah shut her down. "Is that why you don't fight back?"

Their eyes met in the mirror's reflection.

"If I said half the things Mom said to you, you would have shut me up in an instant." Elle said.

A deep breath escaped Norah's freshly lined lips, contemplating whether or not to answer, which was new to Elle. The grandmother she knew never held any quip back.

Instead Norah stood. "Come on. I don't want to be late to the party."

***

The Clubhouse parking lot was crammed with Lincolns, Buicks, Cadillacs and a Lexus. "You know it would be nice if I could meet your friends. You always had to meet my friends growing up."

"You mean boyfriends."

"I mean both."

Norah unbuckled her seatbelt and grabbed her clutch as Elle idled in front of the entrance. Before another word was spoken, the man donning the white wingtip shoes came to Norah's door. He pointed down to the handle, and with an expression of bewilderment Norah nodded.

He opened the door and held it for her with his other hand stretched out akin to a classy hotel doorman's welcome.

"Good evening, Norah." He said in a strong timbre. "Ma'am," nodding to Elle.

Norah turned to her granddaughter after exiting the car with her eyebrows raised. Elle gave a little smirk. Norah whispered "After" then rushed off to her party.

Alone again in the car, Elle sat for a moment. Her hands rounding the steering wheel, she realized she no longer knew what to do on a Friday night. Her Fridays had now become Norah's Fridays, and if Elle was honest with herself she didn't mind it all that much. The lure of a nice restaurant or drinks on the beach lost its luster when she attended alone or became a third or fifth or whatever odd number wheel.

She had forfeited the Friday nights of a beer on the beach with Aaron, at which she lamented why he couldn't pick a vegan restaurant occasionally or why he wouldn't dance with her. It was light, normal banter, but as she played the scenes in her mind she saw his eyes turn downcast when she started in on him.

A small group of people dressed in subpar attire passed by her car to join the party inside. The red dress worn by a gray-haired woman reminded Elle of the last work event she and Aaron had attended, a "save the children" type program Lena Designs supported. The suit she had chosen for Aaron complemented her red and black silhouette dress, but he dressed himself in a navy suit and purple plaid tie that made her want to scratch out her irises. They spent the evening not talking except for brief quips whispered about how boring the speaker was.

Her heart plunged to the car's floorboards as she saw herself through Aaron's eyes, ashamed of how superficial she was, how embarrassed she had become by everyone around her. All the while they were embarrassed by her.

Maybe in the end, Aaron didn't leave her because of the money or kids. Maybe it had just been her. Maybe he'd made up everything else in an attempt to…what? Protect her?

A migraine pinched between her eyes. She couldn't take this wallow in the parking lot, and the desperation to crash the rooftop party was as embarrassing as a purple plaid tie. There was an itch in the back of her throat, a symptom of withdrawal, and she couldn't go without scratching it anymore. She gave in and went shopping.

The boutique lights glittered behind their glass doors, showing off the latest fashions through windows like a clothing red-light district. Her feet moved slowly compared to her usual shopping pace. Her eyes caught a pair of shoes in a white-on-white display, like they belonged in her old apartment, in her old life. It was unlikely she would find shoes on the Boulevard that matched her current peach-tinted life.

The ache for a new blouse began deep in her torso, to feel the feather-weight fabric caress her skin like a lover. She pushed into the next store's entrance like coming up for air. Her fingers brushed the sleeves of a gold tunic. She knew the exact Chanel shoes she would pair with the shirt and a list of jeans popped into her mind as well. But as she grabbed the hanger, a shock rang through her fingers and into her body. With it, the vision of her Trader Joe's brown paper bag with unopened credit card bills. The top folded over neatly hiding away her dirty secret.

Even after Norah had handed her the silver envelope opener, Elle hadn't the courage to use it. "Eventually they'll just write me off, won't they?" She'd asked Norah. "Other companies are sending me more credit cards so it can't be that bad." Unknown phone numbers had started calling and leaving messages that she neither answered nor listened to. And the shock of the metal hanger on her finger was a little warning. The glamorous yet casual gold shirt sprouted lips saying, *Don't let me fool you. You don't really need me.* She wanted to gouge out the impulsive part of her brain with one of the store's metal hangers.

The saleswomen must have seen the strained expression on Elle's face and was heading toward her new customer. But that would be the end; she would give in if someone offered her help or god-forbid a sale. Without hesitation, Elle turned on her peep-toe heels attempting to not meet anyone's glances as she scurried back to her car.

It was too much, this self-reflection that came at inopportune moments. By the time she was parked at the Clubhouse, she already regretted her decision. Checking the clock on her phone, she calculated the time it would take to buy the shirt, maybe even the shoes, and return in time for Norah.

A hard knock on the passenger window made her jump and nearly throw her phone into the dashboard like she'd been caught. When she looked up incredulously, Norah's face peered through the window at her.

"Did you want to come in?" Norah shouted through the window.

"Not tonight." She wasn't open to any other opportunities at self-reflection.

"How was the party?" Elle asked once Norah was seated next to her.

"It was fine." Norah scooted her rump around in the seat, then added, "They don't know how to throw a real party."

Elle couldn't think of anything to say. She really didn't feel like conversing.

"Your grandfather and I used to throw great parties."

Elle glanced over at Norah whose head was leaned back on the headrest, peering dreamily out the window as they drove down the Pacific Coast Highway.

"It's all about the music and the cocktails."

There was no denying the truth of that statement.

"The Clubhouse doesn't even allow cocktails." Norah said.

Elle could see her grandmother glance in her direction. Her silence seemed to be a frustration.

Norah fingered her pearl necklace. "Your grandfather could make a mean Grand Marnier martini."

"That's Aaron's favorite drink." The words came out of Elle like a croak.

Norah didn't act surprised by the words or their presentation. "They would have gotten along well."

***

The burning began in her chest during the drive home. She could feel it behind her sternum, an emotional heart burn.

As Elle pulled the car into the driveway, her heart was pounding fast and loud like the needle of her sewing machine. By the time she helped

Norah inside and up the stairs, Elle's skin was itching. She wanted to claw at it, but she realized where the itch was coming from. An allergy to the white gold of her wedding ring that had developed in minutes. An allergy to anything that reminded her of Aaron, of her lost life, of her ruined marriage. It took effort to *not* slam the door, but she knew how Norah reacted to slammed doors.

Tears stung her eyes in anger more than sadness. Her whole body felt on fire. She wrenched the wedding ring off of her finger.

Why was there a stupid cooling off period? She wanted to sign the papers, mail them in with the ring attached and be rid of everything. She wanted to erase the part of her brain storing images and memories of Aaron. She wanted to be done with self-reflection and self-help and self-betterment. She wanted to hide away from the whole world like she was hiding from the creditors.

Her breathing was erratic until she found a place under blankets and pillows in the corner of the closet to hide the ring under, as though it were alive, speaking to her and had to be suffocated.

A sharp rapping on her bedroom door caught her off guard. There was a relief in opening the door to this claustrophobic room. Norah was on the other side in her ankle-length nightgown and house shoes. Her natural hair sticking out in odd directions startled Elle, having grown accustomed to Norah in her wig.

Her grandmother didn't speak, only sat down, sinking into the cloudlike comforter. She stretched out her hand to Elle, pulling her down next to her, then reaching up and drawing the hair out of Elle's face. Years of gestures identical to this one steadied Elle. There was comfort in knowing that someone was steady and constant in her life.

In the dim luminescence of the moon, Elle found safety and the ability to put words to the questions smoldering inside her. She took a breath then let them out in a whisper, "Why can't my marriage be like yours? Why did I inherit mom's curse?"

At first her questions were met with silence, and though Elle couldn't see Norah's face, she knew Norah was processing an answer.

"Oh Elle," Norah began. Her voice was as quivery as Elle's. "I wish I had the marriage you've seen in pictures. Marriage is never as easy as it looks on the outside. Ours was full of ups and downs, years of neglect and distrust and pain. But we trudged through it."

Elle pictured Norah's hands dirty while working at her marriage the way they were when she worked in her garden. What would the yard look like if Norah didn't put in as much time and sweat as she did? The beauty and color would disappear until only the weeds were thriving.

"I could tell you stories, boy could I. But I never did because I wanted you to see the smiling pictures, and I wanted you to know it was possible."

With her senses heightened in the lowlight, Elle heard her grandmother swallow.

"I wanted that for your mother too." Norah swallowed again prematurely, steadying the cadence of her words. "But something happened—to her."

A story began, and Elle's room seemed to turn into a theater with the light of her imagination projecting the picture like a movie in the dark.

A teenage Charlene finally moving out from her parent's home, starting a summer job. A girl who hadn't had the best of reputations in high school: her miniskirts too short and her liquid eyeliner too thick. The boys liked it, but the girls called names. Her humble apartment only blocks away from her parent's house gave a feeling of safety while still having the independence of a woman. She too dreamed of making her way up the hill to a house by the beach; she only had to find the right path.

She'd continued to hang out with friends left over from high school, and on the beach one night, dancing to the Rolling Stones, Charlene drank a bit too much and wandered off to find the bathroom. It was a free-standing building near a park with swing sets. And after she relieved herself and started back to her friends, a strong arm grabbed her from behind. The man, barely taller than her but solid, dragged her behind the building and raped her.

Elle gasped. Her heart couldn't decide whether to race or to stop. She suddenly realized where the story was leading.

Charlene laid behind the building long after the man was gone. She didn't remember his voice or if he even spoke, only his grunts. Once she got up, she sat on the park swings crying until she had the energy to walk to her friends. Someone drove her home—to her parent's house. She let herself in and sat in the living room alone until morning when Norah made it downstairs for coffee.

Norah had been startled by Charlene's presence, but then once again by her appearance. Sticks and grass in her hair. Makeup smeared down her cheeks. A dead stare in her eyes.

Norah helped Charlene to the bathroom to wash up. They didn't use rape kits back then. This wasn't a thing people talked about and there was no way to know who had done this to her.

Weeks went by and Charlene started to heal ever so slowly, to feel like she had feet again. Norah's husband, Larry, handled the news by drinking and rarely looking his daughter in the eye. But after a couple months, Charlene wound up on Norah's couch crying again.

She was pregnant.

Charlene knew her reputation—one that had some truth in it—and she knew no one would believe her. So she never told anyone. Even Elle.

After the baby girl was born, Charlene had moved back home and set up a nursery in the spare room upstairs that had been hers before. She felt like she was moving backwards, but it was all she could do to survive.

"You see, you are more like her than you know." Norah said as the projection of the story faded from Elle's eyes and turned back to real time.

Tears spotted Elle's shirt, her neck and chest. "Why didn't anyone tell me?"

"She didn't want you growing up knowing you came from such pain or thinking you were unwanted." Norah squeezed Elle's hand, and the physical touch was an electric shock. "Because you were loved so much."

There was no way for Elle to form words. She couldn't even decipher where the vein of anger turned to betrayal then pumped relief in finally knowing the truth.

"And I thought it was best. Everything Charlene did these years was to support you." These were the first words of Norah's louder than a whisper.

Elle snorted.

"There is more than one way to be a good mother." Norah said. "She was given a hard situation, and she did her best. I kept you as much as I could while she went off trying to find the right job so you two could get your own place."

And they had. Elle remembered it. The small one-bedroom apartment with brown floral wallpaper. But she also remembered being kicked out of it.

"She went on job interviews all across the country where expenses were lower." Norah explained. "Mine was the only help she would accept.

I know she always intended on coming back to get you when the money was right."

Norah's grip was strong and steady on Elle's forearm, reminding Elle how wrong she was to think of Norah as fragile or weak. This woman had seen decades of hurt and pain, and not only survived them but shaped herself around them. She may not have been the perfect mother or grandmother, but she had always been there. Availability spoke more than perfection ever could.

"By then your grandfather had long passed and Bruce had moved with his family and I was retired so I had all the time in the world to play with my granddaughter."

Elle formulated a question. "If I was here so much, why don't I remember him?"

"Your grandfather? He was a complicated man to begin with but what happened to Charlene–" She trailed off, and then started anew. "He was angry. Not at all with Charlene but the fact that he couldn't control what happened. And he couldn't look at her. Charlene thought it was because he was ashamed of her—and you—but that wasn't it. He couldn't look at her because it reminded him how powerless he was. And in a way, she inherited that. She learned to control other things."

Elle knew that part; she had lived that part.

"See, what you call controlling, I call coping." Norah added. "Sometimes I think it was the pain that killed him. It was a heart attack of course, but I think inside he was hurting and wouldn't let it out, so it found its own way out."

She patted on Elle's hand again. "Don't ever do that. Don't bury the pain and hurt."

"I think it's too late for that." Elle managed.

A cloud moved in the night sky allowing more moonlight in the room as if on cue.

"You're wrong. You didn't inherit this. We all made choices along the way, good or bad, but it's never too late to change your direction."

Elle thought better of arguing. Instead she snuggled up next to Norah like she had the first night she'd moved back. Against her grandmother, she was warm and safe. Next to Norah felt like home. And the burning in her chest was gone.

18

JOCELYN

Every minute available, Jocelyn snuck Scott's laptop open and read his journals like it was the latest James Patterson novel. While he was in the shower, when he was in PT, during his days at work. She was slowly falling in love with the man on the pages she read. The man she always loved. But when she closed the laptop screen, he was gone. His body walked through their home, but that wasn't who she loved. It wasn't because of the scars or brokenness. She longed for the man in the journals because he was the man she had been waiting for to come home. As though the man at the dinner table with her was an imposter.

The journals called to her, but she pulled herself away to clean the house and keep up with Ian, although it was evident that things were sliding. Not just because of the journals.

Her dry erase board may have been time blocked neatly, but the heavy schedule was nearly impossible. Mornings like this one, she woke at dawn to fill lunch boxes, help dress both males, taxi Scott to work then race to get Ian to Mother's Day Out. And it didn't stop there. Dropping them off began the sprint to finish her errands and chores and cleaning before picking Ian up and übering Scott from work to therapy. Purple crescents draped her eyes when she went without makeup, and today she'd forgotten deodorant.

Evening was closing in. The sun was so low in the sky that it almost made the earth feel off-kilter. Or maybe that was just Jocelyn. She hadn't figured out how to live in her new life yet. If this was her family's new normal, she was certain she couldn't keep up.

Standing in her kitchen, watching the sun return to its other home, she wished she could escape the days just as easily. Dinner had not gone as planned. Cooking for a pre-schooler was different than cooking for a grown man. Even Scott's tastes in food had changed. Her homemade spaghetti sauce was now too watery and he argued with why she put vegetables in everything.

"It's spaghetti," he said. "Why does it have to have bell peppers and mushrooms?" He hadn't said it meanly, but it bruised her. And affected Ian. She saw his brown eyes watch as big, strong, heroic daddy quarantined all the vegetables on the side of the plate. And she wanted to throw the spaghetti noodles at Scott and say, *This is the way it has always been! Why are you ruining everything now?!*

A bitterness festered. Bitterness that she tried every day to push back. She didn't even know who or what or where the bitterness was directed. It wasn't Scott's fault he was hurt. It wasn't the army's fault. But the point was, none of it was Jocelyn's fault. She was the good, supportive wife taking care of life on the home front as they say. And yet she felt punished.

Just rest so you can get better. She told him after the spaghetti fiasco.

But Scott didn't want to rest. When his body couldn't keep up with the energy coursing through him, he fidgeted. The energy pushing him to walk unassisted was a living, breathing entity in their home. The obsession to run again, work out the way he had before, prove to the doctors and everyone, was Scott's mistress. When he wasn't at work or therapy, he was using his pushup bar, or doing chinups on the playground monkey bars while Ian played or attempting squats to mobilize his knee again.

She prayed he wouldn't reinjure what they had spent so much time waiting to heal. Not only his body, but their marriage.

So here she was in the kitchen with dish soap bubbles clinging to her elbows and sleeves, avoiding Scott as much as he was avoiding her. Until she realized what time it was. The bath was supposed to be running for Ian—a must after spaghetti night—but she couldn't hear it. The nights before Mother's Day Out were earlier than usual and he hadn't done his nightly chores. Jocelyn didn't make him do much at his age, but she believed he could still be helpful and responsible within reason for being four. He had a few freshly laundered clothes to put away, clean up the toys left in his room and brush his teeth.

"Ian," she hollered out when she saw his bathroom empty. When there was no response, she hollered a little louder, wiping her hands on a kitchen towel, embroidered with a T.

"He's back here." Scott hollered back.

Closer to the bedroom, Ian's giggles rang out. They emerged as full on belly laughs when she opened the door. There was Scott and Ian sitting on the yellow comforter, her son wearing the spaghetti sauce like a night mask. Orange stains were all over his mouth, cheeks and chin, with a smidgen in his eyebrow. All toddlers were messy, but Ian had never outgrown it.

"Why aren't you in the bath?" Her hand on her hip in typical mom pose.

Ian's eyes fixed on the television screen in front of him, his thumbs moving adeptly over the buttons, "We're playing Lego Star Wars."

Jocelyn glared at Scott, who also found the screen more important than her. "You were supposed to give him a bath, and it's–" She looked at the clock at her bedside. "Eight o'clock! It's already his bedtime."

No one looked her way. Scott kept playing when he answered her, "It's just one night."

"Yes, but he has to wake up early in the morning. And look at him."

Scott looked up and shrugged. "He asked to play video games."

So many responses she wanted to yell at him that she ground her teeth against her tongue until she could choose. *Of course he asked to play video games. He's four.* Or, *Is the new Scott always going to give in to what the four-year-old wants to do?* Or, *I didn't realize I had two children to raise.* But instead she picked, "Well he doesn't make the decisions around here."

Her husband put his controller down and raised an eyebrow at her, "And you do?"

Indignation rose from her toes. "Yes, in fact, I've had to since you've been gone," then inadvertently glancing at his leg, she added, "And pretty much since you've been home."

The sounds of the game had stopped. Ian had paused it and was watching her, sitting next to his dad as if on his side.

"It's one night, Jocelyn. He can stay up a little late *one night*. It's not that big of a deal."

Her voice took on a higher, annoying alarm-clock pitch than she wished when she spoke next, "But it happens to be one night that he has to go to bed on time or he'll be a zombie tomorrow. And I'll pay for it. Any other night would be fine. Just. Not. Tonight."

"Bullshit."

That one word was a punch in the gut. Long ago they agreed never to curse in front of Ian, and they had stuck to always, military or no military. It was like Scott was taking all their family rules, crapping on them, and flushing them down the sewer with that one undermining word.

But he didn't stop his attack there. "Any other night you would have an excuse for him to not break *your* little routine. You can't bend at all, can you? Everything has to be your way. You can't let him have any fun unless you plan it."

The heat of Ian's eyes penetrated her. "That's how *you* feel." She had to catch her breath, grit her teeth. "Don't put your feelings off on him."

Scott shook his head, sounding almost surprised at his realization. "You're ridiculous. You're controlling. You can't let anything go. That's one way to become a bad mom."

"Don't say that! Mom's good mom! Don't say that!" Ian yelled, jumping off the bed and grabbing on to Jocelyn around the thighs, his spaghetti coated face rubbing her pants. "I won't play anymore. I want to take a bath."

Jocelyn's feet were rooted in concrete, unable to move or dodge the words flying across the room.

Scott laughed out loud. "Good job, Joss. Ruining his fun. He asked to play, and now he'll do whatever just to please you."

She bent down and picked Ian up, feeling his heartbeat against her as he rested his head on her chest.

"Come on, buddy," Scott scooted to the edge of the bed and tried to grab Ian from her. "You can take a bath tomorrow. Let's finish our game."

If she had lasers shooting from her eyes, they would have done more damage to him than a thousand RPG's in the war.

Torn between two parents, two worlds, Ian's hold on her loosened. Maybe she was too hard, too tightly wound around her own schedule. If he fell asleep during class tomorrow or gave his teachers hell… But maybe parenting was part leading the bumpy way and part watching them fall. So long as you were there to pick them up, Band-Aid their scuffed knee and kiss away the trails of tears. Four years old just seemed too young to learn that lesson.

In Scott's eyes, Ian seemed like this big kid because he had grown so much while Scott was away. Jocelyn knew how little he still was. Some things could only be learned the hard way. As much as she was white-knuckle gripping, she had to let go. She had to let Scott be the fun play-video-games-all-night parent, and take the hit when Ian was zombified.

"Fine. Go play, Ian." But he didn't grab the video game controller.

"Come on, buddy. We'll finish this level. It's your favorite." To Jocelyn's ears Scott sounded predatory, offering the little boy candy.

The rounded question in Ian's eyes haunted her as he stared at her instead of the screen. He was asking her permission. So she gave it by turning and leaving the room.

Somewhere around 9 o'clock, she heard the game silenced and Scott tell Ian to get his pajamas. She had put his folded laundry and scattered toys away, packed his sack lunch. When she went into his room to say good night, his spaghetti sauce encrusted face and unbrushed teeth had already carried him to dreamland.

An invisible wall kept her from her bedroom and husband that night. What he had said was enough. There was no sense in rehashing. Her husband had changed, that was all, and she didn't like what she saw.

***

Padded steps in the hall woke her. What outburst would she have to wade through this morning? Never before had she dreaded facing her own husband. This man whom she had waited for. Maybe she was still waiting.

When he turned the corner into the kitchen, she didn't turn around right away. She kept cleaning up the pans from Ian's scrambled eggs. After 30 seconds his stare burned through the back of her camisole. She puffed her cheeks, making a face to herself, then turned. She was faced with a more rugged version of the man she married. His milk chocolate eyes softened, and in his flannel shorts and plain white tank, he looked like the stubbly 19-year-old boy she promised to wait for…forever. His strong arm wrapped loosely around his one crutch. He treated it the way a hiker uses a walking stick instead of the item he detested not long ago.

How could everything look so different the next morning? The sunlight revealing her husband after the darkness passed. The opposite effect of waking after a drunken night next to someone you don't know. This man, she recognized.

"Hey," was all he said, but the smirk on his face said he knew he'd already won the fight.

Was her mouth hanging open as she stared at him? She sucked her bottom lip into her mouth. Maybe he *could* see her thoughts on her face. A tug in her belly wanted to reach for him, craved the touch of his skin, but she was stuck. His words last night, his actions had impaled her. He had taken everything she was, everything she spent every day doing and everything that had helped her survive without him, and he made it all inconsequential. Her whole life felt small and naked. She dropped her eyes and grabbed a hand towel from the sink.

"Hey," he repeated, but the smirk was gone. He reached for her arm and almost lost his crutch leaning toward her. "Joss, I don't know why I've been acting this way. I know I'm wrong. I just feel helpless. It's like I was watching us fight last night, and I couldn't get myself to stop or shut myself up. I–I'm sorry,"

Dismissing him would have been easy, even justifiable. She could have poked holes through his excuse until it was swiss cheese. She could, if she didn't believe him. But she knew him. Parts of him were different, parts of him were broken, but his core hadn't changed.

"Can't you forgive me?" His voice was small, and there was a hint of Ian in it.

"Of course," Jocelyn gave no hesitation, but there was a phantom shadow swimming underneath the surface in each of them. "Of course, I forgive you." When he reached for her in relief, she stepped back. "It's just that," How to say it without cutting him the way he had her? "Is that how you feel? Do you think I'm a tight ass?"

"Well, you do *have* a tight ass." He winked at her.

She couldn't help but laugh. "Working out that specific area is a part of my *strict routine*." She did air quotation marks around the last two words, mocking his words from the night before. "But it really hurt what you said. My entire life is my routine."

"It doesn't have to be that way though, does it?"

That simple statement, even after everything had cooled off, weighed more than he could ever know. There was no way to explain that if she let her routine slip, she would lose who she had become all together. The temptation was too great to stop. Like a diet, she couldn't afford to cheat even a bite. Or she'd be lost.

Control. Even as she thought it, she knew what he would say, what anyone would say if they heard her argument. *Control freak.* That's what they would call her. But it wasn't that simple. It wasn't about controlling the things around her. It was being in control of herself. The sky-high schedule she'd created, the endless list of to-do's, gave her mind a place to wander when her toes were on dangerous ground. She knew what to expect in her schedule. Accepting a hairline crack in the surface of her routine, the air could leak out, the water could seep in, and she would drown in her own thoughts. The air was thinning just as she thought of it. Her worst fears had almost happened, and if she let herself stop for a moment to consider them, she might forget how to breath all together.

When Ian finished dressing himself for "school" as he insisted on doing, his shoes were on the wrong feet and the Scott shaped pillow was tucked under his arm.

Scott turned back to Jocelyn and spoke through clamped teeth, low enough that only she could hear. "He lugs that stupid doll around with him all the time when I'm right here."

In those few words, Jocelyn was sad all over again. Even in his trying, he had learned nothing from the night before. He still didn't understand how the familiar had helped she and Ian make it through. She matched his volume when she spoke, "You told him that pillow would keep you with him all the time. That's all he wants. That's all he's ever wanted."

***

"Bye Dad." Ian said through the rolled down window as Scott fumbled getting out the car on his third day back at work. His seat was pushed back as far as it could go, but he still had trouble getting out of the car without bending his leg.

"Bye Ian." He said looking over his shoulder into the back seat, a gesture which came noticeably easier than it had a week earlier. "Bye." He said to Jocelyn, leaning in for a kiss. She wanted passion, but it was a light, obligatory peck.

Watching him from behind as he walked to the front door, working to make the crutches look like accessories instead of necessities, she noticed that the broadness of his shoulders was pulling at the shirt of his uniform.

Her day was both empty and full with both of her guys away. She made her rounds to the PX and Commissary, embarrassed that this was her biggest social interaction.

The day had hardly started for Jocelyn when it was already over and it was time to shuffle Scott from work to PT. Ian fell asleep in his car seat while driving from MDO to Scott's new job with the headquarters platoon, so she waited in the car for him to come out. When he emerged from the doors, he was scowling. He had never been a desk-job kind of guy.

"How was the office, honey?" She tried to sound light as he crammed himself in the car.

"I thought Afghanistan was hell." He jerked the seatbelt across his midsection, then held his hands up to her, revealing a slew of thin red papercuts all over both of his hands. "I was on leave form prep today."

Jocelyn tilted her head, trying her best to hide the smirk that bit at her mouth. "More war wounds."

"Have you heard from Alexis lately? Anything new on Paul?"

The jump from papercuts to Paul and Alexis wasn't lost on Jocelyn. She knew he was thinking of Paul's honorable retirement and the emotional fallout with every leave form he touched.

"Not a lot. Alexis has been taking as many shifts at the bar to make up for his income. He started weekly counseling." Paul had only been off suicide watch for a week or so.

Dropping Scott off at therapy, she craved a read of his journals but cursed inside that she'd left the laptop at home. For a moment it felt like she was having an emotional affair with the man in the journals. But it was her own husband. She scoffed at herself.

Pulling her phone out, she took a second to tap out a quick response to a long unanswered message from Elle Holloway. "How was Ian's birthday party? How are you?"

Ian stirred in the back seat, waking from his brief nap. He rubbed his puffy eyes and pushed out his lips in a waking pout. "I have to go potty." He finally said.

Once she had rushed Ian inside, she decided to wait for Scott outside the PT clinic. Voices came from behind closed white doors. Ian looked up at his mom and hugged his Daddy Doll. The voices were Scott's and Holt's.

"I can't." The growl of Scott's voice.

"Do it anyway." Said Holt's.

"I can't do it."

"Then quit."

Her weight shifted in an attempt to spy through the slats of the door, but only a sliver of Scott could be seen seated on a mat with a green exercise band pulled around his straightened right leg.

Holt's voice returned. "There you go."

Scott grunted, pulling the band back stretching his leg a fraction more.

"You wouldn't quit on your men." Holt said between counting down the seconds of the stretch. "Don't quit on yourself."

Scott's breath came out ragged when he released the band. Pinpricks stung Jocelyn's eyes. She wanted to rush the room and let him borrow another piece of her strength, be the loudest voice cheering him on like she had in his football days. But watching him start the stretch all over again, pulling the exercise band back toward his hips, she knew that no one could do this for him. Only he could dig deep, find his own power.

Taking a silent step back, she patted Ian's back and motioned her head that they would head back to the car. Ian followed. Her shoulders straightened when she felt his hand slip into hers.

A half hour later, Scott exited the Clinic doors. She handed Ian the tablet they'd been playing on. "How'd it go?" She asked as though she hadn't seen or heard anything.

"Fine." He slammed the car door shut.

Not until they were home, after dinner when Scott finished loading the dishes in the washer, he whispered, "Would you still love me if I couldn't dance with you again?"

The words broke her. It was as heartsore as she'd ever heard him. "Stop." She didn't yell. She didn't have the energy to yell.

His voice had been strong. Hers was quiet. Those were their differences in every way. He was bold. She was italics. When he was violent orange fire, she was matte gray. He was magnetic to her, even in middle school. But she often wondered what he saw in her that made him stick. It couldn't be possible that his taste buds craved blandness.

But they had been married too long. There could be no more statements questioning loyalty or love. They weren't teenagers anymore. "You have to stop saying those things."

Then she added, "I want you to know something." A part of her she'd never told him. Another talk left unsaid until now. "I've always wondered what you saw in me. I never thought I was beautiful. I was always awkward and average. But when you looked at me, I felt beautiful. And even though I didn't understand why you thought so, or what you saw that I didn't, I believed you. And it changed the way I saw myself. I may not look at myself in the mirror and think the words, but because you love me and that little boy in there loves me, it's changed what I see. I believe you. Now I need you to believe me when I say I'm here, and I'll always be here."

She used her bare foot to close the dishwasher door, then she grabbed his hands, damp from the sink.

"Dance with me." She placed his hands on either sides of the curve of her waist, leaning in to his body. He balanced himself against the edge of the countertop, and he swayed with her. Hips against hips. Jocelyn tilted her nose up against the curve of his neck. Imagining them on the beaches where they grew up, feet planted in the sand, swaying to the ocean breeze.

He drew her in closer if that was possible.

Then jolting her eyes open, Ian barreled against them, arms wrapped around all their legs, giggling. "Group hug!"

"Be careful," Jocelyn said, about to push Ian back from Scott's leg.

But Scott didn't care. He picked Ian up, the returned strength in his arms making the action easier. Wrapping one arm around Jocelyn's back and holding Ian close with the other, Scott wiggled his fingers under Ian's arms making the little boy shriek with pleasure.

"No tickles!" Ian squealed between giggles. Then when Scott stopped, Ian said "Again!" with a giant smile.

Scott put Ian down, tickling his ribs and said, "Run from the tickle monster!" Off Ian ran, the sound of laughter trailing behind him. But

Scott returned his hands to Jocelyn's waist. "I'll lay him down, and I'll meet *you* in the bedroom."

A familiar twinkle shone from his eyes, the one she hadn't seen since their last Skype meeting.

"Yeah?"

Scott nodded and kissed her cheek. Then he took a step in the direction Ian ran and started roaring like a monster, "The tickle monster is looking for a little blonde boy!"

Ian's cackles could be heard all the way from his bedroom. Jocelyn smiled. This felt familiar.

Rushing to the bedroom, she changed into *the* panties and a lacy bra. Quickly sprayed a bit of perfume on and fluffed her hair, took a deep breath before stepping into the bedroom. Scott was standing just inside the room with the door closed—and locked—behind him. He glowed.

This was how she had imagined them coming together nearly every day he was gone. She'd waited for so long. Stepping closer to him, she placed her hand on his battered chest, taut underneath her fingers. Her eyes fell to the pink scar on his jawline. Gently touching her lips to the edges of it, she felt Scott's breath in her hair.

With his hands along the small of her back, he pulled her around to the edge of the bed and laid on it. Leaning his body over her, his fingers touched the black lace edges of her bra straps. "I like this one." He said with his familiar, wry smile. She smiled back, every emotion bubbling and boiling under the surface of the smile. She was so splendidly happy in this moment and so sick for the time they had wasted getting to this moment. A whimper slipped out of her, but Scott took encouragement from it. He slid the strap from her shoulder and replaced it with his lips. If Scott glanced just right he would see her heart beating through her chest; if he touched her the right way, he would feel the blood racing through her veins, injected with adrenaline.

His hands slid under her, arcing her stomach to his.

Then he stopped abruptly lifting himself off her. "Joss," he spewed her name pained, leaning his forehead against the headboard above her. "I don't think I can–" He broke off.

Humidity clung to her body. She propped herself up on one elbow, almost cheek to cheek with him then. "We'll keep trying." Kissing the line of his collar bone, she felt the flexed muscles like wires under the skin of his protracted shoulder as he held himself above her.

"No." Arms failing, he threw himself down next to her. "I think it's the meds. I want to. I just can't."

His words registered to her. "Oh," her voice revealed more disappointed than she wanted. She was cold now where his body had been. "Okay." Everything had its side effects. Even loving someone.

He punched the headboard and she flinched.

All the built-up tension and excitement had nowhere to go but threatened to release in the form of tears. Another fracture between them. But in order to give proper care to a wound, you have to pull the bandage back and have the courage to look at it. It isn't pretty. Sometimes it's scary. But the desire for change must outweigh the desire for comfort.

"It's okay." She repeated. But she wasn't sure if either of them believed that. Scott's unspoken question hung in the room, *Would you still love me if....?*

19

ELLE

By the time the spring blooms were bursting in their cocoons ready to show their colorful heads to the sun, Elle was used to her knees aching from picking weeds on Sunday afternoon and Norah's house had earned the title of *home*. She'd come home one spring day to find a truck and flatbed trailer parked in front of the house next to Brandon's car. The truck's owner was inside seated next to Brandon at the kitchen table having iced tea with Norah. Elle smiled a "hello" at Brandon, then after the who's-this look that Elle gave, Norah introduced Juan as the "nice young boy who does the yard."

"After all these months of me doing your dirty yard work, now you tell me you have yard man."

Norah laughed, a laugh that made its appearance more often now. "You didn't think I got out there and mowed all that grass myself, did you?" And laughed again. "He does the yard. You do the garden." Norah's energy had returned, and it seemed, so had her inner light.

Brandon, whose Friday appointment with Norah often ran late enough that Elle crossed paths with him, stood from the table. His legs were infinitely long. "I should go."

He patted Norah tenderly on the back, a gesture her grandmother leaned in to. A strand of envy curled through Elle at the way Norah admired him. Here she was the one who had given up everything to help Norah, and she was overlooked.

To ease her conscience, Elle walked him out. He was dressed, as always, in standard blue scrubs and tennis shoes. The first time she'd met him, she thought his neon green shoes, thin-framed glasses and rubber band bracelets were his way of holding on to his youth. He was, after all, old enough to have salt and pepper hair.

"So is that what she does while I'm gone all day? Let yard boys into her house and seduce them with ice tea?"

They both laughed, but Brandon answered the question veiled behind sarcasm. "Norah's one of my most active clients. She goes on walks every day, waters the plants, cleans nearly everything she touches. Things just take her a lot longer."

Holding the door open for Brandon and the black case he rolled behind him, Elle caught herself staring at the V of his back. When he turned, heat rose in her cheeks. She tried to drop her gaze, but he met her with a smile so wide on a narrow face that it seemed to take over. He wasn't laughing at her, he was *seeing* her, which made her cheeks even warmer.

On the porch outside the door, an enormous box blocked the pathway. It was almost as tall as her.

Elle swung her head around to Brandon, raising an eyebrow. "What's this?"

"It was here when I arrived, and it hasn't budged." Brandon said, tilting his head toward the house. "She wouldn't let me move it. Or talk about it."

Before Elle could ask if he knew what it was, Brandon continued.

"I think it's an electric wheelchair?" He said it like a question that Elle should know the answer to, and she did. She had followed up with Medical after her mom left to get that damn chair delivered. After months she had all but forgotten about it. Thrilled at its arrival, she started pulling the edges of it open.

As if she'd been cued, Norah shuffled Juan out the front door. He passed the group wordlessly and headed to his truck, while Norah pointed one crooked finger at the box, said, "I will *not* use that thing," turned and walked away.

Brandon rubbed the bottom of his clean-shaved chin, measuring Elle's reaction. "I'm overstepping my bounds here, and I don't want to get in trouble with my boss, much less Norah." A chuckle lay under those last words. "But I think you should know since selling the car she's been calling taxis to take her around."

No words exited Elle's gaping mouth. In Brandon's tall, lean shadow she felt like a child.

"It's not uncommon for there to be difficulties in letting go of one's independence. Norah's a socialite, and she's taken matters into her own hands." Brandon gestured toward the oversized box. "That doesn't spell independence. It makes her an invalid."

Brandon shrugged like he didn't know what else to say. Empathy swirled in Brandon's dark eyes in a way Elle hadn't felt toward Norah. He was the one person taking Norah's feeling into account. And he was, in effect, a stranger. She envied his ability for such compassion. As far as she had come, there was still so much for her to learn.

Every step as he walked to his car held a casual confidence. Not until he looked back at her from his front seat did she realized she was leaning against the doorframe watching him. He smiled again in a way that made her skin prickle, but she brushed the feeling aside like the pile of crumbs Norah had swept from the floor.

"What was that all about?" Norah asked as she closed the broom in its closet.

Elle shrugged out of her thoughts. "We were talking about you, of course."

Norah clucked her lips. "Shame. He's such a nice young man."

He's got to be a decade older than me. Elle almost retorted. But Norah continued, "And those arms. He can help me up the stairs any time."

"Norah!" Elle shrieked.

There was a sparkle in her eyes that melted the years away and revealed who her grandmother had once been. The young single girl, skin taut and wrinkle-free, hair strawberry blonde with 1940's curls. She was funny and flirty once again. The girl who didn't have to buy her own dinner for months as beau after beau took her out.

"You keep talking about him like that and I'll have to replace him with some middle-aged overweight woman." Elle teased.

"You'd notice his arms too if you were ever here to talk to him for more than five seconds." Norah shuffled toward the front of the house to the stairs. Elle noticed Norah didn't even glance in the direction of the boxed wheelchair as if it weren't there at all. "You should notice his arms.

And his eyes. They brighten when he talks."

"I'm married, Norah. You know that."

"Hmm, I'd thought you'd given up on that one." Norah's gaze focused on the stairs in front of her.

Elle cued up next to Norah, holding her arm out as a support in the only real way that she ever had. Norah's full weight pulled on Elle as she lifted one foot to the next step. She wore her white converse walking shoes today.

"You're the one who told me it was never too late to give up."

With no hesitation in her step or her words, Norah replied, "You're the one who told me it was."

They were halfway up the staircase before Elle could think of a new subject. By then even Elle was out of breath being the one-sided crutch for Norah to lean on.

"Should we maybe unpack that box tomorrow? Give it a try?"

An exasperated "Pfffft," was the only response.

A new strategy came to mind. "Brandon thought it might be good for you." She lied.

Norah huffed. "I don't believe that for one minute. Brandon knows how strong I am. He says so all of the time."

His eyes were in her head. The swirl she'd seen when he had spoken about Norah's need for independence. She heard the word *invalid*. That quickly, she gave in.

"Fine," she consented, "it was just a thought."

Thinking back, Norah was right. Brandon did have nice eyes.

* * *

Overwhelmed didn't describe it. Not just work. Work was the same as always. Life was getting in the way. Her brain was having a hard time juggling the new catalog, the website updates, the fall line in the works, plus Norah's doctor's appointments that Elle was trying to attend, the Medi-cal calls to return the electric wheelchair, the creditors still hounding her about her yet unopened bills.

And the business card sitting in front of her.

With great intentions Jenny had passed along the business card of a divorce attorney her friend used. In the absence of brain function, Elle had shoved the card in her top drawer, but it leered at her every time she opened the drawer. She didn't throw it out, even though she often fantasized about burning a hole in it with a blowtorch.

"Divorce is our business." The slogan on the card read.

Elle wanted to laugh and scream at the same time. Bamboo under the fingernails would be preferred to this. She should be making plans to be out with Aaron for their anniversary.

The date on her desk calendar was encircled with a red heart. No matter what work Lena piled on her desk, nothing erased that stupid heart. Friday would be their seven-year wedding anniversary. What did one do for a wedding anniversary when divorce papers had been filed? Was she to throw a party? Was she to fill herself so full of alcohol that it poured out in her tears while flipping through her wedding album?

Yes. She decided on the latter.

The plan was set. She waited late into the night when Norah was snoring in her typical fashion. The water cup on her grandmother's nightstand was full and the bendy straw was facing her direction so that when she woke in the middle of the night, Norah wouldn't need help getting around for a midnight drink of water. Because Elle was intent on getting trashed. She would probably call in to work the next day.

There was a stockpile of alcohol in the garage, and her wedding album in the closet. Once those two converged, no telling what would happen. Elle hid her phone and tablet from her drunken self, so as to not send any of the awful things that she had become known for.

The appetizer was two shots of Goldschlager Aaron had saved for when she "made it big." But she was done holding on to things. Done saving them for special occasions that would never come. The liquid went down smooth and warmed the deepest parts of her belly.

After that, she lost track.

All she remembered was the unsigned divorce papers. The untouched note still residing in her purse. The business card with its ridiculous slogan.

Driving after drinking was irrational, dangerous, and she knew it. But having impaired judgment makes people do things they know they shouldn't do. Elle had proven that to be true. Phone and tablet may have been hidden, but her keys weren't.

She needed a lawyer. In her drunken state, that's all she knew. She needed a pen to sign those papers because wouldn't it be poetic justice to sign them on the date of their wedding anniversary. And she needed a lawyer. She needed that card with the lawyer's number.

There was no other way. She made it down the stairs without tripping or swaying, so she must not have drunk as much as she thought. Her vision wasn't so impaired that she couldn't get the key in the ignition. Maybe she wasn't drunk at all. She just really needed a pen. And there was one in the drawer of her desk. The same drawer as the business card. With the phone number. Of the lawyer. She needed a lawyer.

The swimming white and yellow lines in front of her car made it hard to focus, and the car stopped a little too abruptly at stoplights. But she made it. She'd forgotten how far away her office was.

Again, she got the office key into the lock on the first try. She was so not drunk.

If this had been Aaron's office, she could have shown up in a trench coat all naked underneath. He would have liked that. That would have been a *happy* anniversary.

The pen. The business card. She rode the elevator up and up until she was nauseous. Once she made it to her desk, she couldn't remember which drawer it was. The first drawer opened easily, but there were only papers in there. She fumbled through them, pulling them out, dropping them on her desk. No business card. No pen. Doing the same for the next drawer and the next. They were nowhere. Maybe they'd been sucked into an abyss. Maybe Jenny took the card back. Maybe a different friend needed it more.

Elle slumped in her office chair and leaned over the desk. She didn't want to concentrate hard enough to drive back home yet. She just wanted to cry until the tears formed ravines in her skin and finally broke her apart, shattered her into the broken pieces that she had become.

If she could just lay her head here for a few minutes, then she'd go back home. Then she could drink off this wretched day.

"Elle,"

There were other words, but she couldn't put them together. They were muffled like sound working its way through a blanket.

She opened her eyes but only saw white. It must have been the comforter from her bed. Her brain was being cracked in half with an ice pick. She closed her eyes again, trying to focus on the words. There were several voices. The television must have been left on.

Her eyes opened again, and she realized the white was the sleeves of her own shirt. Her arm was covering her face. If she moved it then she'd know where the voices were coming from, but her arm weighed more than the entire bed she was laying on. It was then she realized she wasn't lying down at all. She was leaning over, sitting in a chair. Her cheek pressed again something hard, not a pillow.

With pain shrieking through her head, down her neck into her spine, she lifted her head. Loose-leaf paper stuck to her cheek and temple. She peeled it off of her as she strained to open her eyes. The office. The desk. The pen and business card. It came rushing back in a slight fog that burned her brain as much as the light burned her eyes.

"Elle," that voice again. She looked toward the familiar voice. It was Neil from accounting. They'd hung out a few times. But when they hung out, he didn't wear suspenders over his button-up like he was now. Why was he waking her up?

Neil's lips twisted when she lifted her head from her desk. *This* was not her desk. A picture frame showed Neil and his mother. *This* was Neil's desk. The reality of what happened dawned on her slowly. Papers were everywhere, file folders emptied with their contents strewn about, some on the floor, even a few stuck under her shoe. Nope, it was her bare foot. She had no shoes on. She had driven to work with no shoes on.

"Ohmigod, I'm sorry." Her words came out as if they were all one word.

"Whoa," Neil said jerking his head back from her. "You just keep your mouth shut. Breath through your nose." He slung one of her arms around his shoulder. "I'll get you home."

Elle could totally walk on her own, but this was much more comfortable. As they walked away from Neil's messy desk, she saw Lena standing against a wall with one eyebrow perked up like the peak of a mountain. *Shit.* She looked down at her body, at least she was dressed, barring the missing shoes. "I'm really sorry." She repeated to Neil.

His head turned the other way. "Really, mouth shut. And it's okay. I'll just bill you my hourly for how long it takes me to clean up."

Elle woke again with another *I'm sorry* on her mouth. But now she was alone, and she really was in her bed. Hoping the memories that were crashing into her were all just a dream, she pulled the comforter back to see herself still fully dressed in yesterday's clothes, with no shoes. *Shit.* One of these days she would just stop drinking all together. Another blot on her already failing record.

The clock screamed 2:08 in red digital numbers. She let out a sigh and slung her body passed the edge of the bed, making her way downstairs. Coffee. Norah always had coffee ready.

She sulked down the stairs and heard muffled voices from the back porch. The backs of heads bobbed. Brandon in a lawn chair, and Norah watering the plants. Of course. Today was Brandon's appointment.

He turned with raised eyebrows as she opened the screen door. "Hey, it's Sleeping Beauty," he said while standing up to offer Elle his seat. "You look like you could use some coffee." And he was back with a cup before she realized he had left the porch.

The world around her was still foggy, but at least her head didn't hurt as bad. Brandon handed her an aspirin as he pulled up another lawn chair.

"Norah made you an omelet." Brandon told her.

"Since it's your breakfast time," Norah said to acknowledge Elle's presence, but she did so with a wink.

If her eyes didn't hurt so much, Elle might have rolled them at her grandmother's lack of subtlety.

They sat in silence. Only the wind rustled through the branches of the willow trees surrounding them. The area had always seemed so small, but now she appreciated the confined space, the tall trees guarding her from the humiliation just outside their reach.

Silence had never become her. She'd never understood how people could drive with no music or feel comfortable amongst others without talking, but sitting with these two people in silence felt oddly right. Elle let her eyes close, taking in the sounds of water spattering against the leaves, birds chirping from a roost above them unseen, the distant hum of a car passing down the road.

She heard Norah wrap up the hose, return it to its home and go inside. Even though she hadn't opened her eyes, she knew she hadn't been left on the porch alone. Brandon was there. She couldn't hear him breathing, but she could feel him. His arm was inches away from her own, causing her light arm hair to stand on end, his body creating static electricity around hers. Neither of them speaking. Neither of them moving.

Finally, she opened her eyes to take a sip of coffee. He waited in silence. She wondered how much of his life he lived in silence, moving from home to home with the elderly of a generation who were not inclined to fill the air with meaningless words.

And yet he was the one to break the silence. "It gets better," his words ringing through the willow leaves along with the wind.

She moved her head toward him without looking him in the eyes. All she could think about at this moment were those eyes. Why had Norah ever brought them up?

The words hung in the air for minutes before she responded, "You're divorced." It was a statement and a question.

In her periphery, Brandon nodded. His dark hair, stuttered with gray, was cut close to his scalp on the sides, but the longer portion on top he ran his hands through and brushed back away from his face.

She pulled one foot up onto the chair and clutched her knee against her chest. "Yesterday was our anniversary," she said in a quiet voice that wasn't her own. She hadn't told anyone and no one had mentioned it to her, but the words had been bouncing around inside her for days and were eager to escape.

Brandon didn't respond. He didn't say sorry or try to make her feel better or offer advice. He just sat with her. That gesture meant more to her than all the words that could have been said but weren't.

Her watch was inside leaving no way of knowing how long they sat, drinking coffee, in lawn chairs with the sounds of life around them. Eventually Norah broke in.

"Okay kids, tonight's gin rummy so if we're going to do dinner, then we've got to get going." She hollered out the screen door, and when Elle looked over her shoulder, her gran was already dressed and ready.

To Brandon, Elle asked, "Do you have another client or anything?"

His smile came easy, and it revealed long crow's feet that creased the sides of his face. "This is the last stop of the day."

"No kids?" Perhaps Elle was fishing for information.

He shook his head. "Dogs," he said. "It was a short custody battle." Then he laughed with ease. This time she realized how much she liked those lines. They didn't show his age; they showed an enjoyment of life.

"I'm free if you're free." His dark eyes behind the thin-framed glasses lifted to meet hers.

Why? She wanted to ask. *Why would you ever want to spend time with a mess like me?* But no words slipped out. Instead she followed him inside.

***

The dinner and uncharacteristic conversation revealed Norah's intent at an easy distraction since she knew precisely what the date was. She chose the same (non-vegan) buffet place and rehashed the same anecdotes of Elle's love of buffet steak when she was too small to see the top of the buffet line. Brandon welcomed the stories as sincerely as he did the company.

A manager Elle hadn't seen greeted Norah with her usual cup of black coffee and glass of ice water with lime. The owners had become as loyal to her as she was to them.

"You remember my granddaughter, Elle."

Elle opened her mouth to revise the introduction but the man said, "Nice to see you again."

"And this is my," Norah searched for the right word, "Friday companion, Brandon."

Elle's eyes widened, bouncing around the table. With a tilt of his head and slight hesitation, the manager shook Brandon's hand and rushed away, rescued by his managerial obligations.

A chuckle shook Elle's shoulders.

"Whatever is so funny?" asked Norah.

"Your Friday companion?" Elle repeated suggestively. "Sounds a little cougar-ish, don't you think?" With a fleeting look at Brandon, her chuckle erupted into a full laugh. Brandon wrangled his own amusement, but Elle's laugh-tears were contagious.

"Well, what would you call him? My nurse maid?"

Elle caught her breath long enough to share a smirk with Brandon after he took his thin-framed glasses off to wipe his eyes. In unison, another round burst from them both. The other tables were staring at them. For once Elle didn't care what they thought. It felt good to laugh. Refreshing.

Conversation flowed easily across the table listening to Brandon's surprising history of heading to the medical field after being a not-so-great student. They covered movies, game show picks and The Clubhouse gossip over Brandon's four buffet helpings.

"For a thin guy, you eat a lot." Elle quipped as the server cleared the table.

"You should try it." Norah gestured to the half-eaten salad in front of Elle.

"Oh," Elle remembered, "my car is at the office." Instant humiliation returned.

"I'll get a ride home so you all don't have to wait for me." Norah said, by-passing any comment on Elle's situation.

"You need a ride?" Brandon asked. His sly grin was met with an unamused expression. "To your car, obviously."

"I know you have Nice Guy Syndrome, but don't spend your Friday night running my errands." She mentally ticked off her lack of other options. It solidified her humiliation.

His eyebrow arched upward. "My Friday nights are pretty low-key."

Until recently, a low-key Friday would have been Elle's definition of a loser, but paired with an early bird dinner and sweatpants, there was an allure in low-key.

Her thin shoulders pulled into a shrug. "M'kay."

The Killers sprang from the speakers as Brandon started the car but he turned it low as they drove. As a hater of awkward silence, Elle was typically compelled into small talk, but an ease accompanied Brandon. He was as comfortable in the silence as she was among racks of designer silks.

When she stole a glance at him, his thumb casually thumped the steering wheel along to the music. This need for conversation gnawed at her. She sniffed, trying to think of what to say.

"You do that a lot." His words broke her concentration.

"Do what?"

"You sniff like that when you are about to speak."

Elle scoffed. "I do not."

"Either that or you have bad allergies."

She shook her head unconvinced. "Do I really? Nobody's ever told me that before." Although it was nice to be noticed by a man, even if it was a ridiculous observation.

He grinned his answer. That grin. It rivaled his eyes.

After more silence, comfortable silence, they pulled up next to her car sitting alone in the parking lot.

"So this is it?" asked Brandon as he looked across the street to the glass-paned office building. "This is where you make your designs come alive?"

Her confusion confused him. "Aren't you a designer?"

With a snort, Elle said, "No. I'm a glorified secretary."

At her confession, his eyes locked on hers. They were dark, shadowed by the parking lot lights, but they were steady. A piece of her wanted to look away, but the rest of her melted into the warm leather seat under his gaze.

The hypnosis lasted a couple of lines in a song, but it might as well have overtaken the whole evening. In the small space between them, she wanted to retract her answer. *Used to be a designer.* Or *it's a hobby.* Or *I gave up on that.* To explain a part of herself that he had yet to know. But those eyes staring at her. The heat between them in the idling car. It was all too much. Being drawn out of a spell, she blinked as fast as her heart pounded. She couldn't reveal who she really was, what she really wanted. How could she put into words a woman she barely knew anymore.

"Thanks for the ride." She unbuckled her seatbelt and grabbed at her purse, missing the handle the first try. But Brandon didn't move. His body turned toward her, leaning into the console.

For a second, she considered kissing him on the cheek. As a thank you of course, or to test her reading of the situation. But she couldn't. "See you next week," she said as she scrambled out the car door. Did that sound like she expected a repeat dinner? "At Norah's appointment," she amended. But she was rarely at Norah's appointments. "Or whenever." She closed the door before humiliating herself further.

Part of her wanted to turn around and see if he was staring at her, leaning toward her side of the car, but she held off. She conjured the image of a smirk tugging his lips. And she knew she wanted to see that smirk again, as often as she could.

***

The low light bled into Norah's living room, reflecting the tangerine sunset on the photograph-covered wall. Elle's phone balanced on her palm, her feelings just as imbalanced. Aaron. Brandon. One day she was married, the next she was drunk searching for a pen to sign divorce papers and the next she was gazing longingly into another man's eyes. It all felt so wrong. So rushed. So conflicting.

Marissa could make sense of all of this. The girls would lay down soon and Mar being Mar would drive over with two chai teas and sift through Elle's emotions to pick out the rocks while keeping the gold.

With the phone cradled in Elle's hand, she called the one phone number that would always pick up for her.

It rang. And rang. And rang.

"Elle, it's not a good time right now." Heath answered. That *never* happened. Maybe Marissa's kids answered when Mar was on the toilet or in the shower and she'd listen to them yelling through the house. But never Heath. She lowered herself onto the plastic covered couch, feeling the crunch under her thighs.

"I really need her. I'll owe you one, Heath. Put it on my tab."

"Not right now. Can she call you back?" His tone wasn't mad, but somber.

Goosebumps scattered across Elle's arms. "What's going on? Is everything alright? I just want to talk to her."

On the other line, there was fumbling and Marissa's grumbling, "Just give me the phone." Then she was speaking to the phone. "Now's *not* a good time, Elle."

"Are y'all getting freaky? Just say so and I'll—"

"Good god, why don't you let anything go?" Marissa's voice was swallowed by phlegm like having a cold, or...

"Are you crying?" Elle half-shrieked, so worked up that she was almost mad.

Her friend sighed a Marissa sigh that Elle was accustomed to. "Let me guess, you're calling about your anniversary." She sounded exhausted and still phlegmy. "Yep, I remembered. You're going to complain to me about how terrible *your* life is."

But that wasn't it at all. Elle wanted to jump in and defend herself, but she wasn't given the chance.

"I so hoped taking care of Norah would give you a new perspective on the fragility of life. That it would eliminate a smidgen of selfishness, but only you could make Norah's condition *your* problem. Everything is always about you. But other people have lives, Elle. Other people have heartbreak and sadness–" her voice cracked but in Marissa's way she reined it in.

"Why won't you just–" *tell me?* She was going to say but Mar interrupted in an uncharacteristic whisper.

"I had a miscarriage." The words spilled out, matter-of-factly.

Elle gasped. She wished it away immediately, but the sound had vaulted out of her gut. "I didn't know you were pregnant." Elle said, failing to recover from the gasp.

The sigh again. "We hadn't wrapped our heads around it to tell anyone yet."

Elle didn't think she was just anyone.

"Here's the thing, Elle," Mar spoke as if to a child. Or drunk and uninhibited. "I didn't bother to tell you. I wanted to, but you never gave me a chance. Sure you call all of the time, but you don't talk with me. You talk at me. About everything that is so unfair in your life, and not even once have you asked about mine."

The front door clicked shut as Norah entered her home with a smile that fell when she saw Elle's red-stained face.

Marissa's unloading broke for nothing. "It's awful that Aaron left. And this stuff with Norah. I get it, but I stopped trying to fit my life into yours."

In the background, a muffled Heath was talking to her. All else was quiet. Elle wondered about the girls but didn't interrupt to ask. Norah settled next to her. When she placed her crepe paper wrinkled hand over Elle's, that was when Elle realized her own hands were trembling.

When Marissa took a deep breath, this time a whimper escaped. "I didn't tell you I was pregnant," she stopped, perhaps regaining her ability to speak without sobbing. "I didn't tell you because you think I resent my family, that I would rather have a career than each of them. But I'm not like you. I don't want a big career. I want my husband. And I want my kids. And I want–" her words choked and sputtered, "my baby in my arms."

Her cries splintered into shards of glass, each word breaking Elle into tiny pieces with them. "Mar," She didn't know what to say. *I'm sorry* seemed too small a thing, an insult to vocabulary somehow.

She heard Heath next to his wife, his words muffled but the tone and tenderness translated clearly. When too much time passed for Elle to speak again, when it seemed like Marissa had forgotten Elle was listening, when she had given way to the grief that came with a loss Elle couldn't possibly feel equal to, Elle hung up. Norah's hand lingered covering Elle's, rubbing and patting in place of words. Because there were no words for this.

***

Months later after the hurts began healing, Marissa confessed she expected Elle to make a ridiculous statement like, "At least it was so early on that you weren't as emotional." Or "At least it was a surprise and you hadn't been trying," or "Isn't it better than something being wrong with the baby when it's born." All of which, sadly, Elle had thought. She believed she wouldn't have actually said them to her best friend. But with Elle, who could really know.

Hanging up the phone while her friend sobbed into her husband's chest, Elle forgot why she'd called. No thoughts of Brandon re-entered her mind. All focus became how to help Marissa. A sloppy brainstorming list resulted in impersonal, cliché flowers or fruit bouquets. Until an idea materialized as though divinely inspired. She texted Heath that she would watch the girls Saturday night. Tapping her taupe-painted fingernails against her teeth, she stared at her phone awaiting a response. He could think she was irrational or dangerous—being that Marissa assumed she hated kids—or maybe they wanted to share their grief as a family.

Before she completed the thought, a text came back accepting.

A warm afternoon loomed when Elle pulled into the driveway. She readied herself for Marissa's doleful eyes, puffy and red. Instead Heath flung himself through the door before she could approach. His brokenness pierced her. Somehow Elle had forgotten the loss was his as well. His shirt was halfway untucked and hands unsteady as they reached out to shake Elle's.

"Elle," his voice gravelly as he turned his gaze toward the door, "thank you for this."

When his eyes returned to her, they were circled in red and glassy. "I only told Marissa you were coming a few minutes ago." He continued, "I don't think she would have said yes on her own, but I know she needs this. She's trying to stay so strong for the girls, but I don't know if she's processing with them here."

The droop in his voice exposed his own waning strength. Hadn't Heath always been Marissa's rock? And Marissa his? Who would hold him up in his grief? Elle wanted to reach out to him, hold him the way she would his wife. The way Marissa had held her on so many occasions. So she did, in fact, reach out. Elle drew Heath to herself and embraced him between his words.

"Hey, it's going to be okay." She said against his chest.

"I know," he said stoically, but seconds later she felt his faux toughness fade and his shoulders slumped against her.

"I'll take the girls as long as you need me to," Elle said. The hug was bordering on uncomfortable, even with a man she viewed like a brother.

He pulled back with a masculine chin jutting up.

Hailey and Heidi bobbed out the door with backpacks, stuffed animals and purses, then piled into the car, oblivious to what tragedy had befallen their family.

Not knowing any better, Elle shrugged and asked, "So, what do you girls want to do?"

Rapid-fire answers nearly blew her over. "Chuck-E-Cheese! Movie! McDonald's!"

"Tell you what," she said, winking at Heath then looking at the girl's eager reflections in the rearview mirror, "we'll go to the closest one."

Which was McDonald's. Elle couldn't recall the last time she set foot in a McDonald's, but the girls could barely sit still long enough to eat. They ate; they played; they did what any little girls would do at a playground.

"Why aren't you eating?" Heidi asked between hamburger bites and slide runs.

Breathing through her mouth to avoid the smell of greasy meat-ish substance, Elle lied, "I'm not hungry. This is just for you two."

The girls sat with half-eaten food and wrappers scattered on the table, playing with their Happy Meal toys. Tiny dolls with neon pink hair. Hailey at seven and Heidi, the four-year-old culprit of the tragic email, went back and forth, sitting next to each other.

"You are so pink." Heidi started. It seemed sweet.

"You are the pinkest ever." Hailey's doll responded.

Then it got serious and quite a bit louder. Heidi stated, "*You* are pinkalicious!"

"*You are pinkarrific!*" The dolls heads bobbed against each other in intense competition.

"Okay, that's enough," Elle grabbed the dolls away. "Why don't you two wave at me from the very top of the playground?"

Their matching brown ponytails bounded off with even more energy. Two boys playing tag joined with Mar's girls, and the squealing began. That pitch in a room so small was deafening. Elle imagined herself curled up with a glass of wine. And she'd only been at it an hour. Why would Marissa want more children? Then she chided herself picturing Marissa wetting Heath's shirt with her tears, processing the loss of their child. Elle was trying, damn it. She was trying to be selfless.

A couple of tables over, two grandmothers chatted while their boys—presumably their grandsons—were running amuck. Then the boy with hipster glasses and spiked hair ran over to the tables, "Mom," he yelled to be heard over the noise.

Elle didn't register anything after that. She looked at the table of grandmothers and realized that one of them was his *mom*. She had to be at least 60 with a seven-year-old son. In Elle's naivety of children, her estimation of *his* age could be off by a year or two, but the woman's age was spot on, plastic surgery and all.

At her current rate, Elle was en route to that 60-year-old woman's life.

Aaron's words replayed over and over. He was ready for a family when babies were not even on her radar. Was she afraid? Carrying and birthing a child didn't make a mother. Intentions didn't make a mother. Then there were moms like Marissa who loved every minute, even when she wanted to pull her extra-long eyelashes out. If Elle couldn't be that type of mom, then what was the point?

"That's it." In a moment of clarity, she hollered to the girls, "You wanna spend the night with Aunt Elle?"

Hailey and Heidi gawked at her, their large, almond eyes—replicas of Marissa's—shown blank. They wouldn't know how to answer; it had never happened before. But it was about time to find out if she liked children or at least if she could cope with them for one night. Elle owed that much to Marissa. And Norah would welcome the girls with arms wide open and maybe a plate of chicken nuggets and bon-bon's *a la* Elle's childhood.

She tapped Heath a quick text who rebounded with an "Are you sure?" But she was resolute. Bedtime was near; surely she could handle them for the few hours before conking out. Two brunettes with their long, tangled ponytails couldn't be that much trouble.

Granted, Elle didn't account for the ice cream and strawberry soda she had pumped into them. When they tried to jump on Norah's couch and turn Nickelodeon up to volume 65, she announced, "Why don't we make your mom cards?!" Elle knew they were capable since she had received handmade cards from the girls every birthday since they were old enough to hold a glue stick between their chubby fingers.

"Do you have glitter?"

"I want to make mommy a handprint ballerina."

"I can write my own name!"

Their voices blurred together and she couldn't tell which one was saying what, but their enthusiasm told her she was on to something. Norah peeked around the corner of the garage and winked as they piled back into the car to purchase important items like glitter—because they agreed plenty of that was needed—construction paper and glue sticks. Approaching the check-out counter, Elle recalled Aaron encouraging her to hang out with the girls since Hailey was a toddler. Why hadn't she done it?

The white-haired man at checkout commented as the two girls talked over each other to explain what they were making. He winked at Elle, "You have beautiful girls."

She didn't correct him for two reasons. First, they really were beautiful girls. And second, for this one night she could pretend they were family as much as she liked to think of their mom as her sister. Nieces, they were her nieces, and they were a beautiful family.

***

Perhaps the glitter got a little out of hand, sticking to cheeks and toes. Although on Heidi's lush four-year-old eyelashes, Elle perceived why glittery eye shadow was invented. Glitter really does turn a girl into a princess.

When they had each painted pink handprint ballerina tutus—yes, they made Elle join in—and written their names with messages to Marissa, Elle was inspired to sew hearts on them.

"I don't know how to sew." Hailey said.

Her soft words punctuated a memory of Norah leaning over Elle, guiding her child-sized hands along fabric as it rushed through the sewing machine. Elle remember watching her grandmother's age-spotted hands that first time and how they expertly kept the line straight, the blue veins bulging and begging to be poked.

"My gran taught me how to sew." She said to Hailey. "And now I have a sewing machine of my own."

Their eyes lit up even more than the moment the bottle of gold glitter was opened.

"Can I see?" Awe filled Heidi's voice as though she had been offered her own glass slipper.

"Sure!"

Her sewing machine was still boxed up. The girls gladly sifted through the unopened boxes. There was a beauty in watching them discover stowed away treasures. At the first box of fabric, they marveled over the softness of the silk and organza—that Elle seized from their sticky hands—and asked if they could add lace to their mommy's cards.

By the time Elle agreed, Hailey forged ahead in the next box. "What are these?" She pulled out the notebooks Elle had spent her evenings pouring over for years. Notebooks she'd hoped held the key to a blossoming career but were now stored in haggard boxes in a closet.

Hailey opened the gold sketchbook on top, and Elle suppressed the urge to tell her to be careful. Instead Elle studied the seven-year-old's eyes moving over the landscape of the page. It seemed a long time for a seven-year-old entranced in one drawing.

"I like the bottom," she commented of the high-low hem, as if she were a designer herself, "but I think it should be more of a teal color instead of such dark green."

"I like that idea."

The child looked at her with Marissa's almond eyes.

"You might be a future designer yourself." Elle told her.

Hailey clung to the encouragement and turned the page.

The sewing machine search ended at the back of the closet, hidden under hemlines of off-the-rack dresses proving she'd too long given up on her dream. But regret aside, Elle knew her present company would be impressed with the simple sewing machine, and boy, was she right.

***

"Why haven't I seen any of the clothes from your sketchbook?" Hailey asked as the credits to *Frozen* streamed across the television.

Heidi had long since passed out, the three of them curled up in Elle's queen-sized bed. It was almost 10 pm after all. She had forgotten to ask their bedtime. The glittered cards were drying on the windowsill, and the design materials returned to their boxes, to certain neglect.

There was no simple answer to Hailey's question, but Elle tried her best. "I haven't made anything in a long time."

Hailey rubbed her eyes where a piece of glitter held on for dear life, her voice wispy and shy, "I remember you wearing a dress you made to my mom's birthday."

Elle nodded.

"Why don't you make them anymore?" Hailey's small body silhouetted against the brightness of the TV screen. The covert darkness relieved the question's tension.

"That's a complicated answer."

A sleepy hush lulled Elle, until Hailey spoke again, her voice small and fragile. "Could you remember how to make me a costume for my second grade performance?"

Delight pulsed through Elle's heart. She let out a laugh because in that moment it was easier to laugh than cry. "I think I could do that. But only for you."

Hailey's petite frame curled up tighter against her new found friend.

"What is your costume?"

"I'm Mary Todd." She answered flatly.

All Elle could think of was Sweeney Todd and even she knew that was absurd for second grade. "Who's Mary Todd?"

"Abraham Lincoln's wife." In her whispered voice, Elle could practically hear the girl's nose scrunched up.

"You'll be the most exquisite Mary Todd in all of history." Elle answered with a squeeze. Just like that Hailey was asleep. And Elle was going to stay right there, holding both Hailey and Heidi all night long.

20

JOCELYN

"Well, cyber friend, in my message I asked you how *you* were, but you gave me a rundown of Scott and Ian instead. So let's try this again. How are YOU doing????"

Elle's response to Jocelyn glared against her white phone screen. Scrolling up to read the last few messages she'd exchanged with Elle revealed more about herself than she'd expected.

"How was Ian's birthday party? How are you?"

Jocelyn's reply, "Sorry for the delayed response. The party was a huge hit. Scott's dad flew in for the day and stayed a couple afterwards. Scott started back at work this week and Ian began Mother's Day Out. Busy, busy."

Then Elle. "Well, cyber friend, in my message I asked you how *you* were and you gave me a rundown of Scott and Ian instead. So let's try this again. How are YOU doing????"

She positioned her fingers to type out an answer, but they stopped suspended in the air, not knowing what to type. How *was* she doing?

A refinished patio swing creaked under her weight as Jocelyn watched Ian run around catching the bubbles he had blown. Liquid sloshed out of the plastic bottle he held in his hand, but he didn't care. Spills never bothered kids. There was just enough liquid remaining to dunk the wand in again, which he did carefully, then blew more bubbles across the yard.

One lone bubble floated toward Jocelyn. In its curves, she saw the reflection of every color around her, a circular prism. She was that bubble. Tossed by the wind in every direction. Reflecting all the people around her, all the things happening *to* her. All but herself.

How was she? How would she answer that simple question when who she was and everything she did was for Scott and Ian?

Of all the messages from Elle, this one shook Jocelyn most. This woman who had been so caught up in her own life, called selfish by every person close to her, this was the one person who could pierce through Jocelyn's careless words and see that Jocelyn was losing herself. A woman she'd never met.

Even tapping out the words on a screen stung of betrayal. Guilt pooled in her throat, seeped like acid into her stomach. But the words were truth.

> *I'm drowning. That's how I am. If I'm helping Scott, I feel like I'm neglecting my son. If I'm with Ian, I feel like Scott is going through the hardest time of his life alone. I want to be all the things they need from me. But like you said, how am I? I don't even know. I'm sad. I'm scared. I'm exhausted. I'm lost in my own house. I'm alone in my own family. What do I do with that?*
>
> *P.S. Thanks for asking.*

She clicked send.

Never could she imagine saying any of those words aloud, but sometimes you can say things in an email that you would never reveal otherwise.

***

Elizabeth Cryer offered to take Ian to Chuck-E-Cheese for the afternoon while Jocelyn taxied Scott from work to PT. No mom in her right mind would turn that offer down. Although Ian was still gun shy of Chuck-E, not that she could blame him.

Since Ian's birthday party, Elizabeth was a consistent fixture in Ian's week. Like a doting aunt, she stepped in to take Ian to all the kid places that either Jocelyn couldn't afford or was overwhelmed by. Jocelyn wasn't sure if Elizabeth was more interested in helping Ian or if she was stepping in to give Jocelyn and Scott alone time. Either way, *thank you* didn't seem like a big enough statement.

The clinic halls had finally stopped feeling like the setting of a horror movie and were now as familiar as her old high school. On the way to pick Scott up, her phone buzzed. She stopped outside the door to check the message from Elizabeth. A simple text making sure it was okay to leave Chuck-E-Cheese and take Ian to the park to feed Chester the duck. Jocelyn's chest tightened. That used to be her job. She used to get the park dates. She introduced Ian and Chester—from a distance obviously—and remembered the scrunched expression Ian gave when she suggested naming the duck "Donald."

"No, Mom. His name is Chester." As though he had already squawked this over with the duck.

But her role in Ian's days had changed.

She texted Elizabeth back to confirm and asked for pictures.

As she hit the send button, Scott's voice bounded out the door along with Holt's.

"I know you want to do this on your own, Scott. You want to be strong and barrel through. But you need a team here just like you need your men over there."

Jocelyn stayed around the corner plastered to the wall, breathing shallow so no one could hear her position.

"Yes sir. You're my Captain."

"In here, I'm your CO. But I've only got you a few hours a week. What about at home? That woman has got your six. Let her."

A pause hung like a thick fog between them. Then Holt continued, "I've seen it in her eyes, the fight. She wants to fight *for* you. Don't push her out. Don't make her fight *against* you." The thick, silent fog filled her lungs making even her shallow breathing near impossible.

She didn't know if Scott nodded or did nothing, but the tapping of his crutches against the hard floor staccatoed closer. Jocelyn turned the corner still glancing at her phone, pretending she had just arrived, that she hadn't been eavesdropping. "Oh," She looked up with a start when Scott was suddenly in front of her. "How'd it go?"

"I hate this guy." He gestured with his chin behind him while his fists gripped around the crutches.

Holt patted Scott hard on the back. The pat was so strong that she thought Scott would lose balance, but he didn't. He was healing faster than he had shown her.

But there was something more Scott didn't say. He didn't have to form the words. His eyes spoke for him. *Are you going to stick this out, no matter how hard it is?*

She felt like she had been answering that question every day for over a decade. *I'll wait for you. No matter what.*

His jaw ticked, receiving her message. He just wasn't sure yet how to accept it. Jocelyn had never seen him allow someone to be strong for him.

As though he understood the exchange between the couple, Holt turned back to his room with a smile. Like he'd seen this scenario so many times that he knew which marriages could survive and which couldn't. Maybe he did.

At the car, Scott paused. He pulled the crutches out from under his arms and handed them to her, holding himself up in his own strength. "Take these." He said.

"Really?"

"I got some news today."

To anyone else, the statement may have been a jump, but Jocelyn knew the answer would be hidden in what he was about to tell her.

He didn't say anything else until they were in the car. Even then, he didn't look at her as he spoke.

"I got a letter from X's mother." The words were detached. Each its own entity. "He's the kid that died in our ambush."

Jocelyn knew who X was. She sent Scott's letter to his family, but he was on pretty heavy medication at the time so maybe he didn't remember. She'd looked X's picture up on social media. Xavier Martinez, survived by his parents, two sisters and one German Shephard. His mother had sent Scott a thank you note in return to the letter he'd sent. But Jocelyn didn't interrupt Scott. He was open to her, and she wouldn't do anything to inhibit that.

"They buried him in Dallas. She sent a picture and said we could stay with her if we ever came to see him."

"I've never been to Dallas." Jocelyn said when Scott didn't continue. She started the car and decided they would head to the park to meet up with Ian, Elizabeth and Chester the duck.

"I should have been there."

The truth was Jocelyn knew how little soldiers liked going to funerals. No soldier wanted to be reminded what sacrifice their job may ask of them. She reached across the car's console and squeezed his hand.

"I was his platoon sergeant. I should have presented her with his flag." Scott said simply. Jocelyn took a breath, thinking of the crisply folded flag given to X's next of kin. A tiny fracture ripped across her heart picturing Scott completing the tradition.

"There's more."

Her eyebrows raised. "It was a big day."

He huffed air out of his nose almost delivering a laugh. "They're pressuring me for a decision. Medical retirement or reassignment."

That was the sonic boom Jocelyn had not expected. She knew it was the next step after a service member was injured, but she hadn't known there was a question involved for Scott. In her mind, when his enlistment was up, they were done. She envisioned them moving back to California near their families, taking Ian to the beach, having more kids. No more army, no more deployments, no moves to new cities and states where they didn't know anyone. Jocelyn had signed on as milspouse and to army life, but Scott never hinted that he wanted to reenlist. And now? Why wasn't he as done as she was? Wouldn't he want to get back to a normal life—or at least a new normal?

"You–" She stumbled over the words, because she didn't even know what words to say. Everything jumbled. Her eyes barely focused to keep the car in its lane, nevertheless add speech to that action. With a deep breath, she formed words. "When were you going to tell me you wanted to reenlist?"

"When I got home."

She raised her eyebrows. "I thought you hated deskwork."

"I do. But what choice do I have now? Army or not, I'll probably end up behind a desk anyway."

A fire burned in her belly, and with every word he spoke it grew. It raged in her throat, then out her mouth. "So what? You'll end up in recruitment and go off to high schools and talk to the jocks? Tell them, 'You can be like me, bum leg and all. Sign up today.'"

Scott's weight pushed back in the seat. "Wow."

The words burned her tongue even after they were out. With their release, she wanted to cry. She wanted to cry at her husband's broken reaction. She wanted to cry because she meant every word. She wanted to cry remembering George Holt saying, *That woman you have is your team. Let her get your back.* Why would he ever open himself up to her again if she was going to burn him as bad as the shrapnel had in the sands of Afghanistan?

She wants to fight for *you.*

Scott remembered too. "I guess I know what you think of me now. I wondered."

I didn't mean it. She wanted to say, but that was a lie. She hated how ugly the truth could be.

She turned the car early, deciding to return home instead of the park with Ian. He shouldn't see them fighting, again. Her jaw jutted out as though off its hinge. The fire inside her had yet to burn out. Just sitting in the same car with him pressed in on her until she wanted to scream. When she pulled into the driveway of their duplex, Scott fidgeted like he felt the same. He swung the door open before she'd put the car in park, got out and slammed it shut. The sound reverberated through her bones, shaking her palms where they gripped the steering wheel. She exhaled slowly, puffing out her cheeks.

A knock on the window next to her made her jump. Kirk. Jocelyn pursed her lips, steeling herself as she rolled the window down.

"Hiya Joss, everything okay? I saw Scott–" but before he finished his sentence, his body was jerked away from the window and spun around. Then he was falling backward faster than Jocelyn could decipher what was even happening.

Scott stood where Kirk had been, his arm extended, his hand still clenched.

Jocelyn pushed the door open, shrieking. Kirk lay wilted on the ground amongst the leaves. He held his jaw, a red patch against his pale skin.

"Stay away from my wife." Scott spat over Kirk's body. "Stay away from my car. Stay away from my family."

Jocelyn faltered between helping the man at her feet or chasing after the husband who'd stalked into the house with no detectable limp. She stooped down to give Kirk a hand as he lifted himself up from the ground. "I'm sorry." She said, even though the words felt limp.

"No, no–" Kirk started to say, but when his mouth moved, he winced again.

"I'll get you some ice."

She swung the door open, "What the hell were you thinking? That was completely uncalled for."

"Was it?" Scott replied, barely inside the entrance. "If he is that ballsy when I'm home, then what did he do while I was gone?"

"Nothing! Nothing ever happened. He was only ever a helpful neighbor."

"Yeah, I'll bet. Helpful to *my* wife so long as he could fu–"

Jocelyn slapped him across his scarred face. "Don't even say it." Her eyes were wild. "I have known you since the sixth grade. If you don't trust me now, then you never will."

Scott's fist pulsed at his side.

She marched past him to the freezer. "I'm going to take our neighbor ice. Feel free to follow me so that I don't misbehave."

When she returned ten minutes later, Scott's hand was in the freezer, but he closed the door as though he'd been caught.

"Let me take a look at it." She said. Her voice softened as had his expression. Two of his knuckles were swollen and red. "Haven't you been hurt enough lately?"

"Do you think I'm a masochist?" Scott asked.

"Maybe we all are a little." Jocelyn answered. Wasn't that part of the deal, falling in love, knowing the risk of being hurt, accepting the beauty alongside the blood?

The ice pack crackled like pop rocks as it melted against his skin.

"Why does *my* husband have to reenlist? Why can't someone else do their duty for this country now?" Thousands of people did every day, she knew, but just once she wanted to be selfish and keep her husband all to herself.

"If not me, it'll be someone else. It's not like I'll be deployed again like this."

They stood facing each other, each immovable forces.

"It's a job," he said, "one that you used to call honorable."

Yeah, a job where RPGs get shot at you. "It is honorable, but haven't you given enough?"

"What could I lose behind a desk?"

"You tell me. I don't want you miserable the way you have been these last few weeks, and I can't imagine you want it either." Her shoulder slumped around a rock-solid knot forming. "I don't want to live like this anymore."

Scott took her words the way he might take a bullet, standing strong but pain bleeding from his expression. "So what are you saying? That if I reenlist you're going to leave?"

I'll wait for you. Her heart said again. "I'm saying that shrapnel scars aside, you've lost more than you think. I miss the singing and dancing and laughing. I miss our fun."

"I do too," he said, "but my guys are still there, and I know what it's like. I'm home having barbeques and birthday parties and sleeping with my wife. Am I supposed to celebrate? That I'm here and my men are still thousands of miles away, unsure of every day of their life. Do I celebrate that I'm alive even though X is dead?"

He threw the ice pack back in the freezer and slammed the door shut. "I just can't." He said leaving her. She was always waiting. And he was always leaving.

"I wish you would stop walking away from me in the middle of every conversation." She hollered after him, hoping he could hear her through the walls but without the energy to follow him. The weight of her own body suddenly seemed too much to hold upright. She slumped into a chair and got lost in the minutes ticking away.

The sound of a door shut outside—she didn't know how long later—and Jocelyn steadied her heart still pumping anger through her chest. Ian came bounding through the front door smelling like trees and lake scum.

He hugged her around both legs and said, "Mz. Yisbeth say I need a bath."

With a rumple of his soft, thick hair, Jocelyn agreed. "Well, Ms. Elizabeth is right."

"I gots mud on my pants. Just a yiddle bit." He held two dirt-stained fingers up to show how little the little bit was.

"Okay, why don't you put your shoes in your closet and we'll get you into a bath." Jocelyn said as Elizabeth Cryer stepped through the doorway touting her custom camouflage purse on her arm.

"Sorry," Elizabeth said, not a bit frazzled.

Jocelyn started to say, "It's not a big deal," when Ian came running back to her side.

The little mess of a boy asked, "Can you sleep in my bed?"

"Well then where would you sleep?" Jocelyn asked.

"With you, like I used to."

"I think your bed is too small for both of us." Jocelyn said, her eyes bouncing between her son and Elizabeth, embarrassed. As helpful as she had been, Jocelyn never knew when to expect "The Mouth" to return and whisper a tell-all around post.

"But I can't sleep in your room because he's there."

Her throat suddenly felt straw thin. "We'll talk about it after your bath, okay?"

"Otay." Ian answered like it was nothing.

Again she wanted to beg Elizabeth not to say anything, not to even remember this conversation, but she had yet to hear a single strand of gossip about her or her family. Maybe she had misjudged Elizabeth, or maybe for some reason Elizabeth saw them differently, closer to her heart perhaps. Regardless, Elizabeth patted Jocelyn's arm in a way that should have seemed patronizing but somehow didn't.

"Everything will feel normal again. Just hold on." Elizabeth winked one heavily eye-shadowed eye at her. "Even if it's with white knuckles, keep holding on."

Jocelyn only managed a nod.

"I'm a call away if you need anything."

She never chose to lean on Elizabeth Cryer, and yet this woman had been there every step, shouldering much of her burden without ever being asked. As off putting as she seemed, strutting through the post expecting service members to salute her as they would her husband, Elizabeth Cryer showed Jocelyn more of her heart than any other FRG member had.

When Elizabeth let herself out, Jocelyn collapsed against the couch. Ian's voice called for her to start the bath, and she felt herself sinking deeper into exhaustion. No sounds or help came from the bedroom or Scott. Ian made no effort to look for his dad or tell him about his day. The shiny newness of Scott's return had worn off.

A thought slipped across her mind, easily, smoothly like satin across skin. She wished her husband was still deployed. That he was returning with his unit in a few more weeks. In that simple admission, the prongs of guilt stung her and sprung tears. How dare she wish for him still gone when other women were waiting. But if he was, she and Ian would be pining after him, awaiting his call, spraying his cologne on the pillow while she slept with her little boy curled into her.

*****

The email response from Elle Holloway came as Jocelyn awoke. She had taken an over-the-counter sleeping pill to quiet her mind and slept the whole night in Ian's twin size bed. She didn't feel any better. Her head ached and puffy rings clung to her eyes. Lying next to Ian while he slept, she adeptly maneuvered her phone to read Elle's message.

Oh dear Jocelyn. You need some time away to yourself. For me, it would be shopping, and while I'm an expert at that, my ways may not be the best to emulate!! But take time just for YOU! TODAY!!

Even though common sense could have told her that, Jocelyn needed the nudge to take the action. Not the shopping of course. Jocelyn hated shopping on a tight budget; it was more frustrating than enjoyable. She slipped out of bed and, not caring if she woke Scott, entered the bedroom to get her running gear on. She swept her hair in a quick ponytail then headed out the door.

The sun beamed over the horizon when she stepped outside. Fresh air tickled her nose and her feet pounding the pavement made the nerves in her body come alive. She clocked two miles, then rounded the corner to return home. Jogging to a halt in the driveway, a motion in the neighbor's window—Kirk's window—caught her eye. When he saw her, he closed the curtains, and she suddenly felt sorry for not only him but also herself. Kirk lived alone, and maybe he was attracted to her. But in all these months of Scott's deployment, he hadn't so much as flirted. He'd never touched her or pushed his way inside her home. He'd only ever been a helpful, obliging neighbor to a woman whose husband was away. And what was his thanks? A punch in the face by a 6'2" army soldier who was only able to work out his upper body. She closed her eyes, breathing a final outdoor breath before pushing the door open, hoping Kirk really was the nice guy he appeared to be.

Inside Ian and Scott ate cereal at the kitchen table. "Hi Mom," Ian called.

Beads of sweat trickled down her forehead and neared her eye. She downed a glass of water before heading to the shower. Scott came up next to her at the counter to put his empty bowl in the sink. She whispered to him, "You better hope Kirk doesn't sue you. That's not what we need right now."

Scott didn't answer, but that was no surprise. Jocelyn had become accustomed to that, and angry at it. His silence sparked a new pulse of adrenaline that had started to subside after her run.

Slamming her glass into the dishwasher, she nodded at his hand which was even more bruised now. "You should ice that again." Then walked to the shower.

The cold water on her warm skin lent her clarity like the breeze during her running. But she craved more. Elle said shopping. Alexis would recommend a mani/pedi/massage. But like Scott, an anger boiled under the surface of her skin. The cool breeze and the cold shower could only smother it for so long. She needed an outlet for aggression.

Toweling off, she stood in the exact place Scott had the night before deployment. She closed her eyes, saw his broad back, his crisp hairline above his neck, his head bobbing in unison with Ian's while they listened to music. Remembering him the way he had been made her want to cry, but she wouldn't let herself. If she started, how would she reign it in?

She dressed then grabbed a small black case from the top shelf of the closet. The weight of it was lighter than she remembered but the power even stronger. She kissed Ian on the top of his head, told Scott she'd be back in the afternoon, then she walked out the door. Sounds simple enough, but once she was out the door she heard Ian hollering for her, twisting the doorknob trying to open it. "I wanna go with Mom," she heard him crying as Scott tried to console him. "You can stay with me today, buddy."

"I don't wanna stay with you. I wanna go with Mom."

Her chest tightened, but she breathed through it with her back to the front door. She couldn't drown in this. The legendary mom-guilt was pulling at her heels, a weighted anchor dragging her deeper into the darkness. But she fought it. She had to fight for herself, for their family.

She could still hear Ian's phantom crying while she drove.

When she came to the gun range with Scott, she always felt awkward, as though they all knew he was the expert and she was out of place. But this time, alone, there was strength in her stride. She knew what she was doing.

She paid the young man behind the counter who looked as out of place as she usually felt. He pointed her to the lane at the farthest corner. When was the last time she felt this stalwart? Her strength had been dependent upon the others around her and their needs. She was a strong mother for Ian. She was a strong shoulder for Scott. She was a strong friend for Alexis.

But today, she was a strong woman.

With protective gear over her ears and eyes, she looked down the lane at the scarred walls and ceiling that narrowed to her target. Some of the bullet holes in the walls were dangerously close.

Her hands gripped the 941 Jericho handgun that Scott bought for her years ago. She hadn't even seen a gun up close until Scott returned from basic training and brought her to a gun range like this one. Her father had been furious, being that he was against guns altogether, but Scott had held her arms in place gently, patiently teaching her. There wasn't a day that she hadn't felt safe in Scott's care.

The black gun was heavy and weighted in her grip. She wasn't a pink gun kind-of-girl, even though Alexis was. She assumed the proper stance with her feet apart and elbows straight. Released her breath from between her lips, leaned in to the force she was about to unleash, then pulled the trigger. The vibrations electrified her palms and into her bones. One, two, three. Six times she shot at the target and hit just on the edges of the small circle in the right corner, centimeters from where she was aiming. She was rusty but pleased with her results. She continued until every circle on the orange and white target was shredded by holes.

As the gun blasts reverberated through her body in this controlled environment, she envisioned her reactions if someone was shooting at her. With dust flying in the eyes and heavy uniformed gear weighing the body down. With men shouting around and other gunshots popping nearby. With fear pushing itself to the surface but courage taking its place. She invented a person instead of a target. A face. Eyes staring back. Life seeping out through the bullet wound inflicted. Then suddenly the face was Xavier Martinez. She swallowed the images back down.

She dropped the gun back into its case, unloaded, with the safety on. Scott's journals came to life, assaulted her as she tried to shake them from her mind.

Driving straight home, opening the door and walking straight to the bedroom where Scott and Ian sat on the bed playing video games again, she sat next to him and slung her arms around his shoulders and neck. She kissed his cheek with a whispered "I'm sorry."

After he'd laid Ian down and he joined her in the kitchen while she swept up dinner's crumbs, he didn't ask where she'd gone, just simply asked, "Are we okay?"

"I hope so."

"Then why do you look so sad?"

"I'm not sad." She leaned on the handle of the broom. The eloquence to explain what she'd experienced at the gun range evaded her. "I couldn't do what you were trained to do, and I certainly wouldn't be brave enough to return to it."

"You are brave." When his wife shook her head, Scott continued, "You're braver than me in a lot of ways. I rely on a team, guys who have my back. I see the problem and I confront it. I can do that. But I couldn't do what you do here. You've done this all on your own, all while your–" he stumbled between the words, "team member was away. You've raised Ian and taught him everything he knows. And he knows a lot at four. He understands a lot. You're raising a young man to take on the world. That's a bravery I don't have."

"I think you do." She moved to put the broom away. When she turned back to him and saw his unconvinced expression, she continued. "We don't know what's inside ourselves until we are face-to-face with a raging fire that only we can put out." She lifted her hand to his freshly shaven cheek and swiped her thumb across his square chin.

A sadness swarmed in his milk chocolate eyes and brought a revelation to her. "Is that why you don't want to take medical retirement? Because outside of the army, you don't think you're brave enough?"

He furrowed his brow, finding his own words or deciphering his own feelings. "It's what makes me who I am. Just as much as being a husband or a father, I'm a soldier. You take one away, and I'm no longer me."

Propping her arms behind her on the counter, she lifted herself and sat the countertop. "You learn to be a different you. Before you were a husband or a father–"

Scott cut her off. "I was a soldier then too."

Jocelyn nodded. He was getting short with her again, so she drew him closer to her, his body between her thighs, and she kept her voice soft. "But with each new title came a transformation. The same would happen now."

"I can't get out." A crack splintered his voice. Not anger, but resembling fear. "I don't know what to do but the army. It's all I've ever wanted next to being in the NFL when I was a kid and now I can't even run to play football with my son." His nostrils flared, holding back his version of tears. "I mean look at Paul. He retired and he couldn't live with himself. There are so many guys like that."

His head drifted down, but she cupped her hands around his face and beckoned his eyes to meet her. "You aren't like them." She whispered because thrusting away the vision of Scott winding up like Paul took the strength from her voice.

His response was barely words, just a warm breath against her skin. "What if I am?"

The words marinated in her before she released them. Finally, quietly, she answered him. "You know how I know you aren't? Because some people see darkness in war, or even in life, and they are paralyzed by it. But people like you—you know the light is out there somewhere, and you focus on that pinprick of light to find your way."

She thought of his journal entries that spoke of the people of war, their faces, their hopes, their similarities with people all over the world. Even when he wrote of the horrors that he'd seen or fear he'd felt, there was a humanity and compassion for the countries being torn apart by the bombs, the devastation that children should never know. The same light, same focus pushed him through the agony of his injuries, and if he let it, it would bring him out of the darkness of uncertainty to the other side.

"You've always been optimistic. Certain that good could overcome all. That's still in you. I see it when you look at Ian. I see it in your eyes right now." Eyes so deep she could jump in them and swim to eternity.

"That part of me is only there because of you."

"I don't believe that for a second. That part of you is what I fell in love with in seventh grade and again on our first date. And when I married you. And when I had a baby with you." A tear streaked across Scott's cheek as elusive as a shooting star, and a matching one forming in her own eyes. "And even when I walked through the door in the hospital, I saw that hope and light in your eyes. It's still there, Scott Turner. We just have to fight to keep it."

He nodded a rapid cluster of nods. When he opened his mouth, a sob came out and the sound wrecked Jocelyn to her core.

"I need your help," he said, another tear already down to his lips.

She leaned her forehead against his, "You've always had it. We're in this together."

When she kissed him, their tears mingled together. She tasted the saltiness of his lips. The taste of brokenness. The taste of hope.

21

ELLE

The internet search history on Elle's computer at work took a one-eighty in the weeks after Hailey's request. Mary Todd Lincoln was not quite today's version of a fashion icon, but there was enough out there for Elle to work with. After digging through images when she should have been working, Elle stopped on the reproduction of a Mary Todd dress, a purple velvet, bell-shaped dress with white piping and black Chantilly lace sleeves. The image in her mind of Hailey's tanned skin against the dark purple would be stunning *and* historically accurate.

In her insomnia, between her emails with Jocelyn, she sketched the dress and details in her notebooks. The feel of the pencil scuffing against the recycled paper, the scratching sound of shading the drawing. The sounds were so familiar that they warmed her chest.

One sketch sparked another. She jumped into her closet, digging through boxes to find the right fabric. A box of purses never unpacked, a box of scarves she'd forgotten she had. Items from her previous life that were invaluable, now sitting boxed up and forgotten. Waiting to be loved and handled with care. Like her.

An idea formed and by morning every box in her closet and along the far wall was unpacked and laid out on her unmade, unslept in bed. And they stayed that way as Elle set Norah up for the day and went on to work, taking her sketchpad along with her.

Working with and befriending other designers had its benefits. At lunch, she went over the Mary Todd Lincoln sketch with Jenny and a couple designers.

Even rusty Elle only took a week of evenings to measure, draw out, cut the pattern and pin it for an initial fitting with Hailey, then sew and line it. She'd worked in the downstairs living room through Norah's game shows and her grandmother even skipped gin rummy Friday night to help her with the finishing touches.

So when she pulled the dress out of the silver box in front of Hailey's big hazel eyes, the response was worth the exhaustion she felt down to her fingertips. Hailey squeezed her tight around the midsection and skipped to her room to try the dress on.

Marissa gave a tired smile at Elle, still distant since the miscarriage. In Elle's way of diving headfirst into a project, she'd never asked Marissa or even mentioned it to her, and her friend's lack of enthusiasm made her question if she'd done the right thing. They sat in awkward dead air waiting on Hailey, their last conversation hanging between them. Elle wanted to tell Marissa everything, like she used to, about Brandon and her unpacked boxes, but with every lumbering second the opportunity becoming less obvious. Then Hailey was back, twirling and squealing. Even Elle's imagination couldn't picture the dress more beautiful on its owner.

And that, she realized, was what she had been missing. Making someone feel their most beautiful.

Hailey ran back upstairs to show her daddy while Elle followed her friend into the kitchen. There were tinfoil pans of food covering the countertops and take-out boxes overflowing the trashcan, a couple flower arrangements beginning to wilt.

"Sorry for the mess," said Marissa in a stiff, monotone voice. "People keep sending food like there's been a death in the–" her voice trailed off and eyes darkened.

There has been. Elle wanted to say, but with the words came the realization that there *had* been a death in her best friend's family and all she did was let her daughters spend the night and make a dress. Things she should have been doing for years, but nowhere near equal to the circumstances at hand.

"I'm sorry I haven't done more." One sentence that encapsulated Elle's entire life. She could say it to everyone every day and still wouldn't make up for the opportunities she'd lost.

"You should have," Marissa said, and Elle was prepared for a Charlene-style verbal beating. "But it's okay. You couldn't bring him back."

"Him?" Elle asked with a voice matching Marissa's whisper.

Her friend shrugged, "I like to think we got our boy."

The words crushed into Elle, breaking her into more pieces than she knew possible. In all the pain she'd been dealt these past months, they didn't add up to one ounce of what her friend was burdened with. The possibility of a son given and taken away in a breath. A tear dripped down Elle's skin, but Marissa wasn't crying. Her swollen eyes told the story of countless hours weeping behind doors of privacy until there were no more tears allocated for the day.

"I brought you something." Elle set another silver box on the open space of the countertop, all at once feeling how nonsensical the gift was given the timing. "It's not important but a peace offering of sorts."

As she handed the box over, her hand brushed up against Marissa's long fingers shaking ever so slightly, attempting to hide any weakness.

Marissa opened the box and pulled out a brown-on-brown checkered hand bag. "What is this?"

"It's your favorite Louis Vuitton," answering the rhetorical question as her friend touched the soft leather and caressed it with motherly hands. They were hands accustomed to fixing ponytails and placing band-aids instead of handling luxury items. But they deserved their own band-aid, even if it seemed silly.

"I should have given it to you when I bought it, instead of strutting it around in front of you acting like my life was better than yours." Elle's eyes batted around to the kitchen that looked less like a mess in her eyes and more like an outpouring of love. "You have family and people that care about you. And I have a closet full of designer clothes and shoes and handbags." What good was all of that without love anyway?

"I don't understand."

Shaking her head like it was nonsense, Elle answered, "I'm selling them." Her insomniac determination found a website where users sold like-new designer items. "I've already sold one—for a fraction of what it's worth, but still."

Something clicked in Elle when she dug through her boxes. She justified her overflowing closets to Aaron for so long that she had started to believe her own excuses. That she had to dress for success if she was ever going to be a well-respected designer. That each piece made her happy, and she deserved happiness, after all. *I won't feel sorry for you.* Aaron had told her. *Plenty of people have had it worse and aren't drowning in designer brands.*

It was a betrayal of sorts, buying these extraordinary pieces to make herself happy, but leaving them unused and unappreciated. When someone like Marissa who didn't have the money—although in reality neither did Elle—to pay full price could cherish them.

She downplayed it to Marissa with a shrug, "I don't have space in my closet at Norah's anyway, and who knows how long I'll stay there." Maybe the sales would afford her a place of her own. Not the top of the hill, but some dreams took longer than others.

"I'm proud of you," Marissa said.

Elle employed every ounce of self-control to resist spilling the events of her life that her best friend had missed. The story of her mother and her own origin. Brandon and the handful of text messages they'd exchanged, the stolen glances and tension the few times they'd been together since that Friday night. But the timing wasn't right. Marissa needed to heal.

With an embrace that Elle clung to a little longer than she typically would and a kiss to Marissa's cheek, she said, "This isn't supposed to be about me."

Marissa's smile, still weak with sadness and exhaustion, was at least a smile. "But I can still be proud."

***

Arriving home, she bounded up the stairs and informed Norah they were going on an outing. The Dixie cup of medications and vitamins sat by Norah's bed untouched. "Did you take your meds this morning?" Elle asked trying to sound casual.

Norah's typical response, "Of course," with a hint of *I'm not a child* in her tone. The woman whose reactions she had come to know as closely as her own, peppered her with questions about Hailey's dress and Marissa's purse. Elle jetted through the house gathering her sketchpad and tools, food items to squeeze into Norah's picnic basket, then threw it all in her trunk.

But Norah still stood at the top of the stairs. Her lined face usually so confident, this time was unsure of her footing. Elle wished for the strength of a man who could scoop this fragile woman up and cradle her like a baby to the car. Instead she swallowed her impatience and helped Norah step by step. What had become routine after all these months, Elle now viewed through tinted lenses. The woman whose strength had built up again, today seemed weaker somehow. Norah tried to give her granddaughter a grateful smile but it looked more like a grimace as she leaned all her weight onto Elle's forearm.

As difficult as it had been to learn how life could move at Norah's snail speed, Elle found it peaceful this time. She needed to slow down in life, pay attention to things that normally went unnoticed like the pressure of Norah's gold ring pushing into Elle's wrist bone as she held on tighter.

"Was this your wedding ring?" Elle asked as a distraction from the inches of progress they had made.

"Oh heavens, no. We couldn't afford this when your grandfather and I married."

Elle glanced at the ring pressing against her skin, mother of pearl with pencil tip diamonds clustered around it, set in antique gold. "It's beautiful."

Norah let go of the banister with her right hand and patted Elle's arm. "You should have it."

Elle shook her head, but Norah continued. "I'd want you to have it, not your mother. She'd sell it or give it away or lose it. She's never been sentimental." Norah didn't attempt another stair just yet, but instead looked around her as if she could see every meaningful item she owned. "I figure most of this stuff will end up in the junker once I'm gone."

She imagined the painting of the brunette girl standing by the water left in a landfill, broken and rotting. "I wouldn't let that happen," she said once she regained herself.

A glisten in Norah's eyes appeared and just as quickly disappeared before she grabbed hold of the banister again and resumed her belabored trek down the stairs.

Small talk was never Norah's forté and silence between the two women usually won as it did on their drive. They snaked around the neighborhoods of Lomita to the Rolling Hills where Elle had made and lost her home with Aaron, then up the winding roads, up and up to the hills of Palos Verdes.

Elle had taken this drive whenever she wanted to envision what life would be like if every one of her dreams came true. But she realized as they passed mansion after mansion that she had long since stopped dreaming of living here. Those dreams lost a morsel of power with each disappointment until they were hidden so deep that Elle almost didn't recognize them now.

Norah recognized where they were headed when Elle turned onto PV Drive and started directing Elle as she always had. "Go down that way, toward the lighthouse."

Which had been Elle's plan, but she let her grandmother take the lead. She turned toward Golden Cove, knowing there were trails that led to the cliff's edge overlooking the water but Norah would never be strong enough to make it all the way.

"Pull in here," Norah pointed, jumping a bit in her seat. "This is my favorite spot."

They could see the lighthouse like a centurion guard above the water, with a scattering of palm trees as its only company. The sun hung low in the sky, and the orange glow of fire reflected off of the rocky cliff under the lighthouse. Elle had never left the shores of California, but this one nook of the coast made everything seem possible in the world.

Elle helped Norah out of the car to a nearby bench with a quilt to block the chill of the breeze. Norah slipped into her fur coat—the only coat she ever wore these days claiming, "At my age, there's no use saving for special occasions."

"Remember when I used to bring you here?" Norah asked.

An easy smile turned Elle's lips. "I remember being little and just wanting to run down to the water, then getting to the age when I thought it was boring." Elle laughed at her unimpressed teen self. "But one time we came down at sunset like this, and I finally saw the grandness of it all."

Elle's eyes took a panoramic of the scene, the water wading peacefully in this distance. The white of the surf against the shore like lace at the hem of the layered ocean water, dancing to its own rhythm.

"Your grandfather brought me here on a date once in his convertible."

The waning light lit Norah's face in such a way that revealed the beautiful young woman she had once been. Elle knew this story but allowed Norah to tell it as though for the first time. "We had driven up and down Pacific Coast Highway with the top down. Then he brought me here, and we talked until sunrise." Something akin to a giggle was in her grandmother's voice. "He was the first man I stayed out with all night. It wasn't so common back then. But he was never inappropriate. Always a gentleman."

The wind rushed from the ocean in front of them and pushed against Elle. She had forgotten a cardigan. But this familiar story filled Elle with a warmth that kept the chill of the breeze at bay.

"I always imagined Aaron would propose to me here." Elle blurted.

But he hadn't. He'd gone the traditional route of a nice restaurant. Nothing cheesy like hiding the ring in cake. Simple. A ring in a velvet box presented across the table over their glasses of wine. Aaron had always been traditional. She had wanted to fit that mold for him, and maybe she had for a while. But it wasn't enough. Elle was the tofu to Aaron's pallet. Close but not quite the real thing. She believed in marriage. She believed in the strength of a person's will to move past difficult times, the ups and downs in a relationship, choosing that one person every day. She was still choosing him, even when he stopped choosing her.

What could have stopped her breathing like it did in those beginning days, gasping for air like a drowning child, had become her new normal. She'd become accustomed to that ache throbbing inside her heart with every thought of Aaron. And the thoughts of Aaron hadn't gone away. They never really would.

A vision rose inside her like an air bubble exploding in her chest. Their last night before he left. Sitting in bed reading a fashion magazine while he checked emails. She had sifted over this night in her mind a million times, panning for gold, searching for what propelled Aaron to leave. And there it was. A diaper commercial between Jimmy Fallon bits, a mom with two babies, the bedraggled look of exhaustion all over her. And Elle's flippant comment, "I could never do that. I am *not* made for that kind of life." It seemed innocent enough, a comment meant to convey how she couldn't imagine letting herself go unkempt.

But Aaron heard it different. He translated all the times Elle poked fun at Marissa. The ways she complained about babies at her job. How she selfishly spent every penny on herself, not making room for an addition to their family.

Images played over her mind like film of Aaron making funny faces at a stranger's baby to see them laugh; Aaron's niece on his shoulders; Aaron scanning the baby clothes in stores while Elle looked at the shoes that she couldn't afford. She heard her own incensed words *I don't even like babies.*

He had always been traditional. He wanted a traditional family, a wife and children with pets running around in a fenced-in yard. And after spending time with Hailey and Heidi, Elle could admit that maybe someday she wanted that too. But she wasn't ready. Of that she was certain.

The shades of royalty in the sky around wispy clouds gave new perspective to life. An idea propelled her toward the backseat where her bag sat. She picked it up and emptied the contents on the bench next to Norah. She hadn't sketched a portrait in years. But a long time ago, she had drawn a picture of Aaron, the way he was when they were first married. Pencil in hand, she tried it again.

Like muscle memory, her hand drew the outline of his face, prominent cheekbones, uncut hair over the tops of his ears. The pencil swept across the paper drawing his thin eyes. She could see him coming to life on the paper before her, still looking at her with love. A tear snuck down her face, and she felt Norah's cold hand rest on her knee. The wrinkled, age-spotted hand contrasted against Elle's smooth skin, felt like wisdom sat with her, held her in this moment.

It was a grieving of sorts, each stroke that she drew, but with it came a peace that she hadn't realized she needed.

***

The office was exceptionally quiet. Eerily so. Elle glanced at the closed door of her boss' office where a meeting about the new line of baby designs was taking place. She was there for appearance only, and even though it gave her time-and-a-half pay that she desperately needed, it still didn't sit right with her. She should be with Norah not sitting at her cleaned off desk losing at Candy Crush.

She texted Brandon the night before to make sure it was okay to leave

Norah alone while working late. Norah's new fragility concerned her, and though Brandon took her blood and checked her levels weekly, something felt off in Elle. But Brandon said one night would be fine.

In an epiphany-slash-boredom moment, she scoured the bottom of her desk drawer until her hand brushed against the spiral of her sketchbook. She flipped through the pages of her sketches from a fragmented lifetime ago. Everything from cocktail dresses to swimsuits to ridiculous British royalty-style hats. Not all the sketches were sellable, but Aaron was right when he said they were good.

When she came to the last page in the sketchpad, the one of Aaron she had drawn at the look-out point, the ache overwhelmed her. So she flipped to a clean page, pulled out a sharpened pencil, and started sketching haphazardly. At first the pencil strokes were just that, lines on a paper. But before she knew it, her mind played with them, twisting them, shaping them into new images she hadn't planned.

With abrupt force, the closed door next to her opened, and the designers and supervisors poured out as the meeting concluded. Until only Lena remained in her office. Elle turned to her computer, hoping she looked busy, realizing after everyone walked by that the screen wasn't even on. She slumped in her seat. What was the use in pretending anyway? She was playing bodyguard to a closed door.

Just as Elle turned to grab her bag, Lena emerged from her office, Chanel briefcase and Mercedes keys in hand, looking every bit as fresh as she did at her 9 am arrival. "Thank you Elle," she stopped at the edge of her receptionist's desk. "I appreciate you staying here. I don't like having a meeting without someone to watch the phones and doors."

See, bodyguard.

Elle found she had nothing to say.

Lena yawned, abnormally unprofessional of the woman. And when she did, her eyes fell on Elle's notebook. "What are these?" She asked, fingering the edge of the pages.

"Oh," Elle grabbed at them to close the book, but Lena shooed her hand away. "Um, well–" *Lie,* she thought. But she couldn't come up with a good one and fumbled a bunch of *ums* and *hmm* until Lena raised an eyebrow at her. "They are some of my sketches over the years."

"I had no idea you were interested in design." Lena propped herself against Elle's desk with the sketchpad in hand.

Elle wanted to laugh. *No idea? I told you at my interview.* But that was years ago, and Elle had sat behind a desk answering phones without voicing interest in changing jobs. So maybe it made sense.

"Well, I haven't designed baby stuff. Mostly women's clothing." She sounded like a nervous junior high student talking to the high school head cheerleader.

Lena paused a moment, with a piercing stare. "Designers are pitching ideas tomorrow at 10 am. If you'd be comfortable making one or two full color design sketches, I'd like you to pitch them at the meeting. Can you be ready by then?"

Elle's entire world lost color. The edges of her vision blackened and tunnel-focused to a desaturated Lena in the middle. She stumbled over her answer, "Yes, yes of course, I can be ready." And then she amended, "I *will* be ready."

Lena straightened and said, "Good. See you then." After a few steps she added, "For the record, Elle, some of your sketches are impressive."

Elle couldn't move for a full minute, paralyzed by opportunity. She allowed herself that minute, then her brain sprinted ahead. Norah was home, alone. But here, everything was available to Elle's creativity, all night long. She tapped out a text to Brandon: "Have to stay later, maybe all night. Will she be okay?"

He responded in moments: "I'll stop by and check on her."

"You don't have to do that."

"No life, remember. Just dogs."

With a nervous stomach and practically no plan, she set to work. She gathered her inadequate supplies, colored pencils, a new sketchbook, a couple oversized sketch boards for the final product. And as she drew, she prepared her presentation.

At midnight, she made herself a pot of coffee. By two o'clock, the pot was empty and her vision swarmed in front of her, but she wasn't giving up. One finalized design lay before her, reminiscent of the dress she'd made for Hailey with soft purple, white piping and an overlay of black Chantilly lace. Another design, with which she wasn't quite happy, sat next to it.

At her typical insomniac hour, Jocelyn sent her a message. "You up?"

Elle tapped at her phone screen and typed back a quick message. "You're a mom. I'm obviously not. What kind of bedding do kids want?"

"Well, babies don't usually decide their own bedding" was Jocelyn's satirical response. "It's usually a reflection of their parents."

Maybe to someone else that was just a comment, but in Elle it sparked inspiration. *A reflection of their parents.* She knew what to do. And she went to drawing.

Another voice lingered in her ears. *Design what you love*, Aaron had always told her.

There was only one person she wanted to talk to. His reassurance had always inspired her. Although his phone was always on silent these days, she could call just to hear his voice on his voicemail message. When the phone rang, even knowing he wouldn't answer, her stomach knotted, hands sweaty, heart thudding. She almost hung up twice, but she promised herself it would be his voicemail.

"Hello," his airy, slurred, middle-of-the-night voice answered.

"Oh Aaron." She meant to sound surprised, but the words hummed of a broken heart. "It's Elle."

"I know." Of course he knew her voice. "Is everything okay?"

"Yeah," she whispered, somehow feeling that her call would be less intrusive in the black of night if it were only a whisper. "I thought your phone would be on silent."

"It was." He was quiet for a moment. "I haven't been sleeping well. You?"

She let out a pained laugh knowing that feeling all too well. "I haven't slept yet. That's kinda why I called. Something happened, but I didn't want to tell anyone besides you."

He listened. He'd always been good at that. She wished she hadn't taken it for granted.

"It's kinda funny," continuing, "My boss saw some of my scribbles in my sketchpad, and she asked me to pitch some design boards tomorrow morning. So I've been here at the office all night trying to get ready."

"Elle," Aaron cleared his throat, "that's fantastic. Clothes?"

"No. Baby bedding." The words sounded ironic coming out of her mouth. When she closed her eyes, she could almost imagine them having this conversation sitting in bed together as if nothing had changed.

But everything had.

"I always knew you could do it."

Tears stung the corners of her eyes. It could have been the lack of sleep. When she tried to hold them back, they stung her nose in protest. "I know. You're always my champion."

Through the phone she heard the sheets under him rustle, and that simple sound brought along so many memories. His shampoo scent. His morning stubble. The weight of his body on the mattress next to her. She had to stop, open her eyes, pull herself out of the past. "Did we make a mistake?"

After a silence too long for her comfort, "Maybe."

"But it's too late, isn't it?"

She heard him swallow, imagined she heard his heart beating. "I think so."

She exhaled, realizing only then she'd been holding her breath awaiting his answer. Her eyes closed and that pesky tear dripped its way down her cheek and off her chin, and before she could move to wipe its trail away, another one followed. "There was chamomile tea from the kitchen that got boxed up with your stuff. That might help you sleep."

He laughed at that. Finally, the return of the wife he had married. When it was too late to matter. Too little, too late, as they say.

"Good night, Aaron."

"Hey, Elle," he added, "No matter what happens tomorrow, don't quit trying."

The words made her smile. A sad smile, yet hopeful. "I promise."

Up until now, her promises hadn't meant much, but she was trying to change that.

"Good night," they both said.

He had always been her biggest champion. But she had pushed him too hard, too many times until he was just out of her reach. *They* also commented on not knowing what you have until it's gone. She was learning that *they* sucked.

***

The brakes on her car screeched as they turned into the driveway. She came home just long enough to check on Norah and change her clothes so she didn't look like the wreck she was for her first pitch. Face down on her desk lay three completed designs ready to pitch to Lena and the design team. "Hailey's Purple Comet" as she'd named it, "Peaches and

Crème" that reflected the peach pastels of her current bedroom, and a boy and girl version of the army camo with a gold seal and monogram inspired by Jocelyn. Given the time she'd had, she was proud of herself.

Her empty stomach twirled in revolt to even less sleep and food than it was used to. She barely noticed the car parked in front of the mailbox, until she entered the house and saw tennis shoes attached to mile-long legs lying on the couch at 6 am.

The curtained window let in a sliver of morning sunlight across Brandon's face. She sighed, not knowing whether to feel gratitude toward him or disapproval.

It was the longest she'd been able to look at him without being met by an eyebrow raise or a shiver of guilt. Even in sleep, his long features smiled at her. A piece of his long hair lay across his forehead and teased her to push it back in place.

Something stirred him, maybe the creaking of the floorboards as her body shifted. He rubbed his pointed chin as he woke—as unshaven as Elle had ever seen it—which had less gray than she expected. He didn't seem surprised to see her standing over him.

"What are you doing here?" She asked, wanting to chastise but the words came out with a chuckle.

"I felt bad leaving her alone." He brushed the long strands of peppered hair backward in their familiar direction. "Or maybe I wanted you to owe me something."

Their eyes met. His sleepy smile was contagious.

"I'll make you coffee," she said, breaking their locked eyes, "Norah won't be up for hours."

As she prepared the water and one-cup coffee pod, Elle chattered why she'd been gone so late. She felt the heat of his body close behind her, as close as a shadow. The pressure of the water steaming in the coffee pot made a puffing sound. When she turned around, he was there with his typical near-smile expression. Coffee dribbled into the cup at the same rate as her pulse. He looked into her face, but she kept her eyes just south of his. They flickered over the unbuttoned part of his shirt and heat rose to her cheeks, fluttering her eyes back to his.

It had been a long time since she felt the sort of tension that made her heartrate quicken with only a look. This was different for her. She had always been the seductive one, grappling for attention, pursuing until she was satisfied. With Brandon, though, she felt blind-sided. Like he had snuck passed her security guards and smiled his way into the VIP room. But she was taken. She was *married*. She didn't feel free.

With that thought, she grabbed the coffee mug as a shield and handed it to him, stretching her arm out to keep him at a distance. Their fingers brushed as the mug transferred between them, and her breath caught. She childishly scurried away from him, mumbling about changing her clothes. But he could see through her, she knew, and when she looked back at him before leaving the room, she met his amused gaze from over the coffee mug as he took a drink.

She dressed quickly in her designer clothes, made-up face and loose updo. Brandon walked her out, opening the car door for her with a lingering glance once she was in. Elle saw a flash of Aaron carrying out the same motion, like she was living in dual universes.

It was all too soon.

Relief washed the dual vision away. Those few moments with Brandon buried her nerves. Until she rounded the corner toward her office. All at once a stone dropped in her stomach, sitting heavy, constricting her airflow. But she forced each step like walking with ankle weights.

The others before her took two hours, and each minute ate away at her confidence. Her fingers itching to tweak and erase and amend.

Then Lena's voice beckoned her. Elle entered the meeting with a pounding heart, carrying her three presentation boards. The others in the room, including Jenny wearing new henna swirls on both hands, stared at her like she was intruding. No one knew what Lena asked of her the night before.

"Go ahead, Elle," Lena said as her only introduction.

She approached the front of the room, propped up the easel that no one else had used. Suddenly she felt antiquated, not having a computer rendering of her designs.

Once her mouth opened, Jocelyn's words came out. "Every parent wants a room for their child that represents themselves." What did she know of what a parent wanted? The years of mothering she'd observed from Marissa pushed her forward. "They strive to give their perfect baby the perfect environment to thrive and grow, from womb to bedroom."

Her audience's blank expressions stalled her. She had rehearsed this in the bathroom mirror like amateur singers do for the Grammy's. She thought for sure that would earn her a nod or some form of endorsement.

By the end, with all eyes still on her and her presentation boards, she walked out of the room standing straighter and a suppressed smile behind her lips. Not because of how good her designs were or even her presentation—especially since it felt like a fog in her mind. But because she lived out a dream she'd been holding so close to her chest that it had almost suffocated there. Now it was out, breathing, feeding, growing.

***

Time stretched and thinned the way she'd seen vendors by the pier make salt-water taffy, until finally Lena called her into her office. This time Elle didn't approach the meeting like a room on fire but with poise. She sat in the stark white chairs across from Lena's steel gray desk, wearing a firm gaze and sleek bob that slimmed her face.

"I'm sorry Elle," Lena said with no hesitation, "the designs weren't right for us this time. We've gone a different direction."

As much as she hated it, Elle sunk through the gray hardwood floor. She determined no matter what the decision—a verdict that she was almost certain would be against her—she was already a success. But now she struggled to find her footing.

"I know it's disappointing," Lena continued, either reading Elle's shoulder drop or knowing from experience. Lena's manicured hands were clasped together on her desk. "You should know that not one person in this office had a design picked up on their first pitch."

Something Elle hadn't seen before glistened behind her employer's eyes.

"You should be proud."

Elle managed a nod, with lips pursed not in anger or even defeat, but protection over her hopes. She headed toward the exit with a quiet "Thank you," but Lena called her named before she could open the door.

"I may not be a part of the water cooler gossip, but I do catch wind of things. I know you're having a hard time." Experience resonated in Lena's voice. The woman had divorced three men that Elle knew of. "You decide what's most important. No one else can make that choice for you. Then stand by it. But if you so choose, keep designing. You have real talent."

Then she tilted her head and added, "Just maybe not in baby bedding."

Elle let herself laugh. The words felt like sunlight flooding through her, not burying the disappointment but overshadowing it.

For once, she didn't feel the need to dilute this moment by sharing it with someone else. The low or the high. This was a moment to keep for herself.

22

JOCELYN

The throaty laughter of George Holt echoed through the hall as Jocelyn neared the physical therapy clinic entrance. She was early for Scott's pick up after a quick trip to the Commissary. When she stepped closer to the doors, she instantly knew why George was laughing. The song "Can't Feel My Face" rang out from Scott's phone. She had seen him updating his therapy playlist the night before, another symbol of Scott's recovery. He had a song for everything.

"I don't need you to feel your face. I just need you to feel your legs." George laughed.

Scott stood behind a straight-back chair, his cheeks nearly purple and sweat streaking his Metallica shirt like a Jackson Pollock painting. Last time Jocelyn checked in on his therapy, Scott had been holding on to the chair to stabilize himself before a squat, but today he lowered himself parallel to the chair's seat unsupported.

"That's it. Deeper. Go deeper."

"I usually like the dirty talk, but I don't like it from you, Holt." Scott grunted.

Even in their banter, George reminded Jocelyn of a kind-hearted parent. She imagined him with his own children—two boys in high school—the way she was with Ian. She spent time that day working with Ian on writing his name. Only three letters. He was so close to getting the right shapes, but Jocelyn pushed him to try the *a* one more time the way

George always pushed Scott, minus the innuendos. Ian's face of concentration was the same as Scott's too. The squint of their brown eyes, the set of their lips pressed tight in the middle.

Just as Scott grabbed his towel to wipe his face and neck, a man whom Jocelyn recognized entered the clinic from another door. Specialist Boone from Scott's unit. She couldn't remember his first name; it had been so long since anyone used it. Everyone called him Boone. The Company had returned earlier in the week, Jocelyn had overheard. As Boone approached Scott, she tried to read her husband's body language, but could only see the back of his head, and it didn't give off much information. Boone hugged Scott broadly, his arms wrapped around Scott, flat palm thumps against the indention in Scott's back.

When Boone pulled back he continued patting Scott's shoulders and biceps. Jocelyn flinched with each pat, although Scott made no indication that they hurt or imbalanced him. His playlist was still blaring through the room, so Jocelyn couldn't hear their exchange but based on the toothy grin on Boone's face, she'd say they were happy to see each other alive and standing.

Scott wrote of Boone often in his journal, and having read them— twice— and having met Boone before, now seeing him through Scott's eyes, she felt like he was family.

She hadn't realized George Holt was next to her until he spoke. "He's doing well."

"He is." She smiled and nodded nonchalantly. "I just hope it isn't about proving something to the guys," she jutted her chin toward the two unit brothers. Images rolled in her mind of what it would have been like to have Scott return to her whole, walking on his own, able to withstand the weight of her running into his arms. What Ian would be like with his dad if Scott hadn't come home with broken wings. Then came the familiar sting of guilt knowing her struggle was nothing compared to Mrs. Martinez'.

Boone easily bent over, in a way Scott couldn't yet, and picked up a brown bag she hadn't seen before. He handed it to Scott, a United States flag tattoo on Boone's forearm showing from beneath his rolled-up sleeves. From the bag, Scott pulled out what Jocelyn later found out was an Afghany beer, then made a cheers gesture. Their laughter boiled over the music.

George watched them too. "Any motivation that works is good motivation. But he has more to prove to himself than anyone else."

The music stopped and the abruptness caught Jocelyn's attention. Boone and Scott ambled toward her.

"There's the warrior behind the soldier." Boone smiled at her with chapped lips and hugged her, significantly gentler than he had her husband. "We missed this guy. No more karaoke nights with Hooch."

Jocelyn's eyebrows asked the obvious question.

"Almost every night this guy started up karaoke. Songs all over the map, too. Rap and classic rock and R & B. He knew the lyrics to all of them. He might have even pulled out a few love songs and dedicated them to you along the way." He laughed with his whole body. "Made us all vomit."

Laughing and nodding along with them, it described Scott perfectly. It was nice to hear someone else remember Scott before the injury. It was nice to see that Scott emerging more with every laugh, but knowing he'd never truly be the same.

"I'd never done sober karaoke until deployment with Hooch." Boone said. "He's a wanna-be Brian McKnight."

Didn't she know it. But she hadn't heard him sing since he had been home. How had she not realized that until just now? She remembered him singing to their baby when her belly was swollen in pregnancy, his warm breath against her bare skin. Then singing to Ian as a baby, when his ears were still too big for his head and Scott said they were "better to hear me with."

She missed something Boone said about beatbox, the murmur of the men's voices fading to a hum along with the air conditioner and heavy breathing of the other PT patients.

A woman outside the clinic doors whom Jocelyn had seen before wheeled up in her wheelchair. From what Jocelyn had heard, the woman's name was Jo and she'd gone down in a helicopter crash in Iraq. Her right leg had been amputated. Jocelyn excused herself from the memories lapping at her frontal lobe, gesturing to Boone and Scott that she would return.

This could have been Scott, wearing sand-colored cargo pants with the right side pinned back where there was no more leg to fill the fabric.

Once she was standing near the woman, Jocelyn realized she had no idea what to say, but Jo stared at her expectantly. "I wanted to say thank you for your service and your sacrifice." Gratitude could never be expressed enough to someone who had given so much of themselves, yet the feeble words seemed inadequate as they left her mouth.

The woman nodded with grace. "Are you with a wounded soldier?" Jo asked.

"My husband," Jocelyn said, nodding in Scott's direction.

Jo looked at Scott but said nothing. Jocelyn didn't know why but she didn't want to walk away from this woman just yet. She conjured up a question for her, then realized the words had been floating around in her head for such a long time. "Any advice for the spouse at home?"

"Love him," Jo said, fine lines branching out from each of her eyes like spider webs. "Every part of him."

The words were simple yet they crashed into her.

Then the officer added, "Even the parts that may be gone. Love them. Mourn them even. But love *him* as he is now."

Another therapist called Jo to a table at the back of the clinic, Jocelyn stepped back. Thank you seemed vapid, but she said it anyway.

Boone was next to her by then, with Scott. They said their *See you later*'s then she watched Scott working to stand up straight, wrapping his brace around his bare leg, tightening the Velcro above and below his knee, leaving the kneecap exposed like the darkened knot in a tree trunk. *Love him as he is now.*

They exchanged small talk on the drive home, but Scott's left knee bobbed up and down the way Ian's did when watching a movie. At home, she paid the babysitter and walked her out before going to the kitchen to begin dinner. Scott came up next to her and slammed a bulky orange prescription bottle down on the kitchen table in front of her. "Almost forgot."

"What's this?" She asked. Even though there was an obvious answer.

"Today I had the most awkward conversation with my doctor that I could have. But it was worth it. He gave me a new prescription."

A moment or two went by before Jocelyn followed his trail. Then, "Oh," a light inside her came on.

"In a day or two we'll be back at it like the Easter bunny on Good Friday."

Jocelyn scrunched her nose at the reference. Then Ian's voice joined them, "Do I get to see the Easter bunny?"

"When you're older." Scott said, which brought a great whine from his son and roll of the eyes from his wife.

∗∗∗

The two of them hadn't had a night alone since before deployment, so when Scott asked her out to dinner, she thought it was a return to their weekly date nights. She'd dressed in jeans that felt painted on, heels, and a maroon babydoll shirt edged in cream lace—an outfit she'd copied from one of Elle's pictures on social media. And she'd spent more than ten minutes on her makeup. At a glance, her husband looked back to normal. The only evidence was the leg brace over his jeans or the missing parts of his right ear and bottom lip.

Scott drove her to a bar. Which wasn't bad, except as they walked in, Jocelyn recognized faces all around the room. Faces from Scott's unit.

On the outside, none of them looked like they'd returned from a war zone. She could have walked by them in this bar and never thought of the nightmare they had endured, if it hadn't been for Scott gripping their hands and patting their backs. He greeted them with a smile wide enough for a long-lost family member. In a way, that was exactly what they were.

There were a few faces she recognized from the FRG, a handful of wives or husbands whose services member spouses had only just returned home. Then there were the girlfriends who wore shorter shorts than Jocelyn could imagine owning.

Some of the men at the bar were already drunk and Jocelyn gave them a guarded smile as she followed Scott passed the barstools to a table near the back where Boone stood with his...new girlfriend. She was, in fact, in shorts, a button-down shirt with too few buttons and pink cowboy boots. Boone gestured over the crowd to call them over to his table near the stage. That was when Jocelyn realized they were at a karaoke bar. Her insides curdled like cottage cheese. How had she not noticed the neon-lit Karaoke signs blinking from the windows. Scott knew she hated this. What the hell was he thinking?

His hand was on her back as they stepped closer to Boone's table and passed more guys hollering comments at Scott.

She sidestepped one man with a pint of beer sloshing in her direction.

271

Boone stepped between the two of them, then pulled a seat out for Jocelyn at his table.

"It's sure crowded tonight!" Boone yelled to be heard above the crowd.

Jocelyn raised her eyebrows and nodded as Scott sidled up to her.

"You look mad." Scott said.

"No," Jocelyn said, then amended, "I thought it would be the two of us tonight."

"I should have told you."

"Yes."

Hadn't they been married long enough for him to know what he should and should not say? Had he forgotten so much about her? She swallowed, her throat feeling lumpy and dry at the same time.

Boone's girlfriend looked over with a plastered—both drunk plastered and plastered on—smile. "I'm Amber." She said, tossing her long, platinum hair over her shoulder.

Jocelyn couldn't even remember being *that* girl, the take-me-to-a-bar-and-show-me-a-good-time girlfriend. Maybe she never had been. And she thought Scott had appreciated it. That she was an army wife because she was in love with an army man. But her life hadn't revolved around him and his unit and their families. Life hadn't depended on the FRG and the Rear D and the communication that was never coming. Her life had been Scott and Ian. Maybe that's why she was here. Singing, karaoke, this was Scott's kind of thing. If she wanted Scott to appreciate how she had grown and changed, then she had to remember to love him the way he was. All of him. Even the stupid part of him that loved karaoke. But she would *never* be Cameron Diaz in *My Best Friend's Wedding*. She would never sing so loudly and so badly that people cheered.

Someone jumped up on stage and gave their introduction to a terrible karaoke song. She looked up at Scott, who was talking to a bald guy with glasses that she'd never seen. She grabbed his arm, the arm that was home to barely-there scars. His eyes met hers, pleading with her to stay, to understand.

She dropped her hand to her side and grabbed her purse. The instant panic across his face told her he thought she was leaving.

Instead, she tried on her best seductive voice. "Can I buy you a beer, soldier?"

Scott smiled. It was *his* smile, and she couldn't stop herself from melting into the floor.

***

On his third beer and the beginning of Jocelyn's second, Scott jutted his chin out, gesturing to Boone, who stood and headed toward the DJ. Scott leaned over and whispered in Jocelyn's ear but the words were lost amongst the music and mediocre singing blaring from the speakers. All she felt was the tingling of his breath against the curve of her ear, running down the side of her body to her toes. She'd forgotten why she was mad at him for bringing her here.

As Scott stood from his seat, he swept a finger along the edge of her ponytail, barely touching the softness on the back of her neck.

He walked to the stage with strength—any stiffness in his stride was only visible to her eye, but even now she could barely detect it shadowed by his fierce energy. Scott commandeered a microphone first, then Boone followed.

Before the music started, Scott slipped in a few words. "This one's for our brother, Private First Class Xavier Martinez of the 1st Brigade Combat Team, 1st Calvary Division."

"Hooah" army cheers speckled the room.

Jocelyn's heart stuttered when the piano riffs began the elegy. Each solitary note dangled in the air, the bar guests seeming to hold their breath in unison with her.

Then the microphone was at Scott's mouth, his eyes glazing over the crowd while his voice sounded, the words slipping effortlessly from his lips.

I thought of you today, as I walked this dusty road
This road I left you on, this road that leads us home
How long, my friend, how long
I've been walking alone

Then the beat joined the piano, thundering through the speakers. Scott's body rocked with it, hugging the ribs that had been cracked moments before Xavier died.

Amber, Boone's daisy-duke girlfriend reached across the empty seat between her and Jocelyn, grabbing her hand with a knowing smile. Somehow, though, the small touch showed Jocelyn once again that she and Scott weren't alone in their couple's tug-of-war. Every soldier had a girlfriend or wife or family waiting for them, facing the same giants she and Scott were.

The two men's voices blended as though they had rehearsed this for months. And maybe they had during their karaoke nights under their Jalalabad recreation tent. Just not with the same meaning.

I spoke of you today, like you were standing by my side
Your family, my family, we're all missing your light

The lyrics barreled straight through Jocelyn. It could have been Scott who died if it weren't for Xavier. The weight grounded her to the floor. All along he had felt that. But she hadn't listened, she hadn't asked, she hadn't pushed. This, though, felt like a doorway. Like he had brought her to hear this guttural cry. Scott looked right at Jocelyn. His eyes dark shadows under the spotlights of the stage. But she saw them, beckoning her with his words.

Now the same dusty road leads me home

Maybe she still was his gravity. And this long road had brought him home. To her.

How long, my friend, how long

His voice, flawless as glass up until this point, broke on the word "long." He took a breath, with Boone's hand clasped on his shoulder. The piano trilled out its notes. He was no longer on point with the song, but being who he was, he didn't quit. The music ended but Scott was a chattered vessel. The words came bleeding from him anyway.

How long, my friend, how long
I've been walking alone

Frozen in place, the bar was silent after his last word, and it could have been only the two brothers on stage alone, filling the space between them with pain, but also with healing. Because music can do that. It can seep into your skin, drag a feeling out by its hair and strip you of any shield. It can crack you open to see a vulnerability you have never seen before.

In an instant, Jocelyn's body moved before her inhibitions could stop her. Maybe it was the beer, maybe it was his voice ringing inside her. She was at the bottom of the stairs by the stage, and her husband was in front of her, looking at her as she had surged through the room moved by music, dodging tables and chairs, to get to him, to touch him.

And her mouth was on his. She didn't know if she took the steps toward him, or if he came to her, but they were holding each other now.

The room, silent before, erupted in loud *Hooah*'s and whistles. The room, the soldiers, all feeling the moment between a soldier reunited with a lover after war. Even though Scott and Jocelyn had spent weeks together again, this moment was the reuniting. With their lips still pressed together, Scott fist pumped the air at the cheers, which only grew louder at the gesture. It was the same gesture he made at their wedding when Pastor Garr announced "You may kiss the bride."

This kiss, a renewal of vows, a return of the Sergeant Scott Turner she had dropped off at the army airfield to "go to work" 15 months before. As though an imposter had returned, lived in her house, occupied her bed, but now the *real* Scott Turner was home. Like he had, in fact, returned along with his unit. And yet different. And she would love him all anew.

For a moment, the elation of the night turned dark. Was that it? Had he returned to himself now that his unit was back? Was she not enough to help him heal because she wasn't a part of his brotherhood? Were they the ones who had caused his body and his soul to reunite?

But then he was laughing aloud, pulling her to their table, into his lap, then out of the room. Time turned to fog, and so did the poisonous thoughts. She didn't remember them paying their bill, or saying goodbye to anyone. It was all a myriad of his hands on her hips, his lips on her neck, his nose in her hair. And she wanted more. They were in the car, and he was asking if she thought they could sneak in to the house through the backdoor without Ian or the babysitter noticing.

She laughed, loving the bubbly feel of it in her throat. "Our house isn't quite that big!" Looking at the electric green numbers of the dashboard clock, she added, "Ian will already be asleep."

Then they were home, never once letting go of each other's hands. No doubt the babysitter thought they were drunk, but no matter, Jocelyn couldn't remember feeling this happy, this in love, in so long.

Walking down the hall to the bedroom, before the babysitter's car was even out of the driveway, Jocelyn's foot stubbed against a toy—the idea of a toy left in the hallway after bedtime was unheard of when she was home—and it flew against the wall with a loud thud. Giggles bubbled like champagne from her, and Scott shushed her by pressing his mouth against hers. She couldn't stop herself from smiling, her teeth clanking against Scott lips, drunk only on her husband's breath.

Opening the bedroom door, he then wrapped his arms around her waist and easily swung her into the room, then sealed the door shut behind them.

***

With the sheets crumpled at their feet and a layer of sweat glazed on their skin, a laugh bounded out of Jocelyn. Scott shushed her with a quiet laugh as well, but it didn't matter. Her entire body felt energized. In contrast when she looked at her husband, his eyes were groggy with sex. She wiped her hands across his stomach, feeling the blood speeding its way through his body just as it would after one of his big workouts. A smile tiptoed across her face, loving the fact that she put him in this drunk love state.

"Do you need water to replenish your fluids?" She said, grazing her fingertips from his stomach up his chest. His body quaked under her touch.

He cleared his throat, regaining the ability of cognizant speech. "Please."

Without dressing, she slipped out of bed, aware of his eyes on her every movement. His gaze felt as intimate as the hour they had just spent in bed.

In the hallway, she saw the toy but managed to sidestep it. A tiny toy that she could barely see in the dark hallway became a symbol of her letting go inside. Before tonight, she would have rushed around the house to pick up anything left out of place, and then she would have chided herself for allowing a babysitter to take her place even for one night. But now, her thoughts on her husband, it felt right. He *should* come first. He should be more important than a clean house, than every small piece in place. It had been easy to forget while he was away, but when he came home, she hadn't expected anything to have to change. And yet everything had changed. Scott had changed. Their life. Their love. She would have to change along with it. Not only would she have to lessen the "tightness of her ass"—figuratively speaking of course—she would create a new pathway between them. To communicate freely, without being afraid that the other one would somehow love them less.

She knew one way to start.

Returning to bed with a glass of ice water, she propped herself up on her elbow, staring at his profile while he drank, his throat moving the liquid through his body.

"I read your journals on your laptop." She blurted. The honesty was a release of pressure on her chest that she hadn't realized was there. "I mean, not just now. I've been reading them for a few weeks."

"I know. I saw that they were recently opened."

"I thought you would be mad."

"Why write them if they're not going to be read? And I'm not going to read them."

She knew he didn't need to read them, to be reminded of the images that were there every time he closed his eyes, the feelings that were just under the surface of his scarred skin.

"There's still one entry I haven't read."

That admission caught Scott's attention, and he looked at her, revealing nothing in his eyes.

"Because it hasn't been written." She said.

His jaw went to work, clenching and releasing.

"Will you tell me what happened to you that day?" She asked, knowing the clinical description, medical charts, army release statement. But wanting to *know* what happened inside her husband that day. Making love had only been the first part of the two coming together. This could make their return to each other complete.

Scott placed the water glass on his nightstand and rolled on to his back, not saying yes. Not saying anything. She could only hear his exhales. When he began to speak, the words were guarded and quiet, but they cut through the room like gunshots.

"It was a pretty routine mission, but when some of the guys are taking bets on whose gonna be the next one hit like it's a football pool, then you know nothing's routine anymore. Xavier—we called him X because Xavier sounds like a soap star name." Scott huffed out his nose, almost a laugh but not quite. "He always prayed the 91st Psalm over the unit before we'd go out. Even the nonreligious guys would cross themselves because you figure every bit helps."

Jocelyn heard the sheets crinkle under his body as he adjusted his weight on the mattress. She knew he was uncomfortable reliving it.

"We rolled into town, and I could see hesitation on the civilians. You don't know if it's because they know the enemy is there, or because they are the enemy, or because they think *we* are the enemy. We had to stop at an intersection where a car was pulled over, and my instincts pricked. I just—I knew the air was going to explode any second."

There was no way Jocelyn comprehended the amount of fear someone felt knowing they were about to be attacked, ambushed even. Feeling something coming before it even happened, but heading for it anyway. Her heart pounded underneath her naked chest, but her vulnerability was a world away from his.

"Like it was a premonition or something, almost as soon as I thought it, rounds cracked through the air. It was small-arms fire, so we were fully prepared to handle it. I'd been through way more critical and dangerous missions without a hit." His words sounded confused, like they were searching for an answer to an unspoken question.

"Then an RPG flew at us from somewhere between the shops—I don't know where—and I hollered to the guys, but it was already on us. It was like a cloud of lead burst in front of us. It was deafening. I woke up on my back with chunks of metal flying over my head. Xavier was standing over me, trying to drag me to the M-ATV with one hand and shooting the bastards with the other." He said it with pride, but paused in thought. Regret, maybe? Or images he couldn't share.

"I must have gone out again. The next thing I remember, rounds pelted the ground next to me, but I couldn't move." He stopped. The air between them was thick, as though the heat of Afghanistan had joined them in the room along with the memories. "I felt like a coward lying there, pretending I was dead. But I couldn't feel my leg. And," he paused, gulping air. With only the moon as their light, his profile was a silhouette.

She wanted to hear what came next but simultaneously didn't.

Scott swallowed his emotion, the noise loud in the quiet of the room. Then he continued.

"Xavier was laying across my chest. I couldn't go anywhere." His voice caught, but he pushed on. "Blood was dripping out from under his helmet, and I knew. He won the death lottery. He died trying to get me out, when it should have been me getting him out. It was my job. But all I could do was lay there."

In the moonlight streaking through blinds across his face, the trail of a single tear rolled down his temple. It was the first tear she had seen since he'd come home. One small droplet of water that held more weight than a ton of mortar.

All she wanted to do was touch him, hold him, but he was lying so still, like he was still on the grounds of Jalalabad trapped under his own man. Jocelyn knew better than to touch him while he was reliving this moment, better than to disturb the memory that evoked so much pain, anger, death. All she could do was weep with him.

"He was just a kid." Scott's words choked in his throat.

His body convulsed next to her, reverberating the bed in silent sobs. Gingerly she moved her body up against him, and when he didn't pull away, she laid her head on his shoulder. Her hand moved to his forearm where some of the scars memorialized the grief. They lay together, only the thin bed sheet between them, until his ocean of pain receded.

He then grabbed her hand with his own, returning his awareness to the room and acknowledging her touch.

Propping himself on his elbow—a movement that just a few weeks ago, she would have had to help him accomplish—he looked at her, and the light bounced off his face making his eyes glow.

"I've been waiting for the right time to give you something." Turning, he rummaged around in his nightstand drawer then came back with a nondescript box in his hand. "I'm not sure if it's weird or romantic, but I had this made for you."

Jocelyn tentatively took the box in her hand. The Scott who had deployed bought her presents and sent her packages monthly, but this was the first gift from the Scott who returned. She inhaled. Then flipped the lid open.

A necklace lay inside. A locket. But not the average locket. A gold oval the size of a half dollar hung from a thick chain. The inside of the circle was glass. A heart charm floated inside with a small emerald gem, her birthstone. Words in black script on the back layer of glass: *You are my home.*

And shards of metal lay loose-leaf at the bottom, held down only by gravity. Shrapnel pieces.

She lifted her eyes and they met his, brown and heartbreaking.

"I have scars to remember the pain. And the healing." He sucked his bottom lip in between his teeth, waiting for the right words. "I'm not giving you this to commemorate the pain. But to remember that when the shrapnel pieces come out, there's healing." He tapped his finger on the glass of the locket. "These pieces were taken out of me, but some are still in there, coming up to the surface.

"Everyone has their own shrapnel that leaves scars. I don't want to be yours. I want to be part of our healing."

Tears clung to Jocelyn's eyelashes. When she blinked, they fell onto her cheeks. In her hands, the locket felt weighty—not in heaviness but in significance.

"Will you help me put it on?" She held it up for him to unclasp and place around her neck. The chain was cold against the skin of her collar bones, and the circular locket landed in the crevice between them.

Maybe he was right. Maybe everyone has shrapnel explosions in life and pieces of their world that could pierce them and leave them mangled. And we have the choice to either leave the shrapnel inside to cause further damage or go through the pain of pulling the shrapnel out and begin healing.

He said he didn't want to be her shrapnel, but it was too late. He'd already pierced through her. He already left jagged scars. But not every scar was bad. Scott was her shrapnel. He was under her skin. He was everywhere in her, a part of every cell in her body. Sure, he'd caused pain. But he was the cause for her healing too. Scott was her home.

23

ELLE

The call from Marissa came on a Saturday morning while Elle slept. Only slivers of sun poked through the closed blinds above her bed. Elle had spent a few hours in the middle of the night, packaging her two latest sales, one purse and one of her favorite pair of Christian Louboutin shoes. It felt like shopping rehab, wrapping up these pieces of her life—err, former life—in pretty, scented tissue paper and twine with a note to their new owner. Some might think it silly, others good marketing strategy to keep customers coming, but Elle found that it softened the blow to send her beloved pieces off in warmth.

Then night had become morning, and Elle's eyes defied her attempt to open them when her phone buzzed. She threw her hand around the nightstand until landing on her phone and adeptly slid her thumb across the screen to answer, eyes remaining closed. She tried to sound awake when she said, "Hello."

"I woke you." It was Marissa.

Elle realized her friend didn't even know of her insomnia. "It's okay. Is everything alright?" She slurred. There was no point pretending she was alert.

"Can you meet me at Polly's for breakfast?" Her friend's voice wasn't the same, maybe the deadness in it was illuminated over the phone, but Elle took note.

"Polly's?" It was a diner on the edge of Redondo Beach pier where customers sat outside, watching fishermen on the wharf with their poles in the water and locals enjoying the plethora of water sports.

The two had been to Polly's with their husbands over the years, back when Heath and Marissa didn't have kid duty and could get away to a restaurant anytime. Heath and Aaron talked about one day bringing their sons there for breakfast and early morning fishing. It hadn't happened that way.

They tried to continue even when Hailey was a baby, but her attempt to crawl after pelicans on the dirty pier hampered their visits.

Marissa sighed in her way. "For this one day, can't you *not* be vegan?"

Elle laughed. For Marissa and the sake of their friendship, she could try.

***

As expected, Marissa beat her there and was already sipping her coffee. Opened sweetener packets were scattered across the table by the light breeze. The smell of fresh fish wafted up to Elle's nostrils. It was her least favorite part of being near the beach, but she'd become accustomed to it.

When Marissa greeted her, her voice was just as deadened in person as it had been on the phone, and it perforated the edge of Elle's heart.

Her friend waved her hand to the waitress and Elle noticed the thinness of Marissa's wrist. Had she dropped that much weight in their short time apart?

When Marissa had ordered the huevos rancheros, Elle prepared herself for the ugly face she would receive with her own order. "Can I get a bowl of fresh fruit and a side order of the hash browns cooked well done but with olive oil and a pinch of salt?"

Marissa gave a half smile as the waitress tried to keep up. Elle was used to irritating the wait staff of restaurants when she was out with Marissa or Aaron, who refused to go to vegan venues. Marissa had come to think it humorous.

"So how are things?" Marissa asked after the waitress left, shaking her head.

"I don't want to get caught up talking about me." Elle said with a hint of embarrassment.

"I want you to," was her friend quick response, "that's why I called you."

Elle couldn't help but laugh. It made Marissa smile, but the smile didn't reach her eyes.

"I haven't left the house." Marissa shrugged. "Heath's gone to the grocery store for me and cooked dinner. The girls have done all the cleaning, so you know what that means."

Elle didn't really, but she guessed it wasn't good.

"This is the first day I've put on a stitch of makeup or haven't worn dirty clothes." Marissa's voice turned thick and throaty in an instant. "I just don't want to be stuck in mourning anymore."

She looked up from her hands to Elle's face, and there were tears in her hard eyes. For once Elle knew what to say to this broken mother sitting across from her.

Elle tread carefully around the words, swishing each one around her mouth like a taste of fine wine. "You have two other babies who are here, and they need you."

Marissa bobbed her head in short up and down motions, as tears she'd held in a holding pattern started their descent. "That's why I need you to drag me out of this." She rolled her round eyes as she allowed more tears to drip off her eyelashes. "I *know* things have been happening with you, so fill me in."

Don't pity me; distract me. Be my best friend again. Elle heard between her friend's words. She heard it because she had become familiar with the feeling. It was what she hid between her own words whenever she'd reached out too.

"You can be the first to know that I signed the papers," Elle had yet to tell anyone other than the *Divorce-is-our-business* lawyer she'd hired earlier in the week.

Marissa's eyebrows popped up.

"The girls at work want to throw me a divorce party, because apparently that's a thing now. But I don't want to celebrate it. I kind of just want to forget it." Even though that was impossible.

"I'm so sorry. You okay?" Marissa responded unmoving.

The squawk of a seagull preempted Elle's response. She shrugged after stealing a glance at the seagull flying above. "I don't think we're supposed to be okay after tragedy." She met Marissa's hazel eyes, which generated an instant shimmer.

Taking the heat away from Marissa's own tragedy, Elle continued,

"We make mistakes. Slews of them," thinking of all she had learned about herself, Norah, her mother. "The mistakes don't stop just because we change. I think the best we can hope for is to make different mistakes, *better* mistakes."

There was so much she had held back from Marissa. The revelation of her mother's attack, the opportunity she'd had at work, her flirtation with Brandon. There was a relief in talking to her best friend again, but this time over her hash browns and fruit, Elle made the effort to listen as much as she talked.

***

Lena Designs was bustling as the new catalogs were being shipped out, loads of new fabrics being delivered and Elle's fingers were riddled with paper cuts. Even though she was the executive secretary, a day of mail-outs like this called for all-hands-on-deck. More than the sting of paper cuts, though, Elle felt every eye on her like beams of heat each time she set foot in a room, as though everyone knew of her tragic disappointment-slash-failure. *Which one?* she wanted to ask.

Despite Lena's kind words, when she came out to her office to sign off on a contract that needed to be mailed out, Elle was ashamed to meet her eyes. When she finally did, Lena was smiling her no-teeth smile and rubbed Elle's forearm before returning to her office. It felt like pity in the moment, but Elle realized later it was more like experience.

After a full day, she was happy to hear the buzz of her phone. She assumed it was another sale of a closet item, but it was far better.

"Last appointment ended early. Don't want to wait until Friday appt to see you. Plans tonight?" Brandon's text read.

She smiled to herself and looked at the clock. "Hour til I'm off. Suggestions?"

Jenny, with freshly dyed Arial-red dreads, sat in the chair across from Elle's desk. "Haven't seen a smile like that in a while."

"I think I have a date tonight," her voice responded with a quiver. A date, it didn't even sound real to her ears.

Jenny skidded the chair closer until she could set her elbows on Elle's desk. "With who? Do tell!" Her large eyes and full eyelashes peered at her with expectancy.

Elle's phone buzzed again.

Brandon. "I'm thinking about trying the vegan thing. Want to show me the ropes?"

"Seriously?"

"Not for life. Just for dinner."

Yes. She wanted to type but her paper cut fingers wouldn't let her. Was it too soon? She was still in love with Aaron, still dreaming about him, willing to rip up the signed papers if he were to only ask her.

"Ok." She finally typed, then turned to Jenny with wide eyes. Life was about mistakes, wasn't it? Just making better ones.

***

Driving through rush-hour traffic, Elle called to inform Norah she would be eating dinner with Brandon—to which Norah responded, "It's about time!" She reminded Norah to take her evening medications from her Med-plan and that her favorite lasagna was in the freezer.

Sometimes Norah pushed back when Elle micromanaged, but tonight she didn't. "Have some fun." Norah said in the same way she told teenage Elle before a Friday night football game.

Next she called Marissa to squeal like that same high school Elle would about a first date. Marissa laughed, having accepted the reclamation of their friendship.

Then she was at the store, and his car was out front. He was leaning against it with a casual confidence, scrolling through his phone. There are rare moments when someone can be watched unaware, but Elle had caught quite a few of Brandon. It was only the second time she had seen him without scrubs on, without his work badge screaming to keep her distance, to keep their connection professional. But those voices were silent as she stole a moment to study him in a gray t-shirt and jeans, fitted ones that made his legs seem miles long. Never would she have thought she'd find that simplicity attractive until she saw it on him. Maybe she could be a t-shirt and jeans kind of girl.

He looked up in time for her to pull into a parking space, and he strolled to her in long strides, one hand in his jeans pocket. Anyone else walking in such a way would look like he was trying too hard. To Brandon, it came natural. He leaned down to open the car door for her and her stomach twisted.

"Have you been here long?" She nipped whatever flirtatious opening line he might try. She wanted to take this slow, but with his wide smile, she knew how hard that was going to be.

His hair was freshly cut. She could tell by how close the short sides and back were, how she wanted to run her hand up the back up his neck.

Deep breath.

She tried to focus on his small talk. It was hard to know what to ask him, being that he was unable to talk much about work since she was related to one of his patients. "What kind of dogs do you have?" She blurted as they entered the store, realizing too late he was mid-sentence.

Brandon laughed, good natured as always. "Bruiser is a Pomsky. He looks like a Husky but stays small like a Pomeranian. And Harley's a Bulldog."

Once as a child, she asked Charlene for a dog and was told no. Outside of that, Elle wasn't much of an animal person. She thought back to Christmas when she'd seen the pet-owners waiting in line for pictures of their animals with Santa. The image of Brandon being in that line with two dogs pulled back the instant irrational attraction that had surged when she pulled up. Now it was manageable.

"Do you take pictures of them?" She asked, suspiciously.

"Yeah, I have a few." He pulled out his phone.

"I mean, like, family pictures."

"Well, not like professional ones."

She nodded, somewhat satisfied and headed into the store. Brandon pocketed his phone.

"So, what vegan specialty do you have in store for me tonight?" He spoke with trepidation masked by his usual smile.

Elle could have tortured him but she also didn't want to run him off. "Nothing crazy. Salad, pizza and my favorite coconut lemon bars."

His eyebrows raised, surprise having replaced his smile. "Vegan pizza?"

Elle nodded.

"I can do pizza."

The two walked up and down the aisles putting the fresh ingredients in their cart. Standing with him in a grocery store aisle, Elle felt so normal, like they were meant to be doing this. She kept her eyes forward on the rainbow of vegetables in front of her but aware he had one hand on the cart, the other on his hip. The way they were standing together, other shoppers would assume they were a long-term couple. The thought quickened her heartbeat.

"Tofu? I knew you tricked me." His lip curled in mock disgust, when she picked up a small square package of the white substance.

"One pizza with it and one without." Elle promised, working to keep the nerves out of her voice. "You wanted the whole vegan experience."

Not needing to small talk was a first date oddity. But along with Norah's health, small talk had filled up most of their communication for months. She knew of his family up north, parents and two brothers. How he had moved here for college and gotten a local job shortly thereafter. But it was also a nice comfort to not have to always be talking, to just *be* together. That was new for her.

Brandon paid for the groceries claiming he always paid for dinner on a date, and snuck in a bouquet of fresh flowers that he proceeded to hand her with a slight bow. Elle's cheeks warmed as they left the store, then drove their own cars back to his apartment. He attempted to transport the bags all in one load, which was about the time she noticed the way his gray t-shirt naturally clung to his arms and a tribal tattoo on the inside of his bicep she had never seen peek out of his sleeve.

As the groceries were unloaded and fresh foods strewn across his kitchen counter, Elle let her eyes take in everything about his place, the stainless steel, the dark wood floors, the lack of pictures but plethora of books stacked on shelves, the murmur of one of his neighbors and the whoosh of the wind through an open window. His dogs were at his feet in an instant, trying to not get stepped on but used to working around him. She couldn't help but laugh a little. This was his life, and it was comfortable. Even though she didn't want to jump off the cliff into his life, she could see herself as a fixture here.

She went to work on the pizza as he put her flowers in a large mason jar then let the dogs out on the back patio with only a sliver of grass for them to do their business. By the time he returned, her fingers were sticky with dough and there was a patch of almond flour on her pants. He assisted her in rolling out the dough, and even though Elle didn't need the help, she liked his hands on hers, their bodies forced into a tight space.

The coconut lemon cookies were premade and Brandon popped one in his mouth when Elle was busy chopping red bell peppers. She pointed the knife at him playfully, and he put his hands up with innocence, "They are all natural and healthy right? So, they're practically a fruit appetizer."

His apartment filled with the aroma of sautéed peppers, onions, mushrooms and tofu as the pizza cooked in the oven. They sat to eat the arugula and peach salad Elle prepared while Brandon poured the wine.

"Wine and pizza. My kind of guy." Elle said as she held her glass up for him.

There was a comfortable quiet as they ate their salad, which made her self-conscious chewing. Her mind wracked around for conversation dialogue, then finally she dropped her fork on the plate with a clank, laced her fingers together and said, "Tell me something about yourself that I don't know."

With little surprise to Elle, Brandon smiled while he finished chewing. "This is my first date since the divorce." He laughed, then said with sarcasm, "I know it's hard to believe with all my chattiness."

Elle was glad he breached the subject on his own since she was beyond curious.

"How long has it been?"

"Two years," he answered but underneath the matter-of-fact response there was a pain familiar to Elle. She was surprised and saddened to know that the hurt lingered so long.

"Of course it was over long before that." Brandon continued, "Some people divorce because they drift apart, or they cheat, or they can't handle some tragedy that splits them up. We had a little bit of everything."

His story crushed Elle yet imparted an odd sense of camaraderie. He didn't have to say much for her to know his fragmented heart. She didn't know how much Norah had told him or how much he gleaned being around, but panic surged within her. What if he took Aaron's side?

Instead of speaking, she filled her open mouth with salad and bought her courage some time. He didn't ask or try to fill in the air with meaningless words. Just then the timer beeped announcing the pizzas were done, and relief washed over her.

Brandon lifted his nose at the savory scent wafting from the oven. The golden crust was just crispy enough and the vegetables boasted perfectly browned edges.

"So," began Brandon as he sat with the plate of pizza slices in front of him, one with tofu and one without, "if I eat your tofu tonight, on our next date will you eat my steak?"

"That, Sir, was incredibly dirty."

He burst in loud laughter that melted into a cackle, filling his whole face with color.

Elle rain her fingers up the back of her neck to her hairline, pleased with herself. It was easy to make him smile, but she enjoyed making him laugh. This had always been Elle's strong suit in dating, adding to the sexual tension, pushing the limits of flirtation.

"And yes," she answered his original question when his cackle had petered off, "but only metaphorically speaking." Her eyes twinkled at him. "I don't eat steak."

Brandon took a course breath. "Well I don't know whether to end this date now so we can move along to the next or feel insulted that you won't even try my cooking."

Elle winked at him, "I make a mean portabella steak."

But he shook his head. "I don't think that's the same thing."

Their conversation flowed smoothly from there, maybe spurred on a bit by the wine's liquid calm, but she promised herself to not let the buzz take over. Her stunts with Aaron proved how hazardous that was.

She found it easy to be around him, be herself, and her guard set to protect the truth inside of her from coming out began to crumble. They made their way to the patio of the apartment, overlooking the street, where he had soft chairs and clay pottery clustered in the corner. When she asked about them, he told her they were merely conversation pieces which were doing their job.

"My family thinks I'm a workaholic," he answered when she asked if he had any hobbies since pottery proved to not be one. "After the divorce I haven't felt much like going out. I take the dogs to parks and I run, but it takes longer to bounce back than people think."

Elle certainly could relate. She had blamed Norah for feeling disconnected from her old life, but to hear someone put voice to it made her feel sane.

Slouched back in her chair with her feet propped up on the pallet table in front of her, she tilted her head back. "At least your work is noble. I answer phones for a living, do someone else's bidding all day." She heard the alcohol in her voice so she put the glass down on the concrete beneath her.

"Your work doesn't have to be what is noble." Brandon's strong, lean hand reached to her face. His long finger touched the edge of her jaw line. "Your sacrifice to help your grandmother is what makes you noble."

Elle breathed in his words. She wanted to believe them, wanted them to be true. She wanted to be that woman he saw, but she wasn't. "It's sweet of you to say that," she said, shaking her head against his hand, not wanting to relinquish his touch, "but you're wrong. Everything I did was actually self-serving."

The intensity in his eyes darkened. There was a hunger in them that thrilled her and scared her all at once.

"I've seen how you are with her, what you've done for her. It's not self-serving." His fingers electrified her skin.

She couldn't imagine what cases of negligence he had seen. A flicker of sadness in his eyes told her of them. But that didn't change her own circumstances, *Who's selfish now?* It was a family trait, inherited from her grandfather, she supposed, who had been too selfish to let his pride down and accept the broken daughter and fatherless granddaughter waiting to be loved. Did she intend to bring Brandon into that tangled web? Did he deserve that?

There was so much going on in her head, so many reasons she shouldn't be here. Elle leaned forward, putting her elbows on her knees, breaking the connection of his skin against hers.

"He wanted kids," she blurted. Then closed her eyes, hating herself for let the words slip out. "We both wanted a lot of things, different things."

When she turned her head, their eyes locked. She bit her lip and laughed, "It's probably uncouth to talk about your ex on a first date." She put her fingertips over her dry lips, holding in any other unacceptable topics.

His smile returned in all its glory, warming Elle from the inside out. "It's also odd to go grocery shopping on a first date, but we aren't kids anymore. The sheen of dating looks different from adult eyes."

A light breeze rustled around her, catching her hair on her eyelashes. Brandon reached up and swept the hair out of her face as though it was the most natural thing he'd ever done. But it made Elle's pulse quicken.

"Any chance I've turned you into a vegan?" She was becoming the queen of changing the subject, but the night necessitated it. She couldn't allow herself to become enraptured with such ease.

Brandon exhaled, as though he knew her intentions and was disappointed by them. "I could handle it."

His words held double meaning. He knew, and Elle did as well. Brandon wouldn't let the tension go. He held it firm like a rock climber belaying down a jagged cliff.

There wasn't anything else for her to say, so she remained quiet. The evening made sounds around them, a sparrow taking flight from the rooftop, the whir of cars passing on the street ahead, children giggling in a neighboring yard.

Her heart ached at the cheery sound, but not because she wanted children of her own. It was because of her indifference. This man sitting next to her who was a caretaker by nature, she was certain he would eventually come to the same conclusions her husband had. She couldn't take it if Brandon looked at her like she was broken. But maybe she was.

This wasn't what she should be feeling on a first date, not with a man like this, so willing to jump into her world.

Her feelings overwhelmed her, coursed through her blood. She stood before she realized it, and Brandon looked expectant. "I should get home to check on Norah."

Brandon stood too, his body rising and rising until her neck was tilted back to see his tall stature. With a gentle touch, he placed his hands on each of her forearms making parenthesis around her body. "Okay," he said, with a knowing. He sensed her fear just as much as he sensed her want.

In a sudden rush, she grabbed her purse leaving the groceries that were left over from dinner and murmured at Brandon as she hurried out the door. She never heard the door close behind her, so it was safe to assume he was watching her from the doorway as she jumped in her car, but she didn't make the effort to look back, sure that she would turn to stone or crumble to pieces if she did.

Her hands fidgeted against the steering wheel like a junkie in withdraw. She had to get out of his line of sight before she could reach for her phone and make a call for perspective's sake.

The line rang on the other end.

"So," the ready voice of Marissa answered in one ring, "how'd it go?"

"I ran," Elle moaned. She didn't want to sound like her old self, so she took a breath before continuing. "I literally ran out of his house. Away from him. And he didn't do anything wrong." That was the problem. He had done everything right.

"I'm broken, Marissa." Elle said, no tears, just fact. "I'm so broken, and I don't even know where the pieces are. And I'm afraid that Aaron is the only one who could put them back together." Because he knew her. He knew her brokenness and he had mended her in so many ways, helping her passed needing a father, needing a mother. He had become everything for her, and yet she wasn't enough for him. She wasn't even afraid of whether or not Brandon could love her. She'd seen the answer so clear in his eyes, felt it in his touch. "I'm afraid that I won't be able to love anyone else the way I love Aaron. And it's not fair, is it, to ask someone to love me when my heart is already taken?"

Her friend's answer was quiet, not abrupt in Marissa's usual way, but it struck Elle as truth. "Do you remember your first kiss?"

Elle nodded, which of course Marissa couldn't see.

"Remember how perfect you thought it was, but you were only 14, right? You didn't know what the perfect kiss could be. And your first love, seems like it would be forever and nothing would ever measure up. But then you met Aaron."

A car horn honked behind Elle. She looked up to see the red light had turned green. She pulled the car into a parking lot to catch her friend's wisdom, hoping it was contagious.

"This will be the same way. It might take time, but you'll fall in love again with someone. Whether it's Brandon or someone new. This isn't the end, Elle. Endings always feel finite like a period at the end of a sentence. But sometimes where we put a period, there should only be a comma."

Under the parking lot light of a Trader Joe's, Elle's car idled. If she had learned nothing else in these months, she learned the strength in silence. Once she found words, her voice was a childlike whisper, "What do you think I should do?"

A sigh, but not Marissa's typical exasperation. It was kinder. Elle heard a smile translated through it. "I can't tell you what to do, Elle. Too many people have for too long. It's time you answer that question yourself. You pick which door you're walking through, and I will love you and help you and hold you up no matter what."

But Elle didn't want to make her own decisions. It was easier when they were thrust upon her. But her friend was right. She had to jump. Even if she didn't know where she was going to land. Life doesn't always have safety nets, but life does have a way of giving you a hand to grab onto when you've fallen, if you only know where you look.

A sort of autopilot took over her car, and her body, until she was standing at the door. She knocked, louder than expected. For one second, she thought about turning around, hiding in the shadow of the bushes like a teenager pulling a prank. But she stood firm.

Until he pulled the door open. She saw his gray t-shirt and jeans, unchanged. Brandon stood in the doorway looking back at her, watching her eyes move over him. He wore an expression that she couldn't place. Not confusion or arrogance. But confidence, sureness, like he had known all along that she would be at his door when he opened it, that she would be ready for him.

She took one step, then momentum took over and closed the distance between them. With a true urgency, her hands wrapped around his neck and brought his mouth down to hers. She pressed her lips up against his, feeling each nerve that touched and the small space where they parted. His hands were on her hips and pulled her body toward his.

Then he smiled against her kiss. "Welcome back," he whispered against her mouth.

They shared a breath. And she pushed the whole of her weight against him, backing him into the room, and her foot swung the door closed behind them.

Not looking for any safety net this time, she jumped.

24

JOCELYN

The midnight quiet of the neighborhood brought about a rare peace. Sitting atop the duplex roof reminded her of past years, the quiet that only came to her mind up here where the air seemed a little easier to breath and the breeze rustled her hair against her cheeks in an almost romantic way. No clouds in the sky on this night. Just stars, speckled pinholes in a black blanket. She pulled her knees up under her chin, letting her tennis shoes hold her place on the shingled roof.

Sometimes it felt like this was the only way she could think clearly. That down on the ground everything was muddled, but up here, on the roof with only the stars above, her brain had space to roam freely.

Awakened again by insomnia, she'd left Scott sleeping to creep up the ladder to the roof for some moments of solitude. For months, she wished to not spend the night alone. Now she felt a serenity in the quiet. Midnight hours had taught her much about herself. They had become a companion, a friend that she missed.

The ladder up against the edge of the roof shifted. Thinking it was the wind rattling against it, Jocelyn scooted down until she reached it with one foot so that it didn't fall. But as she did, the top of a man's head materialized. She lurched back, but Scott was high enough that his hand gripped the edge of the roof and stabilized himself.

"What are you doing? I thought you were asleep." She whisper-scolded.

"I was. But when I woke up, I couldn't find you. You scared me."

"Well, you scared me." A deep breath eased out the adrenaline burst. "You shouldn't be up here. It's too dangerous for you."

He was over the ladder and on the roof, next to his wife before she finished. "I can do it."

"How are you going to get down?"

"I'll wait until you're at the bottom then jump into your arms."

She rolled her eyes. "Oh great." But she was smiling. This was Scott. Not because his leg was whole or gaining mobility, not because he made it to the top of the roof, but because his light was back. She'd been waiting for it. Again, waiting for him to return to her.

She let the darkness of night mask the tears creeping their way into her eyes.

"Are you cold?"

"No."

"But you have goosebumps." He said, tracing the edge of her arm with his index finger.

"Now I do."

Having dragged a blanket up the ladder with him, he wrapped it around her shoulders. He lifted his face up to the black sky, the same way she had before his unexpected appearance. "It's strange that this sky is the same one I looked at from Afghanistan. Same stars. Less noise."

"I didn't come up here at all while you were gone. I was afraid Ian would wake and not be able to find me." She said, tugging the edges of the blanket around her and scooting closer to him so they could share.

"I came up here the night before I deployed."

That surprised Jocelyn, and her face showed it.

"I threw out some prayers, hoping one of them would catch God's ear." His eyes scanned the sky. "I prayed that I'd come home to sit next to you just like this."

A horn blared in the distance, but neither of them noticed. Jocelyn nestled her head up against Scott's shoulder, a niche that was made just for her. He kissed her hair, pulled up in a knot on top of her head the way she always wore it to sleep.

A hesitation in his otherwise steady breathing told Jocelyn that he had more to say, but she had learned not to push him. She rested right where she was, ever waiting.

"I wish my mom and your dad could have come to visit. It'd be nice to see everybody again. Even Brad and his family." He said of Jocelyn's brother—the two men had never gotten along well, even in high school. They were both too competitive. "I talked to my CO, and I finagled some extra days of leave. I thought maybe being with family would help us decide what we should do about re-enlisting."

Jocelyn's head popped up. He was talking in circles, and she couldn't tell for sure what he was saying. Question marks dangled in her eyes.

"Let's go home." He said.

"Yeah?" She asked. Nothing he could have said would have been better than those three words. "We could take Ian to Disneyland and Knott's Berry Farm and–and the Santa Monica Pier! He's never even seen the beach." She was almost embarrassed to admit it.

Scott laughed. "I don't know if we could fit *all* of that into a couple days, but we'll do what we can."

Giggles sputtered inside her. Lying her back on the roof with knees bent reaching toward the stars, she felt content. "Oh I've missed the beach." She felt the heat of Scott's gaze on her.

"Maybe while we're there, we can look for a place to move back."

She jerked her eyes to his and sat back up. Was he serious? But what she saw in those brown eyes of his was the same seriousness as when he asked her every major statement that formed their lives. *Wait for me. Marry me.*

"Back home," he amended.

"But you never wanted to move back."

He turned his eyes to the stars now. "I never wanted to do a lot of things." When he made those statements, the ones that reached in to times she wasn't present for, she knew what he was remembering. His hand reached for her in a soft caress. "Plans change."

She leaned back against the rooftop again with a contented sigh.

"Does that make you happy?" Scott said, leaning back on his elbow next to her, his hand grazing her stomach.

She nodded. "But most of all *you* make me happy." She pulled her chin up, closing the space between them. He fit his hand under her back and brought her body up to him with strength. His lips brushed hers, soft and cool.

This was how he had proposed to her, sitting up on the roof of her parent's home in Southern California. With only the stars as their witness, he had pulled the simple band with a small solitaire diamond out of his pocket. He didn't even say the typical words. He said, "Thank you for waiting for me." And she hadn't said yes. She had only said, "You were worth the wait." Then he slid the ring on her finger, they had kissed and the rest was the history that led to this moment.

Her words came back to her. *You were worth every single second of the wait.*

***

The bags were packed and Scott was loading them in the car. Jocelyn was a self-proclaimed packing expert. Completed with space saver bags and rolled up clothes, she had packed all three of them in two suitcases with plenty of extra room for any souvenirs acquired on the trip.

Three days of approved leave tacked on to a weekend would give them plenty of time to cram in as many memory-building activities as they could manage. And it all fit into their budget with little squeezing considering the military airline discount and staying at family members' homes. She could hardly contain her excitement.

"Can I take this in my backpack?" Ian asked, holding up his new football and enunciating *backpack* in a way that struck Jocelyn. His vocabulary and pronunciation had grown so much in the last few months.

"You won't be able to throw that around on the airplane. I don't think it's a good idea to bring it."

Ian slumped his shoulders, and Scott looked up from the trunk. "Aw," they said in unison.

"But he wants to throw the football on the beach." Scott said, sounding almost as childlike.

With a wry smile, she shook her head. "Don't get too overconfident, Sergeant. Your leg may be improving, but I don't think it's beach football ready just yet."

She handed him Ian's carry-on full of coloring books and snacks to load in the trunk.

"I can think of a few other things I *can* handle on the beach." He smirked back. As she turned, he gave her yoga pants covered butt a gentle smack. The playful touch made her jump a little and she looked back at him with wide, pleasantly surprised eyes.

"Mom, catch!" Ian threw the football her direction before the words were out of his mouth, but the ball landed three feet to her right.

"Nice try." She said. Maybe she should let him bring it to the beach. He needed all the practice he could get if he was going to be able to throw the ball with his dad once Scott was fully recuperated. There was certainly enough room. "Okay," she relented, "but it goes in the suitcase." She tossed the ball underhanded back to Ian.

Both of her males cheered.

"Now, potty breaks before we leave for the airport." She pointed at Ian...then Scott. Ian laughed.

Her brain jumped back into list mode. She may have chilled out on the color-coded, hour-by-hour schedule that had been removed from the refrigerator, but for her own sanity, she still had lists for everything. Her packing checklist was on the kitchen counter right where she'd left it, a small dried spot of orange juice from breakfast gracing the center. She mentally ticked down all the items. Toiletries, underwear, pajamas, phone chargers, doors and windows locked, and the list went on.

Scott rounded the corner, interrupting her inventory with a kiss. This vacation was already doing them some good, and they hadn't even left yet. What else would the fresh salty air do for them?

"Where's Ian?" She asked.

Scott looked down the hallway toward the bathroom. "I thought he came in with you to go to the bathroom."

Her glance followed his, but the bathroom door was open, light off.

"Ian?" She said, trying to swallow but her throat felt dry. She hated leaving him outside alone. He was four. He didn't pay attention to his surroundings enough. The front yard was cramped, and college students who lived in the duplexes a few doors down always drove too fast on the small street. Not to mention a million other dangerous possibilities that plagued a mother's mind when her child was out of sight.

Bolting through the front door, she hollered his name again, "Ian."

Her son looked up, his eyes inflated like he had been caught, but he had done nothing wrong. He was still throwing the football around and nowhere near the street. Her heart slowed to a normal speed.

"My jacket," she said. With her mind cleared, she remembered what she'd felt like she was forgetting.

"I'll get it." Scott said.

"The lightweight one."

"I know. I'm from California too." He winked at her.

The list was still in her hand, as she slammed the trunk shut. She picked up where she'd left off checking items on her list.

Her subconscious heard the car turn onto the street, but she was trying hard to focus so that nothing else was forgotten. She recognized the sound of the car accelerating far too fast for this short street. Rolling her eyes, wanting to wag her finger at the irresponsible driver, she turned just in time.

She'd imagined it, fearing it in her mind so many times. A bird, a beach ball, a bike, whatever else in the road and Ian running after it. But this time it wasn't her imagination. Ian was throwing the football up in the air, catching it himself, but he missed. The brown leather tapped his fingertips and vaulted backwards on its pointed side. Then bounced some more gaining momentum as it rolled into the road.

As many times as she'd told Ian to look both ways before crossing the street, the words couldn't come out fast enough.

"Ian!" She hollered, but he didn't turn around. His eyes were focused on one thing. His new ball.

"WAIT!" Her legs were in motion, moving without her telling them to, faster than she thought she could travel. For every one of her steps, it seemed like Ian took three, and the car moved forward even faster.

The horn honked. It blared in her ears, but her ears were already ringing with her own voice, screaming his name. "IAN!" She could almost reach out to him. He was bending down to pick up the football, then looked back at her, his eyes bigger than the ball in his hand.

She was one step away. Her arms reached out. In her periphery, she could see the grill of the car, the flash of the headlights. She could hear the screeching of the wheels. She heard Scott shouting behind her.

She pushed with all her might. It was all she could think of. As much as she wanted to grab him and hold him close, she knew it was too late. She shoved with her palms, thrusting Ian's small body to the other side of the road. She didn't see where he landed. It was too late for that. She felt the impact on her right side. The pain wrecking her body, her neck, her head was the last thing she felt. The last thing she saw was the blue sky above her. There was a cloud. The last thing she heard was Scott's voice. Then black.

25

ELLE

Jocelyn!!! I'm so sorry it took so long to respond. I didn't see your message until this morning. And I am so excited that you are coming to visit Cali!!!! I CANNOT wait to meet you in person. At the risk of sounding stalker-ish (although I'm hoping we are quite past that), I've imagined meeting you in person so many times! I know you thought it would be creepy for me to show up at your doorstep, but I'm telling you GO AHEAD! Knock on my door! I want to meet Ian and Scott, too! If that's not too weird.

Let me know what day you can get together and at least let me take you out to dinner!

Elle

26

SCOTT

It wasn't instant. That could have been the hardest part. Although he wasn't sure what the hardest part was anymore. Every day reinvented the word *hard*.

He had run to her side. But later he realized he was too late. He'd always been too late. Too late asking her on their first date. Too late in marrying her. He should have held her and never let go. That was all that spun around in his mind while he held her on that black asphalt road in front of their home, the dented car next to him, pushing Ian back to protect him from seeing the nightmare before them. Scott grasped her face between his hand, her matted hair loose from its bun and sticking to her skin—it's pallor quickly fading, speckles of asphalt and rocks glittering her bloody cheek. He pulled at her. He squeezed her. He shook her. He breathed into her lips whatever life he could muster. He dug every piece of his emergency training the army had given him from the foggy nook of his mind, but nothing changed. She laid on the road, half in his arms, half mangled, pouring blood from the side of her head.

Voices swirled around him. But none of them were Jocelyn's, so how could they matter. Later he was told that the neighbor girl who had been driving was hysterical. She claimed she hadn't been texting, just not paying attention. Kirk had come outside hearing the commotion. He was the one who pulled Ian back from the scene, holding the little boy as he cried for his mom, yelled to his dad. But neither were available to him.

Kirk had the presence of mind to call 911 with a free arm, then attempted to calm the driver down.

They were the onlookers while Scott performed CPR on his wife. In the middle of their front yard. On the day they were supposed to leave for vacation.

***

Scott didn't remember any words he'd spoken. Not to Jocelyn or the driver or Kirk or even to Ian. He only remembered holding the jacket she'd asked him to get and blood dripping from Jocelyn head, the same way it had from Xavier's. His nightmares couldn't distinguish between the two faces anymore.

She was in the hospital for days. They did surgeries on her brain to lessen the swelling after her head had smashed into the windshield and then rebounded onto the asphalt. None of the surgeries worked.

A blur of people met him at the hospital. Guys from his unit. Sgt. Cryer. A woman he'd met at an FRG picnic whose name Scott couldn't remember. Elizabeth Cryer stayed in the waiting room and let Ian sleep in her lap after his little arm had been fitted for a cast. Scott had missed that too, waiting at Jocelyn's bedside. The impact of his mother pushing him out of the way had broken it in two places. Although his heart was broken more than that.

When the flat-line had been drawn, time of death called, and there was no more reason for them to be at the hospital, Scott lingered. He couldn't imagine going back to the duplex. To look up at the line of the roof where they sat and talked. To smell her shampoo when he walked into the bathroom. How could he expect Ian to pick up a football again or play in the front yard where the rust-colored stain of Jocelyn's blood discolored the asphalt.

They had nowhere to go. What was home without Jocelyn there?

Until he was making the calls to family, putting into words what had happened, he had never thought about what it must have been like for Jocelyn to hear what had happened to him. Why hadn't he ever asked? No doubt she expected the worst when she saw the car pulling up. No doubt her stomach felt as hollow as his did now.

Scott had come to terms with the idea of his own death. You only took this job as an infantryman if you were prepared to be shot at. It was part of being deployed. In all Scott's preparations in the army, he had written his own letters, the ones Jocelyn would receive in the case of his death. He had thought about them, what he would want Jocelyn and Ian to know. They had been the hardest words he had ever written on paper.

But not once had he considered her going first. And now she was gone.

Jocelyn's parents flew in, as did his own. But they didn't make it in time. He knew they wouldn't, but he didn't feel like he could tell them to stay home. The loss was theirs too.

So, Ian went to the hotel with them for the night until Scott could get his bearings in their home. He didn't know what else to do, but he couldn't bear to experience Ian walking through that front yard again. Not yet anyway. Maybe not ever.

Ian's eyes searched Scott's face for answers. It wasn't like the boy didn't understand. He'd been there. He's seen it for himself. But he wanted something from Scott, and Scott didn't know how to give it to him. The man was searching for answers himself. He didn't know what to say to his son. He needed Jocelyn there to explain this all to them both. She always had the right words.

How had she done it—explained to this little boy why Scott was gone, slept at night knowing that he may never return?

He felt like an absent father. He'd been gone from this boy's life for over a year, only a moving picture on a television screen, a voice through a speaker. Then with his anticipated return, he was only a fraction of the man and father he wanted to be, physically, emotionally. Now another piece was gone. What was left for Ian?

Driving back to the house, Scott's heart ricocheted in his chest. Stalled at the last stop light before turning onto their street, he waited through green, yellow and red. He couldn't force his foot down on the gas pedal. The images rushing back to him. Her body askew. Her blood the color of dark cherries. The feel of her chest under his hands as he administered CPR. The impassiveness of her lips as he breathed air through her body.

He screamed. Until his throat felt coarse. And smashed his palms against the steering wheel over and over again. Why was life so unfair? Twice, people he loved died only inches away from him. His palms were bruised, but nowhere near as bruised as his heart, so he hit the wheel again anyway.

Then a horn honked behind him. And he forced his car to move forward. That was what he would have to do every day: force himself to move forward.

He questioned everything as he turned onto their street. If they had lived in base housing, maybe this wouldn't have happened. If he could have provided her with a better life, more money...

Then his gaze fell on something unfamiliar, unexpected. A mountain of flowers lined the entrance to their home and cascaded into the front yard. Wooden crosses with ribbons and flowers resembling homecoming mums. A field of bouquets covered the porch, so many that each one flowed into the next, undistinguishable from each other. Scott parked the car and got out in a fog, but not the fog of grief.

There were so many, he didn't know how he could get to the front door without stepping on them.

The latch of the neighboring door opened, and Kirk stepped out onto his own front steps.

Scott didn't look at him but posed the question aloud, "Where'd they all come from?"

Leaning against the brown brick of the duplex, Kirk answered, "They've been coming since yesterday, from all over."

"Who?"

"Everyone." Kirk must have seen the question creasing Scott's brows. "You probably haven't see it, but the story made the news. There was a camera crew out here this morning. People have been coming from all over with all this stuff, some of 'em crying, some with kids, a bunch of 'em in uniform, too."

Scott stepped forward toward the swell of flowers, a tidal wave pouring from his home. At the intersecting point of a cross, there was a framed picture that Scott had seen on Facebook while he was still in Afghanistan of Jocelyn holding Ian.

One of the bouquets had words glued on to the ribbon. He bent down closer to see the words. He felt the stiffness of his knee as he knelt, a slight pain that came nowhere near the pain surging through his core. As he squatted, he pushed his right leg out to the side so it could stay straight. The words on the ribbon came into focus. Wife. Mother. Hero. And hanging from the ribbon was a homemade Purple Heart.

Something deep inside him caved, an internal avalanche, and it brought his body to the ground. Seated now, he pulled the bouquet to himself, held it against his chest the way he'd held Jocelyn's body against his own while she lay lifeless in the hospital bed. He buried his face in the flowers and inhaled the way he had smelled her hair. When the flowers were wet with tears that he didn't even know he'd cried, he put them back in place. He looked up, suddenly aware of his surroundings again, but Kirk was gone. And all Scott could think was, *Ian has to see this.*

When he called and said he was picking Ian up, the whole family wanted to come. Scott didn't care if they did, but he wanted to be the one who drove Ian up to the scene. He wanted to be the one who helped Ian out of the car and shared this piece of Jocelyn together.

The two of them drove up to the same turn they always took, but Scott looked at his son in the rear-view mirror tucked tightly in his car seat. "It's a surprise. Can you close your eyes?"

A four-year-old shouldn't have to experience the kind of worry that crossed Ian's face, but Scott quickly reassured him. "It's a good surprise. I promise."

He realized that because of the outpouring of flowers, he hadn't even noticed the asphalt in front of the house. He hadn't thought to look for the stain. The hope shown at their front doorstep had wiped all those thoughts away.

Parking and helping Ian out of his car seat, Scott made sure Ian's dimpled hands were still over his eyes. The grandparents pulled up behind them, and he heard their quiet gasps and whispers. When Scott set Ian down at the edge of the flower memorial, he whispered, "Okay, open."

In an instant Ian's eyes filled with wonderment. The tallest bouquet that rested against the door was even taller than Ian. In one swift movement, he was reaching for the soft petals, moving one bouquet so that he could see the next. He saw the picture of himself with his mom, and he picked the cross up and held it, looking at it closely. For a moment, Scott second guessed himself, that he should have protected his son's heart, but when Ian looked up at him and smiled through his tears, Scott knew his son didn't need the protection.

"She's so pretty." Ian said, looking back at the picture. Scott could only nod. The words clotted in his throat.

Ian made his way through the mound like it was a treasure trove, reaching out and touching every single bouquet, smelling them, pointing them out to his dad and grandparents.

It was the type of moment Jocelyn would have pulled out a camera and taken a picture akin to artwork. But some memories don't need to be captured on film. Some memories embroider themselves into their owner's very being.

Ian pointed a pudgy finger to the ribbons with the words on it. "What's that say?"

The words came out like shards of glass on Scott's tongue, "It says, 'Wife. Mother. Hero.' Do you know what a hero is?"

Ian nodded. Then after a moment asked, "Can you have more than one hero?"

"Of course."

"'Cause Mom's my hero."

"She's mine too."

"But I still want you to be my hero too."

Scott wrapped his hand around his son's thin shoulder and nodded. "I still want to be." The weight of the job that lay before him rested on Scott. For years, Jocelyn had been the one to teach Ian so many important lessons, but now when possibly the most important lesson of his life lay before him, Scott had to be the one to teach him how to move forward, how to heal. Something Ian had been teaching him since the moment he'd peeled the Doc McStuffins band-aid back and placed it on Scott's leg.

Sometimes healing was as simple as allowing someone to be next to you. The process was long, and you'd never be who you were before. Scott may never be the perfect father, but life wasn't about perfection. Life was about process. Moving along a little bit at a time. Seeing the sun get brighter each day, the stars get closer, and knowing that tomorrow may hold a new pain, but it wouldn't be too much that they couldn't get through it together.

Ian picked up one flower arrangement set in a silver tin planter with an angel. "You know who else needs flowers?" His voice suddenly sounded older than a four-year-old's.

Before Scott could respond, Ian pointed to another duplex down the street. The one of the girl who had driven the car. The girl who had killed Jocelyn.

"I don't think that's a good idea." He said, part anger, part panic.

"But we have so many, and she doesn't have any."

Scott swallowed, biting his lip. Jocelyn had said, *Parenting is full of things we don't want to do but must so that we teach them to be the adults we want them to be.*

Then Ian was next to him, a small version of himself, holding his right hand where white scars still shone under misshapen skin.

"It's what Mom would do."

All Scott could do was nod, even though he wasn't sure he believed it. As they began to walk toward the house, Scott looked back at the two sets of grandparents taking in the scene. Roxanne nodded at him, cheeks wet and glistening in the sun.

Ian knocked on the door. An older woman answered, hair the color of straw streaking down the sides of her face. Scott hadn't even known the girl's name until Ian asked for the young driver. The woman looked at Scott defensively, so he managed to soften his pained face.

Moments later, the young girl appeared in the doorway. Same stringy hair as her mother, but hers was accompanied by gaunt eyes that hadn't slept in days. Scott knew the feeling.

She didn't say anything as she stared at them through the open door. Then Ian held up the flower arrangement. "This is for you."

Her light eyes bounced up to Scott's. When he nodded, she took the flowers from the little boy's grip.

"They smell nice." Ian said, prompting her to smell them.

"Yes, they do." Her voice was as tired as her eyes. "I'm so sorry." She said flatly but sincerely, unable to meet anyone's eyes.

Ian stepped forward and hugged her. "I forgive you." He said, with his face pushed against her slender midsection.

What a boy you raised, Joss.

And the response came as though she was standing right next to him. *It was easy.* She said. *He has so much of you in him.*

Scott sucked in his bottom lip and bit back the sobs that wrenched through him at her voice in his head.

When Ian returned to his side, the young girl looked at Scott. Her face slumped.

He felt words stirring inside him. He couldn't walk away without saying anything. The words jumped out, "Don't let this ruin you." His thumbs pushed into his rough palms, steeling himself as he spoke. "There's been enough loss here." It was the closest he could come to echoing Ian's words. He couldn't use the word forgive. Not yet. But he also knew that one day he would have to, and this was the first step.

That night they slept in their own home. Scott didn't wait for Ian to ask to lay down with him. He laid in Ian's Star Wars sheets with the little boy's body curled up next to him as Ian whimpered for his mommy. Inside Scott whimpered for her too. Because he couldn't go in the bedroom, stare at the walls she had painted, lay in the sheets that only days before their body had been tangled up in. But holding their son until the whimpers turned to sniffles then drifted to dreams where they might meet Jocelyn again, Scott knew he would finally find the sleep that had alluded him.

27

ELLE

Spring was spilling over into summer, and Elle felt it everywhere she looked. Norah's yard was bursting with blooms like a flower shop despite the scarcity of rain this season. Momma the cat was finding the perfect amount of shade under the cypress trees from the beating summer sun, but Elle found the warmth like a reset button. She had spent the winter cloaked in heartache and pain, but heat of the summer was like a beam of hope shining through at her most needed moment.

Elle had seen Brandon every day of the week minus one since their first date. She felt like she was living a secret life, at work all day keeping these trysts a secret from coworkers. It wasn't intentional. But there was a comfort in not having all the details move from one mouth to the next, being exaggerated or misunderstood with each translation, like the childhood game of telephone. There would be implications of a rebound or questions about the divorce date. All unnecessary, in Elle's opinion. Her life could finally be her own.

Norah's 85th birthday was coming up in a month, and Elle was scrolling through party ideas on the computer when Lena called Elle into her office. Behind Lena's desk was a wall of windows, and in the summer sun, even with the darkened tint, Elle found it hard to look at her boss without squinting.

"Elle, I've called you in here to discuss with you some of the decisions that have been made over the last few weeks of meetings. Accounting and

Human Resources have brought some things to my attention." Lena brought her slender hands together, the hands of a woman who used to sew but now only gave direction to others. "Based on our most recent reports, we have decided to restructure the company, which unfortunately means some cut backs and layoffs."

The words fogged Elle's thoughts, leaving only a nervous haze. She swallowed, and a stone dropped to the bottom of her stomach.

"...We have chosen to keep only one receptionist who will take on more responsibilities..."

Lena's words droned on, but Elle stopped listening after "one receptionist" to begin calculating Norah's fixed income minus their expenses, not even adjusting for her personal debts or the cost of her divorce. She wasn't a math major but even she could determine the deficit.

"...In doing so, we are projecting that we can expand our market..."

Elle bit the inside of her lip until it was raw. Just when she had made a huge jump in her personal life, the one stable piece remaining was being pulled out from under her.

"Because I believe in loyalty and seniority," Lena continued, "I'd like to offer you the position of receptionist, which in this structure would be your same position with a different title however a small decrease in pay."

Her breathing quickened, and Elle felt a stinging behind her eyes. *Don't cry don't cry don't cry.* Not here. Not in front of Lena. *Just make it through the meeting.*

A plan scratched at the back of her thoughts. She would decline. There had to be other jobs out there for her, but she would say no to Lena, take control of her life, start designing on her own again. Even if it started small. Everything that Aaron had told her, she would do it now. This was the push she needed.

Lena's fingers tapped against each other as she cleared her throat. She must have noticed Elle's thoughts were elsewhere. After the pause, she continued, "But we both know you don't belong as a receptionist." Her pale eyes twinkled. "If you would like to play things safe and continue as a receptionist, I'm giving you that option. But breaking out into a new market, I want to work with designers I know. Therefore, I'd like to ask you to pitch up some designs for clothing."

Elle stopped biting her lip and inhaled.

Lena's sharp features turned upward in a smile though her tone remained authoritative. "We want to branch out into maternity clothing. What I don't want is boring. I want Hollywood glamour at a stay-at-home mother's price. And I would like yours to be the first designs I see."

There was no way to keep the tears at bay; they sprang to Elle's eyes of their own volition. "Lena," no other words came, so she focused on breathing in and out. In and out.

"After seeing your sketchbook, it excited me in a way that has been dormant for years. But Elle," Lena's voice dropped pitch, her gaze steady. "You would be freelance only."

Panic curled in Elle's stomach.

At the same time, her pocket vibrated. She had forgotten to remove her phone before the meeting. Elle slid her hand into her pocket and clicked the button to send the incoming call to voicemail.

Lena continued, "Should the line be successful, your work may become more consistent. But mostly what I am offering you is experience in the field."

The last phrase laid all the panic to rest. This was the break she had been looking for, what she had told Aaron for years she was waiting to see happen. But with freelance there were no guarantees.

An imagine of herself appeared behind a counter working as a barista during the day, then returning home to sketch and sew until her fingers ached. And the image made Elle smile.

Her phone buzzed once again, but she silenced it along with any apprehensions she felt.

And she accepted Lena's offer.

***

Walking back to her desk, Elle held in the shrieking she felt inside. Every inch of her skin wanted to jump and scream. There was no waiting until break, so she scurried to the hallway outside Lena Designs offices toward the bathroom. Let strangers look at her weird. At least the walls of the bathroom would echo her celebration. She thought of calling one person—Aaron. Pulling out her phone, she saw the missed calls. From Brandon. A surge of guilt ran through her. While she had been thinking of her ex-husband, Brandon had been thinking of her.

No matter. She pushed the green "call back" button without listening to the two messages he left.

Brandon answered after one ring. He fumbled the phone before saying, "Elle."

"You won't believe what I just got offered!" Elle shrieked, unable to hold off her excitement any longer even if she was still in the hallway. A woman looked out through glass doors at her with raised eyebrows, but Elle shrugged her off.

"Elle," Brandon repeated, the word steady, quieted.

Never being good at reading people's tones over the phone, Elle rambled on, "My boss offered me a freelance position designing clothes! I mean its maternity clothes, but it beats answering phones, right?"

"Listen, Elle," Brandon's voice was louder in her ear, and it silenced her. "I'm at the hospital with Norah. She's not doing well."

"Wait, wait," Elle swallowed, trying to absorb his words, but her mouth had gone dry. "Start from the beginning." The hallway in front of her narrowed in her vision, turning longer and skinnier like a horror movie. The floor under her quaked, but she realized it was her own legs unable to hold her weight any longer. She leaned her body against the wall and closed her eyes, trying to focus on the words Brandon spoke until she could move again.

Brandon's voice turned robotic, the way a witness on the stand would give their testimony. It was clear he had run through this speech multiple times already. "I arrived at the home for Norah's appointment, and she didn't come to the door. I called her home number and her cell, but there was no response. She had previously told me where to find the spare key, and I was concerned since she'd always answered, so I used the key to let myself in."

Of all the experiences Elle wanted to repeat, listening to how Norah was found and taken to the hospital had not been one of them. Yet here she was, the second time in less than a year. The emotions, though, oh so different. This time, the words crashed into her.

"I found her by your bed, unconscious."

"Oh my god." The words were a breath coming from Elle's mouth.

"I picked her up and carried her to her bed," an unfamiliar choking caught in his voice, then disappeared. "She came to and started mumbling incoherently. I called for an ambulance. She was in and out, but since they picked her up, she hasn't been awake at all. It's still unclear what happened. I don't–I don't know–" He trailed off.

But Elle didn't need him to finish it. "I'll be there soon."

He said he would text her the hospital and room number.

By force, Elle found her footing and rushed to her office, grabbed her purse and keys, and without letting anyone know where she was headed, left. She could call or text or anything on the way. All she knew in that moment was that she had to get to Norah.

***

Elle hadn't been sick often as a child, but one time she'd gotten the flu as an early teen. She couldn't remember exactly what year, only that it was before she lived with Norah and after she'd gotten that terrible boy haircut. Norah had stayed with her at the house Charlene and Elle rented at the time, made homemade chicken noodle soup and kept a large glass of water with a bendy straw by Elle's bedside until she was well.

Walking into the hospital room, Elle felt at a loss, like she should have brought that chicken noodle soup or one of Norah's bendy straws. Her empty hands fidgeted in front of her as she walked through the open doorway, Elle took a breath. Despite the scent of bleach and hand sanitizer, the room smelled musty.

She looked around the curtain, tiptoeing into the room, unsure if she was ready for what she might see. Her eyes landed on Brandon's tennis shoes and blue scrubs pantleg. His knee was bouncing up and down so fast that Elle felt certain if Norah was awake she would bark at him to be still. When she stepped further around the blue curtain, Brandon saw her and jumped out of his seat. In two steps, he was in front of her, his hands were on her arms, his face so high above her that it shielded her from the glaring fluorescent lights.

But Elle only looked at Norah. If the surroundings could melt away, no more machines or metal bed, no more hospital gown, then Norah would have looked the same as she always did in sleep. She could practically hear Norah's grouchy words, "You get my age and any slip or fall, everybody thinks you're dying."

But this time…

Elle carefully stepped closer to the bed, and Brandon stood behind her like a guard, in case she fell apart and cried like the girls in movies did.

When she came closer, she saw the tube running out the opposite side of Norah's mouth, leaving her wrinkled lips sagging even more. That's when tears stung the edges of Elle's eyes. That's when it became real.

She noticed Norah was missing her new wig. A bubble of panic rose. Norah insisted on being presentable in every situation. Elle dug her hand deep into her oversized purse and fished out a brush. She had heard of hospital patient's hair getting knotted up on the back of their head. Elle may not have brought soup or bendy straws, but she would provide the kind of care she was good at.

She sat at Norah's bedside, placed her purse on the counter behind her. Leaning her chest over the metal railing, she pulled the brush through lock after lock of Norah's fine wisps of hair. Elle gently touch her hands to Norah's chin and cheek to turn her grandmother's head on its side in order to reach the back of her hair. Norah's skin was cold and gave way under her fingers, the collagen in her cheeks melted away by age.

"I don't think she'd be too worried about her hair right now," a woman said from behind Elle. She turned to see a nurse with a chart scooting by to take Norah's vitals.

"My gran would," was all she said.

The nurse smiled, and Elle decided to take the moment to step away, just outside the room. Brandon followed.

"You okay?" He asked, then shook his head. There was no easy answer to that question.

"Have the doctors determined the cause?"

"They've done CT scans and an MRI. They're still testing her heart. Preliminarily, they think it was another stroke."

"I don't understand. She's been taking her Med-Plan. That was supposed to stop this from happening again." *And it's worse this time.* She thought but couldn't form those words.

Brandon nodded his agreement and wrapped his arms around her. She melted into him, tall and strong, a stone wall to lean against when her strength was sapped.

"I need to call my mother." She said against his shirt. His badge clip caught on her hair when she tried to look up at him. "Don't you have other patients? Should you be here?"

Brandon rubbed the sides of Elle's arms like he was keeping her warm in the chill of winter. "Only had one, and I called someone to fill in for me." He bent his head down slightly to meet her eyes. "This is where I should be."

The words warmed the parts of her she didn't realized were cold. Words she had longed to hear. To know she didn't have to go at it alone.

"Do you want me to call anyone for you?"

"No," Elle rubbed her fingertips over her eyebrows, feeling the pressure building behind them at the mere thought of what she had to do. "I need to call her myself."

Elle stepped outside the room and dialed her mother. Charlene's phone rang and rang, then went to voicemail. Elle was fine with that. She said the words that needed to be said, mechanically, not letting them reach her heart, not wanting to feel them.

Uncle Bruce answered his phone. He was shocked, and it touched her that he showed so much emotion since last time around he never showed up. He asked her to keep him updated whether he would need to fly out or not. Elle guessed the last episode wasn't enough to warrant the cross-country flight. She tried to push the bitter thoughts down. Months ago, she would have been just as hesitant to come to Norah's aide.

That was just the issue, though, wasn't it? Norah had sacrificed years of her life, given up her empty nest years for Charlene's misplaced priorities. But no one was there for just Norah.

This time, Elle would be.

***

The beeping of Norah's heart monitor kept Elle aware of the life inside her grandmother. Nothing else changed. Nurses came in, made notes on charts, checked fluids or whatever else they did.

Several hours after she'd made the basic calls to her mother, uncle and Marissa, she realized it was rummy night at the Clubhouse. After looking up the number, she called. Elle knew her grandmother would not approve of her seat being empty without explanation.

Brandon left to pick up a change of clothes for Elle and a small dinner that she could stomach. Elle asked him to bring Norah's wig, too.

A male nurse who looked like he was still a teenager came to draw blood for yet another test and tried to make small talk. But Elle couldn't engage.

She set her phone on the side table nearest her grandmother and started a playlist of Frank Sinatra's hits. The crooner's voice filled the room with invisible waves and Elle couldn't stop the sway of her body. She stared at Norah imagining her grandmother dancing the night away with a martini in one hand and Grandpa Larry in the other.

There was a knock on the door though it was open. Thinking it was Brandon, she didn't get up. But when white wing-tip shoes appeared around the corner, Elle sat up straight. She met eyes with the older man from the Clubhouse whom Elle had chided her grandmother about. The wisps of his white hair laid over his age-spotted head, and a white handkerchief sloped out of the pocket of his sport coat. He shuffled closer to the bed, carrying a vase bursting with white roses, and wore a sweet smile as he handed the roses to Elle.

"Hello dear," his voice rang above the music. Elle reached to turn the volume down but not off.

Elle stood to let him have her seat closest to Norah and moved to the couch. Glancing at her grandmother, she ached knowing how upset Norah would be to let this man see her in such a state. And without lipstick on or her hair done.

"I never got your name." Her casual way was met with a pained expression in the man's eyes.

"She didn't speak of me?" It was both a question and a statement, but either way there was hurt behind it.

"I'm sorry," Elle said. Hoping to lighten the blow, she added, "She was too embarrassed of me to introduce me to her friends. The way I was embarrassed of her when I was a teenager." Elle winked, but her words didn't lessen the furrow of his eyebrows.

"Harold. It's nice to meet you, Elle." He tipped his head toward her. Harold reached forward and grabbed Norah's limp hand, rubbing his this thumb over it in gentle circles. "I have asked your grandmother on a date every Friday night for a year and three months."

Elle's heart leapt. Her lips curved into a smile, though it was accompanied with sadness.

"I always thought she would eventually say yes, so I kept asking." He looked at Elle, and his eyes twinkled. "She was the first woman who could make me laugh the way my late wife did. We were married for 32 years before cancer took her from me. And I didn't think I would marry again, but I would have married your grandmother."

Remembering the fuss Norah had made getting ready for the Clubhouse, the new necklace she had worn, and the flush in her cheeks when this man had opened the door for her. How little she still knew of her grandmother, Elle realized. How complex Norah's heart had been to guard it so from this man, and everyone. How alone Norah must have felt in life to not have someone to share these secrets with. Elle suddenly regretted not pushing harder, not asking more questions, not being the friend that Norah needed, and in return having the friendship of her grandmother.

"I think she would have said yes. Someday." Or at least, Elle hoped.

Harold stayed, never releasing Norah's hand, and told Elle stories of her grandmother that she would never have otherwise learned. The time she crashed a fancy party at a hotel, a cruise she took off the coast of Long Beach to go whale-watching, a road trip out to Vegas for the casinos. All in the last few years. It was clear Harold had loved the adventurous spirit he'd found in Norah, a spirit that Elle hadn't seen in the woman for over a decade, a side she didn't know still existed.

But it sparked stories of her own. Norah taking her to a movie then putting her crooked forefinger to her lips in *shhh* and sneaking Elle into a second one.

The two laughed in a moment that could have brought pain. Harold's hand covered over Norah's with such reverence that Elle wondered if it was the first time he had touched her hand, held it in his own worn palm. Then he kissed the top of Norah's head, unkempt hair and all, and said his good-bye. There was a knowing in the word, that this could be a forever good-bye.

✳✳✳

Time disappeared in this place. Night became morning, day break came without notice. Norah's room had no windows, and Elle slept off and on curled on the stiff couch. Brandon came and went. Carts rolled by, the wheels squeaking against the tile. Nurses talked and laughed, too loud for the conditions. Marissa came, sat next to her on the couch with little conversation. Elle fell asleep leaning against her for a period. Coworkers text and called.

When Brandon returned, Elle assumed it was morning. Someone, a blur to Elle, had brought a menu in for her to order breakfast if she wanted, but the thought of the food rolled her stomach. In a trip to the bathroom, Elle caught a reflection of herself, still in day-old clothes even though Brandon had brought new ones the night before. Mascara and eyeliner bled to enhance the dark circles under her eyes. Her hair almost as ratty as Norah's had been when she arrived. But Elle didn't care.

When she came out of the bathroom having changed her clothes and washed her face, Marissa was introducing herself to Brandon. He gave Elle a weak smile, and she longed for the warmth of his full, wide grin.

"I'm going to step outside to call my mom again." Elle said, grabbing her phone and stepping out into the hallway. Irrational, perhaps, but Elle didn't want Norah to hear the conversation she had with her mother, whether Charlene was willing to stop everything to return to Norah's side. If Norah's mind wasn't as quiet as it seemed and she could in fact hear their voices, Elle wanted her grandmother to believe everyone was there for her, as loving and hopeful as Harold.

Charlene's voicemail answered. Again. Elle scuffed her shoes on the shiny white tiles.

"Hi Mom. I've left like three voicemails about Norah's stroke. Please call me as soon as you can."

She stared at her phone as she hung up, feeling like a lost child abandoned by her mother all over again. She didn't want to do this by herself, the struggle of knowing what to say to the doctors, what questions to ask. She didn't feel grown up enough. For once, she wanted her mother to swoop in and handle this one.

When Elle looked up, a familiar figure stood at the end of the hallway. His hair was disheveled and even at this distance she recognized the green smoothie in his hand from her favorite spot. Aaron moved toward her, wearing an expression mixed with pity and regret. They held awkward eye contact as he walked closer, step by step, but she couldn't look away. She hadn't stared into these eyes for so long.

"Hi." He said once he was but a foot away from her. He stared at her from under his thick eyebrows, but not too thick, not too dark, not too anything. She'd always found them perfect.

"Hi," was all she could say in return.

"Marissa called me." He held the green smoothie out to her. "I brought this for you."

She didn't even wonder what was in it, because he knew her. There was comfort in someone who knew her inside out, the ugly and the, well, not as ugly. He knew every side of her. She didn't have to brush her hair out to impress him or wipe the mascara that might be left. There were no nerves standing here in front of this man, no pretenses. Just truth. And even the ugly truth surrounded her like a warm blanket in a day filled with such uncertainty.

"Hey, Elle, the doctor wants to speak–" a voice came from behind her, Brandon's voice. And the words slowed as he recognized her husband. "with you."

Elle turned to see Brandon in the doorway, his eyes bouncing back and forth between hers and Aaron's. She nodded at him, unsure how to make this moment less uncomfortable—for everyone. Turning back to Aaron, she gestured for him to follow her. She accepted the green smoothie from him, condensation dripping to the ground, with the heat of Brandon's eyes on her.

The doctor was already seated comfortably on the swivel stool just inside the door. He greeted them in a friendly way, as though he wasn't present for a moment that Elle would remember forever. His dark skin contrasted against his white teeth in a smile and nod to each person as they entered the room. Elle sunk inside herself. Her hands wiped the droplet of condensation off the cup, attempting to keep her mind on something concrete.

"Is it alright if I discuss your grandmother's condition in front of everyone present?" Dr. Anderson asked. He'd been on duty since she'd arrived; his shift probably ended soon. But Elle was glad it was the same doctor on duty to finally deliver the news. Anything familiar was welcomed right about now.

She confirmed with the doctor.

Aaron cleared his throat and leaned in close to Elle to say, "Even this guy?" with his thumb pointed back to Brandon. It was obvious Aaron wasn't trying to be subtle.

Heat rushed to Elle's cheeks. Her eyes flickered to Brandon but couldn't hold his gaze long. "Yes," she responded without looking at

Aaron, "he's her home nurse."

The words weighed on her chest like cinder blocks had been put on top of her. She knew it was wrong to reduce Brandon to only Norah's nurse now that their relationship had turned personal. Just a nurse wouldn't have driven Elle back to her car after a night of grief-stricken drinking. Or checked in on her grandmother when she stayed at work overnight. Just a nurse wouldn't have abandoned his own life to help her these last 20 or so hours. Just a nurse wouldn't have changed Elle's outlook on what was possible after signing divorce papers.

Brandon's back straightened, eyes on the doctor. The words had pierced him too, but she didn't know how to take them back, make it right. The doctor was already speaking about Norah and she was missing it, the words droning in the background of her embarrassment. Elle caught Marissa's eyes, they went from wide-eyed to downcast in half a second. Her lips were pressed together as if she was holding words inside them.

Elle had done it again, let everyone down. At least for *that* she could be counted on.

She closed her eyes, trying to focus on Dr. Anderson's rich voice.

"...with her medical history. Her body is not working with us. There are things that we could do, however, she has a DNR on file so that prevents us from moving forward. At this point, we will just have to wait and see how her body responds to the trauma it's been through."

Elle blinked her eyes in quick succession. Not from tears, but suddenly she was exhausted. She should have been feeling more...something. There should have been questions pestering her.

"So you're saying her body is shutting down?" Aaron spoke up, his voice louder than Dr. Andersons's.

Dr. Anderson bobbed his head in confirmation. "It appears that way. The next few hours will tell us a lot."

That caught Elle's attention. "You think she only has hours?"

"No, no," Dr. Anderson amended, "even if her organs are shutting down, it could days or weeks even. Each patient goes in their own time."

She thought some of the pressure inside her would release when the doctor gave her a time frame, but it didn't. Her insides still ached, as if they were no longer whole.

"I'll be back to check on her later, if you have any more questions."

Dr. Anderson said as he left the room, but Elle didn't watch him go. She didn't move, her feet concreted to the ground.

"I know what you're thinking," a voice whispered from behind her. Aaron's. The voice she had longed to speak to her for months, but now felt like prickles against her ears. "You are wishing you'd done more. But you've been there for her more in the last few months than you have in years."

There was no emotion left in Elle's voice, only flat words came out. "I don't know if that makes me feel better or worse."

Aaron's lips smacked. "That's not what I meant."

"But it's true." Those were the thoughts warring inside her. All the years she should have been there. Stories she still didn't know, things about life she had yet to understand, wisdom Norah could still impart.

Instead Elle was an expert at making everything about herself. Even this. Even now. What would Norah be thinking? Had she lived a happy life? Had she held regrets?

An image of Harold tenderly holding her grandmother's hand came to her mind. Norah had always told her it was never too late, and yet this time, for Norah it was.

But it wasn't for Elle.

She turned, but Aaron was the only one behind her. He caught hold of her forearm.

"Where'd Brandon go?" Elle said, almost breathless.

"Who?" Aaron responded, mouth ajar. "Oh, the nurse?"

Elle cringed at the word and pushed passed her husband—ex-husband—she didn't know what to call him anymore.

Brandon was passed the nurse's station, headed toward the elevator at the end of the hall.

She called after him but he only half turned, uncommitted. At this angle, he was the exact image of the first time she saw him. Elle came up beside him and faced him, his glasses glaring against fluorescent lights above his head.

"Don't go." The words made her feel naked.

He scratched at his eyebrow, his eyes flickering above Elle's head. She knew Aaron was behind her in the doorway, watching her movements, but she refused to look. She was no longer obligated to him, just as he had wished. The temptation of resentment licked at her, but she submerged it.

A clattering of high heels and a blur of floral moved in their direction. With a double take, Elle recognized her mother storming toward her, a rolling suitcase accompanying her. Charlene shrieked her name.

Brandon took a steadying breath, his eyes back on Elle's. "Text me if anything changes." He leaned down toward her cheek, but changed his mind as his eyes flickered back to the doorway behind her. In a rush, she wanted to grab him, to kiss him, to escape this place with him and never look back. And she would have, but she couldn't miss this part of Norah's life too.

Her mother breezed down the hall, jostling against her while grabbing her elbow, disregarding Brandon. "Take me to her." Charlene said gushing with dramatic flair.

As she was pulled to Norah's room, Elle looked over her shoulder to catch a glimpse of Brandon, but he was gone.

For the next few hours, days, weeks, however long it was that Norah stayed trapped in this bed, Elle had to be present for her. Nothing else could matter. She had to do this right.

Charlene floated around the room, greeting Marissa and Aaron with a wary eye, and complaining. The lights were too bright, the blanket wasn't warm enough, the nurses hadn't greeted her. Elle made every effort to not roll her eyes at each comment.

"So you got my messages?" Elle asked, having never received a text or call back.

Charlene threw herself across the couch next to Marissa, arranging the two pillows behind her back. "Of course. I scheduled a flight as soon as I heard how serious it was. Bruce is on his way too."

Although she would have appreciated the response and a little warning, this was a battle she didn't want to engage. Aaron took his leave, extending his hand to her, unsure of where it should land, then finally patting her shoulder.

"She looks pale, doesn't she?" It was the first concern for Norah that Charlene had voiced, and even though it was subtle, Elle recognized the fear hiding behind the words. "What is on her head?" Charlene referred to the wig, but Elle didn't respond.

Looking at her mother, the background faded and Elle suddenly saw Charlene, the teen with bell bottoms, cropped top and long straight hair parted down the middle. The girl who frequented the beach and arrived at a party innocent but left it violated, carrying more than grief but the seed of a life she wasn't expecting. Elle's life.

This was the first time she'd been with her mother since knowing the truth about them both. She wasn't prepared to discuss it, nor was it the time, but looking at Charlene through these eyes, her view was different.

A rush of gratitude swelled inside Elle. In all her focus on what Charlene could have or should have done differently, there was one detail Charlene had right. She had become Elle's mother, even if she hadn't been a perfect one. Charlene had given Elle a chance, repeatedly. First at birth but again by living with Norah, Elle had gotten a chance to know her grandmother, to grow in the shadow of her stability. Things that Elle wouldn't change. As much hurt and resentment that had crusted over her opinion of this woman seated before her, at least there was this layer, thin as it may be, of respect.

"I'd like to speak with the doctor. I'm Charlene Webster, daughter and Power of Attorney of the patient." Charlene was speaking to a nurse who had entered while Elle was wrapped in the past. Once Charlene started talking, it was harder for Elle to hold on to the conjured feelings of respect.

"She has a DNR in place." Elle said.

"I know," Charlene answered. "but I want to know who is responsible for this. She was on medications; she was being monitored at home—obviously not well enough."

Elle's ears perked at that backhanded remark and wondered if it was aimed at herself or Brandon. Either way, she didn't like the implication. Marissa shifted on the couch, her eyes bouncing back and forth between the mother and daughter.

Charlene ran her almond shaped fingernails through her hair. Her expression was difficult to read; Elle realized Charlene's eyebrows and forehead seemed frozen in place. She must have received a fresh injection. "I knew *he* wasn't right for the job."

"Who?" Elle asked, but she knew the answer.

"That Brandon." She said his name like a dirty word and wagged a finger toward the hallway where they had seen him last.

At his name, Elle's stomach seized. She knew her mother well enough to know where this was headed.

"He came in all charm and talk. Norah always was a sucker for charming men." Charlene said, shaking her thick head of hair. "When I was there, you know, I caught him giving her the wrong medication."

Elle couldn't believe that. She questioned her mother, but Charlene continued.

"He had the medication mixed up. I should have reported him then."

Lowering herself into the nearby chair, Elle swallowed. "That hardly seems like something to report."

But Charlene went on as though she never heard Elle, although as quiet as she'd been, Charlene may not have. "I promise you he's been doing things around that house that are not in his job description." She crossed her legs, high heel swinging in circles above the tile. "He's probably stolen things, too."

"That's ridiculous." Elle spoke, loud enough that time.

Charlene narrowed her eyes. "Is it? I've heard stories about those in-home workers weaseling their way into their patient's lives just for money or who knows what else. I think I saw it on *Dateline*."

Her next breath shook its way out. Elle remembered the anti-anxiety medication she took when Aaron left. It had been months since she needed one, since she'd felt a crushing weight on her lungs.

"What was he even doing here? He doesn't work at the hospital." Charlene's face twisted into a scowl. "Did Mother have jewelry on when she was admitted?"

Elle shrugged with hesitation. She knew Charlene would find out Brandon found Norah and was alone in the house while Norah lay unconscious waiting for the ambulance. And Charlene would conclude that he had plenty of time to raid the house of valuables.

Brandon's side wouldn't matter. Charlene could badger someone into feeling guilty even when they're innocent. Elle's mother also knew how to take things to the highest authority and strip someone of their dignity in the meantime. She'd seen her mother do it to contractors, other students in Elle's classes, Charlene's own ex-boyfriends. Maybe her experiences had hardened her to the truth, jaded her. But Elle didn't want to see her mother's side. She suddenly just wanted this all over.

Charlene was up, heading to the nurse's station, and even from the room, Elle could hear her boisterous voice checking on her suspicions.

"Do you want me to call him?" Marissa asked. *Warn him* was what she implied.

When Elle shook her head, her brain felt like it toggled against her skull. "I should. But not yet." This had to be explained in person, *I'm sorry you're going to be hounded in your job for who knows how long by a woman out for blood.*

Smoothing her hands over her hair as she reentered the room, Charlene grabbed her purse. "I'm going to head to the hotel. I've got to get these clothes off and change. I smell like an airplane. I'll be back soon." Her sing-song delivery would have suited a vacation arrival better.

With a glance at her own clothes, exhaustion stung the backs of Elle's eyes.

"Can you imagine what else she would do if she found out about *you* and Brandon?" Marissa said biting a nail.

There it was. The sinking inevitability that clutched her stomach. And Charlene would find out. Somehow. Elle knew she would.

28

SCOTT

SOLDIER'S WIFE GIVES LIFE FOR TODDLER SON

Bravery runs in the Turner family. As does sacrifice. Months after Sergeant Scott Turner of the U.S. Army was injured by an RPG explosion in Afghanistan, his wife, Jocelyn Turner, became a hero as well. Pushing her four-year-old son out of the way of an oncoming automobile, Turner saved him at the cost of her own life. The 27-year-old mother died in the hospital on May 22nd from brain contusions. A husband willing to give his life for his country. A mother willing to give her life for her son. A young boy, who has lost so much but understands so little, will grow up knowing his parents are heroes, not only to him, but to all of America...

Scott closed the internet browser on his phone and slammed it down on the table. He couldn't read any more. People kept sending the articles to him, but they all sounded the same, and none of them captured the essence of Jocelyn. Mere words never could.

Within days of her death, Jocelyn's story made national news and went viral on the internet. Magazines were asking for statements from family and friends, Scott's CO and Elizabeth Cryer. There were voicemails and emails trying to contact Scott for a statement, but he didn't know what to say yet. The army had released their statement, but it wasn't Scott's statement, that's for sure.

There had even been an email from a literary agent wanting to represent him should he decide to write a book. He'd gone running four miles to release the anger from that one.

Jocelyn's parents brought her body home to California to be buried near them. He didn't have any reason or energy to fight it. Roxanne planned the funeral. He nodded at every suggestion. He made only one decision. He opted for a closed casket.

At the funeral, there was standing room only. Friends of Jocelyn had a hard time getting seats for all the onlookers thanks to the local news station's coverage. Alexis flew in and sat directly behind him during the service, but he was unable to find the right way to show gratitude for her being there. Jocelyn would have known how to balance the darkness with the images of people fluttering by him, but he couldn't find the way.

He shook a lot of hands. He said, "Thank you," to all the well-wishers. He pulled at the collar of his suit as it suffocated him. But all the time, he kept his eyes on Ian. When the funeral was over and the people dispersed, he and the boy were the ones who had to get on without her. He just didn't have the first thought as to how.

***

From a nearby park, Scott watched the sun descend beneath the triangular roof of his parent's home sometime after the funeral—the days blurred together. He and Ian had walked to the park, not feeling any strain in his leg, only in his chest where a gaping hole had replaced his organs.

"Dad, watch." Ian said as he disappeared into the cavernous slide and reappeared seconds later, landing in the wood chips below.

The fuchsia sky told Scott it was past Ian's bedtime, but this park had caused Ian to smile for the first time in days. Scott envied his son's resilience. Or maybe Ian still didn't quite understand what was going on. Maybe Ian would cry himself to sleep for weeks or months, just as he had the last few days without Jocelyn to lay him down. There were no Mommy Dolls left behind or storybooks recorded with Jocelyn's voice. There was no preparation. Only the black void of night.

And that was when Scott saw their faces. Jocelyn's. Xavier's. Their head wounds oozing blood. Their hands reaching out to him. The dead eyes blaming him.

No one in Scott's family had died before now. No friends in fatal car accidents. No long-term illnesses. No one close to him. He had never known loss. Even in the army, he'd never lost a man before Xavier. Now, the deaths haunted him. The children he'd seen on the streets of Jalalabad, even they came to him in his dreams.

The army prepares a soldier for a certain amount of loss. Some classes. Some textbook scenarios. A therapist if necessary. Scott had been trained to put pressure on a wound, even when it's slippery and bloody. He knew how to make a tourniquet out of random items ala MacGyver. But they don't teach you how to heal a hemorrhaging heart.

He didn't hear his father walk up until Mike's silhouette sat next to him on the park bench. The evening breeze nipped at Scott's neck. California summer wasn't the same as Texas.

Neither of them spoke. Even though they both needed to. They watched Ian scale the mini rock-climbing wall to the top level of the playground.

When Scott's hands started to tremble, he knew the emotions were building up and he needed to say something. The first few words out of his mouth were broken, like he hadn't spoken in years. They felt foreign in his mouth, but he pressed on.

"I don't know what I'm doing, Dad." His neck lost the will to hold itself up, and he hung his head low to his chest. His chin itched where his beard was growing back.

The breath coming from Mike's direction quickened. "None of us do, son."

"She did. She always knew how to reach me." His mind was still so foggy, drugged by loss. "She was what kept me alive. And now she's gone." He hadn't realized he was crying until the remnants of tears stained his shirt.

The army had told them they were strong, that they were brave. But now he knew they were wrong. He'd never been brave. He'd only ever survived to make it home to her.

He scrubbed his face hard with both hands. He dug his fingertips into his eye sockets, pushing the tears back from where they came. Jocelyn was what kept his feet anchored. Jocelyn was everything. Without her…

His dad's gruff voice surprised him. "The way I see it, you've got a choice to make." The sun had disappeared now, but the street lights beamed like spotlights over the park. Ian jumped up and down on the wobbly bridge of the playground. Mike waved back when Ian waved, then continued, "You can leave that boy with a broken dad. Or you can give him everything you've got. Even when you don't think it's enough, it will be.

"You're a good dad, Scott." Mike patted his knee, the undamaged one, even though his whole body felt damaged now. "You're a good man."

Then Mike was up, grabbing Ian and whisking him off to the house, leaving Scott on the bench under the spotlight, feeling like the world was spinning and swirling around him. The only thing left in focus was Ian's little face, looking over his grandpa's shoulder, smiling at Scott. His whole world had changed in a second when the car barreled into his wife, his life, his future. But he had new gravity now. Ian was the gravity that would pull him back.

29

ELLE

Everything was a battle with Charlene. Elle put Norah's wig on, and Charlene took it off calling it ridiculous. Elle played more Sinatra, and Charlene wanted the television on. Elle tried to speak in quiet reverence, but Charlene took loud calls from interested homebuyers.

Marissa brought them both coffee, but Charlene thought it was too weak. She dumped it in trash after drinking less than half. She did, however, comment on Marissa's new Louis Vutton purse.

"I didn't know you could afford bags like that." Charlene said, in her best good-for-you tone.

Elle jumped out of her seat, "We're going out," she exclaimed, grabbing Marissa by the elbow. She hadn't left the hospital in two days, and now was the time.

Her mother gave an oblivious nod.

Once tucked away in Elle's compact car, she groaned. "That woman." The car idled in the parking garage, and Elle shook her head. "I thought knowing what happened to her would make her easier to take. But it hasn't."

"I don't think anything but a bottle of vodka would make that woman easier to take." Marissa delivered dryly.

Elle bubbled with laughter, lying her forehead on the steering wheel and let the laughter take over. It was a gift, Marissa's ability to make her laugh amid utter chaos. A gift more valuable than a Louis Vutton purse.

She rolled her head to the side and looked at her friend, so grateful for this woman who had watched her train wreck and stayed to sweep up the pieces.

"I'm so glad you're here." Elle said.

Marissa lifted a shoulder. "I'm just glad you're back. I've missed this Elle."

Elle nodded.

"Now," Marissa transitioned abruptly, "let's figure out this Brandon issue."

***

The women pulled up to the coffee shop where Brandon suggested they meet after Elle texted him. When Elle asked Marissa again if she was okay to stay in the car, her friend raised an eyebrow. "Are you kidding? I'd love to sit in the car in complete silence with no interruptions and *Mommy, mommy*'s. This is my dream."

Elle smiled. Grateful didn't describe how she felt about Marissa any more. The word wasn't enough somehow.

The clanking of coffee cups against countertops greeted Elle as she walked in. Brandon was already seated in his pedestrian t-shirt and jeans wardrobe which reminded Elle it was the weekend.

He stood as she approached his two-top table. "How's Norah?"

"The same." Elle shrugged, unsure if that was comforting or not. She picked at a napkin sitting haphazardly on the table, the white fibers unraveling in her hands. "I wanted to talk to you about Charlene. Warn you."

Brandon lifted his chin like he was ready for a punch.

"She's out for blood. She wants someone to blame." Elle felt a tingle in her fingers, panic. "We can't give her any ammunition to use against you."

"She's blaming me?"

Elle nodded, ever so slightly. "I think we," she paused knowing that *we* was still such a new, fragile term for them, "should not be something she could use against you."

The revelation was tangible in Brandon's eyes. He shook his head in jagged motions. "No, there has to be a different way around it."

It hurt Elle so deep, a knife to her vital organs, but she knew her mother. She knew the length Charlene would go. "If she can prove that you did anything wrong, it won't matter what it is, she'll use it."

Money was an issue too, though Elle didn't want to admit it for some reason. It would ruin him, and Charlene wouldn't even blink.

"Maybe if we just step back. Maybe after the estate is closed and the inheritance is doled out, maybe she'll go back home and forget about you. Maybe then," Elle's words trailed off.

His hand moved closer to hers. She felt safer in her explanation when there was more space between them. But he scooted his chair by hers and leaned in as close to her as he could get. She felt his body heat warm her, smelled his skin, and the sliver of distance between them infuriated Elle, knowing it had to be this way.

"That's a lot of maybe's." He closed the small distance between them. Elle's breath caught in her throat. She became fully aware of her rapid heartbeat and the people around them. "I know." They were words disguised as a final breath. Then he kissed her, pressing his lips hard against hers.

Her phone buzzed in her pocket, jolting against her hip. Their bodies were close enough that Brandon felt it too. She pulled back from him, moving in opposition to every instinct in her body.

It was Charlene. "You have to get here now. We're losing her."

All words and breath clotted in her throat. *Not yet.* She caught herself. "I'm on my way."

Brandon hadn't taken his eyes off her. "Norah?" He asked.

All she could do was nod.

"Do you want me to come with you?" His hand held her elbow, stabilizing her.

"I think it would be better if you didn't." She saw the way her words stabbed him. It wasn't just Elle. He had a relationship with Norah. He *should* be able to be there once more for Norah. "I'm sorry."

There was a moment when she thought he would ask her to call him, that he would chase after her as she walked out of the door, but he didn't.

***

By the time Elle arrived at Norah's hospital door, she expected to see the staff rushing about, to hear monitors beeping out of control, but she was too late for that. She entered to a stinging silence. Her mother, mascara smudged under her eyes, threw herself across the room into her daughter's arms. "Oh Elle," she sobbed.

They held each other, grounded to that one spot in the middle of the white, antiseptic room, firm in each other's unsteadiness. One moment of shared pain as mother and daughter.

All too soon it was over. Charlene launched into business mode. Phone call after phone call, changing appointments back home, calling Bruce who was stuck in Chicago on a flight delay, then the lawyer who held the will. In between phone calls, she was tapping notes into her phone. Before the end of the day, Charlene had already started planning the funeral, via phone calls with Bruce. As soon as his flight landed, they were working out a meeting with the lawyer early Monday morning to go over Norah's will. Charlene barely gave her older brother a moment to grieve. Maybe it was better that way for the two of them.

But Elle only wanted to get back to Norah's home. Charlene had argued with her about returning to the home of a dead woman, but Elle was returning to *her* home—who knew how much longer she could call it that.

Walking in the house, with a new tint in her eyes knowing that Norah would never return to it, Elle suddenly didn't want to move a thing. She didn't want to move Norah's peach house slippers that were perched by the living room sofa. The brown spot of spilled coffee contrasted on the white coffee pot couldn't be wiped clean yet—it was the last pot of coffee Norah made.

She made her way up the stairs. The floor creaked under her feet and sounded the way her bones felt after nights spent sleeping on the hospital couch.

As she approached the doorway to her bedroom, the scene lay before her where Norah had collapsed, in Elle's room by the bed. She stood there now, cleaning supplies left on the nightstand, a rag with gray dust lines dropped on the floor, her bed made wrinkle-free in a proficiency Elle had never inherited from Norah. The impact wasn't lost on her. Norah's last moments of consciousness were spent taking care of her granddaughter.

Oh how she craved to be close to her grandmother, to curl up next to her, to smell her gardenia scent, to feel the strength in Norah's hug that withstood the fragility of her age-old bones. She slipped into Norah's bedroom. She peeled back the comforter on the opposite side than Norah slept and climbed between the soft sheets, for once relishing the peach hue of this room. She laid her hand on the pillow that was Norah's, remembering all the times as a child she would sleep next to Norah, her hair covered in sponge curlers and a shower cap. A tear leaked out and fell onto the pillowcase, and more threatened to fall. She finally let them.

***

The shrill ring of the rotary phone on the nightstand woke Elle with a start. For a second she was confused to be waking in this room, with daylight glowing against her eyelids. It was her third night to fall asleep in Norah's bed, watch Norah's television, once she even wore Norah's silky pajamas.

The shrill ring repeated itself, like a woman's scream in an Alfred Hitchcock movie. Elle knew it was Charlene. Her mother's voice under pressure sounded much like the shrillness of the telephone. She looked at the clock. It was the morning of Norah's funeral. Charlene was a rock star in her element of staying busy to avoid her emotions. Elle had made sure the service represented who Norah was, her tastes and her relationships.

Already feeling the emotions of the day creep on her, Elle stretched all the way to her toes. The television was still on from the night before, the volume muted. She swung her feet over the side of the bed when she recognized a face on the morning news show. It was a picture she'd seen so many times on social media. Jocelyn Turner hugging her little boy.

"Army wife gives life for son" the headline at the bottom of the screen read. Elle's heart raced. She patted the sheets to find the remote tucked between them and punched the volume up.

"...our own local hero. Jocelyn Brennin Turner grew up just around the corner in Temecula, California until she married Scott Turner who is now a Sergeant in the United States Army." The news anchor continued to tell their story while pictures of Jocelyn and Scott's life flashed on the screen.

Elle grabbed her phone, checked her emails, certain the news was wrong. Jocelyn was supposed to visit this week. They were going to have dinner. Elle was finally going to meet her. This couldn't be right. But internet searches of Jocelyn Turner confirmed the same news. She read articles from the *Fort Hood Herald* and *USA Today*. She couldn't stop reading. Article after article. Her own loss punctuated by the loss that little blond hair boy must be feeling. And Scott. Oh Scott.

She didn't know what she could do, not even knowing the Turner family, never having met Jocelyn herself. And now she would never get to. She looked up Jocelyn's information in her contacts, scrolled through bouquets of flowers on a national florist website. The least she could do was send flowers. And then as silly as it might have been, Elle sent an email. Their whole friendship had been through email, so it seemed tragically appropriate.

> *Jocelyn,*
>
> *I hoped to meet you this week. Instead this week has been full of loss. I never got the chance to tell you how much you've meant to me in these last few months. When I thought no one was for me, you were. Your words of encouragement and wisdom helped me find my way again. My grandmother died this week. And it hurts in a way that I couldn't put into words. Maybe now the two of you can meet instead. Two amazing, selfless women. Give her a hug for me. She gives strong ones, but you can feel them for days. I'm so, so sorry.*

Elle could barely sign her name and hit send with her vision so blurred by tears.

Her clothes for the funeral hung outside the mirrored closet door. When she could wait no longer to get dressed, she slipped into the simple black dress—the only black dress that didn't look like she was attending a cocktail party. Elle glanced at Norah's jewelry box. She fingered the carved edges of the wood until she felt the handle. This jewelry box that she had played in as a child, putting gaudy rings over chubby childhood fingers, layering necklaces of every length over her neck and modeling them around for Norah while her grandmother beamed at her.

One more time she would dress up in her grandmother's jewelry and wear the pearl necklace Norah had told Elle to keep. Tender emotions rising, she sat on the soft cushion at Norah's vanity and looked in the mirror where months earlier she helped Norah with her makeup. The same broken hand mirror lay in front of her perfume. Elle picked the bottle up, sniffed the nozzle and used the fancy, fringed pump to spray a mist on herself. It wasn't her favorite scent, but it was Norah's, and for today that was what mattered.

She pinned her hair back, leaving thin tendrils around her face, and stared at her reflection. She couldn't see Norah in her face. They had never looked much alike. Now she wondered if she looked like her unknown father, if somewhere there was a man sorry for his past who had her same hazel eyes, round and jaded by hurts but ever hopeful that someone would see the person beyond the mistakes.

A car horn honked, and Elle advanced down the stairs to the door. In an instant, the silence of the house burst into activity as Charlene blew into the room like a tornado, followed by Uncle Bruce, followed by the limo driver. Her mother's clothing stunned her into silence, the amount of cleavage Charlene was showing even made Elle's eyes pop out.

Charlene chattered about deliveries to the gravesite where the ceremony would take place. The reception would be here at Norah's home, which had all been prepared the night before, but Charlene rushed through the house one more time to make sure it was perfect.

Aunt Linda was in the limo finishing up her makeup—her lateness was nothing new but Elle was glad to see her and her full coverage dress—and Uncle Bruce slid next to her on the bucket seats. It was an uncomfortable drive, just Elle and her family, who hadn't been together in years.

The limo drove up to the gravesite, and she could feel Norah. Elle nodded as Charlene grabbed her hand, both seated inside the limo looking out the darkly tinted windows. The sun bounced off the white casket, covered in white lilies. Two dozen white wooden chairs sat in a semi-circle around the casket. An ancient tree rose above the setting, looking over Norah's resting place like a centurion on guard.

As Elle was seated on the front row, her favorite picture of Norah from over a decade ago in a fluffy peach sweater stood in front of her, on an easel in a glorious golden frame. Marissa sat with Heath next to her. Elle thought of Jocelyn Turner absently, wished she could have attended that service too. Cars approached, then more, and by the time Charlene waved the minister to begin, all the seats were taken with more attendees standing under the shade of the giant tree.

Harold, with his wing-tip shoes, sat toward the back row and a few others she recognized from the Clubhouse. Aaron, whose hair was shaggier around the ears than she ever would have let it get, and his sister, Rachel sat behind Elle but said little to her. A nurse from the hospital stood to the side with an umbrella blocking the sun from baring down on her back. Elle was surprised at how many people attended. But there was one face she was looking for. Only one and she didn't see it.

Charlene planned for each family member to speak during the service. Elle had argued, not knowing what she would say, but Charlene insisted. Uncle Bruce and Charlene went before her, but she blocked out their words. Her own were hurdling around in her head and if she listened to everyone else's, she'd forget what little she had prepared.

When her turn came, she smoothed her dress down as she stood, unstable in heels that sunk into the dirt underfoot. She made her way to the podium with no notecards because she thought that was corny, but now that this group of faces were staring back at her, she realized how helpful notes would have been.

She cleared her throat, buying herself a couple seconds. "Norah," she started, then realized now was not the time to separate herself from her grandmother—why had she for so long?—so she started again, "My grandmother loved to throw parties. I see some of you from the Clubhouse, and I'm so glad that you are here. But I should tell you that my grandmother didn't think much of the Clubhouse parties." A couple members chuckled. "She believed that the music and of course cocktails made the party, although shrimp cocktail didn't hurt either."

Elle glanced to her right at the casket where the body of her grandmother was locked inside, but not her spirit. She knew that. She had seen the difference in Norah's body at the hospital after the monitors had been turned off and the last bit of life left Norah's skin, painting it the color dough.

"But I disagree, Gran," Elle shook her head as if she heard Norah's voice in her head. "I know that's no surprise!"

The small crowd laughed and Elle smiled with them.

"I think it's the people who make the party." She turned toward the casket. "Living with you for the last few months, you've turned some of my worst days into parties just by being with me."

She thought of Jocelyn, Marissa, Heath, Hailey and Heidi. Grateful for people in her life who had made it so much more bearable.

A young woman under the tree stepped to the side, and behind the woman Elle saw the one face she had searched for: Brandon with his hands in his pockets. He nodded at her with encouragement.

Then she couldn't hold back her tears. She waited a beat and took a deep breath. "And I know if Gran was standing where I am today, she would look out at all of you and realize that *you* make the party. Today wouldn't be the same without each of you, just like each of our lives wouldn't have been the same without Norah." Her eyes fluttered to the soft ground beneath her. "I know mine wouldn't."

That was all. She closed her mouth, to reign in the sob rising, then trudged through the thickness under her shoes back to her seat.

The murmurs of a prayer followed, then some music from some wireless speaker that she hadn't noticed. The music wasn't Sinatra; she did notice that. Each attendee offered their respects, which hurt worse than Elle anticipated. She wanted to be alone, to lean against the casket one time, to stare into Norah's eyes that looked out from the portrait, to somehow feel Norah's presence again.

Elle glanced down the row at her friends. Past the chairs, Heidi was pulling up shreds of grass and piling them in her lap. Marissa was chatting quietly with Rachel. Heath had been cornered by someone Elle didn't recognize. She stood, hoping to not draw attention to herself. Her dear friends, but especially Heath, had been treating her like a fragile piece of china, hovering over her, making sure nothing caused her to shatter.

She chanced sneaking away to find Brandon, hiding from Charlene. But Aaron stood up in her path, awkward with hand in the air hanging between them. "I'm sorry...for all of this." He said, letting his hand fall now that he had Elle's attention. "The timing of all this—well, maybe if I had known this was what was coming, I'd-" The sentence trailed off and Elle knew why. Because what he was going to say wasn't true. He wouldn't have changed anything.

Her control came easier than expected, because she realized, she wasn't angry anymore. "Was any of this ever about me changing? Or was that just an excuse to leave because you didn't think I could?" Her eyes flicked to find Brandon. And he was there, every inch of his tall stature standing at attention, watching her. "Because I have."

Aaron nodded his head. "I know you have."

"That doesn't matter anymore though, does it?"

He didn't answer. He didn't have to.

Elle looked down at his sister, Rachel, who occupied herself on her phone now. The woman whom she had befriended, considered a sister of her own, bore her soul to on several occasions, now wouldn't look her in the face.

Trying to escape, Elle sidestepped her ex-husband. But he wasn't done. His shoes squeaked as he turned to her again.

"Uh, Elle,"

She turned, a hollow pang in her heart. This man whom she had loved for so long, clung to at night, now reduced to someone she wanted to avoid.

"I don't feel right about going back to Norah's for the reception, but I told my lawyer not to fight for the inheritance or anything." His eyes were sincere, brows furrowed like he was doing her a favor.

Elle laughed. She felt eyes on her back. Chatter around her halted. Aaron was ridiculous, and Elle couldn't stifle another laugh as she answered, "That's great." Her shoulders lifted as she looked at him one last time, then turned with a shake of her head.

A lock of highlighted hair fell from its pin and touched her cheek as she approached Brandon. He leaned back against the massive tree trunk that would forever guard Norah.

"Thank you for coming." Elle's words sounded far away.

Brandon nodded, "Of course." He looked around at the landscape of the cemetery. The bright green grass, trees everywhere and a stone angel statue accompanying a nearby grave. "This is the perfect place for her."

"It is." The place reminded her of Norah's backyard, roses and vines. Life was growing everywhere, even in a place so crowded by death. It filled Elle with the glow of hope.

Brandon reached his hand toward Elle's but only brushed the outside of her hand and pinky finger. His touch sent a shiver up her arm then through her whole body.

She sent a subconscious glance over her shoulder toward her mother, as though she was a teenager again hiding a forbidden crush.

"I know what you said," Brandon's voice just above the whisper of the tree leaves. "but–"

The strength to shake her head, to say "No," took Herculean effort. Guilt and grief warred inside of her, clawing at each other to see which one would win. "I won't let her ruin you."

"Don't you see," he said, tilting his head down to meet her eyes in a way that only someone so tall had to. He tucked that wild lock of hair behind her ear. "She already is."

Elle couldn't look in his eyes, those dark eyes that swallowed her whole with one glance, that she wanted to jump in and never leave. "Maybe–" Their conversation stilted by unfinished thoughts.

"Yeah," he leaned back against the tree, distancing his body from hers in a way that made her ache for his warmth. "Maybe." He said with a nod and that smile.

She breathed him in one more time, not knowing if it would be the last, then turned toward the voice calling her name. Her mother's voice, the woman who was always pulling her away from him. Elle walked toward the limo, but this time beckoned Marissa and Heath to join them in the stretched-out car. Charlene opened her mouth to argue, but she closed it with one look in Elle's stern face. She wasn't going to let her mother take anymore away from her today.

30

SCOTT

He hadn't left California yet. He couldn't bear to leave Jocelyn behind. Even though he knew she wasn't there, something drew him to their hometown, their family, where they had met and fell in love. He felt closer to her here.

Part of him wanted to take Ian to Disneyland and Knott's Berry Farm and Santa Monica Pier the way Jocelyn had planned for their vacation. She'd been so excited about their trip. Another part of him was weary at the thought of it. His thoughts were still so jumbled, so confused. He felt like he was walking underwater, holding his breath, trying to see through the constantly moving current around him.

In the flurry, Roxanne had packed his and Ian's suitcase for their trip. Scott hadn't even thought of it. And at the bottom of the suitcase sat his laptop. The last time he'd even used it was in Afghanistan. But Jocelyn had been on it often. She'd confessed to reading his journals, and while that made him feel like he wasn't wearing any skin, he was simultaneously relieved.

Maybe he could find the same relief in journaling again. He'd thought it was ridiculous when he started. What man wrote in a diary? He felt like a preteen girl who wrote her *i*'s with hearts instead of dots. But it had helped him purge the clustered craziness happening around him, and in him.

He opened his laptop once again to let his fingers fall over the keys and see what came out.

When he clicked on the "Journal" file, the modified date had changed. To April. One month before the accident. His palms were layered with sweat when he clicked Open. He was sure it was a fluke. That the date had changed only because Jocelyn had opened it to read. But just in case, he scrolled to the last page.

His nerves were on the outside of his skin. Every inch of him prickled and burned the way he had lying under the rubble of the RPG, under Xavier's dead body.

Then he read the last page:

> Scott,
>
> Who knows how long it will take you to get here. Maybe by now we are old and wrinkly and have grandchildren. You said you never wanted to read these journals again, so there's a chance you'll never see this. But just in case you do, I wanted the last entry to leave you with good after all this pain.
>
> I want you to know that I see you. I see the strong soldier you are, and it makes me stand taller. I see the father you are, and it makes me fall in love with you all over again. I see the husband you are, and I'm a gawky seventh grader again, giddy over you looking in my direction.
>
> But most importantly, I see the man you are underneath all of that. Don't let all you've lost get in the way of all you've gained. You're stronger than you've ever been. I've loved each version of you. And I will always love you, Scott Turner. You're worth it all.
>
> Jocelyn

31

ELLE

The house was even quieter without Norah, somehow. Well, for one, the television was kept at a reasonable volume. Although, the home may never again be as clean as with Norah, Elle did her best to tidy up after the reception. Maybe Norah knew a little secret about cleaning. There was always more to clean, but the freshness of a clean room, like a fresh day, was a beautiful symbol.

The evening before Charlene returned to North Carolina, Elle descended the stairs to find her staring out the front window. It was a familiar scene from long ago. Before her mother's fine lines had appeared, Charlene would stare out the window in a daze twirling her hair around her manicured finger. As a child Elle assumed her mom was waiting, longing for Elle's father to come home and make them a family, because it was her own childhood desire too.

She wondered if her newfound knowledge would set her mother free or only bring back painful memories. All these years of secrets and misunderstandings filled the country-wide gap between them. The simple words "I know; Norah told me," wouldn't close the distance created over decades. It might entice Charlene's distance more, to keep the pain at bay, to not look at the child who knew her secret.

Just as Charlene had protected Elle all these years from this bitter truth, Elle chose to do the same. Protect her mother. It was the least she could do. They may never move any closer or know each other better, they may never fill in the cracks that had formed between them, but they would always remain mother and daughter.

And she could finally give up the hunt for a family. Embrace the one she already had, albeit a few months too late. Make a family of her own—maybe not the traditional sense of husband and children, but a non-blood family.

Elle glanced at her watch then back at her mother. "I'm meeting Marissa for a drink. You want to join us?"

Jolted out of her trance, Charlene smiled. She had to be stunned, being that Elle had never, ever invited her to grab a drink. "I'd like that."

Elle grabbed a six-pack she'd hidden in a corner of the garage, just like she did in high school, and when Charlene almost succeeded in raising an eyebrow, Elle answered, "It's BYOB."

The women hopped in her car and careened toward Palos Verdes Drive to the last place she had taken Norah. This time after she parked, they walked down to the cove by the lighthouse. She tasted the salty air without even opening her mouth. Marissa was already there, balancing on the back of a bench with her feet in the seat. Elle took her shoes off and let the sand cling to her toes, then sat copying Marissa.

Charlene sat with them but properly on the bench. All three looked toward the water, all quiet but the crashing waves. A palm tree reached to the sky behind them.

Shrill laughter echoed off the jagged cliffs around the lighthouse, and the women looked in the direction of the noise. A blond-haired boy, holding a football under his arm, ran into view and straight for the water. A man ambled along behind him, presumably his father, holding the boy's shoes in his hand. The man hollered for the boy, "Just get your feet wet." He walked toward the boy slowly, carefully, with a brace over the jeans of his right leg. For a moment, he glanced toward the woman, put a hand up in a sort of wave, but didn't move in their direction.

"Well, hello." Charlene said in a suggestive growl that only the women next to her could hear.

The little boy tossed the football at his dad, but the throw was short and it landed in the sand.

Elle shook her head. "Mother, don't." She eyed Marissa and nodded in Charlene's direction. Telepathically saying, *Fill her in.* "I'll be right back." She slid down from the bench and didn't bother to put her shoes back on. She headed toward the father and his son.

The Santa Ana winds blew their hair back from her face and Elle masked a shiver by pulling her cardigan tight around her body. When she was in speaking distance of him, she said, "You must be Scott Turner."

He nodded. "Elle Holloway?"

She smiled, "Yes. Thank you for emailing me back."

Unexpectedly, she had received a reply in her inbox to the final goodbye email she'd sent Jocelyn. Goosebumps covered her body while she opened the email, but it was from Scott.

"Well, it was an interesting surprise to find yours and Jocelyn's emails." His eyebrows shrugged over his brown eyes. "I hope it isn't weird that I read them."

"No, it's fine."

"They were gifts, each one of them, to read little pieces from her." He shifted his gaze back to Ian wading in the water with splash patterns on his shorts. "I know it meant a lot to Jocelyn to find a friend in you, even unexpectedly. She didn't have a lot of friends. A lot of people loved her and cared about her, but she didn't trust many people with her thoughts. So, I'm glad she had you to, uh, vent to. Especially at such a hard time."

"Well she did a lot for me too." Elle hated how ineloquent she sounded, but she couldn't possibly put into words how she felt about this woman whom she had never met. "She changed my life through those emails." It sounded so silly, but it was true. "I wish I could have met her in person."

Scott's lips pushed together tight until they turned white.

"But I'm glad to meet you, and Ian. She loved you both so much."

A crisp nod, then he turned his face toward the ocean and let the breeze rush over him. "This is Ian's first time to the beach." He smiled, pushing the hand not holding Ian's shoes—the one housing a gold band on his ring finger—into his pocket. "I know your friendship with Jocelyn started with a gift, so I wanted to give you something of hers, as a thank you for…everything." He pulled a chain from his pocket.

"The locket." Elle said, recognizing it from a picture Jocelyn had sent her, noticing the small charms inside the glass.

Dropping the locket in the palm of Elle's hand, Scott recognized loss and heartache in her. When he spoke, the necklace took on meaning for her too. "I wanted to tell you what I told her when I gave it to her. That we all have shrapnel that leaves wounds and scars. But you know, what those wounds teach us, make the scars worthwhile."

They both looked at the circle encasing the sand, the metal, the symbol of love that was once almost forgotten.

Elle let herself smile at the words, listening to the crash of the waves below them. The clouds stuttered across the sky, welcoming the sunset as it approached. "Thank you."

"We should go." He said, then he called for Ian.

"Are you sure? You want a drink?" Elle pointed a thumb back at the bench, the women with her and her six-pack.

"No," Scott laughed. Ian came running, grabbing the football, throwing it as hard as he could at Scott. "We're heading back to Texas first thing in the morning. But thanks."

"What will you do now?" She asked.

"I'm not entirely sure." He watched Ian clumsily drop the football then pick it back up. "I think I'll start with coaching my son's pee-wee football team. But being back on the California coast makes retirement look pretty good."

"Well if you need help finding a new place, my mom's a master realtor." She pointed over her shoulder.

Ian came up next to Scott then squatted down in the sand, funneling it through his fingers.

"It'll be a few weeks maybe a month before the army can get it all wrapped up, but it'll be nice to be so close to family again."

"Family's important for a kid." Elle thought of all the good things she wished for Scott and Ian's future. All the hope and happiness, all the smiles and little boy laughter, only good memories of the woman they lost, only happy dreams. But she felt awkward telling that to a stranger.

They both turned and went their ways, Jocelyn's locket like a heart in Elle's hand.

She plucked a bottle from the six-pack and popped the cap, the fizzle and foam matching the waves flowing up shore.

"Mmm, he is fine." Charlene dragging the *i* sound out.

Elle twisted the gold chain around her fingers, thinking of Norah and Aaron and Brandon and all that had changed over the last year.

"You know who else is fine?" Charlene continued, "That nurse of Norah's."

Elle's pulse sprinted within her. Marissa met her eyes with caution and a bit of a twinkle.

"What was his name? Brandon?" Charlene asked.

Careful with her reaction, Elle responded, "Isn't he the person you thought was responsible for Norah heading to the hospital?"

"I was upset. It was completely unfounded." Charlene tilted her head to look up at Elle from the bench. "I saw you talking to him at the funeral. There's something between you two."

Without taking her eyes off of her mother, Elle wrapped a hand around one of Marissa's and squeezed. She nodded her answer, not trusting her own voice.

"Was he good to you?"

A shallow breath passed between Elle's lips as she nodded again.

"You deserve to be happy, Elle. If he makes you happy..." Charlene gave her daughter a knowing smile and placed a hand on Elle's knee.

Marissa bent down and plucked Elle's phone out of her purse and tossed it in Elle's lap. "So are you gonna call him right now, or what?"

Elle made a face, but still held the phone in her palms like a beating heart. "I can wait." If she had learned anything from her time with Norah—and Jocelyn—it was to be present in the now.

A seagull squawked, flying overhead. Wind rustling the palm leaves.

"Well the bird thinks that's a load of crap." Marissa cracked.

Charlene shrieked with laughter. Elle smiled at them both, but when she met eyes with Marissa she saw the sun reflecting in her eyes. She leaned down and kissed Marissa on her freckled cheek, then picked up the six-pack from under the bench. "One more drink." She pulled another bottle out for each of the women. They clinked the bottle necks together with a cheers and deep breath.

Life had pierced each of them with their own shrapnel pieces, even left a scar or two. But it wasn't over. Maybe there were more scars to come, more mistakes to be made. Better ones, with better stories to be told. Elle was happy to take life as it came at her now, with these women who had scars of their own, braving the world ahead.

ACKNOWLEDGMENTS

Even as a writer, it's difficult for me to put words to my gratitude for each person who helped in this journey. These little lines at the back of the book are only symbolic of how much you all encouraged, inspired, and challenged me during this process.

First, a thank you to all military personnel and their families who sacrifice more in one day than most of us have to in our lives. This country is great because of you.

To my grandmothers, Leota Burke and Lavena Chavez, who may be gone from this earth but who inspired so many of these pages. For the pearls and the pianos.

Rob Stewart, for taking me seriously even though I felt in over my head and letting me ask you ridiculous questions about the army without laughing at me. This book would not be here without your help.

Melissa Hoy, who set me straight on home care givers and gave me a glimpse of the heart behind the work.

Mom and Dad, for not letting me quit that 9th grade creative writing class. Look, it's working!

Crystal Sparks, for the hours of caffeine and accountability. For encouraging me when I wanted to literally throw it all in the trash.

Angelica Plata and Sally Hall, for the hearts and crying emojis, right along with the critiques and edits. You two reminded me why I do this thing called writing.

Berlin Boutique, for working so hard to bring Jocelyn's locket to life, even more beautifully than I imagined.

My moms group, who watched my kids while I drank loads of coffee and typed streams of consciousness that eventually became this book.

Jude, Rhema, Lucas and Canaan. Being your mother has crafted me into a better writer. You have given me heart, courage, bravery, determination and taught me far more lessons than I have taught you.

Isaiah, I don't know how you put up with my ups and downs, my questions, my uncertainties. But you have kept me standing. And writing. You truly are my home.

ABOUT THE AUTHOR

Jessica Shook writes and has for as long as she can remember. Her first book about a teenage rock band was complete when she was 15 but corrupted on a floppy disk. Regardless, the addiction to writing never subsided, but years later the environment where the inspiration happens certainly changed. Jessica now writes while being a short order cook, taxi driver, diaper changer and anything else her family of six needs.

Jessica lives in Texas with her husband and four children. More information on her writing can be found at jessicashook.com.